THE NIGHT GARDENER

Also by George Pelecanos

Drama City

Hard Revolution

Soul Circus

Hell to Pay

Right As Rain

The Sweet Forever

Shame the Devil

King Suckerman

The Big Blowdown

Down By the River Where the Dead Men Go

Shoedog

Nick's Trip

A Firing Offense

GEORGE PELECANOS

THE NIGHT GARDENER

a novel

Little, Brown and Company New York Boston London

Little, Brown and Company
Hachette Book Group USA
1271 Avenue of the Americas, New York, NY 10020
Visit our Web site at www.HachetteBookGroupUSA.com

First Edition: August 2006

The characters and events in this book are fictitious. Any similarity to real persons, living or dead, is coincidental and not intended by the author.

Library of Congress Cataloging-in-Publication Data

Pelecanos, George P.
The night gardener : a novel / George Pelecanos.— 1st ed.
p. cm.
ISBN-10: 0-316-15650-7 (hardcover)
ISBN-13: 978-0-316-15650-9 (hardcover)
1. Police—Washington (D.C.)—Fiction. 2. Serial murderers—Fiction. 3. Washington (D.C.)—Fiction. 4. Teenagers—Fiction. I. Title.
PS3566.E354N53 2006
813'.54—dc22 2006001286

10 9 8 7 6 5 4 3 2 1

Q-FF

Printed in the United States of America

TO REAGAN ARTHUR

1985

ONE

THE CRIME SCENE was in the low 30s around E, on the edge of Fort Dupont Park, in a neighborhood known as Greenway, in the 6th District section of Southeast D.C. A girl of fourteen lay in the grass on the side of a community vegetable garden that was blind to the residents whose yards backed up to the nearby woods. There were colorful beads in her braided hair. She appeared to have died from a single gunshot wound to the head. A middle-aged homicide police was down on one knee beside her, staring at her as if he were waiting for her to awake. His name was T. C. Cook. He was a sergeant with twenty-four years on the force, and he was thinking.

His thoughts were not optimistic. There was no visible blood on or around the girl, with the exception of the entrance and exit wounds, now congealed. No blood at all on her shirt, jeans, or sneakers, all of which looked to be brand-new. Cook surmised that she had been undressed and re-dressed after her murder, and her body had been moved and dumped here. He had a sick feeling in his gut and also, he realized with some degree of guilt, a quickening in his pulse that suggested, if not excitement, then engagement. An ID on the body would confirm it, but Cook suspected that this one was like the others. She was one of them.

The Mobile Crime Lab had arrived. The techs were going through the motions, but there was a kind of listlessness in their movements and a general air of defeat. The transportation of a body away from the murder site meant that there would be few forensic clues. Also, it had rained. When this happened, it was said by some techs that the killer was laughing.

On the edge of the crime scene were a meat wagon and several patrol cars and uniformed officers who had responded to the call for assistance. There were a couple dozen spectators as well. Yellow tape had been strung, and the uniforms were now charged with keeping the spectators and the media back and away from the homicide cops and lab techs doing their jobs. Superintendent of Detectives Michael Messina and Homicide Captain Arnold Bellows had ducked the tape and were talking to each other, leaving Sergeant Cook alone. The public-relations officer, a moley Italian American who appeared frequently on TV, fed the usual to a reporter from Channel 4, a man with suspicious hair whose gimmick was a clipped delivery and dramatic pauses between sentences.

Two of the uniformed officers stood by their cruiser. Their names were Gus Ramone and Dan Holiday. Ramone was of medium height and build. Holiday was taller and blade thin. Both were college dropouts, single, in their early twenties, and white. Both were in their second year on the force, past their rookie status but not seasoned. They had already acquired a distrust of officers above the rank of sergeant but were not yet cynical about the job.

"Look at 'em," said Holiday, nodding his sharp chin in

the direction of Superintendent Messina and Captain Bellows. "They're not even talking to T.C."

"They're just letting him do his thing," said Ramone.

"The white shirts are afraid of him, is what it is."

T. C. Cook was an average-sized black man in a tan raincoat with a zip-in lining, worn over a houndstooth sport jacket. His dress Stetson, light brown with a chocolate band holding a small multicolored feather, was cocked just so, covering a bald head sided by clown patches of black hair flecked with gray. He had a bulbous nose and a thick brown mustache. His mouth rarely turned up in a smile, but his eyes sometimes shone brightly with amusement.

"The Mission Man," said Holiday. "The brass don't like him, but they sure don't fuck with him. Guy's got a ninety percent closure rate; he can do what he wants."

That's Holiday all over, thought Ramone. Get results, and all will be forgiven. Produce, and do whatever the fuck you want.

Ramone had his own rules: follow the playbook, stay safe, put in your twenty-five and move on. He was not enamored of Cook or any of the other mavericks, cowboys, and assorted living legends on the force. Romanticizing the work could not elevate it to something it was not. This was a job, not a calling. Holiday, on the other hand, was living a dream, had lead in his pencil, and was jacked up big on the Twenty-third Psalm.

Holiday had started on foot patrol in the H Street corridor of Northeast, a white man solo in a black section of town. He had cut it fine and already had a rep. Holiday remembered the names of folks he had met only one time, complimented the young women and the grandmothers alike, could talk Interhigh sports, the Redskins, and the Bullets with guys sitting on their front porches and those hanging outside the liquor stores, could even shoot the shit with the young ones he knew were headed for the hard side. Citizens, criminal and straight, sensed that Holiday was a joker and a fuckup, and still they liked him. His enthusiasm and natural fit for the job would probably get him further in the MPD than Ramone would go. That is, if that little man with the pitchfork, sitting on Holiday's shoulder, didn't ruin him first.

Ramone and Holiday had gone through the academy together, but they weren't friends. They weren't even partners. They were sharing a car because there had been a shortage of cruisers in the lot behind the 6D station. Six hours into a four-to-midnight, and Ramone was already tired of Holiday's voice. Some cops liked the company, and the backup, even if it was less than stellar. Ramone preferred to ride alone.

"I tell you about this girl I been seein?" said Holiday.

"Yeah," said Ramone. Not yeah with a question mark on the end of it, but yeah with a period, as in, end of discussion.

"She's a Redskinette," said Holiday. "One of those cheerleaders they got at RFK."

"I know what they are."

"I tell you about her?"

"I think you did."

"You oughtta see her ass, Giuseppe."

Ramone's mother, when she was angry or sentimental, was the only one who ever called him by his given name. That is, until Holiday had seen Ramone's driver's license. Holiday also occasionally called him "the Ramone," after having had a look at Ramone's record collection on the single occasion Ramone had let him into his apartment. That had been a mistake.

"Nice ones, too," said Holiday, doing the arthritic thing with his hands. "She got those big pink, whaddaya call 'em, *aureoles*."

Holiday turned, his face catching the strobe of the cruiser light bars still activated at the scene. He was smiling his large row of straight white teeth, his ice blue eyes catching the flash. The ID bar on his chest read "D. Holiday," so naturally and instantly he had caught the nickname "Doc" within the department. Coincidentally, he was as angular and bone skinny as the tubercular gunman. Some of the older cops claimed he looked like a young Dan Duryea.

"You told me," said Ramone for the third time.

"Okay. But listen to this. Last week, I'm out with her in a bar. The Constable, down on Eighth . . ."

"I know the place." Ramone had gone to the Constable many times, pre-cop, in that year when he thought of himself as In Between. You could score coke from the bartender there, watch the band, Tiny Desk Unit or the Insect Surfers or whoever, in that back room, or sit under the stars on the patio they had out back, drink beers and catch cigarettes behind the shake, and talk to the girls, back when they were all wearing the heavy mascara and the fishnets. This was after his fourth, and last, semester at Maryland, when he'd taken that criminology class and thought, I don't need any more of this desk-and-blackboard bullshit; I can do this thing right now. But then just wandering for a while before he signed up, hitting the bars, smoking weed, and doing a little blow, chasing those girls with the fishnets. It had felt to him then like he was stumbling. Tonight, wearing the blue, the badge and gun, standing next to a guy he would have ridiculed a few years back, now his contemporary, it felt like he had been free.

". . . and she drops a bomb on me. Tells me she likes me and all that bulljive, but she's dating one of the Redskins, too."

"Joe Jacoby?" said Ramone, side-glancing Holiday.

"Nah, not that beast."

"So who?"

"A receiver. And not Donnie Warren, if you catch my drift."

"You're saying she's dating a black receiver."

"One of 'em," said Holiday. "And you know they like white girls."

"Who doesn't," said Ramone.

Over the crackle of the radios coming from the cars they heard Cook telling one of the men in his squad to keep the

Channel 4 reporter, who was attempting to move under the tape, away from the deceased. "Punk motherfucker," said Cook, saying it loud, making sure the reporter could hear. "He's the one got that witness killed down in Congress Park. Goes on the air and talks about how a young lady's about to give testimony . . ."

"I had a problem with what she told me, I gotta be honest," said Holiday, watching Cook but going ahead with his story.

" 'Cause he's black."

"I can't lie. It was hard for me to forget him and her after that. When I was in the rack with her, is what I'm talkin about."

"You felt, what, inadequate or somethin?"

"Come on. Pro football player, a brother . . ." Holiday held his palm out a foot from his groin. "Guy's gotta be like this."

"It's an NFL requirement."

"Huh?"

"They check their teeth, too."

"I'm sayin, I'm just an average guy. Down there, I mean. Don't get me wrong; it's Kielbasa Street when the blood gets to it, but when it's just layin there—"

"What's your point?"

"Knowin this girl was hanging off the end of this guy's dick, it just ruined her for me, I guess."

"So you what, let her go?"

"Not with that ass of hers, I wasn't gonna let her go. No, sir."

A woman had wandered under the tape while they were talking, and as she approached the body of the girl and got a look at it, she vomited voluminously into the grass. Sergeant Cook removed his hat, ran a finger along the brim, and breathed deeply. He replaced the Stetson on his head, adjusted it, and allowed his eyes to search the perimeter of the scene. He turned to the man beside him, a white detective named Chip Rogers, and pointed to Ramone and Holiday.

"Tell those white boys to do their jobs," said Cook.

"People regurgitatin, fucking up my crime scene . . . If they can't keep these folks back, find some men who will. I'm not playin."

Ramone and Holiday immediately went to the yellow tape, turned their backs to it, and affected a pose of authority. Holiday spread his feet and looped his fingers through his utility belt, unfazed by Cook's words. Ramone's jaw tightened as he felt a twinge of anger at being called a white boy by the homicide cop. He had heard it occasionally growing up outside D.C. and many times while playing baseball and basketball in the city proper. He didn't like it. He knew it was meant to cut him and he was expected to take it, and that made it burn even more.

"How about you?" said Holiday.

"How 'bout me *what?*" said Ramone.

"You been gettin any hay for your donkey?"

Ramone did not answer. He had his eye on one woman in particular, a cop, God help him. But he had learned not to let Holiday into his personal world.

"C'mon, brother," said Holiday. "I showed you mine, now you show me yours. You got someone in your gun sights?"

"Your baby sister," said Ramone.

Holiday's mouth fell open and his eyes flared. "My sister died of leukemia when she was eleven years old, you piece a shit."

Ramone looked away. For a while there was only the squawk and hiss of the police radios and the low conversations of the spectators in the crowd. Then Holiday cackled and slapped Ramone on the back.

"I'm kiddin you, Giuseppe. Oh, Christ, but I had your ass."

The description of the victim had been matched to a list of missing teenagers in the area. A half hour later, a man was brought to the scene to identify her. As he looked at the body, a father's anguished howl filled the night.

The victim's name was Eve Drake. In the past year, two other black teenagers, both living in the poorer sections of town, had been murdered and dumped in similar fashion in community gardens, both discovered shortly after sunrise. Shot in the head, both had traces of semen in their rectums. Their names were Otto Williams and Ava Simmons. Like Otto and Ava, Drake's first name, Eve, was spelled the same way backward as it was forward. The press had made the connection and dubbed the events the Palindrome Murders. Within the department, some police had begun to refer to the perpetrator as the Night Gardener.

ACROSS TOWN, AT THE same time the father cried out over his daughter's body, young Washingtonians were in their homes, tuning in to *Miami Vice*, doing lines of coke as they watched the exploits of two hip undercover cops and their quest to take down the kingpins of the drug trade. Others read bestselling novels by Tom Clancy, John Jakes, Stephen King, and Peter Straub, or sat in bars and talked about the fading play-off prospects of the Jay Schroeder–led Washington Redskins. Others watched rented VCR tapes of *Beverly Hills Cop* and *Code of Silence*, the top picks that week at Erol's Video Club, or barely sweated to Jane Fonda's *Workout*, or went out and caught the new Michael J. Fox at the Circle Avalon or *Caligula* at the Georgetown. Mr. Mister and Midge Ure were in town, playing the clubs.

As these movers of the Reagan generation entertained themselves west of Rock Creek Park and in the suburbs, detectives and techs worked at a crime scene at 33rd and E, in the neighborhood of Greenway, in Southeast D.C. They could not know that this would be the last victim of the Palindrome Killer. For now, there was only a dead teenager, one of three unsolved, and someone out there, somewhere, doing the murders.

On a cool rainy night in December 1985, two young uniformed police and a middle-aged homicide detective were on the scene.

2005

TWO

THE WIRY LITTLE man in the box, sitting low in his chair, was William Tyree. In the opposite chair was Detective Paul "Bo" Green. A can of Coca-Cola and an ashtray holding dead Newports sat on the rectangular table between them. The room stank of nicotine and the crack sweat coming off Tyree.

"Those the kicks you were wearing?" said Green, pointing at Tyree's shoes. "Those right there?"

"These here are the Huaraches," said Tyree.

"Those shoes you've got on right now, you saying you weren't wearing those yesterday?"

"Nah, uh-uh."

"Tell me something, William. What size you wear?"

Tyree's hair held specks of fuzz. A small cut, now congealed, was visible below his left eye.

"These here are nine and a half," said Tyree. "I wear tens most times. You know them Nikes be runnin big."

Detective Sergeant Gus Ramone, watching the interview on a monitor in a space adjacent to the interrogation room, allowed himself the first smile of the day. Even being questioned for murder, even under the fluorescent lights of an interrogation, a man damn near always felt the need to lie about or explain away his shoe size.

"Okay," said Green, his hands folded on the table before him. "So those Nikes you got on now . . . you telling me you weren't wearing those yesterday?"

"I was wearin Nikes. But not these ones, no."

"Which type were you wearing, William? What I mean specifically is, which type of Nikes were you wearing when you visited your ex-wife yesterday at her apartment?"

Green's brow wrinkled as he considered the question. "It was the Twenties."

"Yeah? My son has those."

"They're popular with the young ones."

"The black Twenties?"

"Uh-uh. I got the white with the blue."

"So, if we were to go to your apartment, would we find a pair of white Twenties, size nine and a half?"

"They ain't at my apartment no more."

"Where are they?"

"I put 'em in a bag with some other stuff."

"What other stuff?"

"The jeans and T-shirt I was wearin yesterday."

"The jeans and T-shirt you had on when you visited your ex-wife?"

"Uh-huh."

"What kind of bag?"

"One of those bags from Safeway."

"A grocery bag, says Safeway on it?"

Tyree nodded his head. "One of those plastic ones they got."

"You put anything else in that bag?"

"Besides my clothes and sneaks?"

"Yes, William."

"I put a knife in there, too."

Detective Anthony Antonelli, seated beside an impassive Ramone in the video monitor room, leaned forward. Bo Green, in the box, did the same. William Tyree did not pull back from the space that Green was invading. He had been sharing the box with Green for several hours now, and he had grown comfortable with his presence.

Green had started slowly, small-talking Tyree but dancing around the murder of Jacqueline Taylor. Green and Tyree had gone to the same high school, Ballou, though not at the same time. Green had known Tyree's older brother, Jason, a pretty fair Interhigh baseball player, now with the post office. They had talked about the old neighborhood, and where the best fish sandwich could be gotten in the 1980s, and how the music had been more positive, and how parents watched their kids more closely, and if they couldn't, how the neighbors chipped in and helped.

Green, a bearish man with gentle eyes, always took his time and, through his familiarity with the area and the many families he had come to know over the years, endeared himself, eventually, to many of the suspects in the interrogation room, especially those of a certain generation. He became their friend and confidant. Ramone was the primary on the Jacqueline Taylor case, but he had allowed Green to conduct the crucial interview. It appeared that Green was about to close this now.

"What kind of knife, William?"

"A big knife I had in my kitchen. You know, for cutting meat."

"Like a butcher knife?"

"Somethin like that."

"And you put the knife and the clothing in the bag. . . ."

" 'Cause the knife had blood on it," said Tyree, like he was explaining the obvious to a child.

"And your clothing and shoes?"

"They had blood on 'em, too."

"Where'd you put the bag?"

"You know that Popeyes down there on Pennsylvania, near where Minnesota comes in?"

"Uh-huh?"

"There's a liquor store across the street from it. . . ."

"Penn Liquors."

"Nah, farther down. The one got a Jewish name to it."

"You talking about Saul's?"

"Yeah, that one. I put the bag in the Dumpster they got out back in the alley."

"Out back of Saul's?"

"Uh-huh. Last night."

Green nodded casually, as if someone had just told him the score of a ball game or that he had left the lights on in his car.

In the video room, Ramone opened the door and shouted to Detective Eugene Hornsby, his ass parked against a desk, half-seated, half-standing beside Detective Rhonda Willis, both of them in the big office area of VCB.

"We got it," said Ramone, and both Hornsby and Rhonda Willis straightened their postures. "Gene, you know that liquor store, Saul's, on Pennsylvania?"

"Over there by Minnesota?" said Hornsby, a completely average-looking man of thirty-eight years who had come up in the infamous part of Northeast known as Simple City.

"Yeah. Mr. Tyree says he dumped a butcher knife and his clothes in the Dumpster out back. And he put a pair of white-and-blue Nike Twenties in there, too, size nine and a half. It's all in a Safeway bag."

"Paper or plastic?" said Hornsby with a barely detectable grin.

"Plastic," said Ramone. "It should be there."

"If Sanitation didn't pick up the trash yet," said Rhonda.

"I heard *that,*" said Ramone.

"I'll get some uniforms down there straight away," said Hornsby, snatching a set of keys off his desk. "*And* I'll make sure them rookies don't fuck it up."

"Thanks, Gene," said Ramone. "How's that warrant coming, Rhonda?"

"It's comin," said Rhonda. "Ain't nobody going in and out of Tyree's apartment until we get it. Got a patrol car parked right out front as we speak."

"All right."

"Nice one, Gus," said Rhonda.

"That was all Bo," said Ramone.

In the box, Bo Green got out of his seat. He looked at Tyree, who had sat up some in his chair. Tyree looked like he'd had a fever that had broken.

"I'm thirsty, William. You thirsty?"

"I could use another soda."

"What you want, same thing?"

"Can I get a Slice this time?"

"We don't have it. All's we got like it is Mountain Dew."

"That'll work."

"You got enough cigarettes?"

"I'm good."

Detective Green looked at his watch, then straight up into the camera mounted high on the wall. "Three forty-two," he said before leaving the room.

The light over the door of the interrogation room remained green, indicating that the tape was still rolling. Inside the video room, Antonelli read the sports page of the *Post* and glanced occasionally at the monitor.

Bo Green was greeted by Ramone and Rhonda Willis.

"Good one," said Ramone.

"He *wanted* to talk," said Green.

"Lieutenant said to come on back when you had something," said Rhonda. "Prosecutor wants to, what's that word, *interface.*"

"Rhonda says we drew Littleton," said Ramone.

"Little man," said Green.

Gus Ramone stroked his black mustache.

THREE

DAN HOLIDAY SIGNALED the bartender, making a grand circular motion with his index finger over glasses that were not quite empty but empty enough.

"The same way," said Holiday. "For me and my friends."

The men at the bar were three rounds deep into a discussion that had gone from Angelina Jolie to Santana Moss to the new Mustang GT, their points argued with vehemence, but all of it, in the end, about nothing at all. The conversation was something to hang the alcohol on. You couldn't just sit there and drink.

On the stools sat carpet-and-floor salesman Jerry Fink, freelance writer Bradley West, a residential contractor named Bob Bonano, and Holiday. None of them had bosses. All had the kind of jobs that allowed them to drink off a workday without guilt.

They met, informally, several times a week at Leo's, a

tavern on Georgia Avenue, between Geranium and Floral, in Shepherd Park. It was a simple rectangular room with an oak bar going front to back, twelve stools and a few four-tops, and a jukebox holding obscure soul singles. The walls were freshly painted and unadorned with beer posters, pennants, or mirrors, instead showing photographs of Leo's parents in D.C. and grandparents in their Greek village. The bar was a neighborhood watering hole, neither a bucket of blood nor a home for gentrifiers. It was simply an efficient place to get a pleasant load on in the middle of the afternoon.

"Jesus, you stink," said Jerry Fink, sitting beside Holiday, rattling the rocks in his cocktail glass.

"It's called Axe," said Holiday. "The kids wear it."

"You ain't no kid, hombre." Jerry Fink, raised off River Road and a graduate of Walt Whitman High, one of the finest and whitest public schools in the country, often spoke in double negatives. He felt it made him more street. He was short, had a gut, wore glasses with tinted lenses indoors, and sported a perm, which he called "my Jewfro." Fink was forty-eight years old.

"Tell me something I don't know."

"I'm just askin you why you're wearing that swill."

"Very simple. Where I woke up this morning, I didn't have my own toiletries close by, if you catch my drift."

"Here we go," said West.

Holiday grinned and squared his shoulders. He was as rail thin as he had been in his twenties. The only indicator of his forty-one years was the small belly he had acquired from years of drinking. His acquaintances called it "the Holiday Hump."

"Tell us a bedtime story, Daddy," said Bonano.

"Okay," said Holiday. "I had a job yesterday, a client from NYC. Some big-shot investor looking at a company about to go public. I drove him out to an office building in the Dulles corridor, waited around a few hours, and drove him back downtown to the Ritz. So I'm goin back to my place last night, I'm feeling thirsty, I stop in to the Royal Mile in Wheaton for a short one. Soon as I walk in, I notice this brunette sitting with a couple other women. She had some mileage on the odometer, but she was attractive. We made eye contact, and her eyes spoke a million words."

"What did her eyes say, Doc?" said West tiredly.

"They said, I'm hungry for Johnny Johnson."

This drew head shakes.

"I didn't make my move right away. I waited till she had to get up and take a piss. I needed to get a look at her bottom half, see, to make sure I wasn't settin myself up for some horror show later on. Anyway, I checked her out and she was all right. She'd had babies, obviously, but there wasn't any severe damage to speak of."

"C'mon, man," said Bonano.

"Be patient. Soon as she gets back from the head, I cut her from the herd real quick. It only cost me two Miller Lites. She didn't even finish her beer before she tells me she's ready to go." Holiday tapped ash off his smoke. "I figured I'd take her out to the parking lot across the street, let her blow me or somethin."

"And they say romance is dead," said West.

"But she wasn't having any of that," said Holiday, missing West's tone or ignoring it. " 'I'm not doing it in a car,' she says. 'I'm not seventeen anymore.' No shit, I'm thinkin, but hey, I wasn't gonna turn down some ass."

"Even if she wasn't seventeen," said Jerry Fink.

"We go back to her house; she's got a couple of kids, a teenage boy and his younger sister, they barely turn their heads away from the television when we come in."

"What were they watching?" said Bonano.

"What difference does that make?" said Holiday.

"Makes the story better. Makes me see it, like, in my head."

"It was one of those *Law and Order* shows," said Holiday. "I know 'cause I heard that *duh-duh* thing they do."

"Keep goin," said Fink.

"Okay," said Holiday. "She tells the kids not to stay up too late, 'cause they got school the next day, and then she takes me by the hand and we go up to her room."

The cell phone set on the bar, before Bob Bonano, "the kitchen and bath expert," rang. He checked the display number and did not move to answer it. If it was new business, he would take the call. If it was a customer he had already screwed, he would not. Most of the time he did not take the call. Bonano's business was called Home Masters. Jerry Fink called it "Home Bastards" and sometimes "Home Butchers" when he was feeling expansive.

"You fucked her while her kids were downstairs, watching TV?" said Bonano, still looking at the cell phone, its ringer playing *The Good, the Bad and the Ugly* theme. Bonano, dark with big features and hands, fancied himself a cowboy but looked Italian as salami on a string.

"I put my hand over her mouth when she started to make noise," said Holiday with a shrug. "She almost bit through my paw."

"Quit braggin," said Fink.

"I'm just stating a fact," said Holiday. "This broad was an animal."

The bartender, Leo Vazoulis, wide and balding, with thin gray hair and a black mustache, served them their drinks. Leo's father had bought the building, cash, forty years earlier, and operated it as a lunch counter until he was felled by a heart attack. Leo had inherited the real estate and turned the diner into a bar. He had no nut beyond the taxes and utilities, and made a good living working less strenuously than his father had. This was how it was supposed to go from fathers to sons.

Leo emptied the ashtrays and walked away.

"That doesn't explain the perfume you're wearin," said Fink.

"It's deodorant," said Holiday. "Well, the can says it's a combination of deodorant and cologne. Some shit like that."

"I read an article on it," said West. "It's like a phenomenon."

"This morning," said Holiday, "I'm lyin in this woman's bed, waiting for her to get her kids off to school, figuring out my exit plan. I hear the door slam and her SUV fire up, I get out of the rack, go to her son's bedroom, and spray whatever he's got on his dresser under my armpits. I sprayed some down there, too, you know what I'm sayin? To get her smell off me."

"Axe," said Bonano, like he was trying to remember it.

"Axe *Rejuvenate* was what the can said. It's real popular with the young men, apparently."

"You smell like a whore," said Fink.

Holiday stubbed out his smoke. "Your mother does, too."

They finished their drinks and were served another round. Bonano ignored his cell calls, and Fink took one, promising a Palisades housewife that he would be out "sometime next week" to measure her rec room. Fink ended the call and went to the jukebox, dropped in quarters, and punched up a couple of tunes. They listened to an Ann Peebles tune, and then a Syl Johnson, and when the Hi rhythm section kicked in, they all moved their heads.

"How's the novel going, Brad?" said Holiday, shaking a cigarette out of the deck, nudging Fink on the elbow.

"I'm working it out in my head," said West, who had a gray beard and long gray hair. He had grown the beard after Fink told him he looked like an old lady with all that hair.

"Shouldn't you be up at NewYorka, or whatever that place is?" said Fink. He meant the touchy-feely coffeehouse over the District line, on the corner past Crisfield's. "I see those dudes from your neighborhood up there, sittin with their double lattes, tapping away at their keyboards."

"Wearing berets," said Bonano, embellishing.

"Those guys aren't writing anything," said West. "They're jerking off."

"Not like you," said Holiday.

They talked about the new kid Gibbs had picked up at quarterback. They talked about which one of the Desperate Housewives they'd like to fuck, the reasons they would kick the others out of bed, and the Chrysler 300. Bonano said he liked the lines, but it looked too "booferish" with aftermarket rims. In his mind, it was simply the best description of the wheels. Still, he looked around before he said it. At night the bar patrons here were mostly black, as were the employees. In the afternoons, it was often just them: four aging white alcoholics with no place else to go.

The car thing naturally led to a discussion of crime, and a turning of heads toward Holiday, who had the most firsthand knowledge of the subject.

"It's getting better," said Fink. "Murder rate's half of what it was ten years ago."

" 'Cause they put most of the assholes in jail," said Bonano.

"The violent criminals moved out to P.G. County, is all it is," said Fink. "They got more homicides out there this year than they do in the District. And that don't even begin to talk about the carjackings and rapes."

"It's no mystery," said West. "White and black people with money are moving back into the city and pushing the poor blacks out to P.G. Shit, those areas between the Beltway and Southern Avenue? Capitol Heights, District Heights, Hillcrest Heights . . ."

"Heights," said Bonano, shaking his head. "Like they got castles on the hills and shit. Jesus. And don't even mention Suitland. A fucking armpit."

"It's Southeast all over again, ten years ago," said Fink.

"It's the culture," said Bonano. "How the fuck you gonna change that?"

"Ward Nine," said Fink. It had become either an affectionate or a pejorative term for P.G., depending on who was using it. It meant the county was no different from, and just as bad as, the eastern, crime-ridden, black-populated regions of D.C.

"What do you expect?" said West. "Poverty *is* violence."

"*Really,* Hillary?" said Bonano.

"No one respects the law anymore," said Holiday very quietly. He looked into his glass, rattled the cubes, and downed the rest of its contents. He picked up his cigarettes and cell from the bar and got off his stool.

"Where you goin?" said Fink.

"Work," said Holiday. "I got an airport run."

"Take it easy, Doc," said Bonano.

"Gents," said Holiday.

Holiday walked out of Leo's into a blinding light. He wore a white dress shirt under a black suit. His hat was out in the car.

FOUR

DETECTIVES RAMONE AND Green walked down the center aisle of the Violent Crime Branch offices, a windowless jumble of loosely rowed cubicles and desks, the touch-base home for the dozens of detectives working murder cases and, as was said by some, those cases concerning victims who had not yet died but had been seriously fucked up. As they moved, there were scattered congratulations and some joking at Ramone's expense from the few detectives who were in the office. The comments alluded to the fact that Green had done the heavy lifting and Ramone would get the glory for closing the case. Ramone didn't mind. Everyone had his strengths, and Green's was in the box. He was happy for the assistance — anything to get this to the finish line. Point of fact, in every respect, all had gone smoothly from the start.

The previous day, Ramone had been on the bubble when

a call came in from an apartment house resident manager who had discovered a body lying in the open doorway of one of his units. Ramone caught the homicide as the primary. Rhonda Willis, as close to a partner as he ever had, would assist.

Patrolmen and a 7D lieutenant were waiting in the street when Gus Ramone and Rhonda Willis arrived. The crime scene was in a third-floor apartment on Cedar Street, S.E., one of several boxy units that ran along both sides a short block off 14th and ended in a court.

Several hours later, after the decedent had been sheeted and removed, Ramone and Willis remained in the living room of the apartment, saying little to each other, communicating mostly with their eyes. A couple of uniforms stood outside the door, in a stairwell smelling faintly of marijuana smoke and deep-fried food. As techs and a photographer worked diligently and quietly, Ramone stared at an eating table in an open area off the living room near a pass-through to the kitchen.

The groceries interested him most. They were spilled on the table, coming out of a paper bag. Even the perishables, which meant the victim had just gotten in from the store and had not had time to put the milk, cheese, and chicken in the refrigerator before she had been assaulted. Stabbed near the table, he reckoned, since there were drops of blood on the tan pile carpeting there and a trail of it leading to the door. Then a whole lot of blood on the carpet at the door. That's where she had been, probably holding onto the open door, hoping for help before she had collapsed.

The groceries reached him on another level, too. In the mix of staples were other items she had bought at the store: Go-Gurt and Lunchables, strawberry Twizzlers, Peanut Butter Toast Crunch, and the all-important Cocoa Puffs. All right, so she wasn't exactly a nutrition-conscious mother. She was one of those mothers who spent her dollars on things that would make her kids smile. It reminded Ramone of his wife, Regina, who never failed to bring home treats from the grocery store for their son, Diego, even though he was now in his teens, and their daughter, Alana, seven. He chided her for all her attentiveness to Diego especially, how she let him play her, how she couldn't stay mad at him for more than a few minutes, how she always gave in to his wants and requests. Well, if the worst thing a man could say about his wife was that she loved her children too much, he was doing all right.

The children who lived here had been picked up at school by their aunt, who had taken them to her home. Diego was still picked up almost daily at his middle school by a dutiful Regina, despite the fact that Ramone had told her she was going to make him soft.

It was good that the kids who lived in this apartment had not seen their mother in death. She had received multiple stab wounds to the face, breasts, and neck. A severed jugular accounted for the extreme volume of blood. Defense wounds were manifested in several slashes on the victim's fingers and a clean stab through the palm of one hand. She had voided her bowels, and her excrement had stained her white uniform brown.

Ramone and Willis walked the apartment, careful not to disturb the techs from the Mobile Crime Lab. Though they had yet to sum up their observations to each other, both had come to similar conclusions. The victim knew the assailant, as the front door showed no signs of forced entry. Also, the knifing had occurred twenty feet inside the apartment, by the table. She had allowed the assailant to come inside. This was not a drug-related killing, not a witness murder or retaliation against a relative of someone in the game. Knifings were almost always personal and rarely involved business.

The victim's purse was on the kitchen table but did not contain a wallet or keys. Upon questioning, the resident manager told Ramone that the decedent, Jacqueline Taylor, drove a late-model Toyota Corolla. That car was not now parked on the street. Ramone deduced that the assailant had taken her money, credit cards, car keys, and car. From the perspective of the case, this was a good thing: if the assailant used the credit card, it could be traced. Likewise, a stolen car would make the assailant easier to find.

The decedent was a single mother. There were some articles of clothing, underwear mostly, double-XL T-shirts and thirty-four-waist boxers, in a corner of one of her dresser drawers, indicating a frequent adult male visitor but not a permanent resident. The second bedroom held two small beds, one covered in a floral pattern and the other in printed Redskins helmets. The room was filled with dolls, action figures, stuffed animals, and athletic equipment, including a miniature basketball and a K2 football. Elementary school photographs of the children, a boy and a girl, were in the living room on a side table.

The decedent had worked as a nurse. A uniform hung in her bedroom closet, and she was wearing a nurse's uniform when she was found. The resident manager confirmed that she was an RN at D.C. General. She was there now, lying on a sheet of plastic in the city morgue.

The preliminary canvass produced no witnesses. A security camera, however, was mounted on the roof of the apartment building, pointed at its entrance. If there was tape in the camera and it was rolling, Ramone would be in business. The resident manager, a skinny guy dressed completely in black, told him that the camera was "usually" working. The man had hard liquor on his breath at three in the afternoon. It was a small thing, but it gave Ramone doubt that the camera would be loaded and operable. Still, Ramone would check the camera. He could only hope.

* * *

TO RAMONE'S SURPRISE, THE tape had been loaded and the camera was in perfect condition. A clear image of a man leaving the apartment building was produced, with a burned-in time confirming his exit roughly at the time of the assault.

"That's her ex-husband right there," said the resident manager, watching the replay of the tape over the shoulder of Ramone, the image on the monitor clear as day. "He be comin around here every so often to see his kids."

Ramone radioed in William Tyree's name and had it run through the computerized WACIES program. Tyree had no criminal history and no prior arrests. Not even juvenile.

Ramone and Willis had the victim's sister meet them at the VCB offices to view the tape. While the children stayed in a kid-friendly playroom on site, the sister sat in the video room and identified the man leaving the apartment house as William Tyree, Jacqueline Taylor's second husband. He had been upset lately, the sister claimed, frustrated by his continued inability to find gainful employment. She suspected he had begun using drugs. Also, Jackie had taken up with a new man, a sometime construction worker named Raymond Pace, and this exacerbated Tyree's negative state of mind. Pace had priors, had done time for a manslaughter conviction, and, the sister said, was "not good" with Jackie's kids. Pace's T-shirts and boxers, Ramone presumed, had been the ones in Jacqueline Taylor's dresser drawer.

A watch was put on Tyree's apartment in Washington Highlands until a search warrant came through. Ramone put the Corolla's plate numbers out on the patrol sheets, along with a description of Tyree. He then visited Raymond Pace on his job site. Pace did not seem particularly moved by the news of Taylor's death, and indeed appeared to be as rough a customer as the sister had described. But Pace's foreman and a couple of his coworkers alibied him completely. In any case, the videotape seemed to tell the tale. William Tyree looked right for the murder.

By midnight, Tyree had not turned up. Ramone and Willis had been on the eight-to-four and collected much overtime that day. They went home to their families and returned the following morning at 8:00 a.m. Shortly thereafter, a patrolman made the plates of the Corolla on a Southeast street and radioed in the location.

The Corolla was parked near Oxon Run Park, in a pocket of known drug activity, sellers and users alike. An older resident of the block walked up to Ramone and Willis, standing with uniforms who were dusting the Corolla's door handles for prints, and asked if they were looking for the man who had parked the car. Ramone said they were.

"He went in that apartment house right over there," said the man, pointing a crooked finger at a brick unit set on the rise of the street. "Buncha people in and out all the time, ain't got no business bein there."

"They using heroin?" said Ramone, trying to determine the type of drug personalities he would encounter in the building.

The resident shook his head. "The pipe."

Ramone, Willis, and several uniforms went into the apartment house with unsnapped holsters. They did not draw their guns. Tyree was up on a second-floor landing, standing in a gray cloud with two other smoke hounds.

"William Tyree?" said Ramone, producing a pair of bracelets as he climbed the stairs.

Upon seeing the police officers and hearing his name, Tyree extended his hands, touching them together at the wrist. He was cuffed without incident. In his pockets they found Jacqueline Taylor's car keys and wallet.

Everything had been easy, even the arrest.

IN THE BACKROOM OFFICE of Lieutenant Maurice Roberts, a young, respected boss at the VCB, Ramone and Green sat on a couch, leaning over a phone on a plastic table. The speaker had been activated. Through it, Assistant U.S. Attorney Ira Littleton made redundant points about the arrest and interrogation. Ramone and Green had been practicing Littleton's theories back when Littleton was watching Saturday-morning cartoons in his pajamas. Most homicide detectives had good relationships with the prosecutors in the U.S. Attorney's office. It was a necessity that they interact cordially, of course, but beyond the required spirit of cooperation, genuine friendships were often forged. Littleton, young, relatively inexperienced, and insecure, was not one of the attorneys the detectives respected or considered a friend.

"I'd prefer an explicit, full confession," said Littleton, "rather than a simple admission that he was wearing bloody clothes yesterday."

"Right," said Ramone and Green, nearly in unison.

"We don't have enough to hold him for the murder charge," said Littleton.

"We can charge him for the theft of the automobile right now," said Ramone. "Also, possession of stolen property on the wallet and its contents. That's enough to hold him."

"But I want the murder charge," said Littleton.

"Copy," said Bo Green, looking at Ramone, making a stroking motion with his fist in front of his crotch. Ramone put his thumb an inch away from his forefinger, indicating the probable length of Littleton's prick.

"Get the confession," said Littleton. "And swab him for DNA."

"Not a problem," said Ramone.

"Will he consent to a blood sample?"

"He did," said Green. "And we took it."

"Was he high when you arrested him?"

"He appeared to be."

"That'll show up in his blood."

"Right."

"Any marks on him, anything like that?"

"A scratch on his face," said Ramone. "He says he doesn't remember how he got it."

"His DNA will be under her fingernails," said Littleton. "How much you wanna bet?"

"I'm not a gambling man," said Ramone.

"It's almost a slam dunk. Let's take it to the finish line."

"Well, he's cooperated with every aspect of the investigation so far. Waived his right to an attorney as well. Only thing he hasn't done is come right out and say he killed her. But he will."

"Okay. We recover that Safeway bag yet?"

"Gene Hornsby's on it," said Ramone.

"Hornsby's a good man," said Littleton.

Ramone rolled his eyes.

"God, I hope the garbagemen haven't picked up the trash yet," said Littleton.

"Me, too," said Ramone before he stuck his tongue out at the phone. Bo Green was still lazily jacking his fist.

"We want a win, fellas," said Littleton.

"Yes!" said Green, idly wondering but not really caring if he was being too emphatic in his response. "Anything else?"

"Call me when you get that confession."

"We will," said Ramone, and he killed the button to the speakerphone.

"You hear that?" said Green. "Littleton said Gene Hornsby was a good man. Said it kinda tender, like. Almost sounded like he was sweet on Gene."

"Gene ain't gonna appreciate that," said Ramone.

"Yeah, Gene got a problem with that homosexuality thing."

"You sayin Littleton's an ass ranger?"

"I don't know, Gus. You got a better sense of that than I do. Some might say a sixth sense."

"I'm tryin to work over here," said Lieutenant Roberts, staring at the paperwork on his desk. "Y'all mind?"

Ramone and Green got up off the couch.

"Ready?" said Ramone.

Green nodded. "Soon as I get my man a Mountain Dew."

FIVE

TWO MEN SAT at a bar, drinking slowly from bottles. The day was warm, and the front door had been opened to cool the space and air it out. Beenie Man toasted from the house stereo, and a man and a woman danced lazily in the center of the room.

"Say that name again?" said Conrad Gaskins.

"Red Fury," said Romeo Brock. He dragged off a Kool cigarette and let the smoke out slow.

"That ain't too common a name."

"Wasn't his given name," said Brock. "Red was what he got called in the street, you know, 'cause of his light skin. Fury was on account of the car."

"He drove a Mopar?"

"His woman did. Had personalized plates with her name on 'em, said 'Coco.' "

"All right, what happened?"

"Lotta shit. But I was thinking on this one murder he did. Red shot this dude dead in a carryout on Fourteenth Street, place called the House of Soul. Coco was waitin on him outside in the car. Red comes walkin out slow, the gun still in his hand. He gets in the passenger side real calm, and Coco pulls out the space and drives off like she just taking a Sunday cruise. Neither of them was moving too fast, is what people say. It was like nothing special had gone down."

"Ain't too smart, leavin off a murder with a car got personal plates."

"This man didn't care about that. Shit, he *wanted* folks to know who he was."

"Was it a Sport Fury?"

Brock nodded. "Red over white. Seventy-one, had those hidden headlights. Auto on the tree, V-eight, four-barrel carb. Faster than a motherfucker, too."

"Why they not call him Red Plymouth?"

"Red Fury sounds better," said Brock. "Red Plymouth don't ring out the same way."

Romeo Brock drank the shoulders off a cold bottle of Red Stripe. A loaded revolver sat snugly inside the belt line of his slacks under a red shirt worn tails out. An ice pick, corked at the tip, was taped to his calf.

The business was owned by East African immigrants and located on a soon-to-be-reconstructed stretch of Florida Avenue, east of 7th, in LeDroit Park. An Ethiopian flag was painted on the sign out front, and Haile Selassie's framed image hung beside the wall of liquor behind the stick. The bar, called Hannibal's by the locals because that was the night tender's name, catered to Jamaicans, mostly, which appealed to Brock. His mother, who worked as a maid in a hotel up by the District line, had been born and raised in Kingston. Brock called himself Jamaican but had never set foot on the island. He was as American as folding money and war.

Beside Brock, on a leather-topped stool, sat Conrad Gaskins, his older cousin. Gaskins was short and powerful, with broad shoulders and muscular arms. His eyes were Asiatic and his facial bones were prominent. A scar from a razor blade, acquired in prison, ran diagonally down his left cheek. It did not ruin him with women and it gave men pause. He stank of perspiration. He had not changed out of his work clothes, which he'd been wearing all day.

Gaskins said, "How he go down?"

"Red?" said Brock. "He'd done so many murders, assaults, and kidnappings in three months' time that he couldn't even keep track of who his enemies was."

"Man was on a regular crime spree."

"Shit, police and the Mob was *both* after him in the end. You heard of the Genovese family in New York, right?"

"Sure."

"They had a contract out on his black ass, is what people say. Whether he knew it or not, he killed some man was connected. I guess that's why he left town."

"He was got, though," said Gaskins.

"Everyone gets got; you know that. It's how you roll on the way there."

"Was it the police or the Corleones?"

"FBI got him down in Tennessee. Or West Virginia, *I* don't know. Caught him sleepin in one of them motor courts."

"They kill him?"

"Nah. He got doomed in the federal joint. Marion, I believe. White boys murdered his ass."

"Aryan Brotherhood?"

"Uh-huh. Back then they kept the whites separate from the blacks. Now, you know that some of the Marion prison guards were hooked up with those white supremacists. People say they saw the guards passin out knives to the ABs right before they cornered Red out in the yard. He held them off with a trash can lid for an hour. It took eight of those motherfuckers to kill him."

"That boy was fierce."

"You *know* it. Red Fury was a man."

Brock liked the old stories about outlaws like Red. Men who just didn't give a good fuck about the law or if and when they'd go down. Having other men talk about you in bars and on street corners after you were dead and gone, that's what made a life worth living. Otherwise, wasn't anything about you that was special. 'Cause everybody, straight and criminal alike, ended up covered in dirt. For that reason alone it was important to leave a powerful name behind.

"Finish your beer," said Brock. "We got shit to do."

Out on the street, Brock and Gaskins went to Brock's car, a '96 black Impala SS. It was parked on Wiltberger, a block of bland row houses fronted by stoops rather than porches, a street that looked more like Baltimore than D.C. Wiltberger ran behind the storied Howard Theater, once the local stage for Motown and Stax artists and chitlin circuit comics, the south-of-the-Mason-Dixon-Line version of Harlem's Apollo. It had been a charred shell since the time of the riots and was now surrounded by a chain-link construction fence.

"Looks like they finally gonna make somethin out the Howard," said Gaskins.

"Gonna do it like they did the Tivoli," said Brock. "They tryin to fuck this whole town up, you ask me."

They drove out of LeDroit, into Northeast and down into Ivy City off of New York Avenue. For many years this had been one of the grimmest sections of town, off the commuter path of most residents and so ignored and forgotten, a knot of small streets holding warehouses, dilapidated row houses, and brick apartments with plywood doors and windows. It was the long-time home of prostitutes, pipeheads, heroin addicts, dealers, and down-and-out families. Ivy City was nearly framed by Gallaudet University and Mount Olivet Cemetery, with an opening into the neighborhood of Trinidad, once known as the home base of the city's most famous drug lord, Rayful Edmond.

Now properties were being purchased and refurbished all over town, in places that doubters had said would never come back: Far Northeast and Southeast, Petworth and Park View, LeDroit, and the waterfront area around South Capitol, where ground was set to break on the new baseball stadium. Even here in Ivy City, For Sale and Sold signs could be seen on seemingly undesirable properties. Apartment buildings that had been shells for squatters, shooters, and rats were being gutted and turned into condos. Houses were bought and flipped six months later. Workers had begun to remove the rotting wood, put glass in the window frames, and brush on fresh coats of paint. Roofers hauled shingles and tar buckets up ladders, and real estate agents stood on the sidewalks, nervously aware of their surroundings as they talked on their cells.

"They gonna fix up this shithole, too?" said Gaskins.

"Like puttin a Band-Aid on a bullet hole, you ask me," said Brock.

"Where those boys at?" said Gaskins.

"They always around that corner up there," said Brock. He drove slowly down Gallaudet Street, passing a row of boxy brick apartment structures opposite a shuttered elementary school.

Brock curbed the SS and cut its engine.

"There go that boy Charles," said Brock, chinning in the direction of a thirteen-year-old who wore calf-length shorts, a blue-and-white-striped polo shirt, and blue-and-white Nikes. "Think he slick, too. Duckin my ass."

"He just a kid."

"They all just kids. But they gonna grow tall soon enough. Punk 'em now, and they won't have the mind to rise up later on."

"We don't need to be hurtin no kids, cousin."

"Why not?"

Brock and Gaskins got out of the car and walked down a

weedy sidewalk veined with cracks. Residents sitting on the steps outside their apartments and in folding chairs on lawns of dirt watched them as they approached a group of boys gathered at the intersection of Gallaudet and Fenwick streets. They were corner boys, standing on the spot where they stood on the days when they were not in school, and much of every night.

At the sight of Brock striding toward them, rangy and muscled beneath his red rayon shirt, they turned and ran. The boys moved with more immediacy than they would have had they been pulled up by police. They knew who Brock and Gaskins were and they knew what they were there for and what they would do to get it.

Two of the boys did not run because they realized that running would be futile. The older of the two was named Charles and the younger one was his friend James. Charles led a loosely formed group of teenagers and preteens who sold marijuana exclusively on that particular stretch of Gallaudet. They had started out selling it for fun and because they wanted to be gangsters, but now they found themselves with a growing business. They bought from a supplier in the Trinidad area who had his own retailers, some of whom quietly worked Ivy City, but the supplier did not begrudge them having a corner, as they turned his product and paid as they moved the inventory. Charles's people sold dimes in small plastic bags with tops that sealed.

Charles tried to keep his posture as Brock and Gaskins came up on him. Though James held his ground, he did not look into the eyes of Romeo Brock.

Brock had a foot of height on Charles. He got close in and looked down on the boy. Conrad Gaskins turned his back on them, crossed his arms, and eye-fucked the residents who were watching the scene from across the street.

"Damn, Charles," said Brock. "You look like you surprised to see me."

"I knew you'd come."

"So why you look surprised?" Brock gave him his bright and menacing smile. His features were sharp and angular, accentuated by a precisely groomed Vandyke. His ears were pointed. He liked to wear the color red. He looked like a tall devil.

"I was there," said Charles. "I was where you said."

"No, you weren't."

"You said meet me at the corner of Okie and Fenwick at nine o'clock. I was there."

"I ain't say no motherfuckin Okie. I said Gallaudet and Fenwick, where we at right now. Made it real simple on your little ass, so you wouldn't get confused."

"You said Okie."

Brock's right hand flew up and slapped Charles hard across the face. Charles was knocked back a step, and his eyes rolled some as he took the strike. Tears welled in his eyes, and his closed lips went out like a muzzle. Far as stripping a boy of his pride, Brock knew that the open hand was more powerful than the closed fist.

"Where was we gonna meet?" said Brock.

"I . . ." Charles struggled to speak but could not.

"Aw, you fixin to cry?"

Charles shook his head.

"Are you a girl or a man?"

"I'm a man."

"'I'm a *man*,'" repeated Brock. "Well, if you are, you a poor excuse for one."

A tear rolled down Charles's cheek. Brock laughed.

"Get the money and let's get gone," said Gaskins, his back still turned.

"I'm gonna ask you again," said Brock. "Where was we supposed to meet, Charles?"

"Right here."

"Good. And why you ain't post?"

" 'Cause I ain't had no money," said Charles.

"You still in business, right?"

"I just now bought my stash. I'm fixin to have some money soon."

"Oh, you gonna have some soon."

"Uh-huh. Soon as I move my stash."

"What's that lump in your pocket, then? And don't even try and tell me it's your manhood, 'cause we already established that you ain't got none."

"Leave him alone," said James.

Brock turned his attention to the smaller of the two boys, who couldn't have been more than twelve. He had braids under an NY cap turned sideways.

"You say somethin?" said Brock.

James raised his chin and for the first time looked Brock in the eye. His fists were balled as he spoke. "I said, leave my boy alone."

Brock's eyes crinkled at the corners. "Look at you. Hey, Conrad, this boy here showin some heart."

"I heard him," said Gaskins. "Let's go."

"I'm *here now,*" said Charles desperately. "I wasn't runnin. I been waitin on you to show all day."

"But you shouldn't have lied. Now I'm 'a have to give you your medicine."

"Please," said Charles.

"Beggin-ass bitch."

Brock grabbed hold of the right pocket on Charles's low-riding jean shorts and pulled down on it so violently that the boy fell to the sidewalk. The jeans ripped open at the side, exposing the inner pocket. Brock tore the pocket clean away and turned it inside out. He found cash and some dime bags of marijuana. He tossed the marijuana to the ground and counted the money. He frowned but slipped the money into his own pocket.

"One more thing," said Brock.

Brock kicked Charles in the ribs. He kicked him again, his teeth bared, and Charles rolled over on his side as bile poured from his open mouth. James looked away.

Gaskins pulled on Brock's arm and moved between him and Charles. They stared at each other until the fire went out of Brock's eyes.

"Y'all coulda made this easy," said Brock, stepping back and shaking his head. "I was willin to share. I was only lookin to take half. But you had to fuck up and lie. And now you prob'ly thinking, We gonna get this motherfucker. We gonna come back on him, or we gonna find someone who can, and get righteous on his ass." Brock straightened his shirt. "But you know what? You never will. Y'all ain't man enough to fuck with me. And you don't have anyone to protect you. If you knew someone bad enough to do it, they dead or in jail. If you had someone in your life who gave a fuck about you to begin with, you wouldn't be out here on this corner. So what do you have? Your little-ass, no-ass selves."

The boy on the ground said nothing and neither did his friend.

"What's my name?"

"Romeo," said Charles, his eyes closed in pain.

"We'll be comin 'round again."

Brock and Gaskins walked back to the Impala SS. None of the residents or onlookers had made a move to help the boys, and now they averted their eyes. None, Brock knew, would talk to the police. But he wasn't satisfied. It was too easy, and not worth the effort for a man of his reputation. It hadn't been a challenge, and the payoff was shit.

"How much we get?" said Gaskins.

"Buck forty."

"Hardly seem worth it."

"Don't worry. We gonna step it up from here."

"It's lookin to me that all we doin is roughin kids and shit. I'm askin where we goin with this, cuz. What's this about?"

"Money and respect," said Brock.

They got into the car.

"We'll head back to Northwest," said Brock. "Got a couple more appointments we need to keep."

"Not me," said Gaskins. "I got to be up before the sunrise. 'Less you sayin you need me."

"I'll drop you off at the house," said Brock. "I can handle the rest myself."

Brock made a call on his cell, ignitioned the SS, and drove off.

Soon after he and Gaskins left the neighborhood, a police cruiser came slowly down Gallaudet. Its driver, a white man in uniform, looked at the residents in front of the apartments and at the boy on the corner who was helping another boy, holding his side, to his feet. The uniformed officer gave the cruiser gas and continued on his way.

SIX

HOW IS IT?" said Detective Bo Green, back in the box.

"Taste good," said William Tyree, placing the can of soda on the table.

"Cold enough for you?"

"It's good."

In the darkness of the video room, Anthony Antonelli grunted in disgust. "Fucknuts thinks he's in a restaurant."

"Bo's just making him comfortable," said Ramone.

Green shifted his weight in his chair. "You feel all right, William?"

"Not so bad."

"You still high?"

"I been high for a day." Tyree shook his head in self-disgust.

"When did you get first get high yesterday?"

"Before I got on the bus."

"You took the bus to . . ."

"Jackie's."

"How much crack had you smoked? You remember?"

"I don't know. But it musta hit me good. I was upset to begin with. The rock made me feel, you know, fierce inside."

"What were you upset about, William?"

"Every goddamn thing. I got laid off from my job a year ago. I was a driver for a linen service, you know, one of those companies that deliver uniforms, tablecloths to restaurants, and stuff. I been havin trouble finding a job since I lost that one. It's hard out there."

"I know it is."

"It *damn* sure is. And then, to lose my wife and kids on top of that. I mean, I'm an honest man, Detective. I ain't never been in trouble in my life."

"I know your family. You come from good people."

"I never even messed with no drugs before my luck turned bad. A little marijuana, maybe."

"That ain't no thing."

"And then my wife goes and takes up with a low-ass criminal. Man sleepin in my bed, telling *my* kids what to say and do . . . telling them to shut their mouths and show respect. To *him*."

"It bothered you."

"*Shit*. Wouldn't it bother *you?*"

"It would," said Green, giving him that. "So you smoked some crack yesterday and you went to see your ex-wife."

"She was still my wife. We ain't had no divorce proceedings yet."

"My mistake. I got some bad information."

"We were still married. And I was just . . . I was *angry*, Detective. I'm sayin my head was on fire when I left out the house."

"Did you take anything with you when you left?"

Tyree nodded. "A knife. You know, that knife I told you about."

"The one you put in the Safeway bag."

"Uh-huh. I snatched it up off the counter before I tipped out."

"You carried it on the Metrobus."

"It was inside my shirt."

"And then you walked up Cedar Street with the knife in your shirt and you went to your wife's apartment." When Tyree nodded again, Green said, "You knocked on the door, right? Or did you have a key?"

"I knocked. She asked who it was, and I told her it was me. She said she was busy and couldn't see me right then, and asked me to go away. I said I just wanted to talk to her for a minute, and she opened the door. I went inside."

"Did you say anything else to her when you went inside?"

In the video room, Antonelli said, "No, I just fucking murdered her ass."

"What did you do when you went inside, William?" said Green.

"She was unloading groceries and stuff. I followed her over to where the groceries were at, by the eating table."

"And what did you do when you got there?"

Ramone leaned forward.

"I don't remember," said Tyree.

Rhonda Willis entered the video room. To Ramone she said, "Gene found the Safeway bag in the Dumpster. The clothes and the knife are inside it."

Ramone did not feel elation of any kind. "Tell Bo," he said.

Ramone and Antonelli watched the monitor as Green's head turned at the sound of a knock. The door opened, and Rhonda came half through it to tell Green he had a call he should probably take.

Before Green left the interrogation room, he looked at his watch, then up at the camera, and said, "Four thirty-two."

He returned several minutes later, stated the time the same way, and took a seat across the table from William Tyree. Tyree was now smoking a cigarette.

"You all right?" said Green.

"Yes."

"Need another soda, somethin?"

"I still got some."

"Okay, then," said Green. "Let's go back to your wife's apartment yesterday. After you went inside, you followed her over there to the eating table. What happened next?"

"It's like I said: I don't remember."

"William."

"I'm telling you straight."

"*Look* at me, William."

Tyree looked into the big soulful eyes of Detective Bo Green. They were caring eyes, the eyes of a man who had run the same streets and walked the halls of Ballou High School, just like Tyree had done. A man who had come up in a strong family, just like him. Who had listened to Trouble Funk and Rare Essence and Backyard, and seen all those go-go bands play for free at Fort Dupont Park, just like him, when both of them had been young men. A man who was not all that different from Tyree, who Tyree could trust to do him right.

"What did you do with the knife when you followed Jackie over to that table?"

Tyree did not answer.

"We have the knife," said Green without any tone of threat or malice. "We have the clothes you were wearing. You know the blood on the clothing and the knife is going to match your wife's blood. And the skin under your wife's fingernails is gonna be the same skin got took off your face, from that cut you got right there. So William, why don't we get this done?"

"Detective, I don't remember."

"Did you use the knife we found in the bag to stab your wife, William?"

Tyree made a clucking sound with his tongue. His eyes were heavy with tears. "If you say I did, then I guess I did."

"You guess you did or you did?"

Tyree nodded. "I did."

"You did what?"

"I stabbed Jackie with that knife."

Green sat back and folded his hands on his ample belly. Tyree dragged on his cigarette and tapped its ash into a heavy piece of foil.

"I gotta hand it to Bo," said Antonelli. "He's good with them hootleheads."

Ramone said nothing.

Ramone and Antonelli watched and listened as William Tyree told the rest of the story. After stabbing his wife, he had taken her car and, using all the cash in her wallet, bought more crack. He then proceeded to smoke it in various pockets of Southeast. He didn't eat or sleep all night. He rented Jackie's car out to two different men. He used her credit card to buy gas for the hack and also for cash advances to buy more rock. He stayed high and without a plan, except to wait for the police, who he knew would eventually come. He had never done anything remotely criminal before on the violent end and had no knowledge of the underground. He didn't know how to hide. And if he were to run, he could think of no place to go.

When Tyree was talked out, Green asked him to stand and remove his belt and shoelaces. Tyree complied, then sat back down in his chair. He cried a little, and afterward wiped the tears off his face with the back of his hand.

"You all right?" said Green.

"I'm tired," said Tyree very softly. "I don't wanna be here no more."

"No shit," said Antonelli. "You shoulda thought of that before you killed her."

Ramone did not comment. He knew that Tyree was not speaking about being held in the box. He was saying that he didn't want to be in this world any longer. Green had sensed it, too. It was why he had taken Tyree's shoelaces and belt.

"You want a sandwich, somethin?" said Green.

"Nah."

"I can go to Subway."

"I'm good."

Green looked at his watch, then up at the camera, and said, "Five thirteen." He walked from the interrogation room as Tyree reached for a cigarette.

Ramone's eyes thanked Green as he came out of the box. The two of them and Rhonda Willis walked to their cubicles, situated in a kind of triangle. They were senior detectives in the unit and friends.

Green sat down and Ramone did the same, immediately reaching for the phone to call his wife. He did this several times a day and always when he closed a case. There was still much work to be done on this one, especially paperwork, but for now the detectives would allow themselves a small break.

Detective Antonelli and Detective Mike Bakalis took seats nearby. Antonelli, a Gold's Gym enthusiast, was short, broad shouldered, and narrow waisted. He was called Plug to his face and Butt Plug to his back by his fellow detectives. Bakalis, because of his prominent beak, was called Aardvark and sometimes Baklava. Bakalis was there to type a subpoena into his computer, but he hated to type anything and had only been talking about it all day.

Over the desks of the detectives were corkboards, many displaying photos of children, wives, and other relatives along-side death photos of victims and apprehended but unconvicted perps who had become obsessions. Crucifixes, pictures of saints, and psalm quotes were in abundance. Many of the VCB detectives were devout Christians, others only claimed they were, and some had lost their faith in God completely. Divorce was fairly common among them. Conversely, there were those who had managed to maintain strong marriages. Others were players. Some drank heavily and some were on the wagon. Most had a beer or two after their shift and never developed a problem with alcohol. None of them were types. They weren't in their position for the promise of great financial reward. The job wasn't, for the majority of them, a calling. For one reason or another, they were suited to be homicide police. It was where they had naturally landed.

"Everything all right?" said Rhonda Willis, noticing Ramone's frown as he hung up the phone.

Ramone stood, leaned his back against a divider, and crossed his arms. He was an average-sized man with a good chest who had to work hard at his flat belly. His hair was black, still full and wavy, and without gray. He had a dimpled chin. He wore a mustache, the only thing that identified him as a cop. It was unfashionable for white guys to wear them, but his wife preferred him with it, which was reason enough for him to keep it on his face.

"My kid got in trouble again," said Ramone. "Regina said she got a call from the assistant principal, something about insubordination. We get calls from that school damn near every day."

"He's a boy," said Rhonda, who had four of her own by two different husbands and was now raising them by herself. She spent a good part of her day communicating with her sons via their cells.

"I know it," said Ramone.

"Spare the rod," said Bakalis, distracting himself with a stroke magazine he had picked up off his desk. Bakalis had no kids himself but felt he needed to chime in.

Antonelli, who was divorced, tossed a set of Polaroids onto Bakalis's desk. "Check these out, you want to see something."

They were the death photos of Jacqueline Taylor. In the photos she was laid out on her back, naked on a large sheet of black plastic. By the time the sister had identified her, she had been cleaned up, but these were the shots taken when she had first arrived at the morgue. The stab wounds were most prominent on her neck and one of her breasts, which was nearly severed. Her eyes were open, one more widely than the other, which made her appear to be inebriated. Her tongue was swollen and protruded.

"Look at that hair trail," said Antonelli, putting his feet up on his desk. His trouser hiked up, revealing an ankle holster and the butt of his Glock.

Bakalis studied the photos one by one without comment. The mood was not festive, despite the fact that they had caught a killer. No one could be happy with the results in this particular case.

"Poor old gal," said Green.

"Him, too," said Ramone. "Guy was a solid citizen up until a year ago. Loses his job, falls in love with the pipe, watches his wife shack up with an asshole who parks his laundry in the same place Tyree's kids are sleeping. . . ."

"I knew his older brother," said Green. "Shoot, I used to see William out there when he wasn't nothin but a kid. His people were good. Don't let no one tell you that drugs don't fuck you up."

"Even if he pleads," said Rhonda, "he'll catch eighteen, twenty-five."

"And those kids'll be messed up for life," said Green.

"She must have been some woman," said Bakalis, still studying the photos. "I mean, he was so torn about losing that thing he had to kill it so no other man could hit it."

"If he hadn't been smoking that shit," said Green, "he might have thought straight."

"Wasn't just the rock," said Antonelli. "It's a proven fact, pussy will compel you to kill. Even the pussy you *can't* have."

"Pussy can pull a freight train," said Rhonda Willis.

Bakalis dropped the Polaroids on his desk, then touched the pads of his fingers to the keyboard of his computer. But his fingers did not move. He stared stupidly at the monitor.

"Hey, Plug," said Bakalis. "How'd you like to type up a subpoena?"

"How'd you like to suck my dick?"

The two of them went back and forth for a while until Gene Hornsby arrived with the bag of evidence. Ramone thanked him and got to work on the booking and attendant paperwork, including the entering of the case details in The Book. This was a large tablet detailing open and closed homicides, officers assigned to the cases, motives, and other elements that would be helpful to the prosecution effort and also serve to memorialize basic city history.

By the time the detectives had checked out for the day, they had worked a full shift and three hours of overtime.

Out in the parking lot of the VCB, located behind the Penn-Branch shopping center in Southeast, Gus Ramone, Bo Green, George Hornsby, and Rhonda Willis walked to their cars.

"I'm gonna take a nice hot bath tonight," said Rhonda.

"Don't you need to run your sons somewhere this evening?" said Green.

"Not tonight, praise God."

"Anybody up for a beer?" said Hornsby. "I'll let y'all buy me one."

"I got practice," said Green, who coached a boys' football team in the neighborhood where he'd come up.

"What about the Ramone?" said Hornsby.

"Rain check," said Rhonda, who knew what the answer would be before it came from Ramone's mouth.

Ramone wasn't listening. He was thinking of his wife and kids.

SEVEN

DIEGO RAMONE GOT off the 12 bus near the Metro station and walked over the District line toward his house. It had not been a good day at his middle school, but it had been a typical one. He had caught trouble, like he had caught trouble a couple of times every week since he started going there. He wished he could have stayed at his old middle school in D.C., but his father had insisted he transfer into Montgomery County, and things had not gone too well since.

Mr. Guy, the assistant principal, had called Diego's mother earlier in the day to tell her that Diego had refused to give up his cell phone after it had rung inside the school. The truth was, Diego had forgotten it was on. He knew it was against school rules to have it on inside, but he hadn't wanted to give it up, on account of his friend Toby had got his phone taken away for weeks after a similar thing went down. So he'd told Mr. Guy, "No, I'm not gonna give it up, 'cause it was an honest mistake," and then Mr. Guy had taken him down to the office and called his mother. Mr. Guy had said that he could have suspended him for insubordination and that he was cutting him a break. Some break. Diego was still going to hear about it from his father. Besides, being suspended was more fun than being in school. In that school, anyway.

Diego walked through a short tunnel under the Metro tracks and crossed Blair Road. He wore a long black T-shirt showing the Tasmanian Devil hand-screened by a friend, one of the Spriggs twins. Under the T-shirt he wore a Hanes wife-beater. It was autumn, but still warm enough for shorts, and his were Levi Silvertabs worn a few inches below the knee. Beneath the Silvertabs he wore SpongeBob boxers. His shoes today, one of three pairs of sneaks he owned, were Nike Exclusives, the white and navy.

Diego Ramone was fourteen years old.

His ringer, a Backyard live at the Crossroads thing he had downloaded onto his phone, went off. He unhooked his cell from the waistband of his shorts.

"Yeah," he said into the mic.

"Where you at, dawg?" said his friend Shaka Brown.

"I'm comin up on, like, Third and Whittier."

"You walkin?"

"Uh-huh."

"Ain't your mother pick you up?"

"I took the twelve."

His mother had come by the school, but he knew if he got in the car with her she'd want to take him straight home, go on about homework, all that. After some negotiation, it was agreed that he would take the bus and then foot it into their neighborhood, where, he had assured her, his plans were only to meet Shaka and play a little ball. Taking the bus gave him a sense of freedom and made him feel like an adult. He had promised his mother he'd be home well before dinnertime.

"Ain't like you to walk. Soft as you are."

"Stop playin," said Diego.

"Hurry up, Dago, I got a court."

"I'm comin."

"I'm 'a shred you."

"Yeah, right."

Diego ended the call. Before he could reattach the cell to his belt line, his mother rang him up.

"Hello?"

"Where are you?"

"Near Coolidge," said Diego.

"You meeting Shaka?"

"Told you I was."

"You have homework tonight?"

"I did it in study hall," said Diego. It was just a white lie. He would get it done in study hall the next day.

"Don't stay out too long."

"Said I wouldn't."

Diego hit "end." Having a cell phone was tight, but it could be a curse, too.

Shaka was shooting buckets on the fenced court at 3rd and Van Buren. It was a nice clean court for D.C., with chains and everything, part of the rec center that ran behind and alongside Coolidge High School. There were tennis courts that the adults used, mostly, and a soccer field for the Spanish, and a playground for the kids. Diego had been hanging out here, progressing from the monkey bars to hoops, since before he'd been in Whittier Elementary. He lived with his parents and his little sister, Alana, just a few blocks south in Manor Park.

"You better hurry up," said Shaka, as Diego crossed the court. "I'm fixin to burn these chains off the way I'm droppin 'em."

Diego took off his T-shirt, leaving him in his sleeveless, and wrapped the T around his cell. He placed the package on the side of the court, by the fence.

Diego said, "Lemme see that rock."

Shaka bounced the Spalding indoor/outdoor over to Diego, who took a medium-range jumper that hit the back of the iron and did not drop.

"You ready?" said Shaka.

"Gimme a few more warm-ups. You been out here awhile."

"You gonna need a day of warm-ups to touch me."

"I'm 'a damage you, son."

Before they could go at each other, the Spriggs twins, Ronald and Richard, dropped by the court. After some talk, Diego and Shaka went two-on-two against them. The Spriggs twins were on the hard side and were frequently in trouble with the law for minor crimes like theft, which elevated them in the eyes of other boys their age. Diego and Shaka just thought of them as old friends. They had all known one another since elementary, and now they were going down different paths.

Ronald and Richard Spriggs were tough, but they couldn't ball. Diego and Shaka took every game, and the Spriggs twins left, smiling but not happy, muttering benign threats about "next time" and something about Shaka's sister looking nice as they deep-dipped away toward their apartment over on 9th, the group behind the 4th District police station.

For the next hour, Diego and Shaka went one-on-one. Shaka was a year older than Diego and had a few inches on his friend. His skill level was higher than Diego's as well. But Diego showed heart in any sport he played. The games went even until the last rubber match, which Shaka took. As the ball went through the chains, a reverse layin that Shaka earned with a quick first step, Diego's cell sang out, that "Girls Just Wanna Have Fun" thing, go-go style. He answered it, using the T-shirt it was wrapped in to wipe the sweat off his face.

"Mom," said Diego, reading the caller ID.

"Diego, where are you?"

"At the courts behind Coolidge. I'm with Shaka."

"Okay," said Regina, sounding relieved. Diego had made sure to mention the company he was in because his mother liked and trusted Shaka over all of his friends. "You coming home?"

"I'll be dey soon."

"You'll be *dey?*"

"I'll be *there,*" said Diego, ending the call.

He joined Shaka, sitting with his back against the fence, checking his cell for messages. Shaka wore a T-shirt showing Marley smoking a blunt, right off the *Catch a Fire* cover, but Shaka was not a weed smoker. He had never even tried it. He and Diego talked about it often, and romanticized it some, but they didn't use it. They considered themselves athletes, and Diego's parents and Shaka's mother had drumbeat it into their heads that athletes didn't get high. Of course, they knew this to be untrue. But they also knew that many of the kids they hung with who had begun to drink a little and get blazed had kinda dropped off from playing ball and weren't doing as good in school as they had before. That much they could see for themselves. Diego still played Yes League basketball and Boys Club basketball and football; Shaka, now that he was in high school, knew he had to pick one sport if he was going to be serious about pursuing an eventual scholarship, and had chosen basketball. Both of them had dreams of playing college ball and professional sports.

"You keep them Exclusives fresh," said Shaka, chinning at Diego's Nikes.

"They feel good on my feet."

"Good as they look, those shoes didn't help you none today, though, did they?"

"Couldn't find my shot is all it was."

"Uh-huh. Maybe it's the shoes messed you up."

"I got my eye on the new Forums," said Diego. "Them joints is *wet.*"

"Your father ain't gonna let you get another pair of sneaks."

"If I get my grades up for the quarter," said Diego, "he will."

They talked about girls. They talked about Ghetto Prince, the Sunday-night go-go show on WPGC hosted by Big G, the singer from Backyard. They talked about going to a band show at the community center on New Hampshire Avenue, in Langley Park. They talked about Carmelo Anthony and how he had been unfairly treated in that video thing up in Baltimore. Shaka claimed he had seen NBA star Steve Francis and his friend Bradley over by Georgia Avenue. Steve had come up in the area and was frequently seen back in the neighborhood, talking positive to kids.

"Steve was drivin that Escalade he got," said Shaka, and Diego asked about the rims, and when Shaka described them, Diego said they sounded tight.

The sky had darkened some. They got up to go and collected their things. Through the chain-link fence, they saw their friend Asa Johnson walking south on 3rd. Asa was wearing a North Face jacket that broke midthigh. His head down, his brow wrinkled, he was staring at the sidewalk, taking long strides.

"Asa!" shouted Shaka. "Where you goin, dawg?"

Asa did not answer or acknowledge the call. He turned his face away so they could not see his eyes. As he did, Diego thought he saw something shiny on his cheek.

"Asa. Yo, hold up!"

Asa walked on. They watched him as he turned left on Tuckerman, eastward bound.

" 'Sup with him?" said Diego. "Actin like he don't know us."

"No clue. Kinda warm for him to be rockin that North Face, though."

"He was sweatin, too. Guess he gotta show that new coat off."

"You talk to him lately?"

"Not much this school year. Not since I transferred."

"He playin football?"

"He dropped out."

"Maybe he's just in a hurry to get home."

"He lives in the opposite direction," said Diego.

"Maybe he's tryin to get away from home, then," said Shaka. "Way his father's always pressed."

"Could be he's got a girl up that way."

"You ever know Asa to mess with a girl?"

"True," said Diego. "But I ain't never see you with one, either."

"I never am with just one," said Shaka. "I got a whole stable."

"Where they at?"

"I ain't tellin you."

They came off the court and walked south on 3rd. Down past Sheridan they went along a short commercial strip, past a women's clothing store with African designs, a barbershop, a dry cleaner's, and a ministry. On the next street, at the corner of 3rd and Rittenhouse, they stopped in front of a large warehouse-like structure that was now a banquet and party hall, rented out for anniversaries, birthdays, and general celebrations, called the Air Way VIP room.

"I'm headed over to Fat Joe's," said Shaka. "Play some PS 2. He got the new NC double A."

"My pops won't let me go to Joe's."

"Why not?"

"Joe's father has a gun. You know, that little thirty-two he got?"

"We ain't gonna mess with it."

"My father don't want me in that house."

"Okay, then," said Shaka, tapping Diego's outstretched fist. "Later, dawg."

"Later."

Shaka walked west down Rittenhouse, toward his mother's row house on Roxboro Place. Diego went east, in the direction of a pale yellow stucco colonial fronted by a porch, on a rise halfway up the block.

His father's Tahoe was not in the street. Diego felt that he was nearly a man, but he was still young enough to like the security of knowing his dad was home.

Dusk was near. The dropping sun cast long shadows on the grass.

EIGHT

THE MUSIC OKAY, sir?" said Dan Holiday, checking the rearview, looking at his client, a fit guy in his midforties, relaxing on the right side of the backseat.

"It's fine," said the client, pressed jeans and a top-end blazer, open-neck shirt, black leather boots, a Tag Heuer wristwatch that must have put him back a thousand beans. Guy had one of those expensive hairstyles, too, shooting off in different directions on top, with that flip-up thing in the front. The look said, I don't have to wear a tie like all you other suckers, but I have money, rest assured.

Holiday had watched the guy coming out of his house in Bethesda as he sat out in the black Town Car, waiting. He had estimated his approximate age and, knowing he was some kind of writer (Holiday had been contacted by a publishing house in New York, a frequent customer, for the pickup), figured the guy favored the new wave stuff of his youth, meaning '77 and beyond. Holiday had found Fred, the "classic alternative" program, on the radio before the guy even slid into the car.

"You can change it if you'd like," said Holiday. "You've got your own controls on the back of the seat, right there in front of you."

They were heading out on the toll road toward Dulles Airport. Holiday had his black suit jacket on but had forgone the chauffeur cap, which made him feel like a bellhop. He only wore the cap when he was driving corporate bigwigs, politicians, and K Street types.

Holiday didn't feel the need to be real formal with this particular client, and that was nice, but the music, Christ, it was setting him on edge. Some heroin addict was whooping through the speakers. The writer in the backseat was moving his head a little to the beat as he studied the radio controls mounted in the leather before him.

"You got satellite in here?" said the writer.

"I put the XM unit in all my cars," said Holiday. *All.* He had two.

"Cool."

"Same idea behind GPS technology," said Holiday. "We used it for tracking purposes when I was in law enforcement."

"You were a cop?" This seemed to waken the guy's curiosity. His eyes met Holiday's in the rearview for the first time.

"In D.C."

"That must have been interesting."

"I got stories."

"I'll bet."

"Anyway, after I retired, I started up this service."

"You seem too young to have retired already."

"I had all my years in, even if I don't look it," said Holiday. "Good genes, I guess."

Holiday reached for the slotted plastic piece under the sun visor, extracted a couple of business cards, and handed them over the bench to the client. The guy took them and read the embossed printing on the face of the one on top: "Holiday Car Service," in Old English letters. And below it, "Luxury Transportation, Security, Executive Protection." And then the tagline, "Let Us Make Your Workday a Holiday." At the bottom was Holiday's contact information.

"You do security?"

"That's my main business. My *expertise.*"

"Bodyguard stuff, too, huh?"

"Uh-huh."

Holiday left much of the "bodyguard stuff" to Jerome Belton, his other driver and sole employee. Belton, a former noseguard at Virginia Tech who had blown out his knee in his senior year, took the security jobs, driving high-level executives and third-tier rappers and other entertainers coming through town for shows. Belton was a big man who could affect, when needed, a hard, unsmiling expression, and so possessed the necessary equipment for the job.

Holiday passed a Washington Flyer cabbie on the left and swerved his Town Car back into the right lane. In the mirror he saw the writer slip the cards into his breast pocket. He would probably throw them in the trash at the airport, but you never knew. You built a business by referral, or so Holiday had been told. Once you got them in the car, it was all about presentation. The items in the backseat, pristinely folded copies of the *Washington Post, New York Times,* and *Wall Street Journal,* the tin of Altoids, the bottles of Evian, and the satellite radio, they were all there to leave an impression of service and to make the client feel like he or she was a very special person, to elevate him or her above the cab-and-shuttle crowd. Holiday even kept a copy of the *Washington Times* in the trunk, in case the client looked to be of that fringe.

"So, you're a writer," said Holiday, trying to put a tone of give-a-shit into his voice.

"Yes," said the client. "I'm leaving for a three-week book tour today, actually."

"Must be an interesting way to make a living."

"It can be."

"Is it fun to be on the road like that?"

Do you get much pussy?

"Sometimes. Mostly, it's tiring. The airplane travel takes it out of you."

"That sounds rough."

"Getting through airport security is exhausting these days."

"Tell me about it."

You little girl.

"I dread it sometimes," said the writer.

"I can imagine," said Holiday.

Take off your skirt and paste some hair on your balls.

Holiday said little else for the rest of the ride. He had done his duty and passed out a couple of cards, and now he was finished. He sucked on an Ice Breaker breath mint and thought about his next drink.

He was bored shitless. This was no way for a man to make a living. Wearing a stupid fucking hat.

"I'm going out on United," said the guy in the backseat as they neared the color-coded signs alerting them to the airport entrance.

"Yes, sir," said Holiday.

Holiday dropped the client at his gate and pulled the man's luggage out of the trunk. The writer gave him a five-dollar tip. Holiday shook his small hand and told him to "travel safe."

At this hour, 495 would be a parking lot from Virginia to Maryland. Holiday decided to find a bar and wait out the rush. Get back on the road when the traffic eased some. Maybe find someone to talk to while he put his head where it needed to be.

He found a hotel in Reston a couple of exits back off the toll road. It was in something called a Town Center that looked like a block of chain retailers, eateries, and coffee shops that someone had lifted out of a real city and dropped in a cornfield. On the way to the bar he introduced himself to the concierge and handed him several cards along with a ten-dollar bill. Much of his business came from the hotel trade, which Holiday cultivated with the personal touch.

The bar was fine, sports themed but not too aggressive with it. There were many high tables designed for those who wanted to stand in groups and stools for those who preferred to sit. A bank of windows gave a view of the fake street. Holiday had a seat at the stick and placed his cigarettes and matches on its marble top, cool to the touch. One good thing about Virginia, you could still smoke in a bar.

"Yessir," said the bartender, a low-slung blonde.

"Absolut rocks," said Holiday.

Holiday drank and smoked down a Marlboro. The mostly male crowd was heavy with goatees, Kenneth Cole Reaction slacks, Banana Republic stretch oxfords, and golf shirts for those who had taken the afternoon off. The women were similarly clean and square. In his black Hugo Boss suit, bought off the rack, and white shirt, Holiday looked like a businessman, on the Euro side, slightly more hip than the techies around him.

He struck up a conversation with a young route salesman, and they bought each other's drinks for the next two rounds. It had gotten dark out, Holiday noticed, by the time the salesman went up to his room. Holiday ordered another drink, got it in hand, watched as steam came up off the rocks in the glass. He was relaxed. He was going down that familiar darkened road, and still he had no desire to turn back.

An attractive redhead who would never see thirty-five again took a seat on the stool beside him. She wore a greenish skirt-and-jacket business suit that complemented her hair color and picked up the green of her eyes. Her eyes were lively and told him that she'd be a freak in bed. Holiday took all of this in with a quick glance. He was good at this.

He held up the cigarette burning between his fingers. "You mind?"

He showed her his teeth and the laugh lines around his ice blue eyes. The first look was all-important.

"Not if you let me bum one," she said.

"You got it," said Holiday, and offered her the pack. He struck a match, put fire to her smoke, and blew out the flame. "Danny Holiday."

"Rita Magner."

"Pleasure."

"Thanks for this," she said. "I only smoke on the road, y'know."

"Me, too."

"I get bored." She winked. "It's something to do."

"Sales can be a drag," said Holiday. "Different hotel room every night . . ."

"Bartender," she said, raising her hand.

He checked her out as she ordered a drink. He caught the sun line on her ring finger. Married, but that was fine; it only made them more eager. Her treadmilled thigh rippled as she crossed it over the other. He eyed her open suit jacket, her freckled chest, her small breasts, loose in a black brassiere.

"On my tab," said Holiday to the bartender as she placed the drink in front of Rita.

"You're gonna spoil me," said Rita.

"I'll let you get the next one."

"Deal," she said. "So what line are you in?"

"Security," said Holiday. "I sell trackers, surveillance equipment, wiretap devices, that kind of thing. To police."

He had a friend, an ex-cop like him, who did just that, so he knew enough about it to bullshit her.

"Hmm."

"You?"

"Pharmaceuticals."

"You got any samples you wanna lay on me?"

"Bad boy," she said with a crooked smile. "I'd lose my job."

"I had to ask."

"It's okay to ask."

"It is?" said Holiday.

She drank vodka tonics and he stuck to Absolut on ice. She matched him one for one. They finished his pack of smokes and he bought another. He moved closer to her and she let him and he knew that he was there.

He told her about his most embarrassing moment as a salesman. It was a variation on a story he had told many times before. He changed the details as he went along. He was good at that, too.

"What about you?" he said.

"Oh, God," she said with a toss of her hair. "Okay. I was in Saint Louis last year. I had flown in that morning for a big lunch meeting, and I thought I had cushion time between my arrival and the meeting. So I wore some comfortable clothes on the flight. Comfortable but definitely not appropriate for the meeting."

"I know where this is going."

"Let me tell it. The plane was real late getting in, and I had to pick up the rental car as well. By the time I did it, there wasn't enough time to check into my hotel, change my clothes, and still make the meeting."

"So where'd you change?" said Holiday.

"There was a garage under the restaurant where we were supposed to meet."

"You couldn't use the hotel bathroom?"

"It was real dark in the garage and nobody was around. I changed in the backseat of the rental. I had my top off, I mean completely off, because I had to put on a different bra than the one I had on, and this old guy walks by on the way to his car. Instead of doing the decent thing and walking on, maybe doing a double take, he comes over to the window and taps on it, and he's staring at me, really checking me out . . ."

"I don't blame him."

". . . and he says something like, 'Miss, can I be of any assistance?' "

Holiday and Rita Magner laughed.

"That's what makes the story," said Holiday. "That detail."

"Right," said Rita. " 'Cause otherwise, it's not all that unusual. I mean, it wasn't the first time I've been nude in a car."

"And I bet it won't be the last."

Rita Magner smiled, reddened a little, and knocked back the rest of her drink.

"That day in the garage," said Holiday. "Did you have on the black thong you're wearing now?"

"How do you know that?"

"You're definitely wearing a thong," said Holiday. "And it's gotta be black."

"You're bad," she said.

She mentioned the minibar in her room.

Going up in the elevator, he moved on her and kissed her mouth. She parted her lips, and against the wood-paneled wall her legs opened like a flower. His hand went up her bare thigh and touched the lace of her black thong and beneath it the dampness and the heat. She moaned under his kiss and touch.

An hour later, Holiday was walking back to his Lincoln. She'd been as needy and voracious as he'd expected, and when it was done he left her to her memories and her guilt. She hadn't given him any indication that she wanted him to stay. Rita was now like the others, a prop, a story to tell the boys at Leo's, something for them to imagine and be envious of even as she was wiped from his mind. He'd forgotten her face by the time he turned the key to his car.

NINE

GUS RAMONE CAME through the front door and heard "Summer Nights" coming from the rec room at the back of his house. Alana would be there, watching a DVD, one of her favorite musicals. Judging from the smell of garlic and onions, Regina was in the kitchen, preparing dinner.

They're here and they're safe. This was the first thought that came to Ramone as he walked through the hall. As he entered the kitchen, he thought of Diego and wondered if he was somewhere in the house, too.

"How you doin, little girl?" said Ramone to his daughter, who was standing in front of the television set, dancing, imitating the moves she was watching on the screen. The rec room, which they'd added to the house a few years earlier, opened up off the kitchen.

"Good, Daddy," said Alana.

"Hey," he said to Regina, who had her back to him,

moving a wooden spoon around in a pot set on a gas stove. She wore some kind of athletic outfit, pants with stripes on the side and a matching shirt.

"Hey, Gus," she said.

Ramone put his rig, a clip-on belt holster holding his Glock 17, and his badge case, in a drawer he had equipped for security and locked the drawer with a small key on his ring. He and Regina, and no one else, had keys to the drawer.

Ramone went back to his daughter, now doing pelvic thrusts in the center of the living room, aping the young actor onscreen. The man was smiling lasciviously, dancing in the bleachers, as lean and fluid as an alley cat, his Brylcreemed cohorts egging him on, singing, "Tell me more, tell me more . . ."

"Did she put up a fight?" sang Alana, as Ramone bent down and kissed her on the top of her head, sprouting a mass of thick black curls, an inheritance from her father.

"How's my sweet little girl?" said Ramone.

"I'm good, Dad."

She kept on dancing, thumbs out like Danny Zuko. Ramone went back into the kitchen and wrapped his arms around Regina's shoulders and kissed her on the cheek. He pushed himself into her behind just to let her know he was still in the game. The lines at the corners of her eyes told him she was smiling.

"Is that movie she's watching appropriate?" he said.

"It's *Grease,*" said Regina.

"I know what it is. But Travolta is air-humping over there and our daughter's copying him."

"She's just dancing."

"That's what they call it now?"

Ramone unwrapped his arms and stepped to her side.

"Good day?" said Regina.

"We had a bunch of luck. I wouldn't say anyone feels good about it, though. Man wasn't a criminal. He got crazy behind some crack and killed his wife because he was jealous and despondent. She's in the morgue, he's probably down for twenty-five, and the kids are orphans. Nothing good about that."

"You did your job," she said, a familiar refrain in their home.

He talked to her every night about his workday. He felt it was important, in that those cops who didn't, in his experience, were headed for disasters in their marriages. Plus, she understood. She had been police, though now that seemed like a long time ago.

"Where's Diego?" said Ramone.

"Up in his room."

Ramone looked into the pot. The garlic and onions, cooking in olive oil, were beginning to brown.

"You've got the fire up too high," said Ramone. "You're burning the garlic. And those onions are supposed to get clear, not black."

"Leave me alone."

"The only time that flame ought to be on high is when you're boiling water."

"Please."

"You making a sauce?"

"Yes."

"My mother's?"

"My own."

"I like my mother's sauce," said Ramone.

"You should have married your mother."

"Listen, turn that flame down, will you?"

"Go see your son."

"I plan to. What happened today?"

"He says he didn't know his cell was on. One of his friends called him as he was coming out of the bathroom, and Mr. Guy heard it."

"Mr. Guy-guy."

"Gus . . ."

"I'm sayin, dude has name a like that, he's gonna have some issues."

"He's not the manliest fellow on the planet, I'll give you that."

"And they wanted to suspend Diego for *that?*"

"Insubordination. He wouldn't give up his phone."

"They shouldn't have gotten up in his face to begin with."

"I know it," said Regina. "But it's the rule. Anyway, you gotta act like you're upset with him, I guess. A little."

"I'm more upset with that school."

"I am, too."

"I'll talk to him." Ramone leaned over the stove. "You know, you're burning the living shit out of that garlic."

"Go see your son."

Ramone kissed her on her neck, just below her ear. She smelled a little sweaty, and sweet, too. It was that body oil she liked to wear, with a touch of raspberry in it.

As Ramone walked away, he said, "Turn that flame down some."

"You can turn the flame down your own self," said Regina, "the day you step up to cook."

Ramone went down the hall, the sound of the Thunderbirds and the Pink Ladies singing at his back, and up the stairs to the top floor.

He was having more than second thoughts about the decision to transfer Diego out to a Montgomery County school, but at the time he'd made it he felt he had run out of options. Ramone and Regina had been in agreement that the District middle in their zone was unacceptable. Physically it was in a state of perpetual disrepair, and it was always short on supplies, including pencils and paper. With the school's low lighting, many of the fluorescents and incandescents either dead or nonexistent, and the metal detectors and security personnel stationed at every working door, it resembled a prison. Sure, plenty of money got pumped into the D.C. school system, but, suspiciously, little seemed to funnel down to the kids. And the kids themselves had begun to find trouble, both in school and out. In their zone, with many parents working two jobs and others absent or just not involved in their children's lives, some of the kids had begun to go seriously off track. It wasn't the right environment for Diego, who was not the type of student to self-motivate and was, in fact, attracted to those on the tough side.

Gus Ramone had discussed all of this with his wife, intensely and in private. In the end, they both decided that it would do Diego good to be exposed to a different atmosphere. But even then, when Regina herself became adamant that they make the move, Ramone was not entirely sure that his motives for getting Diego out of the D.C. public school system were pure. The thing that played on his conscience was that the kids in their neighborhood middle school were almost all black or Hispanic.

Regardless, he and Regina had arranged the transfer. To do so, they'd set up a kind of ruse to establish residency in Montgomery County. Ramone had bought an investment property, little more than a cottage, in the then run-down downtown Silver Spring area for one hundred and ten thousand back in 1990, when Regina was teaching and they were a two-income couple. Ramone rented it to a Guatemalan roofer and his small family. He and Regina obtained a Maryland phone number for that address; the calls rolled over to their home in D.C. With that and their ownership papers on the house, they had the necessary tools to claim Maryland residence, which made Diego qualified to move.

But from the start, it seemed as if they had made a mistake. The middle school in Montgomery County had magnet students, and most of these students were white. There was less tolerance for so-called disruptive behavior in this school than there was in Diego's old school in D.C. Laughing or talking loudly in the halls or in the cafeteria was an offense that could often warrant suspension. So could being in the vicinity of, but not directly participating in, trouble. There appeared to be different sets of guidelines for Diego and his friends than for the kids in the magnet and gifted and talented classes. Those mostly white kids were being favored, Ramone surmised, because they were bringing higher test scores to the school. Everyone else in the school fell into the category of "other." When Regina dug and looked into it, she found that black kids in Montgomery County were suspended, demoted, or expelled at three times the rate of white kids. Something was definitely wrong there, and though neither Gus nor Regina was quick to bring up the R word, they suspected that their son's color, and the color of his friends, was indirectly related to the troublemaker tags they were being forced to wear.

All of this occurred in a school situated in a neighborhood known for its liberal activism, a place where "Celebrate Diversity" bumper stickers were commonly displayed on cars. The days Ramone picked up his son at the school, he saw that most of the black students streaming out the doors hung together and walked in the down-street direction of "the apartments," while the white students headed for their homes on the high ground. Sometimes he would sit there behind the wheel, watching this, and he would say to himself, I made a mistake with my son.

Thing of it was, he never did know with certainty if he was doing the right thing for his kids. Those who said they did were delusional or liars. Unfortunately, the results didn't come in until the race was done.

Ramone knocked on his son's bedroom door. He knocked harder and was told to come in.

Diego was sitting on the edge of his bed, a mattress and box spring that lay frameless on the carpeted floor. The football he slept with sat beside him. He wore headphones, and as he removed them Ramone heard the sound of go-go turned up loud. Diego wore a sleeveless T, his arms thin and defined, his shoulders already as broad as a man's. He had the beginnings of a mustache, and his sideburns had been trimmed to resemble miniature daggers. His hair, shaped up every couple of weeks at the barber on 3rd, was close to the scalp and precise. His skin was a shade lighter than Regina's. He had Regina's large brown eyes and thick nose. The dimple in his chin was Ramone's.

"Wha'sup, Dad?"

"What's up with you?"

"Chillin."

Ramone stood over him, his feet spread in the power stance, that cop thing. Diego read it, smirked, and shook his head. He got up off the bed and stood facing his father. He was only a couple of inches shorter than Ramone.

"Let me just tell it," said Diego.

"Go ahead."

"Today was . . ."

"I know."

"It wasn't nothin serious."

"Mom told me."

"It's like they're singling me out, Dad."

"Well, you gave them a reason, in the beginning."

"True," said Diego.

Diego had acted out when he'd first come to the school. He'd felt that he had to show the other students that the new kid wasn't soft. That he was tough, cool, and funny as well. Ramone and Regina had gotten several calls in September from exasperated teachers who said Diego was disruptive in class. Ramone had been pretty rough on him, giving him stern, threatening talks, putting him on restriction, and even pulling him from football practice, though Ramone had not gone so far as not letting him play his weekly game. The tough love seemed to have worked, or Diego had simply settled down on his own. A couple of his teachers had told Regina that Diego's behavior had improved in class, and one even said that he had the potential to become a positive influence on other students, a leader. But the negative first impression he'd left on the principal, a white woman named Ms. Brewster, and her assistant, Mr. Guy, had been damaging. Ramone felt that, at this point, they were targeting his son. Diego, discouraged and unmotivated, was losing interest in school. His midterm grades were lower than they had been at his school in D.C.

"Look," said Ramone. "You say you didn't know your phone was on, I believe you."

"I *didn't* know."

Ramone had no doubt. He and Diego had made a deal from early on: Tell the truth, Ramone said, and I won't go off on you. I'll only get angry if I think you're lying. We can deal with the rest. As far as he knew, his son had always kept up his end of the bargain.

"If you say so, I believe you," said Ramone. "But they've got their rules. You should've let them confiscate your phone for the day. That's where the problem came from."

"They took my friend's phone and he didn't get it back for two weeks."

"Your mother and I would've stepped in and got it back. The point is, you can't fight them. They're bosses. You're going to grow up and get out in the world and you're going to have some bosses you don't like, and still, you've got to do what they say."

"Not when I'm playin in the NFL."

"I'm talking to you serious here, Diego. I mean, *I* have to make compromises to bosses I don't like, and I'm forty-two years old. It's not just part of being a kid, it's part of being an adult as well."

Diego's lips tightened. He was shutting down. Ramone

had given him this speech before. It no longer sounded fresh to Ramone, either.

"Just try to get along," said Ramone.

"I will."

Ramone felt like they were done. He put his hand out, and Diego lightly slapped his fingers against Ramone's.

"There's somethin else," said Diego.

"I'm listening."

"There was a fight the other day after school. You know my friend Toby?"

"From football?"

"Yeah."

Ramone remembered Toby from the team. He was a tough kid but not a bad one. He lived with his father, a cab-driver, in the apartments near the school. His mother, Ramone had heard, was a drug addict who was no longer in his life.

"Toby got into it with this boy," said Diego. "He'd been talkin mess to Toby in the halls and he challenged Toby to a fight. They met down by the creek. Toby said, *Bap!*" Diego slammed his right fist into his left palm. "He stole him with a jab and a right punch. One-two, and the other boy went down."

"Were you there?" said Ramone, perhaps with too much excitement in his voice.

"Yeah. I was walkin home that day with a couple of friends and came up on it. You know I was gonna watch. . . ."

"So?"

"The other boy's parents called the school. Now they're havin what they call an investigation. Finding out who was there and who saw what. The parents want to press charges on Toby. They're talking about assault."

"I thought this kid challenged Toby to the fight."

"He did, but now he sayin he was only kidding around. He sayin he never did want to fight."

"Why is the school involved? It was off their property, wasn't it?"

"They were both walking home from school, still carrying their books and stuff. So it makes it the school's business."

"Okay."

"They're gonna want me to tell how Toby hit this boy first."

"Somebody had to throw the first punch," said Ramone, speaking as a man and not a father. "Was it a fair fight?"

"The other boy was bigger than Toby. One of those skateboarder kids. And he was the one made the challenge. He just couldn't back up his words."

"And it was just the two of them. Nobody ganged up on this other boy, right?"

"It was just them."

"I don't see a problem."

"What I'm sayin is, I'm not about to snitch out my friend."

Ramone didn't want him to. But it wouldn't be right for him to come out and say so, because he had to play a role. So he said nothing.

"We straight?" said Diego.

"Get ready for dinner," said Ramone with a small, strategic nod.

As Diego put on a clean T-shirt, Ramone took in his room. Pictures of rappers cut out from the *Source* and *Vibe*, and a nice photo of a dropped, restored '63 Impala, tacked to a corkboard; a poster from Mack Lewis's gym in Baltimore, a collage of local fighters along with Tyson and Ali, with the saying "Good fighters come to the threshold of pain and cross it fully to achieve greatness" printed on the lower border. On the floor, homemade CDs burned on the house computer, a CD tower, a portable stereo, copies of *Don Diva* and a gun magazine, jeans and T-shirts, both dirty and clean, Authentic jerseys from various teams, a pair of Timbs, and two pairs of

Nikes. On his desk, rarely used for studying, an unread copy of *White Fang;* an unread copy of *True Grit,* which Ramone thought his son would like but that he had never cracked; sneaker cleaning solution; photos of girls, black and Hispanic, in tight jeans and tank tops, taken at the mall and presented to Diego as gifts; a pair of dice; a butane lighter with a marijuana leaf inlaid on its face; and his loose-leaf notebook, with the name Dago written, graffiti-style, on its cover. A cap decorated with his nickname and the numbers "09," his alleged graduation year from high school, hung on a nail he had driven into the wall.

Even with the variation in styles, the advances in technology, and the changes in culture, Diego's room looked much like Ramone's room had looked in 1977. In fact, Diego was very much like his father, in so many ways.

"What're we having?" said Diego.

"Your mother's making a sauce."

"Her sauce or Grandmom's?"

"Go on, boy," said Ramone. "Get washed up."

TEN

HOLIDAY WASN'T DRUNK. It was more like he was tired. He had sweated out most of the alcohol with Rita on top of the sheets. His vision was good, driving down the toll road and then the inner loop of the Beltway from Virginia into Maryland. He felt a little foggy, but he was fine.

He listened to the classic rock station on the satellite radio as he drove. He was not much of a music guy, but he knew his '70s rock. His older brother, whom he'd once idolized, had played his records in the house when they were growing up, and this was the only period of music Holiday still paid attention to or knew. A live track from Humble Pie, Steve Marriott shouting, "Awl royt!" in a slurred cockney accent before the band broke into a heavy blues-rock riff, was playing now.

Holiday didn't see his brother anymore, except when Christmas came around, and that was just so he could visit his nephews, let them know their uncle Doc was still in the world. But the nephews were getting up to college age now, and Holiday suspected the once-a-year visits would be soon coming to an end. His brother was in mortgage banking, lived out in Germantown, drove a Nissan Pathfinder whose only path was the 270 corridor, and had a wife that Holiday wouldn't fuck with the lights out. His brother was far away from the long-haired, cool teenager he had once been, spinning Skynyrd, Thin Lizzy, and Clapton in their parents' basement between bong hits blown out the cracked casement windows. His brother now checked his stocks on the hour and studied *Consumer Reports* before every purchase. Holiday wanted to scream in his face, but it wouldn't have brought his brother back to life.

With his sister long gone and both his parents dead, Holiday was alone. The one thing he had had to get up for, the one thing that had made his eyes snap open in the morning and driven him from the bed, had been taken away. He had been a cop, and then he wasn't. Now he wore a stupid hat, made conversation with people who did not interest him at all, and jockeyed luggage in and out of the trunk of a car.

All because of a fellow cop who wouldn't cut him any slack. A rule follower, like Holiday's brother. Another guy with a stick up his ass.

He didn't feel like going back to his place just yet. He exited the Beltway at Georgia Avenue and took it south into D.C. He still had time to catch one, maybe two, at Leo's before they brought up the lights.

THE RAMONE FAMILY ATE dinner at a table with ladder-back chairs situated in the open area between the kitchen and the rec room. They tried to eat dinner together every night, though this meant many late meals, due to Ramone's erratic schedule. Both Regina and Ramone had come from families who had done so, and they felt it was important. The Italian in Ramone believed that sharing good food was a spiritual thing that transcended ritual.

"Good sauce, Mom," said Diego.

"Thank you."

"Tastes a little burnt, though," said Diego, his eyes lighting on Ramone's.

"Your mom put a flame thrower to the garlic and onions," said Ramone.

"Stop it," said Regina.

"We're playin, honey," said Ramone. "It's real good."

Alana had her face down near her bowl, trying to suck up a forkful of spaghetti. She was an intense eater who thought and talked about food often. Ramone liked to see a grown woman enjoy a meal, and he loved it in his little girl.

"Want me to cut that up for you, Junior?" said Diego.

"Uh-uh," said Alana.

"Make it easier to eat."

"Nope."

"You eatin it like a pig do," said Diego.

"Does," said Regina.

"Leave her alone," said Ramone.

"I'm just tryin to help."

"Worry about yourself," said Ramone. "With those sauce stains on your shirt."

"Dag," said Diego, noticing the splatter marks on his wife-beater.

The talk turned to Diego's homework and his repeated claim that he'd done it at study hall. Then the Laveranues Coles trade and Ramone's assertion that Santana Moss was a sideline receiver only, as he tended to drop passes in the middle of the field when he heard footsteps. Diego, who had a jersey with Moss's name on the back of it, circa the Jets, disagreed.

"Who's Ashley?" said Regina to Diego, apropos of nothing.

"Just a girl at school," said Diego.

"I saw her name on the caller ID," said Regina.

"That a crime?" said Diego.

"Course not," said Regina. "Is she nice?"

"What's she look like?" said Ramone, and Diego chuckled.

"Mom, she's a girl I know at school. I don't have no one special, okay?"

"Anyone," said Regina.

"But you are saying," said Ramone, "you're saying you do like girls."

"Go ahead, Dad."

"I was beginning to wonder."

"It's private," said Diego.

" 'Cause you never talk about girls."

"Dad."

"It's okay to be like that," said Ramone.

"Dad, I'm not gay."

"I'd still love you if you were. *Like* that, I mean."

"Gus," said Regina.

They talked about the Nationals. Diego said baseball was a "white sport," and Ramone told him to look at all the black and Hispanic players in the major leagues. But Diego could not be moved. He told Ramone to check out the faces in the stands at RFK. Ramone agreed that most of them were white but finished by saying that he didn't see Diego's point.

"Dad closed a case today," said Regina.

"What's a case?" said Alana.

"He locked up a bad guy," said Diego.

"This guy wasn't all bad," said Ramone. "He *did* something bad. He made a bad mistake."

After dinner, Regina read to Alana, and Alana, who was coming along in sounding out her words, read back to her. Ramone and Diego watched one of the last regular-season Nationals games on TV. At the end of the seventh, Diego gave his father a pound and went to his room. Alana kissed Ramone and went to her room with Regina, who read to her some more and put her to bed. Ramone cracked a bottle of Beck's and watched the rest of the game.

Regina was washing her face in the master bathroom when Ramone came up and undressed for bed. He noticed her outfit, one of Diego's football team T-shirts and worn pajama bottoms, and read the message: no sex tonight. But he was a man, as dim and hopeful as any other. He wasn't going to let some dowdy old outfit stop him completely. He'd give it a try.

He closed their door and slid between the sheets. She joined him and gave him a chaste kiss on the side of his mouth. He got up on his elbow and tried another kiss, just to feel her out.

"Good night," she said.

"So soon?"

"I'm tired."

"I'll make you tired."

Ramone put his hand inside her pajama bottoms and stroked the inside of her thigh.

"Alana's gonna be in here any minute," said Regina. "She wasn't even asleep when I left her room."

Ramone kissed her. Her lips opened and she moved a little closer to him in the bed.

"She's gonna walk in on us," said Regina.

"We'll be quiet."

"You know that ain't true."

"C'mon, girl."

"How about I just yank you off?"

"I can do that myself."

Regina and Ramone chuckled softly, and she kissed him more deeply. He began to pull her bottoms off, her back arched to let him, when they heard a knock on their bedroom door.

"Damn," said Ramone.

"That's your daughter," said Regina.

"That's not my daughter," said Ramone. "That's a seven-year-old chastity belt."

Five minutes later, Alana was snoring between them in their bed, her small brown fingers splayed on Ramone's chest. It was true that he was a little disappointed. But he was happy, too.

LEO'S HAD A BIT of a crowd, and the music from the juke was turned up loud. Holiday got a couple of head nods as he crossed the floor toward an empty stool back near the kitchen doors. He was known here, so there wasn't that stare thing that went with a white guy walking into an all-black neighborhood bar. It had gotten around the Leo's regulars that he had been a cop who'd been forced out under a cloud. It wasn't entirely true, since Holiday had resigned rather than face the official inquiry, but he let them think what they wanted. Dirty cop did hold a certain mystique. But he hadn't been dirty. He had never been on the take, nor had he worked both sides of the game, like some of those cops who'd come onto the force during that sloppy hiring binge in the late '80s. Hell, he had just been helping out a girl he knew. All right, she was a whore. But still.

"Vodka rocks," said Holiday to Charles, the night tender. Leo was gone or in the back counting out the day.

"Any flavor, Doc?"

"Rail's good." This deep into it, the shelf juice was a waste.

Charles served Holiday his drink. The juke was playing a cover of "Jet Airliner," done in a truly smoking soul-rock fashion. The two gentlemen to the right of Holiday were arguing about the song.

"I know this is Paul Pena," said the first man. "He did it first. I'm askin you, who was the white boy who took it and made it into a big hit?"

"Johnny Winters or sumshit like him," said the second man. "I don't know."

"It was one of them Almond Brothers," said the first man.

"Say it was the Osmand Brothers?"

"*Almond*, and five says it's true."

"Steve Miller Band," said Holiday.

"Say what?" said the first man, turning to Holiday.

"This song's a killer, man."

"Damn sure is. But can you tell my boy who made it a hit?"

"No clue," said Holiday. Pride had made him blurt out the answer, but now that he had, he didn't want to get further involved.

Holiday beat the last-call lights with one more drink. He fired it down and walked from the bar unsatisfied. Thinking about his old life and how he'd left it had blackened his thoughts.

HE DROVE EAST. HE lived in a garden apartment out by Prince George's Plaza, off East-West Highway, and the way to get there from Leo's was south to Missouri and then over to Riggs Road. But he got confused down near Kansas Avenue, trying to cut time on the back streets, and going along Blair he realized he needed to turn back. He made a left onto Oglethorpe Street, thinking he could take it through to Riggs.

He knew as soon as he got onto Oglethorpe that he'd fucked up. He remembered too late from his cop days that this stretch of Oglethorpe dead-ended at the Metro and B&O railroad tracks. He recognized the Washington Animal Rescue League on his left and the printing company below it down by the tracks. And on the right, one of those community gardens, which were fairly common around D.C. This one covered several acres of land.

His cell, mounted in a kind of holster set below the dash, went off. It was Jerome Belton, calling to tell him about his night. Holiday pulled over to the right shoulder of the road, on sand and gravel, and cut the engine. Belton told him a story about a wannabe player he had taken to the Tyson-McBride fight at the MCI Center a few months back, and something about the man's phony gators, which had been flaking off in the backseat of the car.

It was a funny if too familiar story. Holiday had a laugh with Belton and ended the call. Then, on the quiet dead-end street, parked beside the community garden, Holiday leaned his head back and rested his eyes. He wasn't drunk. He was tired.

A light swept across his face, waking him. He opened his eyes. He made out an MPD blue-and-white topped by an inactive light bar, approaching his car from the turnaround at the railroad tracks. The patrolman behind the wheel had a passenger, a perp or a suspect, in the backseat of the car. He wondered where his breath mints were as the Crown Victoria slowly came his way. Holiday did not look directly into the car, though one darting glance registered white police. In silhouette and shadow, Holiday saw the backseat passenger, thin of shoulder and neck. His instinct said adult female or teenager. In his side vision he saw a number on the lower portion of the car's front quarter panel. The police officer passed without stopping, obviously seeing Holiday parked there but not bothering to check him out. The image of the numbers left Holiday's mind, and he thought, "Let it grow," and as this thought came to him he chuckled without apparent reason and drifted back to sleep.

When he woke sometime later, his head was still fogged. He looked out into the garden, which held the black shapes of hastily constructed arbors, staked plants, and low rows of vegetables. A person of indeterminate age, medium height, walked across the landscape. Number One Male, thought Holiday, studying the walk with squinted eyes. Holiday blinked slowly. His vision blurred, and he went back to sleep.

He woke again, confused, but this time only for a short

period of time, as the passing hours had granted him sobriety. The sky had lightened a shade, and swallows dipped and sailed through the sky above the gardens and sang out, announcing the morning yet to come. He checked his watch: 4:43 a.m.

"Christ," said Holiday.

His neck was stiff. He needed to get to bed. But first he had to relieve himself. He grabbed a small Maglite from the glove box and stepped out of the car.

Holiday walked onto a path, using the flashlight to guide him. He put the mini Mag in his mouth as he loosed his meat and let piss stream onto the ground. He looked around at his surroundings, turning his head as he urinated. The light landed on what looked to be a human figure lying unconscious or asleep on the edge of a vegetable garden holding staked tomato plants long since harvested. Holiday tucked himself in and zipped his fly. He went to the figure and turned the light directly on it.

Holiday chewed his lip and got down on his haunches. The light was close in now and made the subject clear. A young black man, perhaps in the middle of his teens, in a winter-weight coat, T-shirt, jeans, and Nike sneaks. A bullet wound, beginning to congeal, starred his left temple. The top of the young man's head was pulped from the bullet's exit, his blood and brain matter thick as chowder. His eyes were bugged from the jolt. Holiday let the light play over the ground. He lighted a wide area on the path and in the garden itself. He did not see any shell casings or a gun.

He focused the light again on the young man. A chain holding some sort of card hung around his neck. It lay flat on the T, face out, between the folds of the coat. It was some sort of identification badge. Holiday squinted and read the name on the badge.

He stood and turned, trying to put as little weight as possible on his feet as he walked back to his car. There was no one on Oglethorpe, and he quickly ignitioned the Town Car and swung it around, going up to Blair Road with his headlights off and then waiting until Blair was completely clear before firing the headlights and going right, toward the 7-Eleven on Kansas. There was a pay phone there, but the parking area was too public and lit, and he went on to the shuttered liquor store up the road, which also had a pay phone in an empty lot that sat in near darkness. There he dialed 911 with his back to the road and got a dispatcher on the line. He did not give his name or location when asked but instead talked right through the dispatcher's repeated requests and reported a body in the community garden at Blair and Oglethorpe. The woman was still talking to him, demanding personal information, as he cradled the phone. Holiday quickly returned to his car, sped out of the liquor store lot, and lit a cigarette. There was something both familiar and unidentifiable about the body that left him energized and on edge.

Once in his apartment he slipped into his bed but did not fall asleep. As sunlight began to bleed through his venetian blinds, he stared at the ceiling. But he did not see the ceiling. Rather, he saw himself as a young man in uniform, standing in a community garden very much like the one he had just left. In his memory, the homicide police T. C. Cook was there, working in his coat and brown hat. He saw the crime scene lit by strobing colors coming off the light bars of the cruisers and the occasional flashes of cameras.

It was like he was looking at a photograph in his mind. He could see the lights, the white-shirt commanders, that reporter from Channel 4, and, clearly, himself and Detective T. C. Cook. Also in the photograph, young and in uniform, he saw Gus Ramone.

ELEVEN

AS DAY-SHIFT workers arrived for their jobs at the animal shelter and the printing company, homicide police and technicians from the Mobile Crime Lab worked around the body of a young man lying in the community garden at Oglethorpe Street and Blair Road. Uniformed officers and yellow tape kept the workers, speculating among themselves and calling friends and loved ones from their cells, away from the scene.

Detective Bill "Garloo" Wilkins, working the midnight-to-eight at the VCB, was on the tail end of it when the call came in from the dispatcher after the anonymous tip. He drove to the community garden with Detective George Loomis, a slope-shouldered man who had grown up in the Section Eights near the Frederick Douglass home in Southeast. Wilkins would be the primary on the case.

As Wilkins and Loomis worked the scene, Gus Ramone

arrived at the VCB offices for the start of his eight-to-four. Rhonda Willis, who liked to come in early, have her coffee, and map out her day, was already at her desk. As usual, they discussed their plans for the shift, as well as any violent-crime activity that had occurred since they had last been on. The unidentified gunshot victim found off Blair Road was mentioned, along with the fact that Garloo Wilkins had caught the case. Ramone had the arraignment of William Tyree on his plate, and Rhonda was to testify in a drug burn case she had closed several months earlier. Ramone wanted to try and catch an interview with a potential witness to a homicide before she went off to her job at the McDonald's over by Howard U. Rhonda agreed to go with him, then ride together over to the Judiciary Center on 4th and E.

The potential wit, a youngish woman named Trashon Morris, turned out to be less than helpful. She had been seen in a club on the fringes of Shaw, hanging closely with a young man who was wanted in a killing later that same night. The young man, Dontay Walker, had been beefing at the club, witnesses said, with a guy who was later found shot to death inside his Nissan Altima on 6th, south of U. Walker was being sought in connection with the killing and so far was in the wind. But when Ramone questioned Trashon Morris, catching her on the way out the door of her apartment building, she could not remember any kind of argument in the club or anything else, seemingly, about that night.

"I don't recall it," said Trashon Morris, never looking Ramone in the eye nor acknowledging the presence of Rhonda Willis. "I don't know nothin about no beef." Morris had extra-long, loudly painted fake nails, large hoop earrings, and big hair.

"Had you been drinking much that evening?" said Ramone, trying to determine her credibility in the unlikely event that she would regain her memory and be called to testify in court.

"Yeah, I'd been drinkin. I was in a club; what you think?"

"How much?" said Rhonda.

"Much as I wanted to," said Morris. "It was a weekend and I'm twenty-one."

"People say you left the club with Dontay Walker."

"Who?"

"Dontay Walker."

"People gonna say what they want to." Morris glanced at her watch. "Look, I gotta get to work."

"You got any idea where Dontay's been layin up since that night?" said Ramone.

"Who?"

Ramone gave her his card with his contact information. "You see Dontay again, or you hear from him, or something comes to mind that you forgot to tell us, give me a call."

"I gotta get to work," said Morris, and walked the sidewalk toward the Metro station down the block.

"Cooperative type," said Ramone as he and Rhonda went to an unmarked, maroon, MPD-issue Impala parked along the curb.

"One of those ghetto fabulous girls," said Rhonda. "My sons better not think about bringing home something looking like that, 'cause you know I'll hit the reject button."

"She's just mad because her mother named her Trashon."

"You name it, it's gonna become it," said Rhonda. "One of those self-fulfilling prophecies you hear about."

At the Judiciary Center, Ramone and Rhonda Willis checked in on the first floor to fill out their court appearance worksheets, then went up to the ninth floor, which housed the Assistant U.S. Attorneys, the federal prosecutors who worked cases from arrest to trial and sometimes conviction. Many homicide police were standing in the halls and sitting in the offices of the prosecutors, a common scene. Some wore nice suits, some wore cheap ones, and others were dressed in sweats. They were there to testify, shoot the shit, report progress on cases, and make overtime. On certain days there were more homicide police in these offices than there were at the VCB or on the street.

Ramone found prosecutor Ira Littleton in his office. They discussed the Tyree case and the arraignment, a conversation that consisted of Littleton lecturing Ramone on courtroom procedure and etiquette. Ramone allowed the younger man to have his say. When he was done, Ramone went to the corner office of Margaret Healy, a hard-boiled, smart redhead in her midforties who headed the team of Assistant U.S. Attorneys. Her desk was overflowing with paper, and paperwork littered the floor. He dropped into one of her big comfortable chairs.

"Heard you made quick work out of that stabbing," said Healy.

"That was Bo Green," said Ramone.

"It's a team sport," said Healy, using one of her favorite expressions.

"Congratulations on the Salinas brothers," said Ramone. The recent conviction of two sibling members of MS-13, a drawn-out murder case, had made a splash in the press due to the growing Hispanic gang problem in and around D.C.

"It was a nice win. I was proud of Mary Yu on that one. She took it all the way."

Ramone nodded and pointed his chin in the direction of a photo on the prosecutor's desk. "How's the family?"

"I suspect they're good. Maybe I'll take some time off this year and find out."

An administrative assistant knocked on Healy's open door and told Ramone that he had a call from his wife. Ramone figured she had been trying him on his cell, but the service was spotty in the building. And if she was being that persistent, it had to be some kind of emergency. Alana or Diego, he thought immediately, and he got up out of his chair.

"Excuse me, Margaret."

He took the call in an unoccupied office. He listened to Regina's emotional but controlled voice. Out in the hall, he saw Rhonda Willis bullshitting with a couple of detectives. He told her about his call and where he was going.

"Want some company?" said Rhonda.

"Thought you had to testify."

"I been informed that I'm not on today's menu. What about the arraignment?"

"I'll come back for it," said Ramone. "C'mon, I'll bend your ear on the way out."

MARITA BRYANT SAW THE squad and plainclothes cars arrive at the Johnson family house across the street from the vantage point of her home in Manor Park. She watched as the large bald-headed detective entered the house, and she kept watching as Terrance Johnson pulled up in his Cadillac, parked it sloppily, and ran to his front door. An ambulance arrived shortly thereafter. Helena Johnson, Terrance's wife and the mother of their children, Asa, fourteen, and Deanna, eleven, was carried from the house on a stretcher and taken away. Terrance came out with her, visibly distraught, staggering as he walked across his lawn. He stopped and spoke to his next-door neighbor, a retiree named Colin Tohey, and was then pulled along by the detective, who helped him into the plainclothes car. The two of them drove off.

Marita Bryant left her house for the Johnson yard, where Colin Tohey still stood, somewhat shaken. Tohey told Bryant that the dead body of Asa Johnson had been found in that big community garden off Blair Road. Helena had collapsed upon hearing the news, necessitating the ambulance. Bryant, who had a daughter the same age as Asa and was familiar with Asa's crowd, immediately called Regina Ramone. She knew that Diego was friends with Asa, and thought Regina would want to be informed. Also, she was curious, as Gus would surely have some further information regarding the death. Regina had not yet heard the news and said that she did not think Gus had, either, otherwise he would have phoned. She ended the call while Marita Bryant was still talking and immediately tried to locate Gus.

"YOUR SON WAS TIGHT with this boy?" said Rhonda Willis, riding shotgun in the stripped-down, four-banger Impala, the most basic model Chevrolet produced. She and Ramone were going up North Capitol Street.

"Diego has a lot of friends," said Ramone. "Asa wasn't his main boy, but he was someone Diego knew fairly well. They played football on the same team last year."

"He gonna take it hard?"

"I don't know. When my father died, he felt it because he saw the grief hit me. But this kind of thing is wrong in a different way. It's just unnatural."

"Who's going to tell him?"

"Regina will pick him up at school and give him the news. I'll call him later. Then I'll see him tonight."

"Y'all talk about the Lord much in your house?" said Rhonda.

"Not too much," said Ramone.

"This one of those times you should."

Rhonda's adult life had been challenging, what with having to raise four boys on her own. The God thing definitely worked for her. It was her rock and it was her crutch, and she liked to talk about it. Ramone did not.

"What's in your gut?" said Rhonda, cutting the silence in the car.

"Nothing," said Ramone.

"You knew this boy. You know his family."

"His father and mother are straight. They kept a close watch on him."

"Anything else?"

"His father's kind of an unyielding guy. Athletics, the classroom, everything . . . He rode his son pretty hard."

"Hard enough to push the kid someplace bad?"

"I don't know."

" 'Cause that can do as much damage as not bein there at all."

"Right."

"You ever have any kind of indication or feeling that the boy was into something wrong?"

"No. That doesn't mean he wasn't. But I got no reason to think he was."

Rhonda looked across the bench. "Did you like him?"

"He was a good kid. He was fine."

"I'm sayin, how did you feel about him? You know, how a man looks at a boy and sizes him up?"

Ramone thought of the times he'd seen Asa on the football field, making half-assed tackles, sometimes moving away from the man running with the ball. He thought of Asa entering Ramone's house, not addressing him or Regina directly, not greeting them at all unless he had to. He knew exactly what Rhonda was going for. Sometimes you'd look at a boy and see him as a man, and you'd think, He's going to be a tough one, or a strong one, or he's going to be successful in anything he does. Sometimes you'd look at a young man and think, I'd be proud if he were my son. Asa Johnson was not one of those boys.

"He lacked heart," said Ramone. "That's about the only thing that comes to mind."

There was something else Ramone had felt sometimes, catching a kind of weakness in Asa's eyes. Like he could be got or took.

"Least I got an honest opinion out of you."

"Doesn't mean anything," said Ramone, mildly ashamed.

"It's more than Garloo's gonna see. 'Cause you know he'll look at that boy and think what he's gonna think, automatic. And I'm not even sayin that Bill's like that. He's just . . . The man's got a dull mind. He likes to take those mental shortcuts."

"I just need to get up there and get a look at things."

"If we ever get there."

"They give all the real vehicles to the regular police," said Ramone.

"We do get the bitch cars," said Rhonda.

Ramone punched the gas, but it only made the engine knock.

THE CROWD AT THE crime scene had thinned of spectators and grown with officials and one print reporter by the time Ramone and Rhonda Willis arrived. They found Wilkins and Loomis standing alongside a nondescript Chevy. Nearby, a white uniformed officer leaned against a squad car. Wilkins had a notebook in one hand and a burning cigarette in the other.

"The Ramone," said Wilkins. "Rhonda."

"Bill," said Ramone.

Ramone scanned the geography: the commercial structures, the railroad tracks, and the backs of the homes and the church on the residential street running east-west on a rise at the far edge of the garden.

"Got a call from the office that you were coming out," said Wilkins. "You knew the decedent?"

"Friend of my son's," said Ramone.

"Asa Johnson?"

"If it's him."

"He was wearing one of those middle school photo IDs on a chain around his neck. His father identified the body."

"Is the father here?"

"Hospital. His wife lost it completely. The father's there with her now. He wasn't looking so good himself."

"Anything yet?" said Ramone.

"Kid was shot in the temple, exit wound at the crown. We found the slug. Flattened, but we'll get a caliber on it."

"No gun."

"Uh-uh."

"Casings?"

"No."

"What're you feeling?"

"Nothin, yet."

Ramone knew, as did Rhonda and Loomis, that Wilkins had already formed a likely scenario and eliminated some of the other possibilities. The first assumption that Wilkins had made, seeing a black teenager with a fatal gunshot wound, was "drug thing." A murder involving business, what some D.C. cops openly called "society cleanses." Darwinism put in motion by those in the life.

Wilkins's thoughts would then have gone to murder in the commission of an armed robbery. Except what would a kid this age have, in this middle-income part of town at best, that could be of any real value? The North Face coat, the one-hundred-dollar sneaks . . . but these were still on him. So this scenario was doubtful. He could have been robbed for a roll of money or his stash. But that would have brought it back to a drug thing.

Maybe, Wilkins imagined, the victim had been hitting some other yo's girlfriend. Or looked at her like he wanted to.

Or it could have been a suicide. But black kids didn't do themselves, thought Wilkins, so that was not likely. Plus, no gun. The kid couldn't have punched his own time card, then disposed of the gun after he was dead.

"What do you think, Gus?" said Wilkins. "Was this kid in the life?"

"Not to my knowledge," said Ramone.

Bill Wilkins had acquired the nickname "Garloo" because of his massive size, pointed ears, and bald dome. Garloo was the name of a toy monster popular with boys in the early to mid-'60s, and Wilkins had received the tag from one of the few veterans old enough to recall the loinclothed creature from his youth. It suited Wilkins. He breathed through his mouth. His posture was hulking, his walk heavy. He appeared to those who first met him to be half man and half beast. The FOP bar kept a construction paper medallion, strung with yarn, with the name "Garloo" crudely crayoned across its face, which Wilkins wore around his neck when he was drunk. In the evenings, he could often be found at the FOP bar.

Wilkins had six years to go on his twenty-five and, having lost the desire or expectation for promotion, was left with only the diluted ambition to hold on to his rank and position at VCB. To do so, he would need to maintain a reasonable closure rate. To him, difficult cases were curses, not challenges.

Ramone liked Wilkins well enough. Other homicide police went to him frequently with questions regarding their PCs, as Wilkins had outstanding computer literacy, facility, and knowledge, and was always ready to help. He was honest and a fairly decent guy. A little cynical, but in that he was not alone. As far as his investigative skills went, he had, as Rhonda said, a dull mind.

"Any witnesses?" said Ramone.

"None yet," said Wilkins.

"Who called it in?"

"Anonymous," said Wilkins. "There's a tape. . . ."

Ramone looked over at the uniformed police officer leaning against his 4D squad car within earshot of their conversation. He was on the tall side, lean, and blond. On the front quarter panel of his Ford were the car numbers, which Ramone idly read, a habit from his own days on patrol.

"We're fixing to canvass," said Wilkins, drawing Ramone's attention back to the scene.

"That's McDonald Place up there, isn't it?" said Ramone, nodding to the residential street on the edge of the garden.

"We'll be knocking on those doors first," said Wilkins.

"And that church."

"Saint Paul's Baptist," said Rhonda.

"We'll get it," said Loomis.

"They got night workers in the animal shelter, right?" said Ramone.

"We do have some ground to cover," said Wilkins.

"We can help," said Ramone, easing into it.

"Welcome to the party," said Wilkins.

"I'm gonna get a look at the body," said Ramone, "you don't mind."

Ramone and Rhonda Willis began to walk away. As they passed the nearby squad car, the uniformed officer pushed off it and spoke.

"Detectives?"

"What is it?" said Ramone, turning to the face the patrolman.

"I was just wondering if any witnesses have come forward."

"None as of yet," said Rhonda.

Ramone read the nameplate pinned on the uniformed officer's chest, then looked into his blue eyes. "You got a function here?"

"I'm on the scene to assist."

"Then do it. Keep the spectators and any media away from the body, hear?"

"Yessir."

As they walked into the garden, Rhonda said, "A little short and to the point, weren't you, Gus?"

"The details of this investigation are none of his business. When I was in uniform, I never would have thought to have been so bold like that. When you were around a superior, you kept your mouth shut, unless you got asked to speak."

"Maybe he's just ambitious."

"Another thing I never thought of. Ambition."

"But they went ahead and promoted you anyway."

The body was not far in, lying in a plot off a narrow path. They stopped well short of the corpse, mindful of altering the crime scene with their presence. A technician from the Mobile Crime Lab, Karen Krissoff, worked around Asa Johnson.

"Karen," said Ramone.

"Gus."

"Get your impressions yet?" said Ramone, meaning any footprints that could be found in the soft earth.

"You can come in," said Krissoff.

Ramone came forward, got down on his haunches, and eyeballed the body. He was not sickened, looking at the corpse of his son's friend. He had seen too much death for physical remains to affect him that way, and had come to feel that a body was nothing but a shell. He was merely sad, and somewhat frustrated, knowing that this thing could not be undone.

When Ramone was finished looking at Asa and the immediate area around him, he got up on his feet and heard himself grunt.

"Powder burns prevalent," said Rhonda, stating what she had observed from seven feet away. "It got done close in."

"Right," said Ramone.

"Kinda warm out to be wearing that North Face, too," said Rhonda.

Ramone heard her but did not comment. He was looking out to the road, past the spectators and the uniforms and the techs. A black Lincoln Town Car was parked on Oglethorpe, and a man in a black suit leaned against the passenger door of the car. The man was tall, blond, and thin. He locked eyes with Ramone for a moment, then pushed himself off the vehicle, walked around to the driver's side, and got under the wheel. He executed a three-point turn and drove away.

"Gus?" said Rhonda.

"Coat musta been fresh," said Ramone. "I'm assuming he got it recently and was showing it off. Couldn't wait to wear it."

Rhonda Willis nodded. "That's how kids do."

TWELVE

CONRAD GASKINS CAME out of a clinic located beside a church off Minnesota Avenue and Naylor Road, in Randle Highlands, Southeast. He wore a T-shirt darkened with sweat stains and faded green Dickies work pants. He had been up since 5:00 a.m., when he had risen and walked over to the shape-up spot on Central Avenue in Seat Pleasant, Maryland. He was picked up there every morning by an ex-offender, one of those Christians who saw it as their duty to hire men like they themselves had once been. The shape-up spot was near the rental he shared with Romeo Brock, a shabby two-bedroom house in a stand of woods up off Hill Road.

Brock was waiting on him in the SS, idling in the lot of the clinic. Gaskins dropped into the passenger seat.

"You piss in that cup?" said Brock.

"My PO makes sure I do," said Gaskins. "She said I gotta drop a urine every week."

"You can buy clean pee."

"I know it. But at this clinic, they damn near search your ass before you go into the bathroom. Ain't nobody gettin away with that bullshit. Why my PO sends me here."

"You be dropping negatives, anyway."

"True. I ain't even fuck with no weed since I been uptown."

Gaskins felt good about it, too. He even liked the way his back ached at the end of an honest day's work. Like his back was reminding him he did something straight.

"Let's get your ass cleaned up," said Brock. "I can't take your stink."

They drove into Prince George's, crossing Southern Avenue, the border between the city and the county, where the dirt was done. Those on the outlaw side knew you could move back and forth across that border and rarely get caught, as neither police force had cross-jurisdiction. They had tried to enlist the aid of U.S. Marshals and ATF officers but as of yet had been unable to coordinate the various forces and agencies. Between the gentrification of the city, which had displaced many low-income residents to P.G., and the disorganization of local law enforcement, the neighborhoods around the county line had become a criminal's paradise, the new badlands of the metropolitan area.

"You all right?" said Brock.

"I'm tired, is all it is."

"That all? You just tired? Or are you pressed about somethin? 'Cause you know I got everything fixed airtight."

"Said I was tired."

"You just mad 'cause you still on paper. You got to pee in a little old plastic cup, and here I am, free."

"Hmph," said Gaskins.

His young cousin was all bravado and had not yet seen the other side of the hill. Gaskins had been on both slopes. He had been involved in the drug trade at an early age. He had been an enforcer. He had fallen on agg assault and gun charges, and had done time in Lorton, and when they'd closed Lorton they moved him out of state. There was nothing about any of it that he wanted to visit again. But he had promised his aunt, Romeo Brock's mother, that he would stay by her son and see that he came to no harm.

So far he had made good on that promise. Mina Brock had raised Gaskins after his own mother died when he was a child. You couldn't go back on a blood oath made to a woman as purely good as his aunt. She was probably on her knees right now, scrubbing the urine from some hotel bathroom floor or cleaning the jam off someone's sheets. She had fed and clothed Gaskins, and tried to slap some sense into him when she had to. She was plain good. Least he could do was look after her natural child.

But Romeo wasn't right. He was inching toward that line and was close to crossing it, and though Gaskins would have liked nothing better than to bail out on him, he felt he was trapped. It sickened him to know where Romeo was taking him, and still he had to stay.

They were driving toward a cliff. The doors were locked and the car had no brakes.

GASKINS SHOWERED AND CHANGED in the single bathroom of their house, a one-story structure fronted by a porch, set back on a gravel drive and nearly hidden among old-growth maple, oak, and one tall pine. A large tulip poplar grew alongside the house. Branches from that tree had fallen and lay on the roof. The home was in need of repair, replumbing, and rewiring, but the owner never visited the property. The rent was small, in line with the physical condition of the house, and Brock always paid on time. He didn't want the landlord or anyone else coming around.

Gaskins pulled a hooded sweatshirt over his head and checked himself in the mirror. The landscape work was keeping him in shape. He had thrown weights in prison regular, so it wasn't like he'd ever fallen off. Compact and with thick, muscular thighs, he had been a pretty fair back in his youth, a low-to-the-ground Don Nottingham type, hard to grab, hard to bring down. He had played Pop Warner in the city but drifted away from it when he got involved with some corner boys in the Trinidad neighborhood, where he'd come up. Coach had tried to keep him in it, but Gaskins was too smart for that. There was money to be made, and all the things that went with it. And he'd gotten those things, too. For a short while. He could have been a fair halfback, though, if he'd stayed past the tenth grade at Phelps. But he had been too smart.

He walked into Brock's room, as messy as a teenage boy's. Brock was sitting on the bed, checking the load of a Gold Cup .45.

"That new?" said Gaskins.

"Yeah."

"What happened to your other piece?"

"I traded up," said Brock.

"Why you got to bring it?"

"I always carry when I work. You gonna need a roscoe, too."

"Why?"

"I spoke to the man," said Brock. "Fishhead gonna give us something for tonight."

"What kinda somethin?"

"Something good, is all I know. The man say we gonna get us some real."

"I shouldn't even be in a car with someone got a gun. We get searched, that's an automatic nickel for me."

"Then stay here. I can find someone else to back me up."

Gaskins looked him over. Boy was headed for prison or a grave, and neither one of those prospects made him shudder. Long as he left a rep behind. Wasn't like Gaskins was gonna stop it from happening. But he had to try.

"What you got for me?" said Gaskins.

Brock pulled a piece of oilskin out from under his bed. Inside the cloth was a nine-millimeter automatic. He handed it to Gaskins.

"Glock Seventeen," said Brock.

"Shit is plastic," said Gaskins.

"It's good enough for the MPD."

"Where'd you get it?"

"Gun man down there in Landover?"

Gaskins inspected the weapon. "No serial number?"

"Man filed it off."

"That there's another automatic fall. You don't even have to be using the motherfucker; they catch you with shaved numbers, you goin back in on a felony charge."

"Why you so piss-tess?"

"Tryin to teach you somethin."

Gaskins released the magazine, thumbed the top shell, and felt pressure against the spring. He pushed the magazine back into the grip with his palm. He holstered it behind the waistband of his jeans, grip rightward so that he could reach it naturally with his right hand. It felt familiar against his skin.

"You ready?" said Gaskins.

"Now you talkin," said Brock.

IVAN LEWIS HAD BEEN called Fishhead most of his life because of his long face and the way his big eyes could see things without his having to turn his neck. It wasn't that he looked like a real fish, but more that he looked liked a cartoon version of one. Even his mother, up to the day she passed, had called him Fish.

He was coming from his sister's place, walking down Quincy Street in Park View, looking at what the new people were doing to the houses he had been knowing his whole life. He never thought Park View would gentrify, but the evidence of it was on every block. Young black and Spanish buyers with down-payment money were fixing up these old row homes, and some pioneer white folks were, too. Shoot, a couple of white boys had opened up a pizza parlor on Georgia earlier in the year. Whites starting up businesses again in the View, that was something Fishhead thought he'd never see.

Not that the gamers had gone away. There was plenty of dirt being done on this side of Georgia, especially down around the Section Eights on Morton. And the Spanish had gripped up much of the avenue's west side, into Columbia Heights. But property owners were making improvements around here, house by house.

Fishhead Lewis wondered how a man like him was gonna fit in this town much longer. Once people put money into their homes, they didn't want to see low-down types walking out front their properties, not even on the public sidewalks. These folks voted, so they could make things happen. Now you had politicians, like that ambitious light-skinned dude, councilman for that area up top of Georgia, trying to make laws about loitering and stopping cats from buying single cans of beer. Shoot, not everyone wanted a six-pack or could afford one. Friends of Fishhead said, "How they gonna discriminate?" Fishhead had to tell them, with money and power behind you, you damn sure could. The light-skinned dude, he didn't really care about folks hanging out, and he didn't care if a man wanted to enjoy himself one beer on a summer night. But he was running for mayor, so there it was.

He turned into an alley behind Quincy, up by Warder Place. There, idling down at the end of the alley, was a black Impala SS. They were waiting on him where they liked to do.

Fishhead did not have a payroll job. He made money by selling information. Heroin users were perfect for such work. They went places other people couldn't go. They heard dope and murder gossip that went deeper than the ghetto telegraph of the stoop and the barbershop. They seemed harmless and pitiful, but they had ears, a brain, and a mouth that could speak. Addicts, testers, cutters, and prostitutes were inside to the extreme, and the best informants on the street.

Fishhead had got something that morning. He had heard about it from a boy he knew, worked at a cut house in lower LeDroit. Boy said some pure white was coming in tomorrow from New York, to be distributed by a man looking to become a player but not yet there. A man not plugged into a network, what they called a consortium, with other dealers. An independent with no one to watch his back but an underling who was hoping to go along for the ride.

Fishhead was looking to get out of his sister's basement. It had been their mother's house, but the sister had managed to claim it, and the inheritance, with the help of a lawyer. Because she did have a conscience, she allowed him a room downstairs, rent-free but with no kitchen privileges and a lock on the door leading up to the first floor. It was not much more than a mattress, a hot plate for cooking, a cooler, and a toilet with a stand-up shower, had roaches crawling on the floor. He didn't blame her for treating him like a dog you didn't let upstairs. All the shit he'd done to disappoint his family, he could understand it. But no man, not even a low-ass doper like him, should have to live like that.

This information he had today was his way out. He had been getting low that morning with his cut man friend when the dude started talking. Matter of fact, Fishhead had just pushed down on the plunger when the news came his way. He hoped he had heard it right.

Fishhead slipped into the backseat of the SS and settled down on the bench.

"Charlie the motherfuckin tuna," said Brock, under the wheel. He did not turn his head but communicated with his eyes via the rearview. "What you got for us, slim?"

"Somethin," said Fishhead. He liked the drama of giving it up slow. Also, he didn't care for Romeo Brock. Slick boy, always looking down from his high horse. The quiet one, his older cousin, he was all right. And tougher than the boy with the mouth.

"Give it up," said Brock. "I'm tired of these bullshit plays. Tired of shakin change out the pockets of kids."

"That's what you do," said Fishhead. "Ya'll rob independents got no protection. Most times, they be kids. If they was men, shit, they'd be connected, and it would come back *on* you."

"Said I'm ready to move up from that."

"Well, I got somethin."

"Talk about it," said Brock.

"Dude name of Tommy Broadus. Tryin to act like he bigtime, but he just startin out. Came to the cut house where my friend works, inquiring about fees, all that. Said he got some white comin in. I'm talking about keys, and I'm hearin it's tomorrow. My friend say this man can be got."

"So? I ain't want no fuckin dope. Do I look like a goddamn her-won salesman to you?"

"He gonna need to pay for the package, right? If he sending a mule to NYC, he gonna send the cash up with him. Seein as how he green with the New York connect, he surely don't have no credit."

"What about guns?" said Gaskins.

"Huh?"

"Even an amateur gonna have something behind him."

"That's on y'all," said Fishhead. "I stay out the mechanics. I'm sayin, some big money gonna come out this man's house this evening and some dope gonna come back in. I'm just passin this along."

"When?" said Brock.

"After dark, but not too late. Mules don't like to make that Ninety-five run when the traffic too thin. Look for a trap car, I'd expect. The Taurus is popular, or the Mercury sister car."

"Where this man stay at?" said Brock.

Fishhead Lewis passed a slip of paper over the bench. Brock took it, read it, and slipped it into the breast pocket of his rayon shirt.

"How you get the address?" said Gaskins.

"Our man ran his name through the database, somethin. Parked on the street, watched him go in and out his house. He stayin in a detached in a residential area. Real quiet around there, too."

"Not too smart, let yourself get seen so easy."

"What I'm sayin. Man that sloppy can get took."

"Where he get the money?" said Gaskins, thinking it through.

"By turning his inventory," said Fishhead, now improvising but trying to sound as if he knew. "This here can't be the first buy the man done made."

"I'm askin, how we know this Tommy Broad-ass fella ain't bein bankrolled by someone with power?"

"'Cause my man at the cut house said he was braggin on the fact that he all alone."

Gaskins looked at Brock. He could see from his eager look that Brock had already decided to go. He was looking at the money, feeling it between his fingers, spending it on women and clothing, a suit in red. What he wasn't doing was thinking it through.

"What's he look like?" said Gaskins.

"Say what?"

"Wouldn't want to take the wrong man."

"My friend say he fat. Too old for the game, but I guess he startin late. Came to the cut house with a woman, had it all in the right places. Had a mouth on her, too. They was arguing over shit the whole time they was in there."

"Anyone else?"

"Not that my man said."

"You gonna earn somethin serious, this plays out," said Brock. "Buy yourself a mermaid or sumshit."

Fishhead forced a smile. His teeth were rotted, and there were scabs on his face.

"I been wonderin," said Brock. "Do it smell like fish to a fish?"

"All day," said Fishhead, who hadn't had a clean woman in years.

"Get the fuck out. We'll take it from here."

Fishhead got out of the car, hiking his pants up as he moved along. Brock and Gaskins watched him walk down the alley, a pit bull barking at him furiously from behind chain-link as he passed.

Brock turned to Gaskins. "What you think?"

"I think we don't know shit."

"We know enough to park ourselves outside this man's house and see what we can see."

"I ain't stayin out late. I gotta be at the shape-up spot at dawn."

Brock punched a number into his cell.

THIRTEEN

RAMONE, RHONDA WILLIS, Garloo Wilkins, and George Loomis methodically canvassed the residents living on the short block of McDonald Place, interviewing those who were home during a workday and leaving contact cards for those who were not. Ramone recorded the pertinent details of his conversations in a small Mead spiral notebook, the same type he had been using for many years.

Nothing significant came from the interviews. One elderly woman did say that she had been awakened by what she thought was the snap of a branch during the night but did not know the time, as she had not bothered to look at her clock radio before falling back to sleep. No one they spoke to had seen anything suspicious. Except for the woman, all, apparently, had slept soundly.

The Baptist church on the end of the block, where South Dakota came in, was unoccupied at night.

Wilkins and Loomis had spoken with the night crew at the animal shelter by phone. They would talk to these workers face-to-face later in the day. But the preliminary conversations indicated that no one at the shelter had heard or seen a thing relative to Asa Johnson's death.

"That ain't no surprise," said Wilkins. "All those fuckin Rovers in there, barking their asses off."

"You can't think in that motherfucker," said George Loomis, "much less hear."

"Still some folks we haven't talked to on McDonald Place," said Rhonda. "They'll be comin home from work later on."

"I suppose the city, or the community organization, or whoever runs this garden's got a list of the people who work all these plots," said Ramone.

"I doubt they do gardening in the middle of the night, Gus," said Wilkins.

"Doubtin ain't knowin," said Rhonda, repeating of one of her most used homilies.

"No stone unturned," said Ramone, adding one of his.

"I'll get that list," said Wilkins.

Rhonda looked at her watch. "You gotta get downtown for that arraignment, don't you?"

"Yeah," said Ramone. "And I need to call my son."

Ramone walked down a path cutting through the center of the garden. He passed plots decorated with lawn ornaments and homemade crosslike signs with sayings like "I Heard It Through the Grapevine," "Let It Grow," and "The Secret Life of Plants" painted on the horizontal planks. He passed things that twirled in the breeze and miniature flags like the kind displayed in used-car lots, and then he was out of the garden and near his car.

Ramone got in the Impala and stared through its windshield. That had been Dan Holiday in the monkey suit, standing by his Town Car. Wasn't any question about it. Ramone had heard over the MPD telegraph that Holiday had started some kind of drive-for-hire business after he'd resigned. His appearance had changed very little since the both of them had been in uniform. A comical little belly on him, but other than that, he looked pretty much the same. Question was, why was he here? Holiday did love being police. He was probably one of those sad ex-cops who listened to the scanners long after they'd turned in their badge and gun. Maybe Holiday was having trouble getting the blue out of his system. Well, he should've considered that before he fucked up.

Holiday's image faded. Ramone thought of Asa Johnson and the extreme fear he had probably experienced in his last moments. He thought of what Asa's parents, Terrance and Helena, were facing. He saw Asa's name and he turned it around and saw it the same way. He sat there for a while, thinking of that. Then Ramone thought of his son.

He cranked the ignition and headed downtown.

HOLIDAY STARED AT HIS drink. He took a sip of it and, before putting the rocks glass back on the bar, another. He shouldn't have gone to that crime scene. He was curious, was all it was.

"Tell us a story, Doc," said Jerry Fink.

"I'm fresh out," said Holiday. He could not even remember the name of the woman he had done the night before.

Bob Bonano came back from the jukebox. He had just dropped quarters into it, and now he was strutting as mournful harmonica and the first solemn bars of "In the Ghetto" came into the room at Leo's.

"Elvis," said Jerry Fink. "Trying to be socially relevant. Who blew smoke up his ass and told him he was Dylan?"

"Yeah," said Bonano, "but who's doing this version?"

A woman began to sing the first verse. Fink and Bradley West, seated beside Holiday, closed their eyes.

"It's that 'Band of Gold' broad," said Jerry Fink.

"Nope," said Bonano.

Holiday wasn't hearing the song. He was thinking of Gus Ramone, standing over the body of the boy. Some cosmic fucking joke that Ramone had caught the case.

"She did that Vietnam song, too," said West. " 'Bring the Boys Home,' right?"

"That was Freda Payne, and I don't care what she did," said Bonano. He blew into a deck of Marlboro Lights and watched as the filtered end of one popped out. "She didn't do this."

Holiday wondered if Ramone had noticed that the boy's first name, Asa, was the same spelled backward as it was forward. How the name was one of those palindromes.

"Then who is it, smart guy?" said Fink.

"Candi Staton," said Bonano, lighting his smoke.

"You only know 'cause you read the name off the juke," said Fink.

"Now for a dollar," said Bonano, ignoring Fink, "what was Candi Staton's big hit?"

Holiday wondered if Ramone had connected the boy with the other teenage victims with palindrome names. How all of them were found shot in the head, in community gardens around town.

Ramone was a good enough cop, though he was stymied, Holiday believed, by his insistence on following procedure. He wasn't anywhere near the cop that he, Holiday, had been. He lacked that rapport with citizens at which Holiday had excelled. And those years Ramone had spent in IAD, working mostly behind a desk, hadn't done him any favors as police.

"No clue," said Fink.

" 'Young Hearts Run Free,' " said Bonano with a self-satisfied grin.

"You mean 'Young Dicks *Swing* Free,' " said Fink.

"Huh?"

"It's one of them disco songs," said Fink. "Figures you'd like it."

"I didn't say I liked it. And you owe me a dollar, ya fuckin Jew."

"I don't have a dollar."

Bonano reached over and pushed down on the back of Fink's head. "How 'bout a dollar's worth of this, then?"

Holiday killed his drink and put cash on the bar.

"What's your hurry, Doc?" said West.

Holiday said, "I got a job."

RAMONE ATTENDED THE TYREE arraignment, returned to the crime scene, took part in some more interviews with potential witnesses, ran Rhonda Willis back to the VCU lot, called Diego on his cell, then went back uptown in his own car, a gray Chevy Tahoe. He drove into his neighborhood but did not go home. He was off the clock, but his workday was not done.

The Johnson house was a modest brick colonial, well maintained, on Somerset, west of Coolidge High School. Cars filled the spaces on both sides of the street. Visitors had been cautiously dropping in, bringing food and condolences to the family, leaving just as quickly as they had arrived. A formal wake and church service would come later, but relatives and close friends felt a more immediate response was necessary. No one could really know what was proper in situations such as this. A casserole or a dish of lasagna in hand was an impotent but safe bet.

Ramone was let into the house by a woman he did not recognize after he identified himself as a family friend first and a police officer second. There were folks sitting in the living room, some with their hands in their laps, some talking quietly, some not talking at all. Asa's little sister, Deanna, was sitting on the hall stairway with a couple of young girls, cousins, Ramone guessed. Deanna was not crying, but her eyes showed confusion.

"Ginny," said the woman, shaking Ramone's hand. "Virginia. I'm Helena's sister. Asa's aunt."

"Yes, ma'am. I'm awful sorry." He saw Helena in her sister, the same strong, mannish figure, the perpetually worried look, as if she carried the weight of knowing that something awful was bound to happen, that to enjoy the moment would be a waste of time. "Is Helena back from the hospital?"

"She's upstairs in bed, sedated. Helena wanted to be with her daughter."

"What about Terrance?"

"He's in the kitchen. My husband's with him." Ginny put her hand on Ramone's forearm. "Have you people found anything yet?"

Ramone barely shook his head. "Excuse me."

He went through a short hall to a small kitchen located at the rear of the house. Terrance Johnson and another man, light as Smokey Robinson, were seated at a round two-person table, drinking from cans of beer. Johnson got up to greet Ramone. Their hands clasped and they went shoulder to shoulder, Ramone patting Terrance Johnson's back.

"My sympathies," said Ramone. "Asa was a fine young man."

"Yes," said Johnson. "Meet Clement Harris, my brother-in-law. Clement, this is Gus Ramone."

Clement reached out and shook Ramone's hand without getting up from his chair.

"Gus's boy and Asa were friends," said Johnson. "Gus is a police officer. Works homicide."

Clement Harris mumbled something.

"Get you a beer?" said Johnson, his eyes slightly crossed and unfocused.

"Thanks."

"I'm gonna have one more myself," said Johnson. He tilted his head back and killed what was left in the can. "I ain't tryin to get messed up, understand."

"It's okay," said Ramone. "Let's have a beer together, Terrance."

Johnson tossed the empty into a garbage pail and grabbed two cans of light beer, a brand Ramone would never normally buy or drink, from the refrigerator. As the door swung closed, Ramone saw magnetized photos of the Johnson children: Deanna playing in the snow, Deanna in a gymnastics outfit, an unsmiling Asa in uniform and pads, holding a football after one of his games.

"Let's go outside," said Johnson to Ramone, and when Ramone nodded, they left Clement at the kitchen table without further conversation.

A door from the kitchen led to the narrow backyard, which stopped at an alley. Johnson was not interested in gardening or landscaping, apparently, and neither was his wife. The yard was weedy, cluttered with garbage cans and milk crates, and surrounded by a rusted chain-link fence.

Ramone cracked his can open and drank. The beer had little more taste than water and probably as much kick. He and Johnson stopped halfway down a cracked walkway that led to the alley.

Johnson was a bit shorter than Ramone, with a beefy build and a square head accentuated by an outdated fade, shaved back and sides with a pomaded top. Johnson's teeth were small and pointy, miniature fangs. His arms hung like the sides of a triangle off his trunk.

"Tell me what you know," said Johnson, his face close to Ramone's. The smell of alcohol was pungent on his breath, and it came to Ramone that Johnson had been drinking something other than this pisswater to get him to where he was now.

"Nothing yet," said Ramone.

"Have ya'll found the gun?"

"Not yet."

"When are you going to start knowing things?"

"It's a process. It's *methodical,* Terrance."

Ramone was hoping his choice of words would help placate Johnson, an analyst of some kind for the Census Bureau. Ramone generally did not know what people did, exactly, when they said that they worked for the federal government, but he knew Johnson dealt with numbers and statistics.

"You, what, tryin to find a witness?"

"We're interviewing potential witnesses. We have been all day, and we'll continue to conduct interviews. We'll talk to his friends and acquaintances, his teachers, everyone he knew. Meantime, we'll wait on the results of the autopsy."

Johnson wiped his hand across his mouth. His voice was hoarse as he spoke. "They gonna cut up my boy? Why they got to do that, Gus?"

"It's hard to talk about this, Terrance. I know it's hard for you to hear it. But an autopsy will give us a lot of tools. It's also required by law."

"I can't . . ."

Ramone put his hand on Johnson's shoulder. "With that, the witness interviews, the lab work, the tip line, what have you, we'll start to build a case. We're going to attack this thing on all fronts, Terrance, I promise you."

"What can I do?" said Johnson. "What can I do *right now?*"

"Next thing you have to do is come to the morgue at D.C. General tomorrow between eight and four. We need you to make the formal identification."

Johnson nodded absently. Ramone placed his beer can on the walk and pulled his wallet. He withdrew two cards and handed them to Johnson.

"We offer grief counseling if you want it," said Ramone. "Your wife's eligible, of course, and your daughter, too. The Family Liaison Unit — their number's on that card right there — is always available to you. The people on staff work with us in the VCB offices. Sometimes it's difficult for the detectives to stay in touch with you, and the FLU folks can give you progress reports and answers, if any are available. The other card is mine. My work number and cell are on it."

"What can I do today?"

"All these visitors here, they mean well, I know, but don't give them the run of the house. If they have to use the bathroom, let them use the guest bathroom, not the one upstairs. And don't let anyone except you and your wife go into Asa's bedroom. We're going to want to give that a thorough inspection."

"What you looking for?"

Ramone made a half shrug. There was no reason to mention the possible evidence of criminal activity.

"We don't know until we get in there. In addition, we're going to interview you extensively. Helena and Deanna as well, as soon as they're ready."

"That Detective Wilkins, he already talked to me some."

"He'll be needing to speak to you again."

"Why him and not you?"

"Bill Wilkins is the primary on the case."

"Is he up to this?"

"He's good police. One of our best."

Terrance saw the lie in Ramone's eyes, and Ramone looked away. He drank off some of his beer.

"Gus."

"I'm sorry, Terrance. I can't even begin to imagine what you're going through."

"Look at me, Gus."

Ramone met Johnson's eyes.

"Find who did this," said Johnson.

"We'll do our best."

"That's not what I mean. I'm asking you personal and plain. I want you to find the animal that did this to my son."

Ramone said that he would.

They finished their beers as the sky clouded over. It began to sprinkle. They stood in it and let it cool their faces.

"God's cryin," said Terrance Johnson, his voice not much more than a whisper.

To Ramone, it was only rain.

FOURTEEN

ROMEO BROCK AND Conrad Gaskins were parked at the entrance to a court, one of the tree-and-flower streets uptown off Georgia in Shepherd Park. This was not the high-end side of the neighborhood, but rather the less-fashionable section, east of the avenue. The court held a group of two-story splits and colonials with faded siding and bars on the first-floor windows and doors.

The house of Tommy Broadus was more heavily fortified than the rest, with bars on the storm door and the upper-floor windows as well. Contact lights, positioned to activate on movement at the center of the sidewalk, were mounted high above the front door. The front yard had been paved to accommodate two cars, leaving only a small strip of grass. A black Cadillac CTS and a red Solara convertible sat side by side in the driveway.

"His woman's with him," said Brock.

" 'Cause the convertible would be her car."

"A man wouldn't drive a So-lara. 'Less he the type of man to suck on another man's dick. That's a girl's idea of a sports car right there."

"Okay. But the Caddy must be his." Gaskins squinted. "He got the V version, too."

"That ain't no Caddy," said Brock. "A seventy-four El-D is a Cadillac. That thing there, I don't know what that is."

Gaskins almost smiled. His cousin thought the world had stopped turning in the '70s. That's when cats like Red Fury in D.C. and a dude name Mad Dog out of Baltimore were legends in the streets. And there were businessmen like Frank Matthews, too, in New York, a black man who beat the Italians at their own game, cut and dealt out of an armed fortress known as the Ponderosa, and owned an estate on Long Island. Romeo would have given a nut to have lived in those days and run with any of them. He dressed in tight slacks and synthetic shirts. He even smoked Kools in tribute to that time. He would have worn a natural, too, if he could. But he had a large bald spot on the top of his dome, and a blowout wouldn't come full. So he wore his head shaved clean.

"Tired of waitin," said Gaskins.

"Just got dark," said Brock. "If the mule coming, he coming now. Like Fishhead said, those boys like to run after sundown, but not too late so they stand out."

"Fishhead said."

"Man got a stupid name, don't mean he can't be right."

A little while later, a car came down the street and slowed as it approached the court. Brock and Gaskins made themselves low as the car passed them and parked, as many other vehicles had done, head-in to the curb. It was a Mercury Sable, the sister to the Ford Taurus.

"What I tell you?" said Brock. "Fishhead gave us gold so far."

Brock put his hand to the door handle.

"What you doin?"

"Gonna rush him and bull on in."

"He might be packing. Then you got nothin but a gun battle in the street."

"So we do what?"

"Think, boy. If he comin out with cash, we *let* him come out. Brace his ass then."

"He still gonna have a gun if he got one now."

"But then he got something worth taking."

A young man, cleanly but not loudly dressed, got out of the Mercury and walked toward the house, talking on a cell and looking around as he went along. He did not see the men in the Impala, as their heads were barely above the windshield line and their car was parked far back at the head of the court. The security lights on the house were activated as he moved up the sidewalk. The barred storm door opened as he neared. Then the main door opened as well. The man went into the house.

"You see it?" said Gaskins.

"Wasn't nobody pulling that door open."

"Right. He called in and it opened by itself. Automatic."

"I smell money," said Brock.

"Wait."

They sat there for another half hour. When the front door to the house opened again, it was not the man who had arrived in the Mercury leaving, but a woman, tall and full up top and in the back, with curls on her head. She carried a small purse in one hand and a cell in the other.

"Uh," said Brock.

"We ain't here for that."

"I know, but *damn*."

They watched her get into the red Solara, fire it up, and back it out of the driveway.

"Don't tell me to hold up, neither," said Brock. "That girl's gonna get us in."

Gaskins didn't object. When the Solara passed them, Brock turned the key on the SS. He powered the headlights, swung the car around, and followed the woman to the intersection at 8th, staying close to her taillights. As she slowed for the stop sign there, he gave the Impala gas, swerved around her, cut in front of her abruptly, and threw the trans into park. Brock jumped out and went around the rear of the Chevy, pulling his Colt as he moved. Her window came down, and he could hear her giving him attitude already as he stepped up to the Toyota and pointed the gun at her face. Her big, pretty brown eyes went wide but only in surprise. She did not seem afraid.

"What's your name, baby?"

"Chantel."

"Sounds French. Where you off to, Chantel?"

"To buy cigarettes."

"That won't be necessary. I got plenty."

"You fixin to rob me?"

"Not you. Your man."

"Then let me be on my way."

"You ain't goin no goddamn where but back in that house." Brock made a motion with the barrel of the gun. "Now, get out the car."

"You got no reason to take that tone."

"Please . . . get out the motherfuckin car."

She killed the engine and stepped out of the Toyota. She handed the keys to Brock, who tossed them to Gaskins, walking their way. Gaskins held a roll of duct tape in his free hand.

"My partner will drive it back," said Brock. "You come with me."

"Look, if you gonna kill me, kill me now. I don't want no tape around my head."

Brock smiled. "I got the feelin we gonna get along."

The woman's eyes appraised him. "You look like a devil. Anyone ever tell you that?"

"Once or twice," said Brock.

IT WAS EASY TO get into the house. Chantel Richards phoned her boyfriend, Tommy Broadus, from outside, and he let her in by pushing a button from a remote in the living room, where he sat with his mule, a young man named Edward Reese. The storm door opened and behind it the main door cracked, and Chantel, Brock, and Gaskins went inside.

They walked into the living room, Brock and Gaskins with their guns drawn. Tommy Broadus sat in a large leather easy chair, a snifter of something amber in his hand. Edward Reese, in white Rocawear polo shirt over big jeans and Timberlands, sat in a chair just like it, on the other side of a kidney-shaped marble table. He was drinking the same shade of liquor. Neither of them moved. Gaskins frisked them quickly and found them to be clean.

Brock told Tommy Broadus that they were there to rob him.

"Clarence Carter can see that," said Broadus, chains on his chest, rings on his fingers, his ass spilling over his chair. "But I ain't got nothin of value, see?"

Brock raised his gun. Chantel Richards stepped behind him. He fired a round into an ornate, gold leaf–framed mirror that hung over a fireplace with fake crackling logs. The mirror exploded, and shards of glass flew about the room.

"Now you got less," said Brock.

They all waited for their ears to stop ringing and for the gunsmoke to settle in the room. It was a nice room, lavishly appointed, with furniture bought on Wisconsin Avenue and statues of naked white women with vases resting on their shoulders. A plasma television set, the largest Panasonic made, was set on a stand of glass and iron and blocked out most of one wall. A bookcase with leather-bound volumes on its shelves took up another. In the middle of the bookcase was a cutout holding a large, lighted fish tank in which several tropical varieties swam. Above the fish tank was empty space.

"Tape 'em up," said Brock.

Gaskins handed Brock his gun. Brock holstered it in his belt line, keeping the Colt trained on Broadus.

As Gaskins worked, duct-taping the hands and feet of Broadus and Reese, Brock went to a wet bar situated near the plasma set. Broadus had several high-shelf liquors on display, including bottles of Rémy XO and Martell Cordon Bleu. On a separate platform below were bottles of Courvoisier and Hennessey.

Brock found a glass and poured a couple inches of the Rémy.

"That's the XO," said Broadus, looking perturbed for the first time.

"Why I'm fixin to have some," said Brock.

"I'm sayin, you don't know the difference, ain't no reason for you to be drinking from a one-hundred-fifty-dollar bottle of yak."

"You don't think I know the difference?"

"Bama," said Edward Reese with a smile. Brock locked eyes with him, but Reese's smile did not fade.

"Tape that boy's mouth up, too," said Brock.

Gaskins did it and stepped back. Brock took a sip of the cognac and rolled it in the snifter as he let it settle sweet on his tongue.

"That is nice," said Brock. "You want some, brah?"

"I'm good," said Gaskins.

Brock drew the Glock and handed it to Gaskins.

"Awright, then," said Brock. "Where your stash at, fat man?"

"My stash?"

"Your money only. I don't want no dope."

"Told you, I got nothin."

"Look, you seen I got no problem using this gun. You don't talk real quick, I'm gonna have to use it again."

"You can do whateva," said Broadus. "I ain't tellin' y'all shit."

Brock had another sip of his drink. He put the snifter down and went to Chantel Richards. He touched a finger to her face and ran it slowly down her cheek. She grew warm at his touch and turned her head away.

Broadus's expression did not change.

"I'll give you a choice," said Brock. "Either you give up your shit or I'm gonna fuck Chantel right here in front of you, understand? What you think of that?"

"Go ahead," said Broadus. "Invite the whole goddamn neighborhood, you got a mind to. They can take a turn with it, too."

Chantel's eyes flared. "Mother*fucker*."

"You don't love your woman?" said Brock.

"Shit," said Broadus. "Most of the time, I don't even *like* the bitch."

Brock turned to Gaskins. "Fix the lady a drink."

"What you want, girl?" said Gaskins.

"Martell," said Chantel Richards. "Make it the Cordon Bleu."

BROCK AND CHANTEL SAT on a king-size bed in the master bedroom upstairs. Atop the dresser were several ornate boxes that Brock assumed held jewelry. He could see many suits, a neat row of shoes, and a set of designer luggage through the open door of the walk-in closet. Chantel drank some of the cognac, closed her eyes, and hit it again.

"This is *good*," she said. "One hundred ninety a bottle. I always wondered how it would be."

"First time you had it, huh?"

"You think he'd ever let me have a taste?"

"Man doesn't care about his woman, 'specially one as fine as you? Makes you wonder."

"Only thing Tommy cares about is this house and all the things he done bought to put inside it."

"That your jewelry?" said Brock, nodding toward the dresser.

"His," said Chantel. "He ain't buy me nothin. That car you saw? It's mine. I pay on it every month. I *work*."

"What else he got?"

"He got an egg."

"An egg."

"One of those Fabergé eggs, he says. Bought it off the street. I told him they don't have no Fabergé eggs on no hot sheet, but he claims it's real."

"I don't want no fake eggs. I'm talkin about money."

"He got it. But damn if I know where it is."

"That boy down there with him, with the smart smile. He come to pick up some cash, right? He mulin some dope back from New York tonight, isn't he?"

"I expect."

"But you don't know where that cash is."

"Tommy wouldn't tell me that. Guess he don't love me enough."

"He do love his stuff, though."

"More than life."

Brock pursed his lips. He did this when he was working on a plan.

"Wasn't much of a yard in the front," said Brock.

"Huh?"

"Is there grass out back?"

"He got some."

"So he got a lawn mower, too."

"It's out there in a shed."

"Wouldn't be electric, would it?" said Brock. " 'Cause that would really fuck with what I'm seein in my head."

GASKINS HELD THE GLOCK loosely at his side. Broadus and Reese sat taped in their chairs, with Reese's mouth sealed. Chantel had poured another drink and was alternately sipping it and inspecting her long painted nails.

Brock came from the back of the house and entered the living room. He was carrying a two-gallon plastic container of gasoline.

"Wh-what you fixin to do with that?" said Broadus.

Brock unlatched the cover on the yellow nozzle and the pressure cap on the rear of the container, and began to shake gasoline out and around the room.

"Nah," said Broadus. "Nah, uh-uh."

Brock poured gasoline over the white-woman statues, splashed some onto the leather-bound books on the shelves.

"Hold up," said Broadus.

"You got somethin you want to say?"

"Cut me free."

Gaskins produced a Buck knife and sliced the tape around Broadus's hands and ankles.

"Y'all motherfuckers just *serious*," said Broadus, rubbing at his wrists.

"Your cash," said Brock.

"You lookin to bankrupt a man," said Broadus. He walked to the television stand and picked up one of three remotes that lay upon it.

Broadus pointed the remote at the fish tank and pressed a button. The tank began to rise out of its base. As it did, a small amount of tightly packaged heroin and what looked to be a great deal of money were revealed.

Brock laughed joyously. The others stared at the bounty with varying emotions. Chantel headed for the stairs.

"Where you goin?" said Brock.

"Get something to put that money in," said Chantel. "*And* my things. What you think?"

She returned with two identical Gucci suitcases and a Rolex President watch, which she fitted to Brock's wrist. Brock let the heroin sit and filled one of the suitcases with cash. He picked it up by the handle, his gun in his right hand.

"Don't," said Gaskins, seeing Brock moving toward Edward Reese, still fully taped. But Brock kept walking, a man intent, pressed the barrel of the .45 to Reese's shoulder, and squeezed the trigger.

Reese shuddered violently and flopped about in the chair. The white Rocawear shirt was shredded and blackened instantly from the powder contact. Then it seeped red. Reese tried to scream but could not get the sound out from beneath the duct tape.

"Smile now," said Brock.

"Let's go," said Gaskins, and when Brock didn't move, savoring what he had done, he shouted the same words again.

"You coming?" said Brock to Chantel.

Chantel crossed the room and joined Brock and Gaskins.

"Say your name," said Tommy Broadus.

"Romeo Brock. Tell your grandkids, fat man."

"You made a mistake, Romeo."

"I got your money and your woman. From where I'm standin, it don't look that way to me."

Out on the street, a spotlight mounted on the door of a car flashed one time. The car turned around in the court and drove away.

"All that gasoline in there," said Gaskins, as they walked to the cars, "and you firing off a gun. Lucky we didn't get blowed up."

"I got nothing but luck," said Brock. "Think I'll embroider a horseshoe on the headrest of my next ride."

"Yeah, okay. But why'd you have to shoot that man?"

"Just a robbery otherwise."

"What you sayin?"

"The words Romeo Brock 'bout to ring out on the street." Brock pulled his keys from his pocket. "My name gonna mean something now."

FIFTEEN

RAMONE FOUND REGINA in their kitchen, leaning against the island countertop, holding a glass of chardonnay. It was early for her to be drinking alcohol. She had grilled chicken, boiled some green beans, and cut a salad, and all of it was ready to go. He kissed her and after their embrace he told her where he'd been and how it had gone.

"You see Helena?"

"No. She was in bed."

"I'll go by tomorrow, bring them something like a casserole so they don't have to think about dinner."

"They're loaded with casseroles," said Ramone.

"I'll call Marita, then. She's a busybody, but she gets things done. Maybe we'll get a schedule together, where a bunch of us can cook something on a certain night and take it over."

"That's a good idea," said Ramone. "Where the kids at?"

"They've eaten. They're up in their rooms."

"I spoke to Diego on the phone. He seemed okay."

"He didn't get too emotional about it, if that's what you mean. But he's been kinda quiet since I told him."

"You know how he is," said Ramone. "He thinks he's gotta be hard, even at a time like this. He holds everything in."

"And you're effusive," said Regina. "By the way, the school sent him home a little early today."

"What now?"

"I'll let him tell you."

Ramone locked up his badge and gun and went upstairs to Alana's room. She had lined up all her plastic horses in a row and was fitting her smaller dolls, Barbies, and Groovy Girls in the saddles. She liked to organize her things.

"How's my little girl?" said Ramone.

"Good, Daddy."

He kissed the top of her head and smelled her curly hair.

Alana's bedroom was always in order, obsessively so, because Alana kept it that way. Unlike Diego's room, which was perpetually a mess. The boy just could not get it together, and not only in his personal space. He couldn't remember to make note of his homework assignments, either. Even when he completed them on time, he often turned the work in late.

"We need to get him tested," Regina had said at one point. "Maybe he's got a learning disability."

"He's scatterbrained," Ramone had responded. "I don't need to pay someone to tell me that."

Regina had had Diego tested. The shrink or whatever she was said that Diego had something called executive function disorder, which was why he had trouble organizing his day and thoughts. It was causing him to lag behind in school.

"He doesn't want to do his homework, is all it is," said Ramone. "I know what that's about."

"Look at his room," said Regina. "You can't tell the difference between the dirty clothes and the clean. He doesn't even know to separate them."

"He's a slob," said Ramone. "So now they got a big name for it. It cost me a grand to learn a new word."

"Gus."

Ramone was reminded of this as he knocked on his son's door, opened it, and saw the explosion of T-shirts and jeans on Diego's bedroom floor. Diego was lying on his bed, his headphones on, listening to go-go as he stared glassy-eyed at an open book. He removed the cans and turned the volume down on his portable player.

"Hey, Diego."

"Dad."

"What you doin?"

"Reading this book."

"How can you read and listen to music at the same time?"

"I'm one of them multitaskers, I guess."

Diego sat up on the edge of his bed and dropped the book at his side. He looked tired, and disappointed that his father was giving him the same old. Ramone could have kicked his own ass for riding Diego on a day like this, but he had done so out of habit.

"Look, I shouldn't have—"

"It's all right."

"You okay?"

"We weren't, like, tight-tight. You know that."

"But you were friends."

"Yeah, me and Asa were straight." Diego made a clucking sound with his tongue. It was something he and his friends did often. "I feel bad, though. I saw him yesterday. We didn't talk or nothin like that, but I saw him."

"Where was that? Where and when?"

"Over on Third, at the rec center. Me and Shaka were playin basketball. Asa was walking down the street, and then he turned up Tuckerman."

"Toward Blair Road."

"Yeah, that way. It was getting late in the day. The sun was fading; I remember that."

"What else?"

"He was wearing a North Face. Musta been new, 'cause it's too warm to be rockin that coat right now. He was sweatin."

"What else?"

"He looked pressed," said Diego. He had lowered his voice and he rubbed his hands together uselessly as he spoke. "We called out to him, but he kept walkin. I wish he would've stopped, Dad. I can't forget the way he looked. I can't help thinking that if we had made him stop and talk to us . . ."

"Come here, Diego."

Diego stood up and Ramone pulled him into his arms. Diego held him tightly for a few seconds. Both of them relaxed.

"I'm good, Dad."

"All right, son."

Diego stepped back. "Is this one gonna be yours?"

"No. Another guy caught it." Ramone stroked his mustache. "But Diego, I would like to ask you something."

"Go ahead."

"Was Asa into anything we should know about?"

"Like weed and stuff?"

"For starters. I was thinking more along the lines of, was he deeper into it. Matter of fact, was he into anything criminal at all?"

"Not that I know. Like I say, we weren't all that tight this past year. I'd tell you if I thought he was."

"I know you would. Anyway, we'll talk some more. Go ahead and read your book. Listen to music while you're doing it if you want to."

"I wasn't really readin that book, tell you the truth."

"No kidding."

"Dad? I got in a little trouble again today."

"What happened?"

"We had this fire drill, and while we were standing outside, this boy told me a joke and I laughed."

"So?"

"I mean, I kinda laughed real loud. They suspended me for the rest of the day."

"For laughing outside of the school."

"It's the rule. Principal got on the intercom before the drill, warned everyone against it. I knew not to do it, but I couldn't help it. This boy just cracked me up."

"You couldn't have been the only kid who was laughing."

"True. Plenty of kids were joking around. But Mr. Guy didn't mess with them. He came right down on me."

"Don't worry about it," said Ramone.

He left his son in his room. Ramone's jaw was tight as he walked down the hall.

HOLIDAY POURED VODKA OVER ice, standing beside the Formica-topped counter of his small kitchen. There was nothing to do but have a drink.

He wasn't into television, except for sports, and he never read books. He'd thought about taking up a hobby, but he was suspicious of men who did. He felt they were fucking off when they could have been doing something productive. There were problems to be solved and goals to achieve, and here were grown men chasing little white balls, climbing rocks, and riding bicycles. Wearing those stupid bicycle-riding clothes, for Chrissakes, like boys wearing cowboy outfits.

Holiday wouldn't have minded talking to someone tonight. He had things to discuss, police-type matters, which went beyond bar conversation. But he could think of no one to call.

He had few friends, and none he could call close. A cop he occasionally drank with, Johnny Ramirez, who had a chip on his shoulder but was all right enough to have a beer with now and again. The guys at Leo's, them, too. He knew some of the residents of the garden apartments to nod at or say hello to in the mornings as they walked out to their cars and their cabs, but none of them were people he'd ask into his place. He lived in Prince George's, not the last white man in the county but feeling at times as if he were, because he had grown up here and it felt like home. The guys he had known were in northern Montgomery or down in Charles County now, or had left the area entirely. He'd run into someone locally on occasion, black men he'd gone to Eleanor Roosevelt High with, now with families of their own, and that was cool. They'd talk for a couple of minutes, twenty years of catch-up in a short conversation, then part company. Acquaintances with shared memories, but no real friends.

Sure, he had his women. He had always had a talent for finding strange. But no one he wanted to wake up next to in his bed. His nights were no more meaningful than his days.

This afternoon, Dan Holiday had driven a man named Seamus O'Brien, who had bought an NBA team after cashing out of a tech start-up in the late '90s. O'Brien had come to Washington to meet with a group of lawmakers who shared his values, and also to have his photo taken with a group of charter school students residing east of the Anacostia River. He had brought them signed posters of one of his players, a shooting guard who had come out of Eastern High. O'Brien would never see these children again or be involved in their lives, but a photograph of him and a bunch of smiling black kids would make him feel as if he were right with the world. It would also look good on his office wall.

Holiday had listened as the man in the backseat of the Town Car talked about vouchers, prayer in school, and his desire to influence the culture of the nation, because what was money worth if you didn't use it do some good? His sentences were peppered with references to the Lord and his personal savior, Jesus Christ. Holiday had helpfully turned the satellite radio to The Fish, an adult-contemporary Christian program, but after one song O'Brien asked him if he could find Bloomberg News instead.

That had been his day. Driving a rich man to and from appointments, waiting for him outside those appointments, and taking him to the airport. A nice chunk of change, but zero in the accomplishment department. Which is why his eyes never snapped open in the mornings when he woke up, as they had when he was police. Back then he couldn't wait to get to work. He didn't hate this job or love it; it was an odometer turning, a ride with no destination, a waste of time.

Holiday took his drink and a pack of smokes out to the balcony of his apartment and had a seat. The balcony faced the parking lot and beyond the lot the rear of the Hecht's at the P.G. Plaza mall. A man and a woman were arguing somewhere, and as cars drove slowly in the lot there was rapping and window-rattling bass, and as other cars passed there was toasting, and from the open windows of still other cars came the call-and-response, synthesizers, and percussion of go-go.

The sounds reached Holiday, but they did not bother him or interrupt the scenario forming in his head. He was thinking of a man who would like to hear the story of the dead teenager lying in the community garden on Oglethorpe. Holiday had a sip of his drink and wondered if this man was still alive.

RAMONE AND REGINA ATE dinner and shared a bottle of wine, and when they were done they opened another bottle, which they normally didn't do. The two of them talked intensely about the death of Diego's friend, and at one point Regina cried, not only for Asa, and not only for his parents, to whom she was not particularly close, but for herself, because she was thinking about how completely and permanently crushing it would be to lose one of her own in that way.

"The Lord oughtta strike me down for being so selfish," said Regina, wiping tears off her face and chuckling with embarrassment. "It's just that I'm afraid."

"It's natural to feel that way," said Ramone. He didn't tell her that he feared for his children also, every day.

In bed, they kissed and held each other, but neither of them took the step to make love. For Gus especially the passionate kiss was always a prelude to something else, but not tonight.

"God is crying," said Ramone.

"What?"

"That's what Terrance Johnson said. We were standing in his backyard, and it had started to rain. Can you imagine?"

"Not unusual for him to be thinking on God."

"What I mean is, you'd think that if your kid died like that, you'd either lose your faith completely or you'd be so angry at God that you'd turn your back on him."

"Terrance is gonna look to God now stronger than ever. That's what faith is."

"You sound like Rhonda."

"Us black women do love us some church."

"Regina?"

"What?"

"You know, Asa's name . . . It's spelled the same way backward as it is forward. It's a palindrome."

"All right."

"You were on the force back when those kids from Southeast were killed."

"I was still a recruit. But, yeah, I remember."

"Those kids were found in community gardens, too. All of them, shot in the head."

"You think this is connected?"

"I have to sleep on it. Tomorrow I guess I'll go ahead and open some files."

"Tomorrow. You forget about it now."

After a while Ramone said, "Diego seems okay. He'll never forget this, but he's handling it pretty well."

"He had a rough day, all in all. On top of everything, they went and sent him home—"

"For laughing during a fire drill. I wonder how many white kids laughed."

"Now, Gus. Don't go hatin on white kids."

"Fuck that school," said Ramone. "I've about had it with that bullshit, too."

"Easy, soldier," said Regina, brushing hair off his forehead and kissing him behind his ear. "Your heart's gonna get to fluttering, you're not going to be able to sleep."

They wrapped their arms around each other, and he felt his breathing slow. And holding her, smelling the scent that was only hers and feeling the buttery skin of her cheek against his, he thought, This is why I am married to this woman.

This is something I will never have with anyone else.

SIXTEEN

THE PASSING OF Asa Johnson made the second page of Metro in the next morning's *Washington Post.* The event carried more weight than the usual one- or two-paragraph mention given black victims under the Crime or In Brief headings, informally called the "Violent Negro Deaths" by many area residents. Johnson, after all, was not a project kid. He was a middle-class teenager, and a young one at that. What made him newsworthy was that his age at death was part of a disturbing trend.

In the middle of the summer, a six-year-old boy, Donmiguel Wilson, had been found gagged, bound, and asphyxiated facedown in a bathtub, dead for several hours in an apartment in Congress Heights. That horrific event had made the *Post*'s front page. The random shooting of Donte Manning, nine years old, while he played outside his apartment house in Columbia Heights, had also warranted extra press, and outrage, back in the spring. The year's murder rate was down, but juvenile murders were higher than they had ever been.

The statistic dogged both the mayor and the D.C. police chief. It wasn't just the bad press that bothered them, though that, of course, added to their anxiety. Everyone, even the most hard-hearted, felt a chill when a child was murdered for no other reason than the fact that he or she had been born and raised in the wrong section of the city. Any time a kid was killed, police, officials, and citizenry alike were reminded that they lived in a world gone terribly wrong.

Still, Asa Johnson's death, not yet officially classified as a murder, did not draw the type of attention or prioritization afforded white victims or black preteens. There were other murders to investigate as well. Several bodies, in fact, had dropped in the past couple of days.

Rhonda Willis had caught one of them, a shooting victim found overnight in Fort Slocum Park, a few blocks west of the community garden on Oglethorpe Street.

"You wanna ride out there with me?" said Rhonda, seated at her desk in the VCB. It was early in the morning, not yet nine. Gus Ramone and Rhonda Willis were pulling eight-to-fours for the next two weeks.

"Sure," said Ramone. "But I need to talk to Garloo first."

"Go ahead. We already got an ID on my decedent. I'm gonna run his name through the system, get some background."

"Let me do this and I'll be ready to go."

Garloo Wilkins was in his cubicle, reading something on the Internet. He closed the screen as Ramone approached. It was either sports or porn sites for Garloo. He was into fantasy baseball and mature women with big racks.

Wilkins's desk was clean, with his files aligned neatly in a steel vertical holder to the side. There were no religious icons, family shots, or photos on his corkboard, except for a Polaroid, taken from an evidence file, of a local go-go keyboardist and murder suspect fucking a young female from behind, smiling as he stared into the camera. The musician had been questioned but never charged due to lack of evidence and witnesses. It had not been one of Garloo's cases, but the whole of the unit had been angered by the suspect's ability to evade arrest, and the photo was a reminder that he was still out there, having fun and breathing free air. Also on Garloo's desk was a lighter lying atop a pack of Winstons. The lighter had a map of North and South Vietnam on it. Wilkins was ex-army but had been too young to serve in that war.

"Bill."

"Gus."

Ramone pulled someone's chair over and had a seat. "What's shaking on Asa Johnson?"

Wilkins reached over and pulled the file out of the holder. He opened it and stared at some unmarked paperwork. Ramone eyed the top sheet. There were no notes scribbled upon it. Usually a well-worked case had notations written in the margins and greasy fingerprints staining the manila. This one was bone clean.

Wilkins closed the file and replaced it. He had recorded nothing in it, but the handling of the file added to the drama he was trying to project. Apparently he had some news.

"We got a probable time of death from the pre-autopsy notes. The ME says between midnight and two a.m. Gunshot wound to the left temple, exit at the crown."

"What about the slug?"

"Came from a thirty-eight. Clean enough to get markings. We could match it if we found the weapon."

Ramone nodded. "Any foreign substances in the blood?"

"None. There was powder residue found on the fingers of his left hand. I'm assuming he raised that hand in some kind of defense before he was shot."

"Okay. That's forensics. What about on the investigative end?"

"Canvasses turned up goose eggs. Except for that old lady, thought she heard the snap of a branch. So no witnesses whatsoever. Yet."

"Anything come up off the tip line?"

"Nada."

"What about the tape of the man who called in the body?"

"I've got it," said Wilkins, pulling a cassette dub from an envelope in his top drawer.

"Mind if I listen to it?"

Garloo Wilkins and Ramone walked back to the audio/video room. On the way they passed Anthony Antonelli and Mike Bakalis arguing over Redskins trivia.

"Art Monk had the most yards receiving in eighty-seven," said Bakalis.

"It was Gary Clark," said Antonelli. "Hell, Kelvin Bryant had more yards that year than Monk."

"I was talking about wide receivers," said Bakalis.

"Clark *was* a wide receiver, dumbass."

Ramone went into the room with Wilkins, fitted the tape in the machine, and hit "play." He listened to the voice of the man calling in the body, and the dispatcher, who was unsuccessfully trying to get the man to identify himself. Ramone rewound the tape and listened to it again.

"What are you hearing?" said Wilkins, seeing a look of discovery, or maybe recognition, pass across Ramone's face.

"I'm just listening for ambience," said Ramone.

"No caller ID," said Wilkins. "It's gonna be harder than my dick to find this guy."

"Uh-huh," said Ramone.

"And you know how hard that is," said Wilkins, grinning to reveal a row of horse teeth. "So hard a cat can't scratch it."

"Okay," said Ramone, not hearing Garloo's words of wisdom but listening intensely to the familiar voice coming from the machine, those long Maryland *O*'s of the P.G. County working-class white boy, the slight slur brought on by alcohol.

"We find the dude who made the call, maybe we got a wit. Shit, maybe he's the hitter," said Wilkins.

"Your words to God's ears," said Ramone. He listened to the recording a third time, removed it from the player, and handed it to Wilkins. "Thanks."

"What, you thought you were gonna recognize the guy's voice or somethin?"

"If you play it backwards at a slower speed, he confesses," said Ramone.

"Wouldn't that be nice," sang Wilkins, channeling Brian Wilson. It actually made Ramone smile.

"What now?" said Ramone.

"I'm going to visit the Johnson home today. Check out the kid's room and shit."

Don't fuck it up, thought Ramone. With those ham hock hands of yours.

"I guess I'll get a list of the kid's friends from his father," said Wilkins.

Don't forget the school, thought Ramone.

"You don't mind I talk to your son, do you?" said Wilkins.

"I did, and he doesn't know anything. But you probably should, for the report. Call Regina at my house, and she'll tell you the best time to come by."

"Thanks, Gus. I know you got a personal thing with this. I'm gonna stay on it."

"I appreciate it, Bill," said Ramone.

Ramone joined Rhonda Willis. On their way out the door, Antonelli asked them where they were going, and Rhonda gave him the courtesy of relating the details on her new case.

"The decedent has a list of priors, some grand thefts,

some drug related," said Rhonda. "WACIES gave me some of the names of his accomplices. They were in that game, too."

"Sounds like a society cleanse," said Antonelli.

"Could be," said Rhonda. "But you know I work them all the same way. 'Cause God made them innocent to begin with. Ain't a one of 'em started out wrong."

She and Ramone went out the door. Garloo Wilkins was smoking a Winston down to the filter, standing on the sidewalk bordering a parking lot filled with personal cars, trucks, and SUVs, and police vehicles.

"Looks like Garloo's goin hard at it," said Rhonda when they were out of his hearing range.

"He's pacing himself," said Ramone.

They found a Ford product and got inside. Ramone let Rhonda drive. He wanted to think about the Johnson case. He wondered why he had not yet mentioned to any of his coworkers, including his partner, that the voice on the tape was Dan Holiday's.

HOLIDAY CARRIED THE *POST* out to his balcony and read the article on Asa Johnson thoroughly. He stubbed out his cigarette and took his coffee inside to the second bedroom of his apartment, which he had outfitted as his office. He had a seat at his desk, fired up his computer, and got online. He went to a search engine and typed in "Palindrome Murders, Washington, D.C." For the next hour he read and printed out everything useful on the subject, some of which came from serial-killer sites, most of which came from the archives of the *Washington Post.* He then phoned the local police union office and got a man on the line who had been a patrolman when Holiday had walked a beat in the H Street corridor. This man gave Holiday the current address of the person he was looking for.

Holiday dressed in his black suit and left the apartment. He had a pickup for an airport run.

THE VICTIM'S NAME WAS Jamal White. He had been shot twice in the chest and once in the head. Burn marks and notable cranial damage indicated a close-range kill. He was on his back, with one leg folded in an unnatural manner under the other. His eyes were open and fixed on nothing, and his top teeth were bared and protruded over his lower lip in the manner of a slaughtered animal. He had been found on the edge of the park at 3rd and Madison. Blood had bloomed and dried on his white T.

"Nineteen years old," said Rhonda Willis. "Did a long juvenile stay at Oak Hill and some D.C. Jail time while he was waiting on sentencing. Car thefts, drug possessions, minor sales pops. No violent crimes on his sheet. He came up near Fifth and Kennedy, so you know what that's about. Residential address is his grandmother's home on Longfellow."

"His family been notified?" said Ramone.

"What there is of one. Mother's currently incarcerated. An addict with multiple larceny convictions. No father of record. There's a few half-siblings, but they weren't living with him. The closest kin is his grandmother. She's been called."

They talked to the patrol cop out of 4D who had arrived first on the scene. They asked him if he had spoken to anyone who might have seen something, or if he himself had seen anything pertinent to the murder, and the patrol cop shook his head.

"I guess we should, uh, seek out some witnesses," said Ramone to Rhonda.

"*Please,*" said Rhonda. "Let's go see Granmoms and allow these good people to do their jobs."

They left the working techs and drove to the grandmother's row house on the 500 block of Longfellow Street. The blinds were drawn on the windows of the front porch.

"She in there having her moment, I expect," said Rhonda. "Allowing herself a good cry."

"You could come back," said Ramone.

"No, I need to do this. Might as well make it now. She might have something to tell me while she's thinking on it." Rhonda looked across the bench at Ramone. "Don't suppose you want to come with me."

"I got a few calls to make."

"Gonna make me fly solo, huh."

He watched her go to the house and knock on the front door. The door opened and there was darkness behind. A hand reached out and touched hers and Rhonda stepped inside.

Ramone called 411 and obtained the number for Strange Investigations, a storefront operation on 9th and Upshur. Derek Strange was ex-police, now private, and Ramone had used him in the past for discreet information. In return he threw bits of meat, occasionally, back to Strange.

The phone rang and a woman picked up. It was Strange's wife, Janine.

"Is the big man in?" said Ramone.

"Working," said Janine. "And rarely here. All you boys like to run the streets."

"True. Listen, I got a name. Can you get me an address and phone? I need business and residence."

"All those toys you police have and you're askin me?"

"I'm not at the toy store," said Ramone. "Daniel Holiday, spell it like a vacation. Goes by Doc. He has a car or limo service, is what I hear. I imagine he'd name it after himself."

"Okay. I'll run it through People Finder. Give me your cell number. I got it on file somewhere here, but I'm lazy."

Ramone gave her his number. "How's your boy?"

"Lionel's in college, praise be. Your lovely wife and kids?"

"All is good. Ya'll still got that boxer?"

"You mean Greco. He's under my desk. Got his chin on my toes as we speak."

"Nice beast," said Ramone. "Call me, hear?"

"In a minute," said Janine.

It was more than a minute, but not much more. Ramone wrote down the information on his pad and thanked Janine. Soon after that, Rhonda came out of the house. She put her sunglasses on immediately, walked to the Taurus, and got under the wheel. She removed her sunglasses and used a tissue to wipe at her eyes.

Ramone reached over and put a hand on her shoulder, massaged her there.

"I guess the old girl took it rough," said Ramone.

"She wasn't but ten years older than me," said Rhonda. "Granmom raised that boy from a baby. Stayed right there by him through all his rough spots, never gave up hope that he would make it through to the other side. Now she's got nothin."

"What was her take?"

"She said he was a good boy who had made some bad friends and unfortunate mistakes. Said Jamal had finally got himself on the straight."

"Sounds familiar."

"I took a quick look at his room. No cash lyin around, and the things he had didn't look all that nice. I didn't see any obvious signs that he was in it. Anyway, we gonna have to go elsewhere to get the deeper story. I got a couple of photos from G-mom, so I can show them around." Rhonda leaned forward, looked in the rearview, and chuckled without joy. "Look at me. All puffy-eyed and stuff. And now my mascara's run."

"C'mon, you look fine."

"I used to. Remember how I looked before I had my boys?"

"You know it."

"I had it goin on, Gus."

"You still do."

"Aren't you sweet." Rhonda opened the folder she held on her lap. "Granmom says he's still best friends with this boy Leon Mayo. His name came up on WACIES as an accomplice in one of those car thefts and a possession beef. We ought to find him, see what he's got to say."

"You're driving," said Ramone. "Or do you want me to? So you can, you know, reapply that war paint?"

"I'm good," said Rhonda. "Sorry you had to put up with my tears. I just got emotional. I can't say why."

"Is it that time of month?" said Ramone.

"You mean that time of the month when you start talkin ignorant?"

"Sorry."

They pulled away from the curb.

HOLIDAY DIDN'T SPEAK MUCH to his client, an Arnold and Porter lawyer, on the run down to Reagan National. Guy was on his cell most of the time and never once made eye contact with Holiday in the rearview the entire ride. To the lawyer, he was invisible, and to Holiday that was fine.

Coming back from 395, he shot through the tunnel and took New York Avenue out of town, where he hooked up with the Beltway in Maryland and ramped off onto Greenbelt Road. He listened to Channel 46 on the XM, a station called Classic Album Cuts, and kept it up loud. They were showcasing ax standards today, starting with "Blue Sky," and Holiday could see his brother, long-haired and higher than Hopper, playing air guitar to that beautiful, fluid Dickey Betts solo, a piece of music that just spelled happiness to Holiday, because his brother had been happy then and his sister was there, happy too, and alive. And then the deejay went right into "Have You Ever Loved a Woman," Clapton and Duane Allman dueling, both of them on fire, and something cold touched Holiday, like the finger of death, but then there came the memories of his family, and Holiday relaxed and let the window down and drove on.

He passed Eleanor Roosevelt High and made a right down Cipriano Road, checking the detail map on the bench beside him as he went along woods and past a Vishnu temple, going right on Good Luck Road on the edge of New Carrollton and making another right into a community known as Magnolia Springs, ramblers and ranchers mostly, some well tended, others in need of care. He found the house he was looking for on Dolphin Road. It was a yellow-sided, white-shuttered one-story affair with a brownish lawn and a late-model Mercury Marquis, the step-up Crown Vic, in the driveway. Holiday smiled, looking at the car. *Once a cop.*

He parked the Lincoln curbside, killed the motor, got out of it, and walked to the house. He passed a dead lilac tree in the yard and wondered why the owner hadn't removed it. He rang the doorbell and found himself straightening the lapels of his jacket as he heard footsteps approaching the door. And then the door opened, and a bald, average-sized black man with a gray mustache stood in the frame. He wore a sweater, though the day was warm. He was well past middle-aged and stepping off the bridge to elderly. Holiday had never seen him without his hat.

"Yes?" said the man, his eyes hard and unwelcoming.

"Sergeant Cook?"

"T. C. Cook, th-that's right. What is it?"

"Have you read the *Post* today? There was a boy found over in that community garden on Oglethorpe Street. Shot in the head."

"Fourth District, yes. I saw the segment on Fox Five." Cook unfolded his arms. "You're not with the media. Some kind of law enforcement, right?"

"I'm ex-police. MPD."

"No such thing as ex-police." Cook's mouth sloped down slightly on one side as he spoke.

"I suppose you're right."

"Television man said that the boy's first name was Asa."

"It's spelled the same way," said Holiday, "forwards and back."

Cook studied Holiday and said, "Come inside."

SEVENTEEN

LEON MAYO WORKED as an apprentice auto mechanic in a small garage on a single-digit block of Kennedy Street. He had been given the opportunity to learn the trade by the owner, who had done Lorton time himself back in the early '90s. The owner's former parole officer, who now had Leon as an offender, had put them together. Ramone and Rhonda Willis found Leon after stopping by to see his mother at the apartment where both of them lived. She had told them that Leon was working, hitting the word emphatically, and gave them the location of the garage.

The owner of Rudy's Motor Repair, Rudy Montgomery, met them with unwelcoming body language and a glare, but he led them to Leon Mayo when they described the nature of their visit. Leon was in a bay illuminated by a droplight, using a sprocket wrench to loosen a water pump with the intention of pulling it out of a beat-to-shit Chevy Lumina. They badged him and gave him the news about his friend. Leon put his fingers to the bridge of his nose and stepped away. They left him to his grief. A few minutes later he emerged from the garage and met them in a lot overfilled with previous-decade sedans and coupes manufactured, primarily, in Detroit.

Leon stood before them, rubbing his hands on a shop rag and twisting and untwisting the rag. His eyes were pink, and he kept them focused on the asphalt. The fact that they had seen him spontaneously break down had shamed him. He was a thin, strong young man who looked five years older than his twenty.

"When?" said Leon.

"Sometime last night, I expect," said Rhonda.

"Where was he got?"

"He was found at Fort Slocum, around Third and Madison."

Leon shook his head. "Why they have to do that?"

"They?" said Rhonda.

"I'm sayin, why would anyone do Jamal like that? He wasn't into no dirt."

"Your records say otherwise," said Ramone.

"That's all past," said Leon.

"It is?" said Ramone.

"We did our thing."

"You stole cars, isn't that right?"

"Yeah. We touted and ran for a while, too, over there on Seventh. To us it was all in fun. We wasn't tryin to make no career out of it. We were just kids."

"Seventh and Kennedy," said Rhonda Willis, who had worked UC around that hot corner for several weeks back when she was plainclothes and on the way up to Homicide. "That was more than just boys playin like they were in the game. They were serious over there."

"There was some like that in the mix. But not us."

"What made y'all special?" said Ramone.

"We caught grand-theft charges on the cars before the drug thing went to the next level. Ain't nothin more complicated than that."

"And you don't have any idea who would have done this to Jamal."

"Jamal was my boy. If I knew—"

"You'd tell us," said Rhonda.

"Look, I'm on paper right now. I come to work every day." Leon held out his greasy hands and looked hard at Ramone. "This is me, dawg, right here."

"What about Jamal?" said Rhonda.

"The same way."

"What was he doing for money?"

"Jamal had steady work as a housepainter. I mean steady. And he was fixin to start his own business, soon as he learned the finer points, you know what I'm sayin?"

"Sure."

"He wasn't never gonna go back. We talked about it all the time. I'm not lyin."

Ramone believed him. "Why would Jamal be walking around late at night?"

"He didn't have no whip," said Leon. "Jamal rode buses and walked all over town. He didn't mind."

"Any girlfriends?" said Rhonda.

"Lately, he was just interested in one."

"You got a name?"

"Darcia. Petworth girl, that's all I know. Pretty redbone he met a while back."

"No last name? No address?"

"She lives with this other girl, a dancer down at the Twilight, goes by the name of Star. Far as I know, Darcia dance there, too. I don't know where they stay at. I told Jamal, don't be fuckin with girls like that, you ain't even know who they runnin with."

"Girls like what?"

"Fast." Leon looked away. His voice was hoarse, a whisper. "I told Jamal that."

"We're sorry for your loss," said Rhonda Willis.

T. C. COOK LED HOLIDAY through the house back to the kitchen, where Holiday had a seat at a table that took up much of the space. As they moved through the living and dining rooms, Holiday noted the disarray and sloppiness that were typical of a man who lived alone. The house was not dirty but had widower's dust on its tables and shelves. The windows were closed and their shades were drawn, holding in the smell of decay.

"Black for me," said Holiday, as Cook poured coffee into a couple of mugs. "Thanks."

A schoolhouse clock was hung on the wall, its time off by several hours. Holiday wondered if Cook had even noticed.

"I don't get many visitors," said Cook, putting a mug in front of Holiday and sitting with his own across the table. "My daughter once in a while. She's living down in the Tidewater area of Virginia. Married a navy man."

"Your wife passed?"

"Ten years back."

"I'm sorry."

"It's a helluva thing, being where I'm at. You know those commercials on the TV, talking about the golden years? And those ads for retirement communities, handsome couples with straight teeth, golf clubs and swimming pools? It's all bullshit. There ain't one goddamn thing good about being old."

"Did your daughter give you any grandchildren?"

"Yeah, she has a couple. So?"

Holiday grinned.

"I'm not even seventy yet. But I had a stroke a few years ago that knocked me on my ass. I guess you can tell, the way my mouth turns down. And I stutter some when I'm searching for words or I get flustered 'bout something."

"That's rough," said Holiday, hoping to end this part of the conversation.

"I can't write too good," said Cook with determination, cataloging his ailments the way old folks tended to do. "I can read the newspaper some, and I do it every morning, but it's a struggle. In the hospital, the doctor said I'd never read again, and that right there made me determined to prove him wrong. My motor skills are fine, though, and my memory is sharper than it was before I got ill. Funny how one piece of the brain gets turned off, the others get more bright."

"Yep," said Holiday. "About the Johnson boy . . ."

"Yeah, you came over here for a reason."

"Well, I was thinking that there might be a connection between the Asa Johnson death and the Palindrome Murders you worked."

"Because of the boy's name."

"And the fact that the body was found in that garden. The kid was shot in the head as well."

"Why?"

"Why was he killed?"

"Why are you here?" said Cook.

"I discovered the body. Well, to be more accurate, I came upon the body and was the first one who called it in."

"Now, how'd that happen?"

"It was late, after midnight. Around one-thirty, I would guess, sometime after last call."

"You'd been drinking?"

"I was more tired than I was drunk."

"Uh-huh."

"I was driving down Oglethorpe, thinking it cuts through to New Hampshire."

"And you hit a dead end. 'Cause it stops down there by the railroad tracks. The animal shelter and printing company on that street, too, if I recall."

"You weren't kidding about your memory."

"Go ahead."

"I have a car service, like a limo thing. I had fallen asleep in my Lincoln, and when I woke up I got out to take a leak in the garden. There he was."

"How long were you sleeping?"

"I'm not sure."

"You were out cold?"

"No. I remember a couple of things. A police car with a perp in the back drove by me slow. And a young black man walking through the garden. The times and the spaces in between are foggy."

"This police officer saw you sleeping in your car and he didn't stop to investigate it?"

"No."

"You get a car number, something?"

"No."

"Have you talked to the MPD?"

"Beyond the anonymous call-in, no."

"So you really don't know anything."

"Only what I saw and read in the *Post.*"

"I'm gonna ask you again. Why are you here?"

"Look, if you're not interested—"

"Not interested? Shit, boy."

Cook made a come-on gesture with his head. Holiday got up and followed him out of the kitchen.

They went down a hall past an open bedroom door and one that was closed. And then a bathroom and toward a third room, from which Holiday began to hear squawk and a dispatcher's drone. Cook and Holiday walked into the room.

It was Cook's office. A computer monitor sat on a desk, its CPU beneath it. On the screen, a police scanner site was up, with the RealPlayer box activated in the top left corner. Holiday knew the Web site, which allowed users access to the dialogue between dispatchers and patrolmen in most major cities and states. He often listened to it himself in his apartment.

A large map of the metropolitan area was thumbtacked to the wall. Yellow pushpins marked the various community gardens of the District. Red pushpins marked those gardens where the three victims of the Palindrome Murders had been found. Blue pins marked their home neighborhoods, the probable streets where they first disappeared. There was one lone green pin among the blues.

"Not interested," said Cook. "Three kids killed under my watch, and you say I'm not interested. Otto Williams, fourteen. Ava Simmons, thirteen. Eve Drake. Fourteen. Young man, I've been haunted by those murders for twenty years."

"I was there," said Holiday. "I was in uniform at the Drake crime scene."

"If you were, I don't remember you."

"No reason why you would. But we all knew who you were. They used to call you the Mission Man."

Cook nodded. "That's 'cause I went after it. Most of the time I got it, too. That was before . . . well, that was before everything about the job got all fucked up. I retired with the Palindrome case unsolved. Hell of a note to go out on, right? Not that I didn't give it my best. We just couldn't get a handle on the killer, hard as we tried.

"The kids had been murdered in different spots from where they were found. They had been re-dressed in new clothes. That made the forensics work tough. All had semen and lubricant in their rectums. None had defensive marks or foreign tissue under their nails. To me it means that he had gained their confidence, or at least convinced them they wouldn't be harmed. He seduced them, in a way.

"All lived in Southeast. All of them had been picked up off the street, headed to the corner market or the convenience stores in their neighborhoods. Nobody saw them disappear or get into a car. It was unusual back then for no one to see anything or come forward, the way folks used to look out for their neighbors' kids. We had a ten-thousand-dollar reward out for any information. We got a lot of bullshit calls, but nothing that led to anything real.

"Had to be a black man for those black children to get into his car. I also figured it was a person of authority. Police, military, fireman, or someone wearing a uniform of some kind. Some said it was a taxi driver offering free rides, but I didn't buy into that. City kids wouldn't have fallen for it. A police or a police wannabe would think to put new clothes on the victims, clean them up, and dump them in various locations. He'd know that would mess us up on the lab work. The wannabe angle was the one that stuck in my head.

"We canvassed friends, teachers, boyfriends and girlfriends, any potential sexual partner. I went to Saint Elizabeth's and interviewed the violent sex offenders they had there at the time. The criminally insane were locked up tight, so they couldn't have perpetrated those murders, but I interviewed them as well. Zombies on meds is all they were. So there was nothing there.

"I caught the first murder. Me and this white homicide police, Chip Rogers, who I considered to be my partner at the time. Chip's now deceased. After the second body they added a few other investigators. Finally, after the third and all the newspaper articles, the mayor ordered a force of twelve detectives, exclusively, to focus on the deaths. I was in charge of the detail. We shot miles of film at those kids' funerals, hoping the killer would post. We stationed squad cars at all the community gardens in the District, around the clock. I'd park my own car near those gardens some nights and just sit there, waiting.

"Some folks in the community said we weren't working the murders as hard as we would have if the victims had been white. I can't lie; that hurt me deep. Everything I went through, coming up in the ranks as a black man. First I wasn't smart enough to be police, then I wasn't seasoned enough to work Homicide. Not to mention, my own little girl was about the same age as those kids in nineteen eighty-five. You think it didn't wear on me? Funny thing was, if you looked at the closure rates of black and white victims in the city at the time, they were exactly the same. We worked all the cases hard. We worked them all the same way.

"And then the Palindrome Murders just stopped. Some say the killer got sick and died or was killed hisself. Could be he went to prison on other charges. I don't know. But I'll tell you this: I still think about it, every goddamn day."

"I didn't mean to offend you," said Holiday.

Cook fixed his eyes on Holiday's. "Why are you here?"

"First thing I ought to tell you is, I didn't retire from the MPD."

"Figured that. You're too young."

"I resigned. Internal Affairs was investigating me on some bullshit allegations, and I walked."

"You sayin you were true blue?"

"No. But I was good police. I'd love to turn up something on this Asa Johnson thing and shove it up the MPD's ass."

"Passion's good."

"I have that."

"Let me see your identification," said Cook.

Holiday showed Cook his driver's license. Cook went to an answering machine on his desk, hit the "memo" button, and recorded a message. "This is T. C. Cook. I'm headed out with a Daniel Holiday, former MPD officer, for a look at the residence of Reginald Wilson." Cook hit the stop button. "It would take me forever to write it, and sometimes I can't read what I wrote. Just leaving a record of my whereabouts, is all."

Cook reached into a drawer, pulled out a micro-cassette recorder, and handed it to Holiday. He then extracted a holstered .38 Special from the same drawer and clipped it on the right side of his belt.

"I got a license; don't worry about that."

"I'm not sayin a word," said Holiday. "I got a piece myself, out in the car. And I *don't* have a license. I'd rather have a gun and get popped for it than not have one and need it."

"Hard habit to break when you been carrying one for so long."

"Where we going?" said Holiday.

"Has to do with that green pin on the map."

On the way out the door, Cook grabbed a faded light brown Stetson with a chocolate band holding a multicolored feather, and put it on his head.

"You can drive, Dan."

"Call me Doc," said Holiday.

EIGHTEEN

RHONDA WILLIS PHONED the Twilight, a titty bar on New York Avenue, and asked to speak to the day bouncer working the door. Officially, the MPD no longer allowed its men and women to moonlight at such establishments, but many still did. The Twilight, with a history of shootings in its parking lot and cuttings inside the walls, used off-duty cops to pat down customers as they came through the entrance, as the sight of a badge on a chain was a deterrent to objection. A certain kind of police, the kind who liked action and fun, was naturally drawn to work that particular bar. The Twilight had the best dancers and music, and the most raucous crowd in town.

"Hey, Randy," said Rhonda, speaking on her cell. "It's Rhonda Willis, VCB."

"Detective Willis."

"You still down there, huh."

Randolph Wallace was a twelve-year veteran, still in uniform, married with two children. Home life bored him, and he avoided it. Instead, when he wasn't on the MPD clock, he worked a few shifts a week at the Twilight. He drank free and sometimes had relations with the club's dancers.

"Yeah, you know," said Wallace.

"I need an address on a dancer you got named Star. She stays with a girl name of Darcia. Cell number, too, if you can."

Wallace said nothing.

"It's in connection with a murder investigation," said Rhonda.

"This ain't really right," said Wallace. "I got to work with these people, Detective."

"What, you want me and my partner to come down there and get it?" said Rhonda with a small laugh, just to keep things friendly. "Wonder how much cocaine and smoke is trading hands in those bathrooms as we speak. All that sex for money, too. We could get the folks in Morals involved, that's what you want."

"Detective—"

"I'll hold on while you get that for me."

A few minutes later, Rhonda had the address and cell number for Shaylene Vaughn, whose stage name was Star, and the full name of Darcia Johnson and the number of her cell.

"Thank you, Randy. Be safe." Rhonda ended the call.

"Did you just threaten a fellow police officer?" said Ramone.

"He doesn't need me to hurt him," said Rhonda. "He gonna fuck up his marriage and his career his own self, working in that place. I just don't know what people are thinking sometimes."

They were parked near Barney Circle. Rhonda got onto the Sousa Bridge and drove over the Anacostia River into Far Southeast.

The address provided by Randolph Wallace was on the 1600 block of W Street, near Galon Terrace. Ramone and Rhonda Willis parked and walked by neighborhood kids on their bikes and young women sitting on concrete steps, holding babies and talking. Some teenage males and men in their twenties slowly drifted as the two police officers got out of their car. Ramone walked by a young man wearing a black "Stop Snitchin" T-shirt who was holding the hand of a little boy. The shirts, popular in the D.C. area and in Baltimore, were an explicit warning to those citizens who were thinking of giving information to police.

"Nice message to send the kid," said Ramone.

"Mm-huh," said Rhonda.

They entered a three-story apartment building of brick and glass and went up an open stairwell to the second floor. They stopped at a door marked 202.

"My hand's tender, Gus," said Rhonda.

"What'd you do, drop your wallet on it?"

"Give it the cop knock, will you?"

Ramone made a fist and pounded his right hand on the door. He did this several times, waited, and did it again.

"What is it?" said an annoyed female on the other side of the door.

"Police," said Ramone.

The door opened. A young woman wearing short shorts and a sleeveless pajama top stood before them. She was voluptuous and toned but had unhealthy skin and skin tone. She had a diamond stud in her nose and the remnants of glitter makeup on her face. Her eyes were swollen, and one cheek held the markings of a pillow's edge.

"Shaylene Vaughn?" said Rhonda.

"Yes?"

"We're with the Violent Crime Branch of MPD. This is my partner, Sergeant Ramone."

"May we come in?" said Ramone. He had been holding

his badge out for her to see. Shaylene nodded, and they went inside. The living room was empty except for a full ashtray on the carpet and a single plastic chair.

"Is Darcia Johnson in?" said Rhonda.

"She somewhere, but she's not here."

"Where?"

"She been stayin with her boyfriend."

"Who is that and where does he live?"

"I don't know, really."

"You don't know his name?"

"Not really."

"Mind if we have a look around?" said Ramone.

"Why?"

"Looks like you just woke up," said Rhonda. "Could be she slipped in while you were sleeping. Maybe she's in the back or somethin and you aren't aware of it."

The girl lost her innocent face, and for a moment hate flashed in her eyes. Then she lost that, too, as quickly as it had come, as if it were mandatory that she use every item in her emotional toolbox. She swung her head sloppily toward the back of the apartment. "She ain't here. Go ahead and see, you want to."

Ramone went to the galley-sized kitchen, and Rhonda went back to one of the bedrooms. Both stepped warily, but not from fear. The apartment stank of various kinds of smoke and spoiled food.

In the kitchen Ramone saw open boxes of sugar-rich cereal but no other edible goods. He opened the refrigerator, which held no milk or water and only one can of orange soda. Roaches stood in the sink, their antennae wiggling, and on the electric stove top, where a dirty sauce pot sat. Half-eaten fast food had been dumped in a trash can filled to the rim.

Ramone joined Rhonda in a bedroom. On the floor was a mattress topped with distressed sheets and a couple of pillows. A large-screen television sat on a stand, pornographic

DVDs scattered around it. CDs were stacked near a portable stereo on the carpet. Also on the carpet were thongs, sheer tops, and other articles of cheap-looking lingerie.

Rhonda made eye contact with Ramone. They moved into the second bedroom, a mirror image of the first.

Back out in the living room, Shaylene Vaughn stood sullenly. Rhonda took out her pad and pen.

"Who pays the rent here?" said Rhonda.

"Huh?"

"Whose name is on the lease of this apartment?"

"*I* don't know."

"We can find out by calling the rental company."

Shaylene tapped her hand against her thigh. "Dominique Lyons. He pays for it."

"I thought you didn't know his name," said Rhonda.

"I just now remembered."

"You have a job. Can't you afford to pay it?"

"Me and Darcia give him the money we make from the club. He holds on to it for us."

"Is he Darcia's boyfriend?" said Rhonda. "Is he yours?"

Shaylene stared at Rhonda.

"Does Dominique have a street name, anything like that?" said Ramone.

"Not that I know."

"Where's he stay at?"

"Huh?"

"Does he have an address?"

"Said I didn't know."

"Where were you late last night . . . say, after midnight?"

"Dancing at the Twilight till, like, one thirty. And then I came home."

"Alone?"

Shaylene did not answer.

"What about Darcia?" said Rhonda.

"She was working there, too."

"Was Dominique at the Twilight as well?"

"Maybe he was. He could have been."

"Do you know a Jamal White?" said Rhonda.

Shaylene looked down at her bare feet and shook her head.

"What's that?" said Rhonda.

"I know some Jamals. I ain't know their last names."

Rhonda breathed out slowly and handed Shaylene her card. "My number's on there. You can leave a message, day or night. I'm looking to speak to Darcia and Dominique. You're not going anywhere, are you?"

"No."

"Thanks for your time. We'll be seeing you again."

"Take care," said Ramone.

They left the apartment, glad to breathe fresh air, and got back into the Ford.

"Trick pad," said Rhonda, settling under the wheel. "That's all that is."

"And you think Dominique Lyons is their pimp."

"Maybe. I got to run him through the system first, see what he's about."

"Jamal White falls in love with a dancer-slash-ho, her pimp doesn't like him cutting into his girl's action, and boom."

"I like it so far." Rhonda stared out the windshield. "At one time that girl in there was a baby that someone held and sang to at night."

"If you say so."

"And look where she is now. Not that I blame her for giving her love to a man. You know, devoting all my time to my sons and this job, it's easy for people to forget that I'm still a woman. Even a Christian woman like me, well, every once in a while I have the need for some penis."

"For real?"

"This Dominique Lyons fella, though, he must have one special penis. I'm talkin about the kind of penis that could make a girl dance naked in a bar and give up her hard-earned money to him at the end of the night. The kind of penis that could make her prostitute herself in a roach-infested crib with no furniture or food or drink, and make her feel like she's a loyal queen. I'm sayin, that must be some extraordinary penis."

"Okay."

"Gus?" Rhonda Willis turned the key on the Ford. "I do *not* need that kind of penis."

HOLIDAY AND COOK WERE parked in the Town Car three houses down from a white-sided ranch-style home in Good Luck Estates, a clean middle-class community off Good Luck Road in the New Carrollton area of Prince George's County. A late-model Buick sat in the driveway. The curtains of the house were charcoal gray and drawn closed.

"He doesn't live but ten minutes from my own house," said Cook. "Makes it real convenient for me to drop over here and watch him."

"Tell me about him," said Holiday.

"Reginald Wilson. He'd be close to fifty now."

"You say he was a security guard?"

"At the time of the killings, yes. We were interested in men who could be mistaken for cops because of their uniforms."

"Why him?"

"After the third murder, we questioned all the security guards who worked in the area, and then, on the second round, went back to those who lived in close proximity to the victims. Wilson was a guy I personally interviewed. There was something missing in his eyes, and I backgrounded him. He had done some brig time in the army for two incidents of violence, both against fellow soldiers. He managed to come out with an honorable discharge, which allowed him to apply to the MPD and the P.G. County force. Neither would take him. His intelligence wasn't the issue. In fact, he scored highly there. He had flunked the psychiatric."

"I'm with you so far. Good IQ, bad head. So now he's gonna show the police force they made a big mistake by, what, killing kids?"

"I know," said Cook. "It's a stretch. I had no evidence of anything, to tell you the truth. Not even a pedophilic history at that time. Just a hunch that this guy was wrong. I felt like I had seen him before, maybe at one of the crime scenes. But my memory wasn't helping me out. Neither did the killer. Remember, there were no fibers found on the bodies, not even human hair follicles or fibers from the carpets of homes or cars. No foreign blood cells. No tissue under the fingernails. The bodies were clean. The only thing left behind was semen in their rectums. And there wasn't a way to match that 'cause there was no DNA testing in eighty-five."

"So he left behind some jizz. Did he take anything?"

"You're pretty bright," said Cook.

"I can be."

"There were small cuts of hair missing from all three of the victims' heads. He kept souvenirs. That was a detail we never released to the press."

"Did you ever get into his place?"

"Sure, I interviewed him at his crib. I remember noting that he had almost no furniture, but he did have a monster record collection. All jazz, he said. Electric jazz, whatever that means. Damn if I could ever get into that shit. I like instrumental stuff, but you better be able to dance to it."

"So what happened?" said Holiday, losing patience.

"A month after the third murder, Reginald Wilson fondles a thirteen-year-old boy who's wandered onto his job site, a warehouse near an apartment building where the boy stayed, and gets charged. While he's in the D.C. Jail, waitin on his date, some dude calls him a faggot or somesuch thing, and Wilson takes him down forever. Beats him to death with his fists. Couldn't even plead self-defense, so now he draws real time. Inside the federal joint, he's marked as a short eyes and kills another inmate who came at him with a single-edge. Now he gets more years heaped on top of the original."

"The murders stopped when he went away."

"Right. For nineteen years and change. He ain't been out but a few months and now they started again."

"It's possible he's the one," said Holiday. "But the only thing you've really got is that Wilson's prone to violence and is sexually attracted to kids. Pedophilia's a long way off from murder."

"It's a kind of murder."

"You won't get an argument from me there. But basically you've got nothing. We'd be hard-pressed to get a warrant to search his house. That is, if we were still police."

"I know it."

"Does he have a job?"

"Man's on paper, he got to. Takes cash at an all-night gas-and-convenience station down on Central Avenue. Works different shifts there, including the late. I know, 'cause I tailed him, more than once."

"We could check with his PO, get his hours, talk to his employer. See if he was working the night Johnson was killed."

"Uh-huh," said Cook with no enthusiasm.

"That's no palace," said Holiday, looking at the white rancher, "but this is a pretty fair neighborhood for a guy like him to land in right out of prison."

"It's his parents' house. They died while he was in the joint, and as he was their only child, it went to him. There's no nut on it; all he has to do is pay the taxes. The Buick's not his, either."

"No shit. Got to be his father's. Only old men drive Buicks." Holiday winced. "I didn't mean—"

"There he is," said Cook, who had not taken offense and had kept his eyes on the house.

Holiday saw the curtain on the bay window part and, behind it, the indistinguishable face of a middle-aged man. It looked like a shadow and disappeared as the curtain drifted back into place.

"He's seen you out here?" said Holiday.

"I don't know if he has or hasn't. And you know what? I just don't give a morning crap. 'Cause eventually he's gonna make a mistake."

"We need more information about the Johnson death."

"You saw the body."

"I was at the crime scene, too, the next day."

"Damn, boy, did you speak to anyone?"

"Not yet. I know the homicide detective who caught it. Guy named Gus Ramone."

"Will he talk to you?"

"I don't know. Me and the Ramone have a history."

"What'd you do, fuck his wife?"

"Worse," said Holiday. "Ramone was in charge of the IAD investigation that was trying to take me down. I didn't let him finish the job."

"Beautiful," said Cook.

"That guy's strictly by the book."

"Be nice if you could talk to him, just the same."

"He pulls that stick out of his ass," said Holiday, "maybe I will."

NINETEEN

After a couple of bonefish sandwiches with hot sauce and tartar from an eat-shack on Benning Road, Ramone and Rhonda Willis drove to the Metropolitan Police Academy, set on Blue Plains Drive in a clear tract of acreage between the Anacostia Freeway and South Capitol Street, in Southwest. They passed the K-9 training unit, located on the grounds, and the barracks where both of them had once stayed, and parked in a lot nearly full of cars and buses.

The academy looked like any high school, with standard-sized classrooms on the upper floors and a gymnasium, swimming pool, and extensive workout facilities below. Veteran police, including Ramone, used the weight room and pool to stay in shape. Rhonda's vanity had shrunk with the birth of each successive child, and she had not exercised in many years. If she managed to put together a half hour of free time, Rhonda felt that a hot bath and a glass of wine were more valuable to her physical and mental health than a visit to the gym could ever be.

Entering the building, they noticed that the trim and rails had been painted a bright, almost neon shade of purple.

"That's soothing," said Rhonda. "Wonder what committee of geniuses decided to use that color."

"I guess Sherwin-Williams was all out of pink."

They badged a police officer inside the entrance and proceeded up to the second floor. It was afternoon, and many cops were in shorts and sweats, using weight machines, treadmills, and free weights before reporting to their four-to-midnights. Ramone and Rhonda stood on a landing overlooking the gymnasium.

"There's the man I'm looking for," said Ramone. "He's showin them something he learned at Jhoon Rhee."

In the painted lane extending out from under a basketball hoop, a uniformed officer was demonstrating to a large group of recruits the proper stance and motion of a punch. His left hand came up choplike to protect his face as he threw a right, turned his hip into it, and pivoted his rear foot. The group then attempted to copy his action.

"That was us, not too long ago," said Rhonda.

"They got a higher class of po-lice comin in now. You need a two-year associate's degree to get accepted these days."

"That would have prevented me from getting in. And you know, they'd have pushed away a good cop."

"It does stop the retards from joining the force."

"Gus, someday you gonna learn the correct terms for this new century we're in."

"Okay. The mental defectives."

"You see those Caucasian girls down there?" Rhonda nodded at the numerous white female recruits on the floor. "They get out on the street, most of 'em gonna wash out or land behind a desk in about two weeks."

"Now, why you gotta go there?"

"You know that blond lieutenant, the girl you always see on television, that spokeswoman? She never did walk hard pavement in any of the hot wards. Made her name protecting those pale gentrifiers from the negroes loitering on the sidewalks in Shaw. The MPD just keeps promoting her 'cause that porcelain skin and blond hair look good on camera."

"Rhonda."

"I'm just sayin."

"My mother's white."

"She's Italian. And you know what I'm sayin is true."

"Let me catch this guy," said Ramone, as the instructor disbanded the group of recruits.

"I'll meet you downstairs."

Ramone took the stairwell, passing the doorway to the indoor swimming pool. As it always did when he descended these stairs, the movie in his head rewound to his first full year on the force. It was through the frame of that same open doorway that he had gotten his initial look at Regina, standing in her blue one-piece suit on the pool's edge, looking into the water, preparing to dive. The sight of her, muscular but all woman, with shapely buttocks and nice stand-up breasts, had literally stopped him in his tracks. He was not a guy who was particularly adept at talking to the opposite sex, nor did he have the striking good looks to compensate for his lack of game, but he was not afraid, and he walked right into the pool area, introduced himself, and shook her hand. Please let her be as nice as she is beautiful, he thought, as his hand gripped her smooth fingers and palm. Her big brown eyes drooped a bit with her smile, and, swear to God, he knew.

She wasn't a cop for long. Six months of training, another month of riding with someone experienced, then a year as a rookie on patrol, and Regina had had enough. She said she realized the first week on the street that it wasn't for her. That she wanted to help people in some way, not lock them up. She went back to college, got her education degree, and taught for a few years at Drew Elementary in Far Northeast. When Diego was born, she changed up again and became a full-time mother and part-time school volunteer. In his prayers at church, Ramone sometimes gave thanks for Regina's ill-advised decision to join the MPD. Ramone knew that if he had not been walking down those stairs that day, passing by that door, and if she had not been contemplating that dive, he would not have what he had today. And to him, what he had was everything. Not that he wasn't fully capable of fucking it up.

The strange thing was, he hadn't even planned on marriage and a family, but they had come to him, and it was right. All because of the path he had taken one afternoon, and a woman who had hesitated before entering a pool. Like most folks, he wasn't always certain about the existence of a higher power, but he damn sure did believe in fate.

Ramone crossed the gymnasium floor. He caught the eye of the instructor, John Ramirez, and waited until the last recruit had gone toward the lockers. Ramirez, with a weight-room chest and arms, gave him a weak handshake and cool eyes.

"Johnny."

"Gus. Enjoying the new job?"

"I been at it for a while now."

"Must be more satisfying to lock up bad guys than your fellow officers, right?"

"It was all the same to me. If they're wrong they're wrong, you know what I mean?"

It wasn't true. Ramone had always known the import and consequence of going after cops who had abused their powers or committed minor crimes. But he wasn't going to let a guy like Johnny Ramirez, a hothead who had gone from street cop with insecurity issues to gym teacher with a badge, beat him up about his stint at IAD. Ramone had learned how to investigate cases there, done his job with competence but not vengeance, and used the experience as a bridge to Homicide.

"Not really," said Ramirez. "I really don't know what you mean."

Generally, Ramone had not had any trouble with his fellow officers when he'd worked Internal Affairs. Most cops did not want to be around other cops who were unclean because they tainted the straight ones by association. He had never been fish-eyed by other uniforms, had never heard the words *rat squad* uttered in his presence, and had never had a police move off his bar stool when Ramone stepped up to the stick. IAD was a necessary element of policing, and most cops accepted it. Ramirez was a former drinking buddy of Holiday's, and he simply didn't like Ramone because of what had happened to his friend.

"Listen, I don't want take up too much of your time. I was wondering if you've seen Dan Holiday lately. If you guys were still friends . . ."

"Yeah, I've seen him. Why?"

"I'm just looking to get up with him. It's a private matter."

"Oh, it's private. He runs a limo service; maybe that helps."

"I heard."

"But I don't have his number or anything. Shouldn't be too hard for you to find it, though."

"Okay, Johnny. Thanks."

"You want me to tell him you're looking for him, in case we cross paths?"

"No, don't do that. I wanna surprise him."

Of course, Ramone knew that Ramirez would call Holiday straight away, which was why Ramone had sought him out. He wanted Holiday to think about it before he came up on him. It would eliminate the bullshit half of the conversation if Holiday knew.

"See you around, Ramirez."

Ramone found Rhonda at the turn of the stairwell, looking at a wall covered with the framed photographs of MPD officers killed in the line of duty. She was standing before the photo of a genial young policeman she had known well when both of them were in uniform. He had been shot to death during a seemingly routine traffic stop. Rhonda's eyes were closed, and Ramone knew that she was saying a prayer for her friend. He waited until she turned to him, unsurprised at his presence.

"You get what you needed from Ramirez?" said Rhonda.

"Officer Ramirez was just telling me how much he admired my work in Internal Affairs."

"So you're not gonna tell me."

"Oh, all right. I was asking him out on a date. One bottle of pop and two straws, something like that."

"Okay, then. I need to get back to the office, do some background on our boy Dominique."

Ramone said he'd take her there.

BECAUSE OF ITS PROXIMITY to the majority of the dropped bodies in the city, the Violent Crime Branch of the MPD was located in Southeast, but the offices of most of the other specialized units, such as Morals, Sex Assault, and Domestic Violence, were in the same facility as police headquarters, at 300 Indiana Avenue, Northwest. Ramone arrived at the building soon after leaving Rhonda in the VCB lot and picking up his Tahoe. He went straight to the offices of the Cold Case Squad.

Unsolved homicides moved from VCB to Cold Case after three years. Some homicide police disparaged the work of cold case detectives, as most of the old murders that got "solved" had little to do with investigative prowess or forensic science and more to do with criminals offering up unexpected information in exchange for a reduction in their sentences. These same homicide detectives who felt that the cold casers hadn't earned their closes were conveniently forgetting that this was how many warm homicide cases got put to bed as well.

Ramone had no such resentment. The members of the Cold Case squad were not the sexy, sunglasses-wearing hotshots with toned bodies and beautiful faces seen on TV, but rather were middle-aged men and women with paunches, families, and credit card debt, doing a job, just like those in the VCB. He had worked with some of them in other capacities through the years.

He found Detective James Dalton at his desk. Ramone had done many favors for Dalton in the past and hoped for the same in return. Dalton was lean, with gray hair, a white dude with Chinese eyes. He had grown up in northern Montana, come to D.C. in the '70s intending to do social work, and wound up as police. He often said that he had gone from one small town to another when he moved to Washington. "More people, same attitude."

"Thanks for doing this," said Ramone.

"File was already pulled," said Dalton. "We're waitin around on the ME's report before we decide if it's something we ought to be involved with. You weren't the only one to notice the similarities."

"If you've been around long enough . . ."

"Right. File's over there on the desk. It's a big one."

"That's what *she* said."

"Huh?"

"Dumb old joke."

"You're not the primary on this, are you?"

"Garloo Wilkins," said Ramone. "I knew the decedent. Friend of my son's. You mind if I look it over and take some notes?"

"Go right ahead. I'm outta here."

Perfect, thought Ramone.

For the next two hours, Ramone read the extensive case files on the Palindrome Murders. Included in the official police reports were archived news reports from the *Washington Post* and a long historical piece from the *Washington City Paper*. Dalton had given him the opportunity by clocking out, so Ramone burned copies of what he thought he might need on the office Xerox, counter to policy. He put the copies in an empty brown file container that Dalton had helpfully left on the desk, and carried it under his arm from the headquarters building to his Tahoe.

Under the wheel, he dialed Wilkins's cell.

"Hey, Bill, it's Gus."

"What's going on?"

"I think you should call the ME and order a sex kit on the Asa Johnson autopsy."

"They'll do it without my order."

"Call them anyway and make sure it's done."

"Why?"

"We all just want to be thorough."

"Right."

"Anything today?"

"I spoke with the principal at Asa's middle school. But I'm having a little trouble with the boy's father. I wanted to go by the house and get into Asa's room, but Terrance Johnson told me he wanted you to have a look at it first."

"I apologize, Bill. They've been knowing me for a while, is all it is. I'm going to swing by their house later and while I'm there I'll set him straight."

"It's my investigation, Gus."

"Absolutely. I've got a few more calls to make this afternoon. We can talk when I see you."

"All right, buddy. Take care."

Ramone ended the call. No reason to mention the possible connection to an old, unsolved series of homicides. He told himself that it would just cloud Garloo's mind.

Ramone headed uptown.

TWENTY

ASA JOHNSON'S MIDDLE school was in Manor Park, blocks from the Johnson house, blocks from Ramone's. His son, Diego, had walked there when he'd still been registered, but now he walked the mile into Maryland and caught a Ride On bus to his school in Montgomery County. It seemed unnecessarily complicated to make his son go through all those moves to get to his new destination, given the closeness of the neighborhood school to their home. Of course, Ramone didn't really mind that his son had to break a sweat to get to school. He was simply dipping his toe back in the waters of rationalization for moving Diego back into the District's public-education system.

Ramone thought about this, and other things, walking down the hall to the administrative office. The bell had sounded, ending the last class of the day. The kids around him, mostly black and some Hispanic, were laughing and cutting up, stowing books and retrieving bags from their lockers, preparing to bust out and head home. They moved around roaming security guards. With its wire mesh–covered windows, dim lighting, and constant police-like presence, the place had the feel of a juvie hall.

Ramone saw kids he recognized, from both the neighborhood and Diego's football team, and a couple of them acknowledged him with either a "Mr. Ramone" or a "Mr. Gus." They knew he was police. Some of them did not look him in the eye because of it, but most were friendly and showed him respect.

A few of these kids, especially those with a deficient home life, had already gone off the rails. Others were on the edge. Most would do fine.

Ramone had nothing but respect for teachers. He was married to one and knew what they experienced, not just with unruly kids, but also with angry, unreasonable parents. There were few professions more challenging than middle school educator, but still, what these teenagers needed most was for their teachers and administrators to not give up on them. This was the most critical period of their lives.

One thing about this school, thought Ramone, looking at the faces around him. These teachers see behavior, not race and class.

But then, walking by the open doors, he noted the physical conditions around him: the walls in need of paint, the bathrooms without doors or working toilets, the buckets placed below leaking ceilings, and the lack of supplies. He was reminded of the reasons he and Regina had moved Diego out of D.C.

It was hell, trying to figure out what was right for your child.

Ramone went into the administrative office, identified himself to one of the assistants, and explained that he had called ahead and made an appointment. In a short while, he was seated across the desk from Ms. Cynthia Best, the school principal, an attractive dark-skinned woman with straight posture and knowing eyes.

"Welcome back, Mr. Ramone."

"I wish it was under better circumstances. How are things going?"

"We brought in a special counselor yesterday to help the students come to terms with Asa's death."

"Any takers?"

"A couple of students came in. They were curious more than anything. Or perhaps they were looking for a novel way to get out of class. I sent them back, gently."

"Ms. Best, have you heard anything? Any rumors that have come from the student body filtered through the teachers?"

"Nothing beyond the usual conjecture. You know these kids like to romanticize the lifestyle, but there has been very little in the way of drug rumors in this case. As for the teachers, they have a pretty good feel for what's going on in their students' lives. They've met the parents; they spend time with the kids every day. None of Asa's teachers have offered any speculation, either fact-based or theoretical."

"Did you tell them I would be here?"

"I spoke to his math and English teachers to get you started. They should be waiting for you. If you need to see the others, phys ed, health, science, whatever, I can make it happen."

Ms. Best pushed a piece of notepaper across the desk, showing the room numbers and names of the teachers. Ramone folded it and put it in his jacket pocket.

"You've heard from Detective Bill Wilkins? It's his case, officially."

"Yes, he phoned me. He asked that we not empty the contents of Asa's locker until he gets a look at it."

"That's good," said Ramone, beginning to think that he had underestimated Wilkins.

"Would you like a look yourself?"

"After I talk to Asa's teachers." Ramone tapped his pen on

the small spiral notebook in his lap. "I'm curious. You say the student grief over Asa's death was not exactly overwhelming."

"I didn't mean to imply a negative."

"I didn't take it that way. I'm just looking for your impression of Asa."

"I had very little contact with him these past two years," said Ms. Best. "We spoke only a few times. He was quiet, not a disciplinary problem. I wouldn't call him spirited. He was neither popular nor unpopular."

"You're saying, what, he was kind of a nothing kid."

"*You* are."

"Please, this isn't for the record. You can speak freely."

"Asa wasn't the type of student who left a strong impression on me. That's the most honest assessment I can give you."

"I appreciate it."

"How's Diego?" said Ms. Best.

"There've been a few bumps in the road at that county school, to tell you the truth."

"He's always welcome back here."

"Thank you, Ms. Best. I'll go see those teachers now."

"Good luck."

Ramone found the room of Asa's English teacher up on the second floor. No one, neither student nor adult, was inside. Ramone had a look around to kill some time. There were balled-up scraps of paper on the floor and overflowing trash cans. The desks and chairs, which looked to have been in use since the Depression, were misaligned in barely detectable rows.

On the blackboard, the teacher had written quotes from Dr. King, James Baldwin, and Ralph Ellison. There were also two notes, one an announcement of an upcoming test and one reminding students to update their journals. Ms. Cummings, the English teacher, did not show, and Ramone left the classroom.

Mr. Bolton, Asa's Algebra I teacher, was waiting for Ramone in room 312. In contrast to the English teacher's, Bolton's classroom was orderly and trash-free. He rose from behind his desk and moved around it to greet Ramone.

Bolton was a man with deep chocolate skin in his late thirties who wore plain-front slacks, a wrinkle-free oxford, and monk-strap loafers. The clothes did not seem to be expensive, not surprising given Bolton's anemic salary, but there had been some thought behind the outfit. Ramone had been expecting a nerd, but instead saw a well-built man who was fastidiously dressed and cleanly shaven. His rather large, oddly shaped nose would prevent anyone from calling him handsome. His eyes were large and bright.

"Detective Ramone?" said Bolton.

"Mr. Bolton." Ramone shook his hand.

"Call me Robert."

"Okay. I won't take up much of your time."

"I'm happy to help."

Ramone produced his notebook and pen. "When was the last time you saw Asa Johnson?"

"In my classroom, the day of his death."

"That would have been Tuesday."

"Correct. And then that same day, after school."

"What, he had detention or something?"

"No, nothing like that. He came in to get extra work. He was into math, Detective. He actually liked to solve problems. Asa was one of my best students."

"What did you give him?"

"Just some extra-credit problems. Work sheets, things of that nature."

"Did you notice if he was upset in any way that afternoon?"

"Not that I could detect."

"Can you . . . did you ever have the suspicion that he was into anything wrong?"

"I'm not sure what you're getting at."

"I'm not really reaching for anything in particular. I'd just like your thoughts."

"It's a fallacy to believe that most of the young people in the District are into unlawful activities. You have to realize, the vast majority of these students have nothing to do with stealing cars or dealing drugs."

"I do realize that."

"They're kids. Don't stereotype them just because they're African American and live in D.C."

African American. Years ago, Diego had told him, "Don't ever call my friends that, 'cause they'll just be laughing at you. We're *black*, Dad."

Ramone gave Bolton his cop smile, which was a smile in name only. "I live in this neighborhood, sir."

Bolton folded his arms across his chest. "People sometimes make erroneous assumptions. That's all I was saying."

Ramone wrote the words *defensive* and *asshole* on his pad.

"Anything else you can think of that may be pertinent to the investigation?" said Ramone.

"I'm sorry. I've gone over it in my head many times. To me he was a happy, well-adjusted young man."

"Thank you," said Ramone. He shook Bolton's strong hand.

Ramone went back downstairs and found Andrea Cummings in her classroom. Ms. Cummings was young, still in her twenties, tall, leggy, and dark of skin. She was plain upon first look but straight-up pretty when she smiled. She gave Ramone a nice one when he entered the room.

"I'm Detective Ramone. I thought I might have missed you."

"Lord, no. I've got work to do here after school. I was just up in the lounge, getting a soda."

Ramone dragged a chair over to her desk and had a seat.

"Careful with that," said Ms. Cummings. "It's gotta be sixty years old."

"They should put some of this stuff in a museum and get it out the classroom."

"*Please.* We're out of paper and pencils right now, too. I buy most of the supplies you see here with my own money. I'm telling you, someone is stealing. Whether it's lawyers or contractors or just management, someone is lining their pockets, and it is straight theft. *They're stealing from kids.* You ask me, whoever it is, they oughtta burn in hell."

Ramone smiled. "Say what's on your mind."

"Oh, I've never had a problem with that."

"You from Chicago?"

"You *know* I can't lose that accent. I grew up in public housing, taught in my neighborhood my first couple of years out of Northwestern. The facilities were well below average, but I have never seen anything like this."

"I bet your students like you."

"Hmm. They're starting to. My philosophy is, scare them in the beginning of the semester, give 'em that face of stone. Let them know who's in charge straight away. They can like me later on. Or not. I want them to learn something here. That's how they're going to remember me."

"What about Asa Johnson? Did you have a good relationship with him?"

"Asa was all right. I never had any problem with him doing his work. His behavior was fine, too."

"Did you like him?"

"I cried when I heard the news. Any time a child is killed you can't help but be moved."

"But did you *like* him?"

Ms. Cummings relaxed in her seat. "Teachers have favorites, the way parents have favorite kids, even if few want to admit it. I can't lie and say he was one of mine. But it wasn't because he was bad."

"Did he seem happy to you?"

"Not particularly. You could see that something was weighing on him just by looking at his posture. Plus, he rarely smiled."

"Any reasons you can think of?"

"God forgive me for speculating."

"Go ahead."

"It could've been his home life. I met his parents. Mom was quiet and deferred to her man. The father was one of those macho dudes, trying to overcompensate. I'm just being honest. Couldn't have been any fun for Asa to live in that house, you know what I'm saying?"

"I appreciate your honesty," said Ramone. "Do you have any reason to believe that he was into any kind of illegal activity?"

"None at all. But then, you never know."

"Right." Ramone looked at the blackboard. "I wouldn't mind getting a look at that journal of his, if you have it."

"I don't," said Ms. Cummings. "They turn it in at the end of the semester, and when they do I just check to see if they've made an effort. I don't read the journals, is what I'm saying. My job is to make sure they're doing some work. They do that, they've accomplished something."

Ramone extended his hand. "It's been a pleasure to meet you, Ms. Cummings."

"You, too, Detective," said Ms. Cummings, reaching across the desk. "I hope I've been of some help."

Ramone left the building, went out to his Tahoe, and extracted a pair of latex gloves, stowing them in his jacket pocket. He returned to the school, revisited the administrative offices, and, accompanied by a security guard, walked to Asa's locker. The security guard read off a piece of paper and executed the combination of the built-in lock. He stepped back as Ramone, now wearing the gloves, inspected the locker's contents.

A couple of textbooks sat on the top shelf. There were no

papers wedged between the covers of the textbooks and no loose papers or anything else lying on the metal floor. Middle school kids typically taped photos of sports heroes, rappers, or movie stars on the inside of their locker doors. Asa had taped nothing to his.

"You done?" said the security guard.

"Lock it up," said Ramone.

He had hoped to find the boy's journal, but it was not here.

TWENTY-ONE

TERRANCE JOHNSON OPENED his front door to let Ramone in. Johnson's eyes were rimmed with red, and he reeked of hard liquor. Johnson shook Ramone's hand and held it too long.

"Thanks for seeing me," said Ramone, drawing back his hand.

"You know I'm gonna cooperate."

"I need you to be just as cooperative with Detective Wilkins, Terrance. We're all working together on this, and he has the lead."

"If you say it, I'll do it."

The home was eerily quiet. There were no human voices or sounds from the television or radio.

"Helena in?"

Johnson shook his head. "She's staying with her sister for the time being. Took Deanna with her, too. Helena can't bear to be in this house right now. I don't know when she gonna be right with it."

"There are stages of grief. It'll get better."

"I know it," said Johnson with an annoyed, careless wave of his hand. He stood staring straight ahead, his mouth slightly open, eyes clouded with a glaze of alcohol.

"You need to take care of yourself, too."

"I'll rest easier when you clear this up."

"Can I have a look at Asa's room?"

"Follow me."

They went up the center-hall stairs to the second floor. It was a typical colonial for the neighborhood, three bedrooms and one full bath upstairs. Johnson led Ramone into Asa's room.

"Who's been in here since his death?"

"Me and Helena," said Johnson. "Deanna, I expect. I did like you told me to. I didn't let anyone else in."

"Good. I'm also thinking about the days leading up to Asa's death. Did he have any friends or acquaintances in his room that you can remember?"

Johnson considered the question. "I was at work during the daytime, of course. I'd have to ask Helena. But I can say almost certainly that the answer is no."

"Why are you so sure?"

"The past six months or so, going back to the end of last school year, I guess, Asa wasn't hangin with anyone special."

"He wasn't tight with anybody?"

"He'd drifted apart from the ones he used to hang with. You know how kids do."

Girls do that more frequently, thought Ramone. Boys tend to hold on to friendships longer. But he knew that what Johnson was saying about his son was true. Diego and Asa had been friends once, to the degree that they saw each other almost every day. Diego had not even spoken about Asa, until he was killed, for a long time.

"You need me here?" said Johnson.

"That's okay," said Ramone. "I'll be fine."

Johnson exited, and Ramone had a look around as he removed his latex gloves from his jacket pocket and fitted them on his hands. The bedroom was cleaner than Diego's had ever been. The bed had been made. One poster, the obligatory Michael Jordan in a Bulls uniform, hung on the wall. Asa's few football trophies, sitting atop a freestanding shelf filled with a surprising number of books, had been awarded for team accomplishment, not for individual effort.

Ramone went through the dresser drawers. He looked in Asa's closet and searched the pockets of his jackets and slacks. He ran his hand beneath the lower edge of the dresser and underneath the box spring of the bed. He did not find anything that Asa might have been concealing. He did not find anything that he thought would be pertinent to the investigation.

Ramone went through Asa's book bag, a one-strap JanSport. Inside were a day planner, a young-adult novel, and an Algebra I textbook with no papers between its covers. Asa's journal was not in the bag.

Ramone tried to put on a left-handed baseball mitt he found in the closet, but he could not fit it.

A computer monitor sat atop Asa's desk. Ramone settled into the chair and pulled out a drawer on rollers that held a keyboard, mouse pad, and mouse. He moved the mouse across the pad, and the monitor's screen lit up. The screen saver was a plain blue field, and the icons were numerous, with Microsoft Outlook, Word, and Internet Explorer among them. Ramone was not an expert with computers, but there were PCs in his home and office, and he was familiar with these programs.

He clicked on Outlook and got Asa's e-mail site. Numerous messages appeared, but upon inspection, all of them appeared to be spam. He went into the Deleted and Sent files and found the boxes empty. He did the same with Journal, Notes, and Drafts, and got the same result. Ramone went online, got the Yahoo! opening screen, and clicked on Favorites. Asa had few sites listed in the column. Most were of the game and entertainment variety, and a few seemed to deal with the Civil War and local Civil War forts and cemeteries. Ramone went to Word and checked the files labeled "Asa's Documents." Everything saved appeared to be school related: essays and papers on science and history, and many dealing with the themes and characters of books.

It was odd that there was so much scholastic material and nothing of a personal nature on the computer of a teenage boy.

Ramone got out of the chair and stood in the center of the room. He removed his gloves as he looked at the walls, the bookshelves, and the top of the dresser. History told him that he had learned something here today, even if it had not yet come to him. But it was always frustrating to be at this stage of inertia in an investigation.

He went downstairs to a silent first floor. He found Terrance Johnson in the backyard, seated in a lawn chair, a can of beer in his hand. Ramone found a similar chair, folded and leaning against the house, and carried it over to where Johnson sat.

"You gonna join me?" said Johnson, holding up the can.

"I don't think so, thanks. I've still got some work ahead of me."

Ramone settled in.

"Talk to me," said Johnson. His pointed white teeth peeked out below a sweaty lip.

"I don't have anything solid to report yet. The positive news is there's no reason to believe that Asa was involved in any kind of criminal activity."

"I knew that. I kept that boy straight."

"Did he have a cell phone? I'd like to get a look at his incoming and outgoing calls."

"Nah. I already told Detective Wilkins, we didn't think Asa was ready for the responsibility."

"That's how Regina and I keep track of Diego."

"I didn't need to look for him. I didn't let him go to parties, sleepovers, or nothin like that. He was *home* at night. That's how I knew where he was."

Ramone loosened his tie at the neck. "Asa kept a journal, apparently. It would look like a notebook, or even a regular hardcover book without a title, with blank pages inside. It would be very helpful if I could locate it."

"I don't recall seeing anything like that. He did like to write, though. He liked to read a whole lot, too."

"Lotta books in his room."

"Too many, you ask me."

How could there be too many books in a teenager's room? thought Ramone. He would have been pleased if Diego had been interested in just one.

"I didn't mind the boy reading," said Johnson. "Don't get me wrong. But I was a little worried about him, focusing on just that. A young man needs to be well-rounded, and that goes beyond being book smart or getting good grades in school."

"You're talking about athletics."

"Yeah."

"I heard he had dropped out of the football program."

"I was upset with him when he quit it, I'm not gonna lie. If you're competitive out on the playing field, you're gonna be competitive in life. Plus, it's a tough world out here now. I didn't want that boy to turn soft. You got a son; you understand what I'm saying."

"I guess it was doubly disappointing to you. I mean, you played a lot of football when you were coming up, didn't you?"

"When I was a kid. I played here in the city. But I had an ankle that got broke and then kept breaking on me. By the time I got to high school, I couldn't compete. I would have been a good player, too. My body betrayed me, is what it was."

Ramone remembered Johnson at their sons' football games. He was one of those fathers who frequently second-guessed the coaches and vocally berated the referees. He'd often see Johnson talking to Asa on the sidelines, telling him to find some heart, telling him to hit somebody. Always telling him what he was doing wrong. Ramone had seen the hurt in Asa's eyes. No wonder the boy had lost his desire to play. His father was one of those guys who demanded his son be the athlete that he himself never was or could be.

"I bought him that new North Face coat he was wearing," said Johnson, looking at the weedy patch of grass at his feet, his voice gone low. "Two hundred dollars and seventy-five. I made a deal with him, told him that if I bought him that new coat, he was gonna have to go out for football the next season. Summer tryouts came and he had some excuse for why he didn't want to play. Too hot, he wasn't feeling up for it . . . all that. Boy, I gave him hell. Told him how ashamed I was of him." Johnson's lip trembled slightly. "I said to him, you gonna sit up in your room like some kinda faggot while other boys gonna be out there on that football field, turning into men?"

Ramone, embarrassed and also a bit angry, did not look at Johnson.

"When was the last time you saw him?" said Ramone.

"I work a seven-to-three, so I'm back here around the time the boy gets home from school. He was headed out and I asked him where. He said, 'I'm going for a walk.' I said, 'It's too warm out for you to be wearin that coat. And you know you shouldn't be wearing it anyway, 'cause you broke an agreement we had.' "

"And?"

"He said, 'I love you, Dad.' " A tear broke loose from Johnson's eye and rolled down his cheek. "That's all he said. Asa left out the house right after that. The next time I saw him, he was cold. Someone had put a bullet in my boy's head."

Ramone looked at the sky and the shadows lengthening on the grass. There were few hours of light remaining. He rose from his seat.

DIEGO RAMONE HAD BEEN kicked out of the fake 7-Eleven in Montgomery County that afternoon by a guy, looked like some kind of Punjabi to him, who worked behind the counter. He could have been a Pakistani or even one of those Shiites. Dude had a turban on his head, was all Diego knew.

"Get out," the man had said. "I don't want you in here."

Diego had been with his friend Toby. Toby was topped by a black skully, and both wore their jeans low and had drawstring-style bags on their backs. Diego had wanted to get a Sierra Mist before he got on the bus headed back to the District.

"Wanna buy a soda," said Diego.

"I don't want your money," said the man, pointing to the door. "Out!"

Diego and Toby had hard-eyed the man for a moment and left the store.

Out on the sidewalk, on the avenue lined with apartment houses, Toby held up both of his fists and affected a boxer's stance. "I shoulda introduced him to thunder and lightning."

"You notice he didn't come around the counter."

"He was a bitch," said Toby.

It wasn't the first time Diego had been tossed from a store for being young and black. He'd been rousted by the police here, too. This city had its own force, and they were known to break hard on kids who lived or hung down by the apartments. One weekend night Diego and Shaka were walking home from a party when a couple of squad cars came up on them. The officers inside the cars jumped out and shook the two of them down. They were put up against one of the cars and searched. Their pockets were turned inside out. One of the officers, a young white dude named O'Shea, had taunted Shaka, telling him to go ahead and say one thing out of line, just one thing. O'Shea said that he'd really like it if Shaka would lip off to him, but he figured he wouldn't, because Shaka was soft. Diego knew that Shaka, who could go with his hands for real, could have taken this man in a fight. But they kept their words to themselves, as Diego's father had told them to do when dealing with police, and let it pass.

The next morning, when Regina went to the station to complain, she was told that Diego and Shaka had fit the description of two young men who had stolen a car earlier that night. "The exact description?" said Regina. "Or was it just two black youths?"

That night, Diego heard his parents discussing the incident.

"They're scarecrows," said Ramone, his term for fake police.

"I do not like that neighborhood," said Regina. "With the bumper stickers on their cars."

" 'Celebrate Diversity,' " said Ramone. "Unless diversity is walking down your street on a Saturday night."

Diego and Toby went along the strip near Toby's building.

"They gonna talk to you tomorrow," said Toby.

"Who is?" said Diego.

"Miss Brewster, I guess," said Toby. "Mr. Guy said they doin an investigation. They prob'ly lookin to throw me out of school, 'cause the parents of that boy I stole are making all kinds of noise. I might get expelled this time or sent up that school they got for problem kids."

"That was a fair fight."

"I know it. But they lookin for evidence so they can toss my ass. My father's Kirkin out over that bullshit. He wants to sue the school."

"My father's mad at that school, too," said Diego.

"You ain't gonna say nothin to Brewster and Mr. Guy, right?"

"Nah, dawg, we're straight." They pounded fists. "See you at practice."

"All right, then."

Diego walked toward the bus stop, looking back at the fake 7-Eleven. Thing was, he and Toby *had* shoplifted a candy bar or two out of that place in days past. But the dude with the turban didn't know that. How was he gonna discriminate?

At the bus stop, Diego got a call from his mother.

"Where are you?" said Regina.

"About to get on the twelve. I'll probably stop at the courts, shoot around some. I got practice tonight."

"Do you have homework?"

"I did it in study hall," said Diego. He had done half of his homework, so it was only half a lie.

"Don't be long," said Regina.

"Okay."

"Love you."

"Love you, too, Mom," said Diego in a real low voice, so the guy sitting in the bus shelter next to him could not hear.

Just about then, the Ride On rolled up and came to a stop. Diego boarded the bus.

RAMONE PHONED REGINA AND told her he'd be out for a while longer. He asked about Alana and Diego, and she told him that Alana was up in her room and Diego was playing basketball over by Coolidge. Ramone was in the neighborhood, so he drove over to the courts.

Diego saw him first. His head came up as he heard the sound of the Tahoe approaching, recognizing the way it cried on its shocks. Diego was in the middle of a two-on-two, him and Shaka against the Spriggs twins, Ronald and Richard losing as usual and talking smack about their opponents and their relatives like they tended to do. Earlier, they had discussed Asa and speculated about his murder. The Spriggs boys had seen him that day, as had Diego and Shaka. No one knew a thing about the killing, but they wanted to talk. All of them felt some guilt, as in the last year or so they had turned their backs on Asa to varying degrees. In truth, he had turned away from them, too. Still, it just hurt. They considered themselves to be tough city kids, but this was the first of their childhood friends who had met death.

Gus Ramone walked up to the courts. With his Ray-Ban aviators, his dark blue suit and rep tie, and his black mustache, he looked every inch a cop. He shook Shaka's hand and said hello to Ronald and Richard, correctly identifying them by name, though they were identical twins. He could tell the difference because Ronald had more playful, intelligent eyes. He'd known this group of Diego's friends for ten years, going back to when they were little boys.

Ramone put his arm around Diego's shoulders and the two of them drifted down to the street. Diego returned to the court a few minutes later, and Ramone got in the Tahoe and drove off.

"Detective Ramone," said Shaka. "Man looked serious today."

"Thought he was gonna take you down to the station, somethin," said Ronald Spriggs.

"What he want?" said Richard.

He told me to get home before dark. He asked me how school went today. He told me he loves me. The same way my mom always does before she hangs up the phone.

"Nothing much," said Diego to Richard. "He just told me to beat you Bamas to within an inch of your lives."

"Your mother's a Bama," said Ronald.

Diego said, "Lemme see that rock."

TWENTY-TWO

RAYMOND BENJAMIN LIVED in a freshly built, well-appointed condominium off U Street, between 10th and 9th, in the new Shaw. All of the furnishings and electronics on display had been paid for in cash. Benjamin's IRS form stated that he was self-employed as a "certified used-car dealer." More accurately, he made trips to northern New Jersey several times a month to buy high-end, low-mileage automobiles at auction for clients back in D.C. With his expertise at the process, he was able to purchase a Mercedes-Benz, Cadillac, BMW, or a Lexus at up to ten thousand dollars less than it could be had on a retail lot. In exchange, he delivered the car himself, detailed and in fine running condition, for a thousand-dollar fee.

At a glance, Benjamin was a respected, legitimate businessman. It had been five years since he had completed his prison term on a trafficking beef. He was no longer on paper and appeared to be clean.

Benjamin's hands may not have touched drugs anymore, but they did touch drug money. He had remained in contact with the sons of his old New York connect, a Colombian now in prison, and Benjamin continued to broker and sometimes bankroll transactions between Washington distributors and the source up north without becoming directly involved. He was as adept at getting the best price on heroin as he was at negotiating down the price of cars, and the quality of the dope was consistently high. His commissions were formidable and afforded him a continuation of the lifestyle he had become accustomed to when he was a top-level dealer himself.

The risks were relatively low. His assistants made the calls and spoke in a kind of code, a variation of Pig Latin that Benjamin had developed, when they were on the line. They used disposable cells, difficult if not impossible to wiretap, when conducting business over the phone. At thirty-five, Raymond Benjamin was finding life better than it had ever been.

Except for days like today. Benjamin's older sister, Raynella Reese, was in his condo, standing over him where he sat in a deco-style armchair. Raynella had one hand on her hip and was pointing a finger of the other at his face. She was a very tall woman and, like all of her siblings, was named in some manner after the man who had fathered them, Big Ray Benjamin, in his day a well-known numbers man on the 14th Street corridor.

Also in the room was Tommy Broadus, sitting in a similar chair that was bending under his weight. Broadus stared down at his shoes.

By the door stood two Benjamin employees: Michael "Mikey" Tate and Ernest "Nesto" Henderson. Officially, they were employed as sales associates of Cap City Luxury Vehicles, but they served Raymond Benjamin in a variety of capacities.

"He gonna be fine," said Benjamin, attempting a calming gesture with his hands.

"Oh, he fine, huh?" said Raynella Reese, her hyperemotional voice working against the warm colors Benjamin had chosen for the room.

"The bullet went clean through," said Tommy Broadus.

"Shut up, fatty," said Raynella. She turned to her brother. "Where is Edward now? I want to see him for myself and make sure he's good."

"He restin," said Benjamin. "The doctor took care of him."

"You mean the *dog* doctor," said Raynella. "Ain't that right, Raymond?"

"Doc Newman is straight," said Benjamin.

"He's a veterinarian!" said Raynella.

"True," said Benjamin. "But he is straight."

For a high fee, Dr. Newman treated gunshot victims in the city who did not want to go to hospitals. He ran a veterinary clinic on Bladensburg Road, heading up toward the Peace Cross in Maryland. He often left scars, due to the stitching he used, but he was a master of irrigation. Few of his patients died of infection or loss of blood, and in general he did good work.

"He's all right," said Broadus. "They got him sleeping in the back room."

When he *can* sleep, thought Broadus. With all them dogs barking and shit.

"How did this happen?" said Raynella. "And I don't want to hear from the Michelin Man over there. I'm askin *you*, Raymond."

"Someone got some information on the transaction Tommy was gettin ready to make. What we're thinking is, it was someone at the cut house who learned about the deal and then passed it on."

"You was braggin on yourself when you went to that place, I expect," said Raynella to Broadus.

"I told him to make sure everyone knew he was alone on this," said Benjamin. "That he bankrolled it hisself."

"What he do, give out his home address?"

"I never did," said Broadus.

"I don't know how they figured where he stayed at," said Benjamin. "But look, we gonna find all that out."

"You goddamn right you gonna find out. 'Cause my son Edward is lyin in a, a *dog pound* with a hole in his shoulder, and some motherfucker's gonna have to pay the dinner bill." Raynella's eyes were bugged and fierce. "That's not just my son we're talking about. That's your nephew, Raymond."

"I know it," said Benjamin, wiping at his forehead as if it carried sweat, though he was not perspiring and it was cool in the room.

Right about now, Raymond Benjamin was thinking that buying and selling cars at auction was a relatively stress-free way of making a living. Knowing full well, even as he idly considered giving up his other activities, that the income from his legitimate business would never be, for a man like him, enough.

He had to choose his clients more carefully, is what it was. He had met Tommy Broadus when he got him that Cadillac CTS, six months back. And then Broadus, who knew who Benjamin was and his history, had told him that he was looking to take the plunge. Benjamin had had his doubts about Broadus, but he would take a hefty cut, not to mention the vig on his principal, if all went well. Also, he had seen it as an opportunity to indoctrinate his nephew Edward, who had been bothering him about getting into the business, with an older, nonviolent man in a deal that looked to be money.

And then the boy, with that smart mouth of his, had to go and lip off to a man holding a gun. Big sis was conveniently forgetting what he had tried to do for her son. Matter of fact, it was his sister who had been on him to "take care of" his nephew for some time. And now Raynella was getting all siced over the consequences, here in his living room.

"We gonna take care of it, Raynella," said Benjamin. "That's my fifty Gs they took, too. You know I can't let none of this pass."

"Man who shot Edward said his name," said Broadus. "We do have that."

"Romeo Brock," said Benjamin.

"They was two," said Broadus. "Another man, short and muscled-up."

"You get an address or cell number with that name?" said Raynella. "Do you know anyone who knows this motherfucker who call himself Romeo?"

"He ain't exactly in the phone book," said Raymond.

"Then *exactly* what you gonna do? I was you, I'd go down to that cut house and start cuttin on some throat."

"That wouldn't work," said Raymond. "I got to do business with those people long-term. I *will* find out who talked, eventually. But I can't afford to sever that relationship at this time."

"So what then?"

"For now, there's a better way. Tell her, Tommy."

"This Romeo Brock," said Broadus, nearly mumbling, not looking Raynella in the eye, "he took a woman I been seein with him when he left out my place."

"He snatched your girl out from under you, huh?"

"That pussy had cobwebs on it, anyway," said Broadus, unable to humble himself even for the purpose of a serious discussion. "The point I'm making is, the girl got a job and she too proud to quit it. Won't be hard to track her from there to where Brock layin up."

"Today?" said Raynella.

"She off today," said Broadus, trying not to picture Chantel with Romeo Brock, celebrating what they took.

"She's gonna be at work tomorrow," said Benjamin, standing out of his chair and stretching his six-foot-five-inch frame. "We know where it's at. We already checked it out."

"We?"

"Me, Mikey, and Nesto," said Benjamin, patiently nodding to the two young men who stood by the door.

"Well, get on it!" said Raynella with a horrible shriek.

"I plan on it, Ray-nelle," said Benjamin.

"Quit plannin and do it."

Benjamin slowly rubbed his fingers up and down his temple. "You tryin to give me a migraine, girl."

ROMEO BROCK PARTED THE curtains of his bedroom window. He saw his cousin Conrad walking home from the shape-up spot he went to every morning, out there on Central Avenue. He was passing through the shade of the big tulip poplar and heading for the front door.

Gaskins had sweat stains on his T-shirt and his khaki Dickies held marks from the grass and shrubs he'd been cutting on all day. The man looked spent. Brock felt sorry for him, almost. He'd been out there in that autumn sun since daybreak, while he, Romeo Brock, had been in the cool of his house, drinking champagne and smoking a little get-high with a woman who was all woman. She was like one of those horses you admired while the trainer walked it around the track.

Brock let the curtain fall and looked over at the bed. Chantel Richards was sleeping on top of it, wearing one of his rayon shirts, unbuttoned to show her bra. She wore a lacy black thong to complement the brassiere. Beside the bed was the open Gucci suitcase, showing cash. Beneath Chantel was some of the cash, tossed there by Brock. They had fucked on it earlier.

He remembered seeing this movie on television when he was younger. Steve McQueen, baddest white man ever walked in front of a camera, played a dude who robbed a bank and then took off with his girlfriend, running from the Mob, the law, and a vengeful man who had worked the heist. Toward the end of the movie, before guns and gunmen interrupted, McQueen and his girl had begun to make it on a bed of money, and Romeo Brock at that moment had said in his mind, I will do that with a woman someday my own self. This girl in the movie, she was too skinny for Brock's taste; matter of fact, she looked like a chicken with black hair. But there was something about her, he had to admit. Still, Steve's girl wasn't even on the same playing field as what he had in this bedroom right here. He couldn't have dreamed that he, Romeo Brock, would ever be with a woman as fine as Chantel Richards, drinking White Star, bottom-knocking that thing on a bed of clean sheets and green.

He looked at her for a moment, sleeping there. Brock, dressed in his boxers and nothing else, lit a Kool and tossed the match into a tire-shaped ashtray. He closed the door softly behind him as he left the room.

Brock went down a hall, the kitchen behind him, passing Gaskins's bedroom and the bathroom, and came out into a large living-and-dining-room area where Gaskins was standing.

"Tough day?" said Brock.

"Yeah," said Gaskins, looking him over with a mixture of amusement and disgust. "How 'bout you?"

"Go on, cuz. Tryin' to act like you don't wish you were me."

"Sure, I'd like it. Lie around in a dark room all day with a fine woman, drinking whatever it is you drinking that's coming off your breath, smoking what I smell in the air. I'd like to try a little herb again someday, when I get off paper. I used to enjoy getting my head up."

Brock hit his cigarette and let the smoke out and in, French style. "So why don't you?"

" 'Cause I got to work. I don't mean I have to report to a job, which I do. I'm sayin I got the need to go to work every day."

"You shouldn't anymore. We got money."

Gaskins shook his head. "You missin my point, Ro."

"Cousin, we are rich."

"Not hardly. We got to cut up the pie. And I know you gonna buy some things with what's left. Before long, you'll be looking for more."

"And I'll get it. The same way I got what's in that bedroom."

"And how you think that story's gonna end?"

"Huh?"

"Every story's got an ending," said Gaskins.

Brock, his mouth open as he breathed through it, looked at Gaskins with waxed eyes. Then he smiled. "You just *too* damn serious. Here we are with everything, and you talkin doom."

Gaskins could see it was useless explaining it to the boy. Some of them were just thick. And anyway, who was he to bust on Romeo's groove? His young cousin would see it in the end. Too late, but still.

"All right, Romeo. All right."

"There you go."

"You hear from our man?"

Brock nodded. "He say he'd see us soon. I told him the money was safe."

Gaskins stripped off his T-shirt. His face said thirty, but his body said nineteen.

"I'm gonna have a shower," said Gaskins.

"Take a cold beer in there with you."

"I think I will."

Gaskins went to the kitchen to find that brew. Brock returned to his bedroom.

Chantel Richards was up, pulling the bottle of Moët out of an ice bucket set on the dresser. She poured champagne into a tumbler and had a sip.

"I wake you?" said Brock. He took a last drag off his Kool and stubbed it out in the ashtray.

"It's okay. Been a while since I had a nap in the afternoon. It felt good."

"You all rested?"

Chantel looked his way and gave him a crooked smile. Her hair, done up earlier, had kind of tumbled out and was lying in curls on the shoulders of his red rayon shirt. She tipped the glass back and let some into her mouth. She did not swallow. She placed the tumbler on the dresser, walked over to Brock, and spit the champagne onto his bare chest. Drops of it rolled off his pecs and down his stomach. She held his hips and licked the bubbly from his abs and then moved her tongue up to his chest.

"Girl," said Brock in a clipped way. It was hard for him to catch his breath.

Chantel stepped back and removed the shirt. She peeled it off one shoulder and then the other. Her bra was fastened by a small hook between its cups, and she unfastened it and let her breasts swing free. Her thumbs worked her lacy thong down her long legs and to her manicured feet. She stepped free of the panties and kicked them away.

Chantel sat down naked on the edge of the bed, where fifties and hundreds lay scattered on the sheets behind her. She parted her legs and showed herself, unshaven and slick. Brock's mouth went dry. He liked a woman natural.

Chantel touched both of her purple nipples with her fingers and made circles there. Her aureoles bumped out and her nipples became erect.

"Golly," said Brock, as a boy would when seeing a woman in the altogether for the first time.

"How you want it?" said Chantel.

"Turn around," said Brock. "Rub that money on your face and kiss it some."

"I can do that," said Chantel.

"*Please* do," said Romeo Brock.

TWENTY-THREE

RAMONE PHONED REGINA on the way back down to the VCB offices, told her he'd seen Diego at the basketball courts and that their son had promised to be home before sundown. He said he'd be working late and that she should not expect him for dinner, but if she thought of it maybe she could put some of whatever she prepared aside for him. He'd heat it up when he got in.

"What were you thinking of making, by the way?"

"Pasta," said Regina.

"What kind of pasta?"

"The kind comes out of a long box and slides into a pot of boiling water."

"Don't overboil it. Eight minutes, tops."

"Now you gonna tell me how to boil spaghetti?"

"Last time you had it on the stove for twelve minutes and it tasted like mush."

"Come home and cook it, you want it perfect."

"Al dente, baby."

"Don't baby me."

"I was thinking of you today," said Ramone.

"Yeah?"

"In that blue bathing suit, standing on the edge of the academy pool."

"I couldn't fit in that suit today."

"You look better now, you ask me."

"Liar."

"I'm serious, honey. Neither one of us is in our prime. But I'm saying, when I look at you through my eyes—"

"Thank you, Gus."

"You think, tonight?"

"We'll see."

Ramone, heading down South Dakota Avenue in the neighborhood of Langdon, phoned the office and got Rhonda Willis, still on the job. She said that she had some things to tell him, and that Bill Wilkins was in the office and looking to speak to him, too.

"I'm ten minutes away," said Ramone.

He parked in the lot behind the Penn-Branch shopping center and entered the offices. Some of the detectives from the morning shift were mingling with the new-shift men and women, crowding one another's cubicles. They were exchanging information and bullshitting about nonpolice matters. Some of the officers who were done for the day were collecting overtime and others were trying to stay out of bars or simply unwilling to face the loneliness, unhappiness, duties, or plain boredom of their home lives.

Ramone saw Rhonda Willis seated at her desk, Bo Green towering over her, both of them having a laugh. He made a one-minute gesture with his finger to Rhonda and kept walking, negotiating detectives, plainclothesmen, and a woman from the Family Liaison Unit. He passed Anthony Antonelli, seated with his feet up, his Glock holstered on his ankle. Antonelli was holding out an overtime form to Mike Bakalis, whose hands were in his lap.

"C'mon, Aardvark," said Antonelli. "Sign my eleven-thirty, will you?"

"Put your tongue in my tar pit," said Bakalis, "and I'll think about it."

Bill Wilkins was seated before his computer, tapping at the keyboard. Ramone pulled a chair over.

"What do you have?" said Ramone.

Wilkins handed him a manila folder. Inside it was the ME's findings on the Asa Johnson autopsy. Ramone began to read it.

"The slug was a thirty-eight."

"They're running it through IBIS?"

"Yeah. We'll see if the markings match to any other murder guns. He died of the gunshot wound to the head, no surprise there."

Left temple, read Ramone.

"He wasn't asphyxiated or drugged or anything else. No foreign substances, alcohol, or narcotics in his body."

"He was killed at the scene," said Ramone.

"Looks like it. Probable time is on there." Wilkins paused, watching Ramone, seeing his eyes flare and then grow dull. "You got to it."

"They found semen inside him," said Ramone. His voice was weak. He was sickened, not only for the child but for the parents, too.

"Keep reading," said Wilkins.

The ME had detected lubricant along with the semen. There were no signs of rectal tearing and there was only minor bruising.

Ramone read the entire report and dropped it on the desktop before him. He thought of the victims of the Palindrome Murders, the traces of semen found inside the kids, a baffling lack of violent entry, evidence of consensual anal sex.

On the other hand, the sex could have been initiated after the victims' deaths. Ramone had to consider the possibility that Asa might have been violated in this way as well.

"They found that stuff in him," said Wilkins. "Like KY jelly or something."

Ramone stroked his black mustache. "I read it."

"It doesn't look like he was raped."

"Doesn't prove he wasn't, either."

"I'm only sayin."

"Right."

Wilkins let Ramone have a moment.

"I went through the boy's bedroom," said Ramone, having collected himself. "His locker as well."

"Anything?"

"Nothing pertinent that I could see. He had a journal, apparently, but it seems to have disappeared. In light of this report, we need to prioritize finding that journal."

"When I spoke to him, Mr. Johnson said there was no cell phone."

"That's right."

"Did Asa have a home computer?"

"There was a PC in his room. I didn't find much personal stuff on it. The Sent and Deleted e-mail boxes were empty. His Favorites column had listings for games and Civil War sites. Nothing else."

"Did you go into History?"

"Uh, no."

"You got a teenage son," said Wilkins. "You better get hip to this shit. You can delete your e-mails and the Internet sites you visit and bookmark, but it's still in the computer, in History, unless the kid wipes it out. The really careful kids program their PC to automatically delete the history every day. Sometimes every seven days, or monthly. It's like brushing your trail away. But if Asa didn't do that, whatever he was into should still be in there, somewhere. It's pretty easy to dig it out."

"For you."

"I'll take care of it." Wilkins tapped the eraser end of a pencil on his desk. "What else you get?"

Ramone hesitated. "Nothing I can think of right now."

"This thing with the boy," said Wilkins. "Someone's gonna have to go over the autopsy with the family."

"I'll talk to the father, the time comes."

"I can understand if you don't want to. It's my lookout."

"No, it's on me." Ramone stood.

"Heading out?"

"Goin home," said Ramone.

He stopped at Rhonda's desk and had a seat on the edge of it. Bo Green was gone, and Rhonda was looking at a mess of papers like they had been powdered with anthrax.

"That looks fun," said Ramone.

"You got some paperwork on your desk, too, Gus. Not that you go by there anymore."

"I'm hoping my secretary will do it."

"You get up with Garloo?" said Rhonda.

Ramone told her about the ME's findings and described his day.

"Now you," said Ramone.

"I ran Dominique Lyons. Our boy's got quite a history. Agg assault, which took, and attempted murder, which didn't. Scheduled witnesses did not testify; possible intimidation noted. He was a suspect in two other murders, but those never went to trial. No weapons recovered, no wits. So what I did was, I got a photograph of Lyons from out the files and took it and the photographs of Jamal White, our victim, and I drove down to that classy bar on New York Avenue where Darcia Johnson and Shaylene Vaughn, Ho Number One and Ho Number Two, dance nekkid."

"I think they wear G-strings at the Twilight, if memory serves. Technically, they're not in their birthday suits."

"They're close enough. So I go down there and have a

talk with our police officer friend, Randolph Wallace. Man who works the door when he's not in uniform?"

"He's your friend now, huh?"

"We're not exactly backslappin buddies. But he was very cooperative. Seems our friend Dominique Lyons was in the club last night, and guess what? So was Jamal White. Officer Wallace knew of Lyons straight away because he frequents the Twilight and often leaves with either Darcia or Shaylene, and sometimes both."

"And how'd he remember Jamal?"

"Jamal was seated at the bar. Dominique had some words with Jamal, more like a taunting kind of thing, and Jamal left out the place by hisself. About an hour later, Dominique and Darcia went bye-bye as well."

"Together?"

"Uh-huh. I'm thinking Jamal took the bus down New York, transferred uptown to the Seventh Street–Georgia line, and was walking back home from Georgia Avenue when he was shot."

"You like Dominique Lyons for the murder."

"I liked him enough to put his name out on the sheets. And could be we got a witness in Darcia Johnson, too."

"That would be nice."

"I tried calling Darcia's cell number, but she's not answering the phone."

"No shit."

"What I also did was, I've got an officer placed over there by the girls' apartment, around Sixteenth and W?"

"Dominique knows we're looking to talk to him. You think he'd go there?"

"If Shaylene was trickin up in there last night, and it looked to me like she was, he's gonna want to get his money sooner or later."

"Okay. You said you had something you wanted to see me about. So what else?"

"This is a long play, but look: the slugs recovered from Jamal White's body were thirty-eights. Garloo tells me that Asa Johnson also died from a thirty-eight."

"And?"

"Same-caliber weapon used in killings just a few blocks apart within twenty-four hours. And you know a thirty-eight revolver is not the gun of choice for these young ones. I mean, it could be a coincidence, but it's worth looking into."

"So, for shits and grins, you're saying we should compare the markings. See if the bullets came from the same weapon."

"I ordered the tests."

"What in the world would connect a guy like Dominique Lyons to Asa Johnson?"

"I'm not saying they are connected. But we might as well look at everything."

"You tell Garloo?"

"I'm fixin to," said Rhonda.

"Okay," said Ramone with a long exhale. "Okay."

"You look like you could use a drink."

"I could."

"There's that place down on Second, got those booths. They play that Quiet Storm stuff at night. You remember that bartender, the one with the heavy hand?"

"I'm going home," said Ramone.

"Suit yourself, handsome. Keep your cell on for further developments."

Out in the parking lot, where he could get service, Ramone activated his cell and dialed the number he had gotten from Janine Strange earlier in the day.

"Hello."

"Dan Holiday?"

"Speaking."

"It's Gus Ramone."

Holiday did not respond. Ramone listened to dead air and then took the lead.

"You want to come down to the offices and make an official statement?" said Ramone. "Or should I send a car out to get you?"

"Neither," said Holiday after another block of silence. "You wanna meet someplace neutral, I can do that."

"Just you and me?"

"There'll be someone else."

"I got no time for attorneys."

"He's not a lawyer," said Holiday. "You'll remember this guy. But I don't want to spoil it for you."

"Always gaming."

"You want to meet or not?" said Holiday.

"Where?"

"There's this bar—"

"Uh-uh. I want you sober."

Ramone gave him the location. Holiday said he'd see him there.

TWENTY-FOUR

RAMONE DROVE DOWN Oglethorpe Street and put the Tahoe behind Holiday's black Town Car, parked across from the animal shelter. He could see Holiday and another, much older man standing in the community garden by the yellow tape that was still strung at the crime scene. The sun had dropped, as had the temperature. Some of the garden was shrouded in shadow and some was tinted golden by the dying light.

As Ramone came upon them, he recognized the old man. His photograph had run in the newspaper stories included in the file he had copied from Cold Case. There had been extensive details about him in the *Post* regarding his command of the squad investigating the Palindrome Murders, as well as in the later follow-up story in the *City Paper*. And then there was his Stetson. Ramone would not have forgotten that.

As he reached them, Ramone could see that Cook had aged badly, a result of possible health issues. His mouth drooped on one side, indicating a stroke.

"Sergeant Cook," said Ramone, extending his hand. "I'm Gus Ramone. Nice to see you again."

"You must have been a young man when we met," said Cook.

"We never met, officially. I was fresh fish out of the academy. I knew you by your reputation." Ramone acknowledged Holiday. "Dan."

"Gus."

Up close, Holiday's preserved looks did not completely hold up. He had a drinker's sallow complexion, the lined face of a smoker, and that belly, noticeable on his skinny frame.

Ramone and Holiday did not shake hands.

"You called in the body," said Ramone.

"That's right."

"Tell me about how that came to be."

"Long and short of it, I had pulled over on this street sometime after midnight, say, one-thirty."

"Had you been drinking much?"

"A little. I fell asleep in my car, woke up a few hours later, got out to take a leak, and found the corpse. I went up Blair Road and called it in from a pay phone outside the liquor store."

"You touch the body? You do anything to foul up the scene?"

Holiday smiled tightly at the question. "I wouldn't."

"I'm just asking because you were, you know, sleepy."

"The answer's no."

"You hear a gunshot at any time?"

Holiday shook his head.

"What else?" said Ramone. "What do you remember seeing that night?"

Holiday looked around at nothing. Cook said, "Tell him."

"I woke up a couple of times after I dozed off," said Holiday. "You know, that driftin-in-and-out thing. I didn't look at my watch. It's all kind of hazy."

Because you were drunk.

"Tell me what you saw," said Ramone.

"A patrol car drove by me, up from the dead end. There was a perp in the backseat, behind the cage. Thin shoulders and neck."

"Male cop?"

"White male."

"Did he stop to check you out?"

"No."

"You get a car number?"

"No."

"How do you know the passenger was a perp?"

"I don't."

"What else?"

"Later, I saw a Number One Male walking through the garden. Young, I'd say, from the energy in his movement."

"How did you identify him as black?"

"It wasn't dawn yet, but the sky had lightened some. I can tell you he wasn't white. There was his hair, too. He was doing that dip thing in his walk. I knew."

"You say you saw this guy later. How much time between the patrolman and the young man?"

"Don't know."

"Okay. And then, what, you fell asleep again, woke up, and got out to take a piss."

"That's pretty much it. I had my mini Mag with me. I read the kid's name off his school ID. I put it together with the other elements and called on Sergeant Cook."

"You called Sergeant Cook because of the Palindrome Murders."

"Right."

"That's why you're here?" said Ramone, looking at Cook.

"You can't ignore the similarities," said Cook.

"Or the differences," said Ramonc.

"Which are?"

"I'll get to that." Ramone turned back to Holiday. "Doc, I'm assuming you and others can account for your whereabouts that evening before you pulled over on Oglethorpe."

Holiday thought of the bar in Reston, the young salesman he had drunk with, and the woman, registered at the hotel. Also, there were the two men arguing about the Paul Pena record and the bartender he had spoken with at Leo's.

"I'm good," said Holiday. "But I'm not a suspect, am I, Gus?"

"Just trying to protect you."

"You're looking out for me, huh?"

Ramone bit down on the edge of his lip. He had expected this, and he supposed he deserved a little bit of it, too. But he wasn't going to take more than a drop.

"Are you the primary on this?" said Cook.

"No, I'm assisting. Actually, it's a little deeper than that. The decedent was friendly with my son. He was a neighborhood boy, and I know his parents."

"Anything so far?" said Cook.

"No offense, sir," said Ramone, "but I'm gonna ask that you go first."

"That's not too sporting of you."

"What would you have done when you were out there? I'm a police officer working a live case, and you two are civilians. Okay, ex-cops, but that won't cut it if I go up on charges or if this gets fucked up in court. You know the rules."

Holiday muttered a "bullshit" under his breath. Ramone ignored it, keeping his eyes on Cook.

"W-we don't have anything new," said Cook. "I did have a strong suspect on those old murders. A fellow named Reginald Wilson. No hard evidence, just a feeling."

"The security guard," said Ramone. "I read the files."

Cook appraised Ramone with his eyes. "He went to prison twenty years ago for fondling a boy and stayed in because of his violent nature. Wilson came out recently. I still like him for those old killings. I think he needs to be investigated."

"That's it?"

"So far, yes." Cook pointed his chin toward Ramone. "Now you."

"This is where I'd normally say, Thanks for the chat, but any information related to this case is confidential."

"But?"

"Out of respect to you, Sergeant, I'm going to give you something. And also because I want the both of you to leave this alone and let the police do their jobs."

"That's fair," said Cook.

"First, said Ramone, "the similarities. The name Asa is a palindrome, obviously, and he was found in a community garden, as were the others. As you know, he died from a gunshot wound to the head."

"What did the autopsy show?" said Holiday. "Was he molested?"

Ramone hesitated.

"Was he?" said Cook.

"There was semen found in his rectum," said Ramone. "The parents don't know—"

"What we say here stays here," said Cook impatiently. "Was it a rape?"

"There was no tearing and very little bruising. Lubrication was apparently used. It's possible that the sex was consensual. Or it's possible that it occurred after his murder. Possible."

"Like the others," said Cook.

"But the differences are hard to ignore," said Ramone. "Asa Johnson was not killed elsewhere and dumped in the garden. He was not held captive for several days before his death, and he hadn't been re-dressed. He wasn't from a low-income home. He lived in a middle-class neighborhood on the opposite side of town from Southeast."

"Was there hair missing from the boy's head?"

"If there was, it wasn't noted in the report."

"You still gotta look at Reginald Wilson," said Cook. "The man needs to be checked out. What y'all do with DNA now, if you had a sample from him you could match it up with what was found in the Johnson boy."

"Or it could exonerate him," said Ramone.

"So be it, then," said Cook. "Aren't you curious?"

"You can't just force him to give up a sample. You've got to have evidence linking him to Johnson in some way. A hunch isn't enough."

"You don't need to tell me that, young man."

"I'm saying . . . Look, all of this is moot if he couldn't have committed the crime, isn't that right?"

"You mean if he's got an airtight alibi."

"The man does have a night job," said Holiday. The comment drew a cold glance from Cook.

"You know where he works?" said Ramone to Cook.

"I do. It's out on Central Avenue, in P.G."

"If it'll put your mind at ease, I'd be happy to check it out."

"Now?"

Ramone checked his wristwatch. "Okay. Let's do it now and put this to bed."

The three of them walked from the garden. They passed the whimsical plot with the spinning flags and the signs reading "I Heard It Through the Grapevine," "Let It Grow," and "The Secret Life of Plants."

"Little Stevie Wonder," said Cook, inadvertently showing his age. "They were gonna mention one of his records, they could have picked a good one."

"I think it's 'cause of the garden theme," said Ramone helpfully.

"Really?" said Cook.

Holiday, feeling that cold thing touch his shoulder, stopped and looked back at the signs, then followed Ramone and Cook to the cars.

"You mind driving?" said Ramone to Holiday.

In the Town Car, Holiday took his hat off the seat beside him and put it on the floor behind his feet.

THE GAS-AND-CONVENIENCE store was on the stretch of Route 214 known as Central Avenue, running out of the District from East Capitol into P.G. County. Across the avenue was a shopping center that had seen better tenants come and go. Night had arrived, but the light of the lot was bright as day. Tricked-out SUVs and dual-piped imports occupied the pumps. Ramone heard a go-go tune coming from one of the vehicles, recognizing it as a song his son had been playing of late, a group called UCB. He wondered if Diego had gotten home before dark, as he had promised.

"You goin in?" said Holiday.

"Yeah," said Ramone, remembering why he'd come. "Wilson, right?"

"Goes by Reginald, not Reggie," said Cook.

"This shouldn't take long."

Ramone slipped out of the backseat. They watched him cross the lot, chest out, shoulders squared, the bulge of his Glock visible inside the jacket of his blue suit.

"Ramone," said Holiday. "Motherfucker is ramrod straight, *isn't* he?"

"Some just look like police," said Cook. "I was the same way."

"Lookin ain't being," said Holiday.

They sat there for a while, not speaking. Holiday reached into his jacket for his smokes, thought better of it because of the old man's health, and left them alone.

"Man's got to be pumping sixty dollars' worth of gas into that thing," said Cook, looking at a young guy filling his Yukon Denali. "When it's three dollars a gallon, you'd think they'd downsize."

"There's never a gas crisis in America," said Holiday, "even when there is one."

"Gasoline and television. Two things folks in this country will not do without."

"You know those apartments, Woodland Terrace, down on Langston Lane?"

"Government housing," said Cook. "I had quite a few dealings down in there."

"Some of those people are paying eleven dollars a month for their apartment, subsidized rate. And then they pay eighty dollars a month for cable service and HBO. Talk about sucking on the federal tit."

"You had that area?"

"Shit, I walked and rode patrol in One, Six, *and* Seven-D. I'd work any district, anytime. People *knew* me. They'd see my car number and wave. Drug dealers and their grandmothers, too. Not like our boy Ramone. Pulling desk duty while I was out there on the line."

Cook removed a pack of sugarless gum from his jacket, slid one out, and offered Holiday a stick. Holiday waved it away.

"What happened between you two?" said Cook.

"I was on the fringe of this thing," said Holiday. "I just got caught up in something bigger that was happening at the time."

"*How*'d you get caught up?"

"Ramone had an IAD case, an investigation into a group of vice cops who were being paid off by pimps to leave their girls alone. The undercover guys were having trouble making arrests because the prosties were being tipped off."

"Were they?"

"I had heard that a couple of the vice guys were on the take. Sure."

"So?"

"IAD was surveilling the stroll where these girls walked. Taking photographs from UC cars and shit. They got me on camera, talking to this white girl, name of Lacy. More than once."

"What were you doing with her?"

"I talked to her regular, used her for information and just as my ear to the street. Prostitutes see things out there. *You* know that. Plus, we were friendly, like."

"I doubt her pimp was happy about that."

"He would have been furious if he'd known. This guy didn't play. Dude named Mister Morgan, a real cool killer."

"Was Lacy his bottom?"

"He told her she was. But he'd get violent on her, and sometimes she needed to get away. I'd buy her coffee once in a while, like that."

"What happened?"

"Somehow, Ramone got Lacy to come in from the cold and testify against the vice guys. She was a heroin addict, and she was tired of it and tired of being in the life. Lacy knew exactly who was and who wasn't dirty in Vice, and she was Ramone's prize. He dangled witness protection in front of her, the whole ride. But, see, he fucked up. They should have grand juried her when they had her in the offices, but they let her go back to her pad to get her things. There was a squad car waiting out front of her place, but she must have gone out the alley or something."

"They lost her."

"Yeah. Ramone and his crew found a witness who noticed me talking to Lacy later that day. That was the last time anyone saw her."

"What did you and Lacy discuss?"

"Wasn't important," said Holiday. "Look, I wasn't on the

take and I wasn't corrupt. The only thing I can tell you is, with regards to that girl, I did what was right."

"Ramone was going to bring you up on charges?"

"He was, and I walked. So fuck him."

"There he is," said Cook.

Ramone was moving across the lot.

TWENTY-FIVE

REGINALD WILSON'S NOT our man," said Ramone, seated in the back of the Lincoln. "Not on this one, anyway."

"Who'd you talk to?" said Cook.

"The owner-slash-manager. Guy named Mohammed."

"And he said what?"

"Wilson pulls various shifts. That night he was working the ten p.m. to six a.m. He was working the night Asa was killed."

"This Ach-med, he actually see Wilson on the job?" said Holiday.

"He did see him, until midnight, when Mohammed went home. But even if he hadn't, there's visual proof. He keeps a security camera running all the time in the place. Says he's been robbed a couple of times. I looked at a sample tape. The way he's got the camera placed, whoever's working the register is always in the frame, as long as they're behind the counter. If Wilson had left the job site, it would have showed up."

"Sonofa*bitch*," said Cook.

"I can find his parole officer," said Ramone, "confirm his work schedule, all that. But I don't think it's necessary, do you?"

Cook shook his head.

"What now?" said Holiday.

"I'm gonna need a statement from you at some point," said Ramone. "Nothing to worry about. You're clear."

"I wasn't worried," said Holiday.

"Least you can rest easy, Sarge," said Ramone.

Cook said nothing.

"Let's get a beer or somethin," said Holiday.

"Drop me at my car," said Ramone.

"C'mon, Ramone. How often do we see each other? Right?"

"I'll have a beer," said Cook.

Ramone looked over the bench at Cook. He seemed small, leaning against the door in the front seat of the car.

"Okay," said Ramone. "One beer."

RAMONE WAS FINISHING HIS third beer as Holiday returned from the bar with three more and some shots of something on a tray. Ramone and Cook were seated at a four-top near a hallway leading to the restrooms, listening to Laura Lee singing "Separation Line" from the juke. They were in Leo's, which was fine with Ramone, as it was close to his house. Hell, if it came to it, he could walk. But he hoped it wouldn't come to that. He had picked up his Tahoe from the garden on Oglethorpe, and he intended to drive it home.

"What is that?" said Ramone, as Holiday set the shot glasses down on the table crowded with empty bottles.

"It ain't Alizé or Crown or whatever they're moving these days in this place," said Holiday. "Good ol' Jackie D, baby."

"Been a while," said Cook. "But what the hell." He threw his shot back without waiting for a glass-tap or toast.

Ramone had a healthy sip. The sour mash bit real nice. Holiday downed his completely and chased it with beer. He and Cook were drinking Michelob. Ramone was working a Beck's.

"What time is it, Danny?" said Cook.

Holiday looked at the clock on the wall, within easy sight of all of them. Then he remembered the schoolhouse clock in Cook's house, off by several hours. It came to him that Cook wasn't wearing a watch. The reason being, he couldn't read the time.

"You can't see that?" said Holiday.

"I still got some trouble with numbers," said Cook.

"I thought you could read."

"I can read some. Newspaper headlines, and the leads if I work at it. But I couldn't get my numbers back."

"You had a stroke?" said Ramone, knowing the answer from Cook's appearance but trying to be polite.

"Wasn't too serious," said Cook. "Knocked me down some, is all it did."

"How do you use a phone?"

"It's hard for me to make outgoing calls. My daughter spent a few hours programming my speed dial on my home phone and cell. And then there's the call-back button. I also have this El Salvador lady, comes once a week to do things for me I can't do myself. Her visits are part of my veteran's benefits. She makes appointments for me, writes checks, all that."

"They have, like, voice-activated phones available, don't they?" said Holiday.

"Maybe they do, but I don't wanna go down that road. Look, all a this bullshit is frustrating, but I've seen people got more health problems than I do. I go down to the VA hospital for my checkups, there's a lotta dudes in there way worse off than me. Younger than me, too."

"You're doin okay," said Holiday.

"Compared to some, I'm fine."

Holiday lit a Marlboro and blew the exhale across the

table. He was no longer self-conscious about having a cigarette in front of Cook. The bar was already thick with smoke.

"Felt good working today," said Cook.

It felt the same for Holiday. But he wasn't about to admit it in front of Ramone.

"You were one of the best," said Ramone, pointing the lip of his shot glass at Cook.

"I *was* the best, in my time. That's not braggin, it's fact." Cook leaned forward. "Lemme ask you something, Gus. What's your closure rate?"

"Me? I'm up around sixty-five percent."

"That's better than the department average, isn't it?"

"It is today."

"I was closing almost ninety percent of them in my best years," said Cook. "Course, it wouldn't be that high now. I read the writing on the wall when crack hit town in eighty-six. I could have worked a few more years, but I got out soon after that. You know why?"

"Tell me."

"The job changed from what it was. The feds threatened to turn off the money faucet to the District unless the MPD put more uniforms on the streets and started making more drug arrests. But you know, locking people up willy-nilly for drugs doesn't do shit but destroy families and turn citizens against police. And I'm not talking about criminals. I'm talking about law-abiding citizens, 'cause it seems like damn near everyone in low-income D.C. got a relative or friend who's been locked up on drug charges. Used to be, folks could be friendly with police. Now we're the enemy. The drug war ruined policing, you ask me. And it made the streets more dangerous for cops. Any way you look at it, it's wrong."

"When I started out in Homicide," said Ramone, "there were twenty detectives working four hundred murders a year. That's twenty cases each year per detective. Now we got forty-eight detectives on the squad, each working four or five murders a year. And it's a lower closure rate than when I came in."

"No witnesses," said Holiday. "Not unless the victim is a kid or elderly. And even then, it's not a given that anyone will come forward."

"No one talks to the police anymore," said Cook, tapping his finger on the table. "That's what I'm sayin. Neighborhoods are only safe if the people who live in them work with the law."

"That's over," said Holiday. He took a long swig of his beer. He dragged on his smoke and tapped off the ash.

They had another round the same way. Ramone was feeling the alcohol. He hadn't gone this deep in a bar in a long time.

"'Monkey Jump,'" said Cook, as an instrumental came strong out of the Wurlitzer. "Junior Walker and the All-Stars."

"This place is all right," said Ramone, looking around at the different age groups and types in the room.

"Gus loves all the peoples," said Holiday.

"Shut up, Doc."

"One thing about Leo's, you *can* meet some ladies in here," said Holiday. "Just look at that thing right there."

A young woman came out of the hall and crossed the barroom floor. She was tall and had back on her that many men in the bar were in the process of appreciating.

"I'd kill that," said Holiday.

"Nice way of puttin it," said Ramone.

"I'm just a man who likes his licorice. Nothin wrong with that."

Ramone drank beer down to the waist of the bottle.

"Whatsa matter, Giuseppe, did I offend you? Or is it that you don't think a *woman of color* would want to get with a man like me?"

Ramone looked away.

"Gus is married to a sister, he tell you that?" said Holiday to Cook.

"Shut the fuck up, Holiday," said Ramone in a tired and unthreatening way.

"You say he married your sister?" said Cook, trying to cut the chill.

"My sister's dead," said Holiday. "She died of leukemia when she was eleven years old."

"It's a joke," said Ramone to Cook. "He played that one on me when we were in uniform. It wasn't any funnier then."

"I'm not joking," said Holiday.

Ramone and Cook waited for the rest, but nothing came.

Cook cleared his throat. "So, you're married to a black woman, Gus?"

"Last time I checked."

"How's that working out?"

"I guess she's gonna keep me."

"No bumps in the road?" said Holiday.

"A few," said Ramone.

"Just a few?" said Holiday. "Rumor was you were having, what do they call that, *fidelity issues* a while back."

"Fuck your rumors. Who told you that, your boy Ramirez?"

"I don't remember. It could have been him. It was just something that was going around."

"Bullshit."

"Johnny said you dropped in on him today at the academy."

"Yeah, I saw him. Ramirez was wearing his pink belt. Teaching recruits how to block a punch. The proper stance and all that. Another guy who rose to the bottom."

"You mean like me."

"I didn't say that."

"You could work another twenty and you'd never be the police that I was."

"You shouldn't drink so much, Doc. Your mouth overloads your asshole when you do."

"What's your excuse?"

"I gotta take a leak," said Ramone, and he got up out of his chair. He went down the hall.

Cook had watched and listened as they went quietly back and forth through forced smiles and tightened jaws. And now Holiday was relaxed, his hand wrapped loosely around the bottle of beer.

"You were pretty rough on him," said Cook.

"He's got thick skin. He can take it."

"You know his wife?"

"I met her a long time ago. She was police for a short while. Nice-looking woman. Smart. I hear they've got a couple of good-looking kids, too."

"So what's the problem?"

"There isn't one. I just like to aggravate him. Guy marries a black woman, he thinks he's Hubert H. Humphrey and shit."

"He didn't bring the subject up. You did."

"I'm just having a little fun with him," said Holiday. "That's all it is."

Ramone came back from the head but did not sit back down or touch what was left of his beer or shot. He pulled his wallet and dropped twenty-five dollars on the table.

"That ought to cover me," sad Ramone. "I'm out."

"I'm just curious," said Cook. "You never did say if you had any suspects."

"I don't know much of anything yet," said Ramone. "That's the God's honest truth. But listen, you guys are done with this, right?"

Holiday and Cook both nodded lamely. It was hardly an oath.

"Pleasure to spend some time with you, Sarge," said Ramone, reaching out to shake Cook's hand.

"You, too, Detective."

Holiday put his hand out. Ramone took it.

"Gus."

"Doc."

They watched him walk from the bar, a slight list in his step.

"He knows more than he thinks he knows," said Cook. "It just hasn't come to him yet."

"Still wouldn't mind beating him to it," said Holiday.

"Well, we didn't exactly say we'd stay out of it."

"Did he ask a question? I was just nodding my head to the music."

"So was I."

"You want another beer?"

"I've had my limit," said Cook, watching the same woman Holiday had remarked upon, now talking to a man at the bar. "You go on. I'll just sit here and dream."

RAMONE NEGOTIATED THE SIDE streets leading to his home. He drove the Tahoe a little recklessly, taking turns abruptly, going way too fast. Some were more careful when they had a few beers and liquor in their system, but Ramone on alcohol had always been both aggressive and sloppy. Fuck it, let some 4D uniform pull him over. He'd badge him and go.

Ramone wasn't angry at Holiday. The comments about his wife were weird and cheap, but they hadn't been directed toward Regina. Rather, he'd been insinuating that Ramone had married a black woman to make some kind of statement. Which couldn't have been more off the mark. He'd fallen in love with Regina by accident. They had been lucky in their compatibility, like any couple who made it, and their marriage had survived.

Ramone hadn't even thought too deeply about their color difference in a long time, certainly not since the birth of their children. Diego and Alana had erased anything having to do with that. It wasn't that Ramone didn't "see color," that most ridiculous of claims that some white people felt they had to make. It was just that he didn't notice it in his kids. Except, of course, to notice how handsome they were in their skin.

It was true that in the late '80s, when they had married, they had run into some of that old negativity at holiday gatherings and around town. Early on, Ramone and Regina had agreed to jettison any family members and so-called friends who gave off that vibe, neither of them having any desire to reach out to or "understand" folks who were still that way.

Not that the two of them were untainted. Ramone freely admitted to having remnants of racial prejudice inside him that would never go away, as did Regina. They were products of their upbringing and time. But they also knew that the upcoming generation would be much more liberated of those prejudices, and because of that it was likely that their family would be strong and fine. And it seemed to be so. It was rare for Ramone to catch anyone in the D.C. area double-taking him when he was out with his wife and kids. And when they did, it didn't dawn on him immediately that his family was being noticed because of their different shades. His first thought was, Is my zipper down? or, Do I have something stuck between my teeth?

It didn't mean his kids weren't going to face racism out in the world. He saw evidence of it damn near every day. It was hard for him to sit on his hands when his son got slighted due to his blackness or the way he dressed. Because what could you do, put every convenience store clerk up against a wall who had told his son to get out the shop, or threaten every township-quality cop who tried to bust Diego down? You had to choose your spots. Otherwise you'd go crazy behind the rage.

Ramone wasn't trying to make any statements. It was difficult enough just to get through his day-to-day.

He pulled to a stop in front of his house. Regina's Volvo was parked in the driveway, and she had left the porch light on as well as the light in the upstairs hall. Alana slept better knowing the hall was lit. He looked up at the light in Diego's window. Diego was probably still awake, lying in his bed with his headphones on, listening to music. Thinking of a girl he liked or daydreaming of catching the long ball as the seconds ticked off the clock. All was good.

He sat behind the wheel of the SUV. He was close to drunk and as confused as he had ever been about Asa's death. He had seen something that day, or heard it in an interview. It was glancing at him like a flirtatious woman. Now Ramone was waiting on the kiss.

His cell phone sounded. He read the name on the caller ID. Ramone hit "talk" and put the phone to his ear.

"What's goin on, Rhonda?"

"Got something, Gus. You know that ballistics test I ordered?"

"Talk about it."

"The markings on the slugs recovered from the bodies of Asa Johnson and Jamal White are a match."

"You sayin—"

"Yeah," said Rhonda. "They came from the same gun."

Five minutes later, Ramone entered his house. He locked up his badge and gun, went up the stairs, checked on Alana and Diego, and then walked into his bedroom, locking the door behind him. He went to the bathroom, gargled mouthwash, brushed his teeth, and swallowed a couple of aspirin. Back in his bedroom, he stumbled while taking off his pants and heard Regina stir in bed. He removed his boxers as well and dropped them on the floor. He turned off the bedside lamp and slipped naked under the sheets. He got close to Regina and kissed her behind her ear. In the darkness, he kissed her neck.

"Where you been, Gus?"

"Place called Leo's."

"You drunk?"

"A little."

Ramone slid his hand under the elastic band of Regina's pajama bottoms. She did not resist him. He began to stroke her and she guided his fingers to a better place, and when he found it she made a small sound and opened her mouth. Ramone kissed her cool lips. She pulled her bottoms down further and kicked them away. He got up on one elbow, facing her, and she took him in her hand and rubbed him against her inner thigh and as she turned into him she pressed the head of his cock onto her warm, flat belly.

"Remember me?" said Ramone.

"You do feel familiar."

That night, they made love intensely.

TWENTY-SIX

THE NEXT MORNING saw a buzz of activity in the VCB offices. Two bodies had dropped overnight, and assignments and pairings were being discussed. Also, it was Friday, so detectives were preparing for the increase in fatalities that came naturally with the weekend. Added to that was the fact that it was both a government payday and welfare check day, which meant higher alcohol and drug intake in the evening, which generally resulted in an uptick in violent crime.

Ramone, Bo Green, and Bill Wilkins stood around Rhonda Willis, seated at her desk like the queen bee.

"How'd you know?" said Wilkins.

"I didn't," said Rhonda. "It was a long shot, but hey. I'll take it."

"I don't see what connects Asa Johnson to Jamal White," said Ramone. "Dominique Lyons had motive with the White killing, but why would he do Asa?"

They thought about it without conjecture. They stared at Rhonda's desktop and up at the drop ceiling.

"Twenty-four hours between the two killings," said Green. "Could be two different shooters."

"Like the gun got passed on or sold," said Wilkins.

"Or it was a hack," said Green. "Whoever killed Asa Johnson rented it to Lyons."

"It happens," said Wilkins.

Ramone looked at Rhonda.

"Well, we need to find Mr. Lyons, regardless," said Rhonda. "Then it will all become more clear."

"Any action on W Street?" said Ramone.

"He hasn't posted at the apartment yet. Neither has Darcia."

"What's your day plan?"

"I'm gonna go call on Darcia's mother over in Petworth. See if she can scare up her daughter or point me to her. I don't know, maybe lean on Darcia's friend Shaylene a little harder. Just do a little door-knockin, Gus."

"The old-fashioned way," said Wilkins.

"Y'all?" said Rhonda.

"Bill's gonna get into Asa's computer," said Ramone. "I'll be up in the neighborhood. I'm not done there."

"You want some company?" said Bo Green to Rhonda.

"Always nice to have some size with me," said Rhonda, nodding at Green's huge frame. "Gives me confidence."

"Stay in touch," said Ramone.

BILL WILKINS AND RAMONE split up in the lot, agreeing to keep in contact during the day. Ramone found a blue Taurus that he knew ran reasonably well, then drove to a Starbucks at 8th and Penn and bought a coffee. He was feeling poorly and thought the caffeine might cure him.

He phoned Cynthia Best, the principal of Asa's middle school, on his way uptown.

"Ronald and Richard Spriggs," said Ramone.

"The twins," said Best. "I know them well."

"I was hoping to pull them out of class for a few minutes, with your permission. I'd like to speak with them if I can."

"Just a minute." Principal Best put him on hold and soon came back on the line. "They took a long weekend, apparently."

"Sick?"

"Don't know. We called their mother at work when they didn't show up for first period and informed her of their absence. It's standard procedure. We've found it's the best deterrent to truancy."

"Do the twins miss much school?"

"I wouldn't describe them as model students, Detective."

"I know where they live, but I need an apartment number. Could you give it to me?"

"I'll transfer you to someone who can."

The Spriggs twins lived on 9th, between Peabody and Missouri, in a group of brick apartments surrounded by a black iron, spear-topped fence. Across the street was another community garden, and in sight was the former Paul Junior High, now a charter school still carrying the name. An Eiffel-like radio tower behind the 4th District police station, and a smaller one beside it on the same side of 9th as the apartment house, were the neighborhood landmarks.

Ramone found the Spriggs unit and knocked on the door. Ronald Spriggs opened it, wearing a T-shirt with a character drawn on it in permanent glitter, a guy in a sideways baseball cap holding what looked to be a ray gun. The sleeves had been cut into thin strips at the shoulder and braided tightly, ending in tiny balls, the kind of ornamental touch found on a lampshade. Ronald had talent as an artist and an eye for design, and Diego owned a few of his custom T-shirts. It was Ronald's hand that had drawn the "Dago" logo on Diego's caps.

"What I do, Mr. Gus? Jaywalk or somethin?"

"Nothing that serious. I just wanted to talk with you and your brother about Asa."

"Come on in," said Ronald.

They went down the hall. In the living room, the blinds had been drawn and the air was still. Richard was sitting on a worn couch in the dim light, playing Madden 2006 on Xbox. Ramone recognized the game, as the sound track was often running in his own house.

"Richard, Mr. Gus is here."

Richard Spriggs didn't turn his head. "Hold up." His finger worked the controller with dexterity.

"Put it on pause," said Ronald. "So I can come back and punish you later on."

Richard continued to play. They had programmed a Broncos-Eagles matchup. An animated version of Champ Bailey intercepted a Donovan McNabb toss intended for TO.

"Shit," said Richard.

"*That*'s a blower," said Ronald mockingly.

"I'm 'a smash you, Ronald."

"Yeah?" said Ronald. "When?"

Richard locked the game on pause, and the television screen went blue. Ramone had a seat on an armchair facing a coffee table where the Xbox unit and controllers were, along with an empty Doritos bag and several open cans of soda. Ronald sat on the couch beside his brother. Richard wore long shorts fray-cut at the bottom, something like Dogpatch by way of D.C. Ramone guessed that these were another of Ronald's creations.

"What, both of you guys caught the bug or somethin?" said Ramone.

"Half day," said Ronald.

"They had those teachers' meetings," said Richard with a smile.

"They transfer you to truant squad, Mr. Gus?"

"Not my department. I'll let your mother deal with it."

"She was tweakin after the school called," said Ronald.

"We told her we were sick," said Richard. "Musta ate somethin bad, 'cause both of us got a stomach thing."

Ramone just nodded his head. He'd known these two most of their lives. They weren't bad kids. They could handle themselves if they had to, but they weren't into violence or provocation. They lived with their mother, who was busy with both a full-time and a part-time job, working to support them and also to give them electronics, games, and things with labels that other boys had. It was a struggle to earn the money needed to buy Nike, North Face, and Lacoste products for her sons, and it kept her away from the apartment and further from their lives. Ramone and Regina, capable of making the same mistakes as anyone else, felt the pressure to do the same for their kids, and often succumbed to it, knowing it was wrong.

In their mother's absence, and in the complete absence of a father, the Spriggs twins were beginning to find trouble. Their actions were not different or more serious than the minor thefts and vandalism Ramone and his friends had perpetrated when he was their age. They were boys with adrenaline, burning it off the wrong way.

The Spriggs twins knew things, as they spent a lot of time out on the street. When Diego's bike had been stolen out of their yard, Ramone had turned to Ronald and Richard, who had returned it without comment that night. Ramone hadn't asked them how they had retrieved the bicycle, nor had he forgotten what they'd done. This past winter, Richard and Ronald had been taken into the 4D station for boosting items off the porches of nearby homes. Ramone had gone there with their mother and got them off without charges.

He worried about them, but only passively, because they were not his sons. Richard, who lacked motivation and direction, was the one who would probably find himself in deeper water as the years went on. It would be a shame if Ronald, who had the tools to do something special with his life, followed Richard out of loyalty and blood.

"So, about Asa," said Ramone.

"We don't know nothin about Asa," said Ronald. "We sorry for what happened to him and all, but you know . . ."

"You guys hung with him, right?"

"Not so much anymore."

"Why not?" said Ramone. "Something happen between you all?"

"Not really," said Ronald.

"Why'd you stop hanging out, then?"

Roland and Richard exchanged glances.

"Why?" said Ramone.

"He ain't like to do the stuff we do," said Ronald.

"Like what, knockin down old ladies and taking their purses?"

"We ain't never did that," said Richard with an embarrassed smile.

"I'm playin with you," said Ramone.

"I'm talking about regular stuff, like ballin," said Ronald. "Goin to house parties and band shows."

"Gettin with girls," said Richard.

"His father wouldn't let Asa come out, anyhow," said Ronald. "I don't know, we just kinda stopped seein him around."

"What else?" said Ramone.

Richard, the cockier of the two, clucked his tongue in his mouth. "He got soft."

"In what way?"

"He changed from how he was. Asa got to be all about books and shit."

"You think there's something wrong with that?" said Ramone.

"Sayin, I ain't about to spend all my time at a library."

"He was carryin a book the day we saw him, matter of fact," said Ronald.

"What day?" said Ramone.

"The day he was killed. Me and Richard was headin towards home. We had just come from playin ball with Diego and Shaka."

"Where were you, exactly?"

"We were a couple of blocks behind Coolidge. I guess we were on Underwood."

"And which way was Asa headed?"

"Towards Piney Branch Road."

"Did you guys talk?"

Ronald thought about it. "We said hey, but he kept goin. I asked him, 'Where you off to, son?' He answered me, but he didn't stop."

"What was his answer?" said Ramone.

"The Lincoln-Kennedy Monument is all he said."

"The Lincoln Memorial?"

"*Monument*," said Ronald.

"Did you see the title of the book he was carrying?" said Ramone.

Ronald shook his head. "Nah."

"Wasn't no title, stupid," said Richard.

"Say it again?" said Ramone.

"Book ain't have no words on its cover," said Richard. "I remember, 'cause I was thinkin, that's a strange-ass book."

It was a journal, thought Ramone.

"Don't tell our mom we was playin the Xbox," said Ronald.

"We told her we'd be studying," said Richard.

"You shouldn't lie to your mother," said Ramone. "She's a good woman."

"I know it," said Ronald. "But if we said the truth, that we didn't feel like goin to school today, she'd get all pressed."

"I ain't tryin to get slapped," said Richard.

Ronald nodded at the lower portion of Ramone's suit jacket. "You carrying your Glock today?"

Ramone nodded.

Ronald smiled. "Good stoppin power, right?"

"Hope you guys feel better," said Ramone, putting a business card down on the table as he stood. "Get some rest."

Out in the car, Ramone cranked the ignition and drove in the direction of Terrance Johnson's home with the intention of meeting Bill Wilkins, who would now be deep into Asa's computer. Going east on Peabody, he got a call on his cell.

"Regina."

"Gus . . ."

"What's wrong?"

"Don't get upset."

"Tell me what's wrong."

"Diego got suspended from school."

"Again?"

"That thing about his friend Toby and the fight he got into. Mr. Guy said he was an uncooperative witness and then some kind of jive about insubordination."

"Bullshit."

"Also, Mr. Guy mentioned that the principal has some questions about our residential status."

"I'm guessing they found out we live in D.C."

"Whatever. I'm going to pick up Diego now. I spoke to him on the school phone, and he's upset. I guess I'll try to talk to the principal when I get there."

"Just pick him up," said Ramone. "*I'll* go talk to the principal."

"You ought to chill before you roll up there."

"Get Diego," said Ramone. "I'll call you later."

Ramone curbed the Taurus. He phoned Bill Wilkins, at the Johnsons', on his cell.

"Bill, it's Gus. I'm not gonna get over there for a while."

"I'm into Asa's history files," said Wilkins, his voice low. "There's something you should have a look at."

"I will when I get there. Meantime, you ever hear of a Lincoln Monument?"

"Uh-uh."

"See if you can find some reference to that in there."

"Okay, but Gus—"

"I'll talk to you later," said Ramone.

He drove toward the Maryland line.

TWENTY-SEVEN

RHONDA WILLIS AND Bo Green sat in the living room of a nicely maintained row house on Quincy Street, in the Petworth area of Northwest. They had cups of coffee set before them on a French provincial–style table. The house was clean and its furnishings tasteful and carefully selected. It did not look like the home of a girl who danced at the Twilight and ran with a murderer, but this was the place where Darcia Johnson had been raised.

Her mother, Virginia Johnson, sat on a couch. She was an attractive woman, light of skin and moderately freckled, dressed stylishly and properly for her age. An eleven-month-old boy sat in her lap, making sounds of contentment. He was smiling at Bo Green, who was making faces at him.

"What's she done, Detective?" said Virginia.

"We're looking to speak to a friend of hers," said Rhonda. "Dominique Lyons."

"I've met him," said Virginia. "Speak to him about what?"

"It's regarding a murder investigation."

"Is my daughter under suspicion of murder?"

"Not at this time," said Green. Squeezed into a small chair, he looked like the bull who'd decided to have a seat in the china shop.

"We know that Darcia and Dominique spend time together," said Rhonda. "We've been to the apartment she shares with Shaylene Vaughn, over in Southeast. And we know where Darcia works. But she hasn't shown up at those places for the last couple of days."

"Have you heard from her?" said Green.

"She called last night," said Virginia, her finger being held by the boy. "She was checking up on little Isaiah here. But I don't know where she was calling from."

"Is Isaiah hers?"

"He came from her."

"Is Dominique Lyons the father?"

"No. Another young man who's no longer in the picture."

"We've got no fixed address on Lyons," said Green. "Any ideas?"

"I'm sorry, no."

Green leaned forward, picked up his coffee cup off the saucer, and had a sip. The cup was hand-painted, delicate, and looked endangered in his huge hand.

"I'm sorry about bothering you with this," said Rhonda, her empathy genuine.

"We thought we did everything right," said Virginia Johnson quietly.

"You can only try."

"This neighborhood is changing now for the better, but it wasn't always this way, as you're well aware. My husband grew up here in Petworth, and he was adamant about sticking it out until the bad wind blew past. He said that two strong, watchful parents and our involvement with the church would be enough to keep our kids out of trouble. Mostly, he was right."

"You have other children?"

"Three others, all grown. All attended college, all are out there in the world, doing fine. Darcia is the youngest. She was tight with that girl Shaylene since grammar school. Shaylene was into drugs and promiscuity starting at thirteen. She was never right. God forgive me for saying that, 'cause most of it wasn't her fault. She had no home life to speak of."

"That'll do it," said Green.

"But it's not everything," said Virginia. "You can be here all the time, give them all the guidance and love they need, and still, they go ahead and jump off that bridge."

"Does Darcia have a close relationship with her son?"

"She cares for him very much. But she's not fit to be his mother. I had my twenty-five in with the government and I took early retirement. My husband's career is strong, so we can afford to get by on one job. The two of us will raise Isaiah. Unless things change."

"Like I said, Darcia's not a suspect in this crime," said Green.

"But we are going to have to bring her into our offices," said Rhonda. "She might be a witness."

"Does she drive a car?" said Green.

"No, Darcia never did get a license."

"So chances are," said Rhonda, "Dominique would be driving her around."

It was not a question. Rhonda Willis was thinking out loud.

"Did that young man kill someone?" said Virginia.

Rhonda nodded at Bo Green, a suggestion that he answer Virginia, and also that they begin to press.

"It's a strong possibility," said Green.

"It would be a good first step," said Rhonda, "to get Dominique Lyons off the street and away from your daughter."

"We've got her cell phone number," said Green.

"But she isn't answering when we call," said Rhonda.

"Maybe if she thought her son was sick or somethin like that," said Green.

"She'd be concerned enough to come on by," said Rhonda.

"I'll call her," said Virginia Johnson, using a soft towel to wipe some drool off Isaiah's chin.

"We'd appreciate it," said Rhonda.

"She'll come, too," said Virginia, now looking at Rhonda. "She does love this child."

RAMONE WAS IN THE waiting area at his son's middle school in Montgomery County, sitting next to a black father about his age. He had arrived ten minutes earlier and told an administrative assistant that he'd like to speak with Principal Brewster. When told that he would need an appointment, Ramone had badged the woman, informed her that he was Diego Ramone's father, and said that he'd wait until he was called. The woman had told him to have a seat.

Ten minutes later, a tall thin woman in her late forties emerged from a hallway leading to offices. She came around the counter, smiling, and looked around the waiting area, going to the black man and extending her hand.

"Mr. Ramone?" she said.

"I'm Gus Ramone."

Ramone stood and shook her hand. Ms. Brewster had a humorless long face, what newspaper feature writers called "equine" when they meant "horsey." She seemed to have too many teeth. Her forced smile had faded, but she managed to bring it back. Her eyes, however, had not recovered. She had met Regina several times but never Ramone. It was obvious that she had expected him to be black.

"Please come with me," said Ms. Brewster.

Ramone followed her. He checked out her backside, because he was a man, and saw that she was light an ass.

Mr. Guy was seated in one of three chairs in Ms. Brewster's office. The assistant principal held a clipboard tight to his chest. Unlike Ms. Brewster, he had an ample behind, and a belly and girl-tits to go with the package.

"Guy Davis," he said, extending his hand.

"Mr. Guy," said Ramone, pointedly using the ridiculous name Davis had chosen to be addressed by the students. He shook Mr. Guy's hand and had a seat before Ms. Brewster's desk.

Ms. Brewster settled into her chair. She glanced at her computer screen, couldn't resist clicking her mouse to check something, then looked at Ramone.

"Well, Mr. Ramone."

"Detective Ramone."

"Detective, I'm glad you came by. Something has been brought to our attention, and we intended on bringing you in to discuss it. Now's a good time."

"First let's talk about my son," said Ramone. "I'd like to know why he was suspended today."

"I'll let Mr. Guy explain it to you."

"There was an incident," said Mr. Guy, "between a student, Toby Morrison, and another student recently."

"You mean they had a fight," said Ramone. "I know about it."

"We have reason to believe that your son was a witness to it."

"How did you come to that?"

"I interviewed several students," said Mr. Guy. "I conducted an investigation."

"An investigation?" Ramone gave Mr. Guy a small and meaningful smile.

"Yes," said Mr. Guy, looking at his clipboard. "I brought Diego in to discuss the events that transpired, and he refused to answer my questions."

"Let me get this straight in my mind," said Ramone. "Diego was a witness to a fair fight off school grounds that I understand was between two boys. Nobody ganged up on the other boy or anything like that."

"Essentially, that's right. But the other boy was hurt in the altercation."

"What, exactly, did Diego do wrong?"

"Well," said Ms. Brewster, "for one thing, he did nothing. He could have stepped in and stopped the fight, but he chose to watch it instead."

"You're suspending him for an inaction?"

"In effect, yes," said Ms. Brewster. "That and insubordination."

"He refused to answer my questions in the course of the investigation," said Mr. Guy.

"Bullshit," said Ramone, feeling heat come to his face.

"I'm going to ask that you refrain from that sort of language," said Ms. Brewster, her fingers laced together, her hands resting on her desk.

Ramone exhaled slowly.

"Diego could have helped us sort this out," said Mr. Guy. "Instead, he hampered our efforts to get to the bottom of the incident."

"You know something?" said Ramone. "I'm glad that my son didn't answer your questions."

Ms. Brewster blinked rapidly, a nervous tic that she had, up to this moment, managed to control. "Certainly you of all people should understand the value of cooperation in matters such as this."

"*This* is not a homicide. Boys get in fights. They test each other and find out things about themselves that they carry the rest of their lives. And it wasn't a case of bullying, and no one was seriously hurt."

"The boy was punched in the face," said Mr. Guy.

"That's one way to lose a fight," said Ramone.

"I can see we're looking at this from wildly different perspectives," said Ms. Brewster.

"I didn't raise my son to rat out his friends," said Ramone, looking at Ms. Brewster, deliberately not addressing Mr. Guy. "Now Toby Morrison will know what kind of friend Diego is to him and he'll always have his back. And Diego will have respect out in the street. That's more important to me and my son than your regulations."

"Diego's protecting a dangerous kid," said Ms. Brewster.

"What's that?"

"Toby Morrison is a dangerous young man."

Now I know what you're about, thought Ramone.

"He's a *tough* young man, Ms. Brewster," said Ramone. "I know Toby. He plays on my son's football team. He's been over our house many times, and he's welcome there. If you don't know the difference between dangerous and tough —"

"I certainly do know the difference."

"I'm just a little curious," said Ramone. "I'm sure there are some white kids in this school who have also gotten into fights from time to time. Have you ever sat in this office and described those kids as dangerous?"

"Please," said Ms. Brewster with a small wave of her hand. Her smile was joyless and sickly. "I'm the principal of a school that's over fifty percent African American and Hispanic. Do you think they would have brought me in here if I didn't have an empathy and understanding for minority students?"

"Obviously, they made a mistake," said Ramone. "You separate these kids by test scores. You see color and you see problems, but never potential. Pretty soon it starts to become a self-fulfilling prophecy. And having a black man doing your hatchet work for you doesn't excuse any of it."

"Now wait a minute," said Mr. Guy.

"I'm talking to Ms. Brewster," said Ramone. "Not you."

"I don't have to take this," said Mr. Guy.

"Yeah?" said Ramone. "What are you gonna *do?*"

"In any event," said Ms. Brewster, still collected, "this is all moot. In the course of Mr. Guy's investigation, a student informed us that you and your family do not live in Montgomery County but rather reside in D.C."

"Would you like me to show you the deed on my house in Silver Spring?"

"A deed makes no difference to us if you don't actually live in the house, Detective. You and your family reside on Rittenhouse Street in Northwest—we've confirmed this. In effect, Diego is illegally attending this school. I'm afraid we're going to have to terminate his enrollment, effective immediately."

"You're kicking him out."

"He is disenrolled. If you'd like to appeal—"

"I don't think so. I don't want him here."

"Then this conversation is over."

"Right." Ramone got out of his chair. "I can't believe they'd put someone like you in charge of kids."

"I'm sure I don't know what you're talking about."

"I believe you. But that doesn't make you right."

"Good day, Detective."

Mr. Guy stood. Ramone brushed by him and left the office. He had a spring in his step. He knew he had been aggressive and needlessly insulting, and he did not feel sorry at all.

RAMONE CALLED REGINA FROM the parking lot. Diego had come home briefly, picked up his basketball, and gone out the door. He wasn't angry, Regina said. Just quiet.

Ramone drove over the District line down to 3rd and Van Buren. He parked, left his suit jacket in the car, loosened his tie, and walked up to the fenced court. Diego was shooting buckets, wearing shorts too big for him, a wife beater, and his Exclusives. He spun in a reverse layup, gathered up the ball, and tucked it under his arm. Ramone stood three feet away from him and spread his feet.

"I know, Dad. I messed up."

"I'm not gonna lecture you. You made a choice and you did what you thought was right."

"How long am I out for?"

"You're not going back there ever," said Ramone. "They found out we used the Silver Spring address to get you in."

"So where am I gonna go?"

"I've got to talk with your mother. I expect we'll put you back in your old school for the rest of the year. Then we'll figure something out."

"I'm sorry, Dad."

"It's okay."

Diego looked out across 3rd. "Everything, this week . . ."

"Come here."

Diego dropped the ball and went into his father's arms. Ramone held him tightly. He smelled Diego's perspiration, the Axe he sprayed on his body, that cheap shampoo he used. He felt the muscles of his shoulders and back, and the heat of his tears.

Diego stepped out of Ramone's embrace. He wiped at his eyes and picked up the ball.

"Want to play some?" said Diego.

"You got me at a disadvantage. You in your eighty-dollar sneakers and me in my brogues."

"You scared, huh?"

"To eleven," said Ramone.

Diego took the ball out. It was over, really, with his first step off check. Ramone tried to beat him, but he could not. Diego was a better athlete at fourteen than Ramone had ever been.

"You goin' back to work like that?" said Diego, nodding at the sweat stains on Ramone's shirt.

"No one will notice. Women stopped looking at me five years ago."

"Mom looks."

"Occasionally."

"Five dollars says I can make it from thirty feet out," said Diego.

"Go ahead."

Diego banked it in off the glass. He flexed his arm, kissed his biceps, and smiled at Ramone.

That's my son.

"You didn't call backboard," said Ramone.

"I'll take that five."

Ramone paid up. "I'm outta here. Got a long day today."

"Love you, Dad."

"Love you, too. Call Mom if you go anywhere, let her know where you are."

Ramone went to the Taurus and got under the wheel. Before he turned the key, Rhonda Willis called him on his cell. They had Dominique Lyons and Darcia Johnson in the boxes down at VCB.

"I'll be right there," said Ramone.

TWENTY-EIGHT

DARCIA JOHNSON'S MOTHER called her to say that her baby was feverish and having difficulty with his breathing. The detectives and uniformed backups who had been radioed for assistance had little time to get in place: within a half hour, a black Lexus GS 430 came up Quincy, stopping in front of the Johnson house. Inside, watching from the upstairs bedroom window, Virginia Johnson phoned Rhonda Willis, seated with Bo Green in the maroon Impala parked up the street. Virginia told Rhonda that the woman getting out of the Lexus was her daughter Darcia and, from what she could make out, the driver of the vehicle, memorable because of his braids, was Dominique Lyons. As Rhonda listened she nodded to Bo Green, who was on his radio with the sergeant in charge of the uniformed officers. Green told the sergeant to go.

Two squad cars suddenly blocked the east and west access to Quincy Street as uniforms on foot emerged from the

Warder Place alley with guns drawn, yelling at the driver of the Lexus to step out of the vehicle with his hands visible. The action was loud and swift, meant to shock and defuse any potential situation completely. Based on Lyons's history, Rhonda was taking no unnecessary risks.

Darcia Johnson sat down immediately on the steps of her parents' row house and covered her face with her hands. Dominique Lyons did as he was told and got out of his car, his hands raised. He was cuffed and put into the back of a squad car. Darcia, also cuffed, was led to a different car. The Lexus was searched thoroughly. No weapons of any kind were recovered. Roughly an ounce of marijuana was found beneath the driver's-side seat.

Virginia Johnson emerged from the house holding Isaiah. She looked at her daughter in the squad car and saw fear and hate in Darcia's eyes. Virginia asked Rhonda if she could come with them, and Rhonda told her that it would be fine.

"We got a playroom set up for kids," said Rhonda. It was Rhonda, in fact, who had pushed for the funding of such a room on the VCB premises. The idea of a waiting area for spouses, girlfriends, grandmothers, and children whose relatives were being arrested or questioned regarding murder-related business had entered few of her male colleagues' minds.

"I'll have my husband meet me there," said Virginia.

"This is gonna be good for your daughter in the end," said Rhonda. "You did right."

DAN HOLIDAY STOOD IN the community garden on Oglethorpe Street, smoking a cigarette. He had a job later in the day and was dressed in his black suit. He had come because he knew that the answer he was looking for was here.

The crime scene had reverted to the state it had been in prior to Asa Johnson's death. Someone had taken the yellow tape down and disposed of it. A few citizens were out in the garden, idly working their plots but socializing mostly, as full autumn had come to Washington, and the vegetables had been harvested and the growth of flowers and other plants had slowed.

Holiday walked to his car. He had positioned it exactly where it had been parked as he had drifted in and out of sleep the night he discovered the body.

He sat behind the wheel of the Lincoln and finished the rest of his Marlboro. He took a hit, examined the butt in his fingers, and hit it again before flipping it out into the road. He watched the smoke ripple up off the cherry smoldering on the asphalt.

Holiday glanced over in the direction of the fancy plot with the used-car-lot flags and propellers, and the signs with song titles related to plants and botany. He had felt that cold finger the day before, passing by the signs.

Let It Grow.

Those were the words that had come to his mind when the patrol car had passed by, sometime in the night. But at the time, he hadn't yet seen the sign.

Holiday squinted, staring at nothing, thinking of the white policeman and the perp in the backseat of the car. Then he saw his brother, playing air guitar and high, long-haired and long ago, in the basement of their parents' house in Chillum.

"Fuck *me*," said Holiday.

He laughed shortly, pulled his cell along with Gus Ramone's card, and made a call.

"Ramone."

"Gus, it's Holiday."

"Okay."

"Hey, man, I'm at the garden. On Oglethorpe? I came up with something."

"Go ahead," said Ramone.

"The patrol car, the one I saw that night? The car number was four sixty-one. As in *Ocean Boulevard*."

Ramone did not comment. He was trying to bring up a

visual in his mind. The mention of the car number had immediately triggered something in his memory.

"It came to me 'cause my brother was a Clapton freak," said Holiday.

"That's fascinating," said Ramone.

"Should be pretty easy to check the Four-D logs, right? See who took out four sixty-one on the midnight that date?"

"Except that I'm busy. I'm heading down to VCB right now. We've got a couple of live ones in the box."

"You get me the name of that patrolman, me and T.C.—"

"You're not police."

"That cop could be a witness. You're gonna want to talk with him, aren't you?"

"*I* am," said Ramone. "Not you."

"Me and Cook, we could, you know, check it out. With you bein' so busy and all."

"You got no fuckin idea what my day is looking like," said Ramone.

"All the more reason," said Holiday.

"No," said Ramone.

"Hit me back," said Holiday, and ended the call.

Holiday got out of the car. He lit another smoke, thinking, He'll call me with what I need. I saw it in him last night. He felt sorry for the old man and deep inside he knows he did me wrong. He's not a bad guy, basically, always colors inside the lines, but that's not awful. He won't keep me out of this, even if it's against the rules.

Fifteen minutes later, Ramone called.

"I thought about it," said Ramone.

He had, in fact, found his memory. The cocky blond patrolman who had been at the Asa Johnson crime scene was leaning on car number 461 when Ramone had first arrived. And he remembered the name on the uniform's faceplate: G. Dunne. But he wasn't going to give it up to Holiday. Doc and the old man were running on passion and desperation.

Passion was always a positive. It was their desperation that worried Ramone.

"And?" said Holiday.

"I'd be nuts to hand over that information to you. It's not gonna happen."

"I don't need you. I'll find it my own way."

"Just do me a favor and don't act on anything unless you talk to me first."

"Got it," said Holiday.

"I mean it, Doc."

"Understood."

"That includes conducting your own investigation," said Ramone. "Impersonating a police officer is a serious crime."

"Don't worry, Gus, I won't turn you in."

"You're a funny guy, Doc."

"Thanks for calling me back."

Holiday hit "end." Then he dialed the number for T. C. Cook that he had programmed into his phone. Cook picked up on the second ring. Holiday thinking, The old man was waiting for me to call.

T. C. COOK SAT AT his kitchen table, drinking a cup of coffee. From back in the office, he could hear the squawk, dispatcher's voice, and patrolman's response coming from the Internet site on his computer. It was often the sole sound in his otherwise quiet house. The woman the VA sent, the El Salvador lady, she made some noise around here, livened things up. He looked forward to her visits, but she only came once a week.

Mostly, his days were long on boredom. He got up early, made out what he could of the newspaper, then spent time in his office or the workshop in his basement, looking for something to do. He waited for his mail around noon and took longer than necessary to prepare his lunch. He fought off but often succumbed to an afternoon nap. He tried not to watch too much television, though that was something he could do without frustration. But it was a passive activity, all take and no give. Cook was someone who had always lived for goals, and now he had none.

He wasn't mentally weak. He had more reason than most to be unhappy, but he would not allow himself the out of depression. There was little upside for him to getting out of bed in the morning, but he did so and dressed before breakfast, as a man would who was headed off to work.

Getting involved with the church was an option, but he wasn't much of a Jesus type. His wife had been a devout Baptist, a woman of strong faith. Some police clung to God, but the job and what he had seen produced the opposite effect on Cook. Now that he was closer to death, it would have been easy and understandable for him to fall back into churchgoing, but also, he felt, hypocritical. He had not been an attentive or particularly model husband, but he had loved his wife and been faithful to her, and if there was a God, and if indeed He was good, Cook believed that He would see fit to put him and Willa together again, whether Cook attended Sunday services or not.

Cook stared into his empty coffee mug.

His doctor had said to have only one cup a day, if he had any at all. That caffeine made his heart race, and Cook didn't need that. Thing of it was, the doctor had also told him that the likelihood of his having another stroke was high, and when it came, it could be worse than the last. Wasn't like not having a second cup of coffee was going to prevent that.

His circulatory system was fragile, the doctor said. No, I cannot tell you how long it will be before "the next event." Could be weeks and it could be years. All those decades of smoking and poor diet. We wish we could do more for you, Mr. Cook. Another operation would be too risky. Unfortunately. Continue to lead an active but careful life. Take your medication. Bullshit piled on top of bullshit, on and on.

Cook looked over at the kitchen counter. He had one of those organizers, two pills in each compartment, separated by days of the week. So he wouldn't forget a day, or forget he had taken the pills already and swallow double the dose. This is what it had come to for him. If he lived past the next stroke, he would probably be one of those dudes, had dead arms and legs. Then the VA would have someone dropping by to bathe him. Put one of those bibs on him while he ate. Send some poor immigrant lady to wipe his old man's ass.

He'd sooner eat his gun. But that was a thought for another day.

Holiday had called. Cook had then phoned an old friend in the 4th District whom he had mentored in the early '80s, now a commanding officer. Cook told the lieutenant that an officer in 4D had done his niece a kindness and she wanted to write a letter commending him, but she could only remember the number she'd seen on his car. Cook had no niece, and the lieutenant's hesitation told him that he sensed the lie, but he gave the information out to Cook just the same. When Cook asked about the officer's schedule, the lieutenant told him, after a long pause, that he was on an eight-to-four that day.

Holiday would come, and they could get to work. The young man carried heavy baggage, but he had energy and fire. Maybe the two of them would turn over the right rock.

Cook went out to his car, a light gold Mercury Marquis with a blue-star FOP sticker on the rear window, and opened the trunk. He suspected that he and Holiday would be working a tail late in the day and that they would take two cars. He knew what was in the trunk, knew he had not moved its contents, but he was a little bit excited and wanted to have a look at his things.

He kept the car maintenance items here, including oil, antifreeze, jumper cables, brake and power steering fluid, shop rags, a tire patch kit, and a pneumatic jack. There was one Craftsman box holding standard tools and another holding a 100-foot retractable tape measure, duct tape, 10 × 50 binoculars, night vision goggles he'd never used, a box of latex gloves, a friction-lock expandable baton, a set of Smith and Wesson blued handcuffs, a variety of batteries, a digital camera that Cook did not know how to operate, and a Streamlight Stinger rechargeable steel-cased flashlight, which could double as a weapon. Also in the trunk was a steel jimmy bar.

All was in place. Holiday would not be by for a while. Cook decided to go back in the house and pull his Hoppe's kit and .38. He had time to clean his gun.

MICHAEL "MIKEY" TATE AND Ernest "Nesto" Henderson sat in a pretty black Maxima, the new style with the four pipes coming out the back, in the lot of a strip mall on Riggs Road in Northeast D.C., not far from the Maryland line. There was a dollar store, pawnbroker, liquor store, Chinese-and-sub shop, check-cashing joint, papusa place, and two hairstyling shops. One specialized in nails and the other, called Hair Raisers, was known for braids and hair extensions. Chantel Richards was employed at Hair Raisers. Henderson could see her through the front window, standing behind a woman in a chair, both of them running their mouths as Richards did her job. It was Henderson who was doing most of the surveillance. Tate was leafing through the latest *Vogue.*

"Damn, she fine, though," said Henderson.

"That is a lot of woman," said Tate, looking up. He was wearing big jeans, a long-sleeved Lacoste shirt, and matching shoes with the little alligators stitched on the sides.

"She tall, too," said Henderson, who wore a blue Nationals cap, the away game version, not because he followed baseball but because the color matched his shirt. The cap was tilted slightly on his head.

"Her hair makes her look taller than she is," said Tate. "Plus, she might be wearing high heels. These fashion girls like to get that height thing goin. Makes 'em look more slim."

"She fat where it counts."

"She dresses right for the type of body she got."

"Where you read that, in that girl magazine?"

"I'm just sayin. She got that effect she was going for." Tate noticed women's clothing, their shoes and jewelry, how they carried themselves, all that. He was interested, was all it was. But he didn't talk about it much around Nesto, who thought that reading magazines about such things, and indeed reading of any kind, was gay.

"I worry about you, son."

"I'm just admiring her effort, is all."

"Yeah, well, we been admiring her long enough."

"I ain't happy about it, either. My ass hurts from sittin out here, too."

"Sure it don't hurt from something else?"

"Huh?"

"Has someone been puttin their pork inside you?"

"Fuck you, dawg."

"You read them fashion magazines all the time; I worry."

"Least I *can* read."

"While you gettin pounded from behind."

"Go on, Nesto."

They were coworkers, but they had little in common. Michael Tate had arrived at where he was as a transfer point to someplace else. He was like all those waiters in New York he'd read about, who weren't waiters for real but actors who were on the way to being movie and television stars. That's how Tate thought of himself. He wasn't about working a minimum-wage thing, though, until he blew up. No way was he going to leave out his house without a nice outfit on or money in his pocket, because he was like that. So here he was.

His older brother, William, now incarcerated, had been in the trade with Raymond Benjamin when both of them were young, and when Benjamin had come uptown from prison, he had put Michael on. But Michael Tate was smart enough to know that the money, as good as it was, was just walking-around money compared to what those clothing designers made. If soft-ass rappers could do it, shit, why couldn't Michael Tate?

Question was, how did you go from here to there? He guessed the way to start was to work on getting his GED. But that was a conversation he would have with himself another time.

For now he was stuck with Nesto Henderson, in a shit-on-your-shoe parking lot, keeping an eye on a young woman who probably had hurt no one. Being called a faggy by this Bama who got no pussy himself but who felt the need to call him names because he read magazines. To top it off, his stomach was growling, too.

"I'm hungry," said Tate.

"Go over there to that slope house and get a steak and cheese, then. Matter of fact, get me one while you're at it."

"How you so stupid? You don't never buy a sub from a place got Chinese food, too. And you don't never eat no Chinese from a place sells subs."

"I'm not having no Pedro food," said Henderson, speaking of the papusa place.

"Look, she ain't goin nowhere for a while. She got her client to take care of, and anyway, it's too early in the day for her to get off. Let's find someplace and eat some real food, come on back later."

Henderson looked at Chantel Richards, admiring the movement of her hips as she listened to the music they were playing in the shop. "Shame if we had to kill her. Ain't too many champions walkin around like that."

"We just supposed to follow her to where she layin up with that Romeo."

"I'm just sayin, we might have to." Henderson nodded at the ignition. "Come on, let's go."

Tate started the Nissan and pulled out of their space. He stopped at the yellow up on Riggs and was careful to use his turn signal at the intersection beyond. There were live guns under the seats, and he did not want to risk being pulled over by the law.

Nesto Henderson had put work in. Least, he claimed he had. Michael Tate could take care of himself and physically protect Raymond Benjamin if he had to, but he hadn't signed up for the doom squad. After all, Benjamin had told him that he was done with that part of the game himself.

I ain't about to kill no woman, thought Michael Tate. That ain't me.

TWENTY-NINE

THE BOX WAS stuffy, as it always was. Dominique Lyons sat on a stool bolted to the floor. Its seat was deliberately small and would be uncomfortable to sit on for a man of size. Lyons had not been leg-ironed to the stool's base. At this point in the interview Detective Bo Green, seated across the table, was still Lyons's friend. They had been talking for just a short while.

Lyons wore an Authentic Redskins jersey with Sean Taylor's name and number, 21, stitched on the back. The Authentics went for one thirty-five, one hundred forty on the street. The brand-new Jordans on Lyons's feet retailed for a hundred and a half. Lyons's jewelry, a real Rolex, rings, diamond earrings, and a platinum chain, were of five-figure value. When Green asked him what he did for a living, Lyons said that he had a car-detailing business on the street where he lived.

"I see you're a Taylor fan," said Green.

"Boy's a beast," said Lyons, tall of trunk and long limbed. He had broad shoulders and an angular, handsome face. His braids were long and framed his cheekbones. His eyes were deep brown and flat, a taxidermist's ideal.

"He attended Miami, so that ain't no surprise. You know those Hurricanes *always* come to play."

Lyons nodded. He looked blandly into Bo Green's eyes.

"You played Interhigh ball, didn't you?" said Green. He was taking a shot due to Lyons's height, weight, and athletic build. Green knew that some coach had gotten a look at Lyons at one time in his life and tried.

"Eastern," said Lyons. "I was at D-back."

"Corner or safety?"

"Free safety."

"That would have been when, the late nineties?"

"I ain't play but one year. Ninety-nine."

"The Ramblers had a team that year, I remember right. Shoot, I think I saw you play. Y'all did go up against Ballou that year, didn't you?"

It was a lie and Lyons read it. But his ego could not let it die.

"I started varsity my sophomore year."

"You look like you can hit."

"I was *pan*cakin younguns," said Lyons.

"Why you only play one season?"

"I graduated my sophomore year, too."

"Took the early out, huh?"

"I guess I'm one of them young prodigies you hear about. I was on the accelerated plan."

"Football's a good game. Useful for some as well. You might've parlayed it into something else if you had hung with it."

"Guess I shoulda talked to my guidance counselor. If I could find one."

"I coach a football team in Southeast," said Green, his tone patient and unwavering. "Me and some other fellas I came up with down around that area. We got three weight divisions. If the boys come to practice regular and show me their report cards every quarter, and if they get passing grades, I guarantee they'll see time on the field. I don't even care if they got skills."

"So?" said Dominique Lyons.

Bo Green smiled ferally at the man on the small stool. "You funny, man. Anyone ever tell you that?"

"Sayin, that's a good story. But we ain't here to socialize. Unless you gonna charge me with something, you need to let me out this piece, 'cause I got things I got to do."

"You've been charged with marijuana possession," said Green.

"I'll cop to that," said Lyons. "That's like, what, a parking ticket in this town. So give me my discharge papers and my court date, and I'll be on my way."

"Like to ask you some questions while I got you here."

"Regardin what?"

"A homicide. Victim was a young man name of Jamal White. You know him?"

"Lawyer," said Lyons.

"All's I'm askin is, are you familiar with that name?"

Lyons stared at Green.

"You're correct, Dominique. You got a right to bring in an attorney. But you know, that lawyer advises you not to talk to us, it's gonna ruin the opportunity you got for leniency later on. I mean, if you were to cooperate, give us some information that would be helpful to this homicide investigation, for example, that marijuana charge you caught today, most likely it's gonna go away."

"I seen that TV show," said Lyons.

"What's that?"

"You know the one. Where that white dude gets the suspects in the interview room and talks them out of their right to an attorney, like, every week for ten years straight? And then pushes that yellow pad across the table and tells the suspect to write out his confession? And then the suspect does it? Yeah, I seen it. Trouble is, ain't no motherfucker I know ever been stupid enough to do that. Maybe in New York they ignorant like that. But not in D.C."

"You *are* smart, Dominique."

"Said I was."

"Like Doogie Howser."

"If you say so."

"We're talkin to your girlfriend Darcia."

"That right?"

"She as smart as you?"

Bo Green got out of his seat. He looked down at Lyons, who was examining the table in front of him. His hands, steady throughout the interview, were rhythmically tapping the table's scarred surface.

"I'm gonna grab a soda," said Green. "You want anything?"

"Let me get a Slice."

"We don't have that. How about Mountain Dew?"

Lyons nodded shortly. Green glanced at his watch, then looked directly into the camera mounted in a corner of the ceiling.

"Eleven twenty a.m.," said Green before he left the box.

Bo Green waited for the door to shut behind him with its audible lock. He walked into the adjacent video monitor room, where Detectives Ramone and Antonelli sat, Antonelli with the Sports section open in his lap. On one screen was Dominique Lyons, still staring at the table, shifting his bottom, trying to find a comfortable spot on the seat. On the other were Rhonda Willis and Darcia Johnson, seated in box number 2. Ramone was focused on that screen. Rhonda's soft, steady voice came from the speakers.

"Anything?" said Green.

"Rhonda's taking it slow," said Ramone.

"Trick-ass bitch ain't said nary a word yet," said Antonelli.

"I love it when you talk like that, Tony," said Green. "It's so street authentic."

"That is some nice booty, though," said Antonelli.

"There's an expression you don't hear much these days," said Green. "Been a few decades, come to think of it."

"Your boy Dominique," said Ramone. "He's real cooperative."

"That's my buddy," said Green. "After this is over we gonna go, like, on a camping trip, somethin. Sit around a fire and sing 'Kum Bah Ya'."

"I don't mean to be negative," said Ramone, "but I have the feeling Dominique's not going to confess."

"He's seen that TV show," said Green. "Anyway, let me get on out of here and find him a Mountain Dew."

Green exited the room as Ramone continued to watch the screen. Rhonda Willis was leaning across the table, a lit match in her hand, bringing fire to Darcia Johnson's cigarette.

"Says here *Lee*-Var Arrington's not one hundred percent," said Antonelli, his eyes on the newspaper. "He's *doubtful* for this Sunday's game. Ten million a year, or whatever it is, and he doesn't have to go to work 'cause his fuckin knee hurts. Me, I got hemorrhoids like grapes, hanging between my ass crack, and I show up every day. Am I missing something or what?"

"It's possible," said Ramone.

In box number 2, Rhonda Willis blew out the match.

Darcia dragged on her cigarette and tapped ash into a foil tray. She was freckled, with hazel eyes. Her body was full and ripe. Having a baby had not ruined her figure. In fact, it had made her more voluptuous, an asset in her job.

"Tell me about Jamal White," said Rhonda.

Darcia Johnson looked away.

"It's okay to talk about Jamal," said Rhonda, repeating the boy's name deliberately. "I know about your relationship. Jamal's friend Leon Mayo? He told us you two had a thing."

"Wasn't no thing," said Darcia. "I'm with Dominique."

"Jamal was sweet on you, though."

"He could have been. I ain't know him that well, really."

"No? The man who works the door down at the Twilight is a police officer. He says you two were talking at the bar the night of Jamal's murder."

"I talk to a lot of men down there. I get paid to. That's how I get tips."

"And by dancing."

"Sure."

"What else?"

Darcia didn't answer.

"I been to that place you stay with Shaylene Vaughn," said Rhonda, her tone free of aggression or animosity. "I got eyes."

"So?"

"Do you give Dominique all the money you earn?"

Darcia dragged on her cigarette.

"Is Dominique Lyons your pimp?"

Darcia exhaled a stream of smoke into the small room.

"I'm not judging you, girl," said Rhonda. "I'm just tryin to find out what happened to that young man. I met his grandmother and I saw her tears. His people deserve to know, don't you think?"

"Jamal was just a boy I knew."

"If you say."

"I'm sorry that he got killed. But I don't know nothin about it."

"Okay."

"Can I see my baby now?"

"He's with your mother in the playroom we got. Your father's there too, I expect."

"Isaiah's not sick, is he?"

"He's fine."

"My mother lied to get me arrested, then."

"She lied to help you, Darcia. She did right for you and your son."

"How's it gonna be right between me and my baby when I'm in lock-up?"

Darcia hit her smoke and stabbed it dead in the ashtray. She rubbed at her eyes.

"About Jamal."

Darcia made a small wave of her hand.

"Take your time," said Rhonda.

"We done, far as I'm concerned."

"Not yet. I'd like to get up out of here my own self, but we still got some things we need to discuss. Unfortunately, I caught this homicide. . . ."

"You can't hold me on no marijuana charge."

"Gonna take a little while to process the paperwork."

"This some bullshit. You *know* it is."

Rhonda let Darcia have her anger and watched as it passed.

"You all right? You ain't sick or nothin like that, are you? You comin down off a high?"

Darcia shook her head.

"That's good," said Rhonda. "Listen, you want a soda, somethin?"

"I'll take a Diet Coke, you got it."

"Gonna have to be a Pepsi," said Rhonda. "That work for you?"

Darcia nodded. Rhonda stood, looked at her watch, then looked into the camera lens and said, "Eleven thirty-five a.m."

Rhonda walked from the room, waited for the door to lock behind her, and got a Diet Pepsi from the vending machine. She carried it to the video room, where Ramone and Antonelli sat watching Bo Green and Dominique Lyons on screen number 1.

"Where my whip at?" said Lyons.

"Prob'ly on the way to the impound lot," said Green.

"Better not be one scratch on it," said Lyons, "or y'all gonna have a lawsuit on your hands."

"That is a nice Lexus," said Green. "What is that, the four hundred?"

"Four thirty," said Lyons.

"Were you driving that the other night?"

"What night you talkin about?"

"The night Jamal White was murdered," said Green.

"Who?"

"Jamal White."

"I ain't familiar with that name."

"You had a confrontation with him at the Twilight the night of his death. We have a witness."

"Lawyer," said Dominique Lyons.

Green folded his hands across his huge torso, sat back in his chair, and stared straight ahead.

"Bo looks kinda sad, doesn't he?" said Antonelli.

"That's frustration," said Ramone.

"You see a young man who's keeping his mouth shut," said Rhonda. "I see one who's talkin his ass off."

"For real?"

"Let me get back in there and do my thing."

"You need an assistant?" said Antonelli. "I know how to loosen a young woman's tongue. All it takes is the Plug charm."

"And plenty of alcohol," said Ramone.

"I got this," said Rhonda. She left the room.

Ramone turned down the sound on screen 1 because there was nothing to listen to of value. They waited for Rhonda to get back in box number 2. She had a seat and pushed the can of soda across the table to Darcia. Rhonda let Darcia pop the tab on the can and take a long pull. She lit Darcia's next cigarette.

"I got four sons," said Rhonda, pulling back the match.

Darcia smoked her cigarette.

"Four sons," said Rhonda, "and no man. I'm not complainin. The boys had two different fathers, but neither one of them was what you'd call a family man. I showed the first one the door, and when the second one couldn't be true I told him to go out the same way. I don't get a penny from either of them to this day and I wouldn't take it if it was offered to me. I ain't sayin my boys wouldn't have been better off with a good man around the house, but we didn't have that option. It was hard, I'm not gonna lie. It's been a struggle and it'll continue to be, but we're doing all right. We're gonna be fine.

"You look at me, Darcia, and I know what you see. Middle-aged woman with a little bit of belly on her and clothes from JCPenney. Bags under my eyes and flat shoes. I haven't been to a nice restaurant in five years and I can't tell you when I last went to a real party. Wasn't too long ago I looked something like you. I *had* it, too. In the eighties they used to send me undercover into clubs where the big drug boys were throwin down. I'm talking about the R Street Crew, Mr. Edmond, all of 'em, 'cause the brass knew young men with money would want to talk to me. I walk down the street today, I'm lucky to get a second look. That's how fast it goes away, darling. And then what you got?

"I'll tell you. You got the people you love and who love you back. I look at my sons and I don't regret a minute of the time I spent with them. I don't even mind the way I look in the mirror, 'cause I know it don't mean all that much in the end. My purpose wasn't this job or the paycheck or anything you can buy. It was raising my family. Knowing they ain't never gonna leave me in their hearts. You understand what I'm sayin?"

"Go ahead, Rhonda," said Ramone, watching the monitor.

"You got an opportunity to step off this road you're on," said Rhonda. "Get yourself cleaned up and start raising your baby right, your own self. Like your good mother and father did for you. Back up off of those type of men you been with and start new. We can help. We got this witness security program where we put you in an apartment, away from where you been. We'll set you up."

"I don't know anything," said Darcia. The ash had lengthened on her cigarette. She had stopped smoking it and she had yet to tap it off.

"How you gonna protect that man? He's in another interrogation room right now, schemin you."

"No he isn't."

"Shoot. You think you're his bottom baby? Fancy man tells that to Shaylene and every other young girl he fuckin and robbin. Don't you know that? And now he's in there sayin that it was you had the idea to kill Jamal."

"That's not true."

"True or no, that's how he's gonna testify. He might have pulled the trigger, but he'll get the lesser charge if the premeditation was comin from you."

"I didn't want to hurt Jamal. Why would I?"

"I don't know. You tell me."

"Jamal was good."

"*Tell* me, Darcia. You can. You're no killer. You got the same good in your eyes I saw in your mother's. The law gonna charge you with accessory to a murder, and you're gonna do real time behind it, and for what? You didn't hurt nobody. You couldn't. I know this."

A tear broke free from Darcia's right eye and rolled down her cheek.

"Talk to me," said Rhonda. "I can't help you unless you do. I know you're tired of where you're at. Isn't that right?"

Darcia nodded.

"Tell it," said Rhonda.

Darcia crushed her cigarette out in the ashtray. She watched the smoke curl up off the foil.

"Jamal brought me a rose that night," said Darcia. "That's all he did wrong."

"And what happened then?"

"I was talking to him at the bar, and Dominique saw him give it to me. It wasn't like Dominique was jealous or nothin like that. But he knew that Jamal and me . . ."

"Jamal wasn't a customer. He was your boyfriend."

"I wouldn't let Jamal give me money. That's what set Dominique off. I ain't even think of Jamal like that. He was nice."

"Did Jamal and Dominique have words in the Twilight?"

"Dominique was tryin to punk him. Jamal stood his ground, which only made things worse. Then Jamal tipped on out. I knew the bus lines he rode and the way he walked home. Dominique made me tell him, and he made me come along. I was scared not to. I didn't think Dominique was gonna hurt him bad. I thought he might try and rough him some, but nothing like what he did. In the back of my mind I thought I could stop him if I was there."

"Did Dominique Lyons shoot Jamal White?"

"He rolled up on him at Third and Madison, on the park side. Dominique got out of his Lex and shot Jamal three times."

"Darcia, this is a very important question. I know the doorman pats everyone down for weapons when you go in that place. So it's unlikely that Dominique was strapped inside the Twilight. Did he have a gun in his car?"

"No."

"No, *what?*"

"He didn't have no gun at that time. When we left out the Twilight, he drove to see this man. The man he met sold him a gun."

"That night?"

"Yes."

"Shit," said Ramone, in the darkness of the monitor room.

"Looks like Dominique wasn't your shooter," said Antonelli.

Ramone said nothing and rubbed at his face. The door opened, and Detective Eugene Hornsby, rumpled and in ill-matched clothes, stood in the frame.

"Garloo's pulling into the parking lot, Gus," said Hornsby. "He says he needs to speak with you right now. He's got something to show you. For some reason he wants you to come outside."

"Mother*fucker*," said Ramone, getting quickly out of his seat, extreme agitation on his face.

"Shoot the piano player," said Hornsby. "Not me."

THIRTY

BILL WILKINS WAS seated in the Impala, the driver's side door open, one foot out of the car and on the asphalt. He was having a cigarette and blowing the smoke away from Ramone. Ramone was in the passenger bucket, looking through the papers that Wilkins had brought in a manila jacket.

"You got this, what," said Ramone, "out of the History files of his computer?"

"It's basically the sites Asa was visiting the week before his death. He had an automatic delete programmed for every seven days."

"This is . . ."

"Those are just examples of the home pages," said Wilkins. "You get deep into the contents, it's really raw. Take my word for it, it's explicit. Men-on-men stuff, basically. Dick shots, anal penetration. Cocksucking. Jerking off is a big number, too."

"Asa was gay."

"That's a bet."

Ramone stroked his black mustache. "I guess I've suspected it since the ME's report. I don't know why I didn't look at it dead on. I suppose I didn't want it to be true."

Wilkins pitched his cigarette out into the street. "I don't mean to be flip about it. I was real sorry when I saw this come up. You knowin the kid and all."

"You did well."

"I wish I had uncovered more. I mean, there's no correspondence in there. He was careful about his e-mails or he didn't use the format to communicate. Men pick up boys in those chat rooms, that's how they connect. I've done it myself." Wilkins caught Ramone's look. "With women, Gus. Married women, mostly, you want the truth. They're the easiest to, you know, meet. The wonder of the Internet."

"Did you talk to Terrance Johnson?"

"Hell, no. Not about this. He was intoxicated, anyway. Askin me about the investigation, did we find the murder weapon yet, all that. I was backpedaling out of there with this file tight under my arm. I printed out those pages and booked."

"Drunk at nine in the morning."

"Can't say I blame him," said Wilkins.

"You know, he asked me if we'd found the gun, too."

"You don't think—"

"No," said Ramone. "What's the motive? Terrance Johnson can be a class-A jerk. But there's no way he killed his son." Ramone looked blankly through the windshield. "This explains the Civil War stuff, all that."

"Huh?"

"All those sites Asa visited, about the local forts and cemeteries."

"Right. Prime locations for fag hookups."

"I imagine two people would arrange the meet through the Internet. A teenage boy doesn't have his own place to go, and a lot of the older guys, I would think they don't want some kid being seen entering their house. Hell, a lot of these chickenhawks are probably married."

"Fort Stevens would be a good one. Thirteenth and Quackenbos? It's not far from the Johnson house. All those embankments and, what do you call 'em, *parapets* you can hide in."

"They don't have a Lincoln-Kennedy monument up there, do they, Bill?"

"Never heard of it. I mean, President Lincoln was fired on during that famous battle they had there. The only time he was on a live battlefield during the Civil War. But there's no memorial there for that, none that I can recall. Maybe in that national cemetery they got, up the road."

"On Georgia Avenue?"

"The one that Venable Place backs up into. It's just a tiny graveyard. That's where they buried the soldiers who fell in that battle."

"Bill, you're—"

"I know. You guys think I'm all about pussy and PBR. I like to read, is what it is. I'm telling you, I read my ass off when I'm at home."

Ramone gathered his thoughts. "You know what's bothering me, don't you?"

"What?"

"All right, Asa was gay. But what's that got to do with his murder?"

"You don't think we're any closer?"

"I do, but I'm not seeing it."

"What about Rhonda's suspect?"

"That's the thing," said Ramone. "Dominique Lyons's girlfriend is in the process of fingering him for the Jamal White killing. But she says he didn't purchase the gun until the night he did Jamal. Asa got dropped the night before."

"So we find the dude who sold Lyons the gun."

"Rhonda's working on it as we speak."

"Sarge?"

"Huh."

"You said I was doing a good job on this."

"You are."

"I been putting in a ton of overtime on it."

"Okay."

"Will you sign my Eleven-thirty when we get inside?"

"Kiss my ass," said Ramone.

He looked at his watch. It was past noon.

RAMONE AND WILKINS ENTERED the video monitor room. Bo Green and Antonelli were seated, watching Rhonda Willis and Darcia on screen 2. On screen 1, Dominique Lyons was alone in the box, his head on the table, his eyes closed.

"What's going on?" said Ramone.

"Bo gave up on the shitbird," said Antonelli. "Rhonda got it all out of the girl, anyway."

"What about the gun?"

"Dominique took the cylinder out of the revolver and tossed it over the rail of the Douglass Bridge. Then he doubled back and threw the rest of it over the rail of the Sousa. It's in pieces in the Anacostia River, forever. But the girl gave us a name and location on the seller. Guy by the name of Beano. Eugene's running it now."

"Look at Dominque," said Green with disgust.

"Fucknuts is takin a nap," said Antonelli.

"You know what the captain says," said Wilkins. "If they can sleep in the box, they're guilty. 'Cause otherwise they'd be screaming their asses off about how we made a big mistake."

"Let him sleep," said Green. "Young man believes he's gonna walk out of here free. But he ain't goin no goddamn where but the joint. I'm gonna stick around just to see the look on his face when we tell him about his future."

"What about the girl?" said Wilkins. "They gonna charge her?"

"We need to talk to the prosecutor," said Green. "But I imagine, what with all the cooperating she did, and her testimony, she's gonna pull probation. Rhonda promised her WitSec. It's a start."

"Like that little ho is gonna turn her sweet ass around," said Antonelli, "just in time for Mother's Day."

"Don't you ever shut up?" said Ramone.

As Rhonda recorded the time for the camera, Ramone and Wilkins left the room. When they were gone, Antonelli looked over at Bo Green.

"What the fuck did I do?"

"I guess he just don't like assholes," said Green. "Damn if *I* know why."

Ramone and Wilkins met Rhonda Willis at her cubicle. She and Ramone exchanged a look, and then he lightly touched her arm.

"Nice work."

"Thanks."

"You've put in a full day."

"Uh-huh. And you?"

"It's been interesting, so far. My son got bounced from his school. I went there and peed on the principal's desk, and then I questioned the assistant principal's manhood."

"You're quite the diplomat."

"Also, Bill here found some things on Asa Johnson's computer that pretty much prove Asa was gay."

"You must have had a feeling."

"I did."

"But what's it got to do with his murder?"

"I don't know if it has anything to do with it. I'm hoping the two of us can find the dude who sold Lyons the gun and figure this shit out."

Eugene Hornsby joined the group. He had run the name Beano through WACIES. The program had the ability to cross-reference the street name and bring up the given name, last known address, and priors. Hornsby passed out copies he had made after printing out the information. He had found two Beanos, but one was currently incarcerated.

"Aldan Tinsley," said Hornsby. "Our man has a sheet indicating a history of receiving and selling stolen property. Plus one recent arrest for driving while intoxicated."

"Darcia said that she and Dominique met him in an alley behind a street off Blair Road," said Rhonda. "She didn't recall the cross."

"The LKA is in the two-digit block of Milmarson," said Hornsby.

"That's right near Fort Slocum," said Wilkins. "Where Jamal was found."

"And a stone's throw from the community garden on Oglethorpe," said Ramone.

"I gotta call my sons," said Rhonda, "make sure they're straight."

"Meet you out in the lot," said Ramone.

RAMONE AND RHONDA WILLIS drove uptown in a Taurus. They were on South Dakota Avenue, headed for North Capitol via Michigan, the best route north through Northeast. Ramone was forcing the Taurus up a hill as Rhonda applied lipstick using the vanity mirror behind the passenger-side visor.

"Shame about Asa," said Rhonda. "Shame his parents got to add that to their grief as well."

"You don't know the half of it," said Ramone. "One of the many things Terrance Johnson did to his son was to call him a faggot. Wonder how he's gonna live with that."

"Do you think Johnson knew?"

"No. He was just being ignorant."

Milmarson Place was a short block of well-tended brick and shingled colonials running from Blair Road to First Street, between Nicholson and Madison. It was a one-way going west to east, so Ramone came in from Kansas Avenue and Nicholson. A complicated system of alleys connected the streets, with alleys breaking in on both sides up by First. Ramone turned into an alley entrance and followed it around, horseshoe-style. They passed freestanding garages, wooden and chain-link fences, overturned trash cans, and several dogs of the pit and shepherd mix variety, standing and barking or quietly lying in the small backyards. This section of the alley came out near Blair. When they emerged they saw a parked 4D squad car facing west. Ramone put the Taurus along the curb behind it. The Tinsley residence was on the opposite end of the street.

Rhonda grabbed a walkie-talkie. She and Ramone got out of the Ford and were met by the uniformed patrolman, who had stepped from his car. He was young and blond, and had a crew cut with a cowlick. The name Conconi was on his chest plate. Rhonda had radioed ahead for assistance.

"Arturo Conconi," said the young man, extending his hand.

"Detective Ramone, and this is Detective Willis."

"What do we have?"

"Booster name of Aldan Tinsley," said Ramone. "We think he might have sold a gun that was later used in a homicide. There's no history of violence."

"No reason to take a chance," said Conconi.

"Right. You got good eyes?"

"Pretty good."

"Watch the house from here," said Ramone. "If Detective Willis calls you, move into the alley."

Conconi pulled his radio off his utility belt. He and Rhonda set their frequencies.

"They call you Art or Arturo?" said Rhonda.

"Turo gets it."

"All right, then."

Ramone and Rhonda walked down the block.

"One of your countrymen," said Rhonda.

"Don't hold it against him," said Ramone.

They walked up concrete steps to a concrete porch fronting a brick house at the end of Milmarson. Rhonda chinned toward the door.

"Give it the cop knock, Gus."

"Your hand still hurting?"

"From countin all my money."

Ramone made a fist and pounded on the door. He tried it again. The door opened, and a man in his midtwenties appeared. He was Ramone's height, with a large head, long arms, and a skinny torso. He wore a We R One T-shirt out over jeans. He had a cell phone to his ear.

"Hold up," he said into the phone, then looked at Ramone. "Yeah."

Ramone and Rhonda took one step into the foyer. Ramone badged the man as Rhonda looked over his shoulder, trying to determine if there was anyone else in the house. She thought she heard movement from somewhere in the rear.

"I'm Detective Ramone and this is Detective Willis. Are you Aldan Tinsley?"

"Nah, he's not in at this time."

"Who are you?"

"I'm his cousin."

Ramone tried to match the man in front of him to the photograph he had seen on the sheet. He looked like Aldan Tinsley. He could have been his cousin, too.

"You got some ID?" said Rhonda.

"You still there, girl?" said the man into the phone.

"I'm gonna ask you to end that call, sir," said Ramone.

"I'll hit you back," said the man into his cell. "Police up in here lookin for my cousin."

The man clipped his cell on his belt line.

"Can we see some identification?" said Rhonda.

"What's this regarding?"

"Are you Aldan Tinsley?" said Ramone.

"Look, you got a warrant? 'Cause if not, you stepped into my house, and that's trespassing."

"Are you Aldan Tinsley?" said Ramone.

"Look, fuck y'all, okay? My cousin ain't here."

"Fuck us?" said Ramone. He felt himself smile.

"I'm sayin, this shit ain't right. I really don't have the time for it, so you gonna have to excuse me."

The man tried to close the door. The detectives stood still, and the door swung toward Rhonda and clipped her shoulder, knocking her off balance. Ramone kicked the door back violently and stepped full into the house.

"That's assault," said Ramone.

He grabbed two fistfuls of the man's T-shirt and danced him across the room. He put him up against a wall. The man struggled under Ramone's grasp and tried to twist free, and Ramone lifted him off his feet and tripped him, and as he was falling Ramone put more into it and slammed him down onto the hardwood floor. Ramone heard Rhonda on the radio, calling the patrolman. He reached for his cuffs and turned the man over, noticing the blood on his lips and teeth from when his face had hit the wood. Ramone put his knee in the man's back as he fitted the cuffs to his wrists.

The man muttered something obscene under his breath. Ramone told him to shut his mouth.

An older woman walked into the room. She carried a dinner plate and a rag she had been using to dry it. She stared at the man lying cuffed and bloody on the floor.

"Beano," she said with disappointment in her voice. "What you done now?"

"Is this Aldan Tinsley, ma'am?" said Ramone.

"My son," said the woman.

Ramone looked over at Rhonda, who had not bothered to unholster her Glock. She wiggled her eyebrows at him, the signal that she was fine.

Arturo Conconi came through the front door, his hand on the grip of his sidearm.

"Put this gentleman in the back of your car," said Ramone, "and follow us down to VCB."

"Why'd you have to rough me?" said Tinsley. "You split my lip and shit."

"You shoulda said your name," said Ramone. "We asked you nice."

"Would've saved you some hurt," said Rhonda.

Rhonda apologized to the mother for the trouble. Ramone and Conconi led Tinsley from the house.

THIRTY-ONE

T. C. COOK SAT in his office, several files open before him. The victims of the Palindrome Murders each had their own. He had compiled a fairly complete record of their lives, including photos, both of the family variety and individual and group shots from school. He knew that there were those in the force, especially during his last months of service, who thought he had crossed the border from diligence to obsession. But someone had to be on it.

Cook had stayed directly connected to the case for a couple of years. By the third killing, anger in the Southeast community had focused on the police force, the presumption being that the case was not being prioritized because the victims were black. Cook eventually earned the residents' trust. He had advised a neighborhood citizen task force with tips on how to keep their kids safe. Then concerns about drug murders began to supersede those related to the child killings, which had seemingly stopped, and the talk at the meetings turned to matters regarding gangs, dealers, and crack cocaine. As for the relatives of the victims, they formed a group called Palindrome Parents and met twice a month, more for therapy than anything else. Cook attended these meetings as well.

But after a year or so he lost touch with them. One couple, the mother and father of Ava Simmons, was separated from the start. Another got divorced soon after the murder of their son, Otto Williams. The father of Eve Drake committed suicide on the second anniversary of the discovery of his daughter's body. The mother had become close to catatonic and was committed to a mental institution the following winter.

Cook studied the photographs. Otto Williams, a smart young man who liked to build things, wore eyeglasses, and, despite his nerdy appearance, was popular with his peers. Ava Simmons, thirteen when she was murdered, with the body of a girl in her late teens, funny, sassy by all accounts, not much of a student but street smart, and devoted to her grandmother, who lived in the family's house. And Eve Drake, the double-Dutch girl who had traveled to tournaments and won awards that she proudly displayed in her immaculate room.

Cook felt their presence in the room.

The doorbell rang out. Cook went to the front of the house and let Holiday inside. Holiday was wearing his black suit.

"Why didn't you call me?" said Holiday.

"I c-couldn't get the number right. You need to program it into my speed dial. Might as well do that now."

"Did you talk to your lieutenant friend?"

"I got it. Come on in."

They went into the kitchen. Cook poured Holiday a cup of coffee while Holiday programmed Cook's cell.

"Thanks," said Holiday, as Cook put the cup of coffee before him. "What do you got?"

"The officer's name is Grady Dunne," said Cook. "Six-year veteran. White dude, like you said."

"Is he working tonight?"

"He's on the eight-to-four today. We can catch him clocking out."

"Beautiful," said Holiday. "I've got an airport run that should take me a couple of hours. I can be at the station by four, no problem."

"We just gonna follow him?"

"A double should do it. It's harder to burn a tail like that."

"We'll see what he's about," said Cook.

Holiday reached into each of his jacket side pockets and pulled out two Motorola professional-grade walkie-talkies. He put them on the table.

"I bring these when I'm working a team with my security business," said Holiday. "Six-mile capability. The beauty is, they're voice activated. You can drive and use them at the same time."

"And no numbers for me to mess up."

"We'll be golden."

"I've got some good binoculars in the trunk of my Marquis. Maybe you better take 'em. You can ID him as he comes out of the station."

"Right." Holiday looked at the clock on the wall, its hands off by hours. He got up out of his chair, took the clock down, flipped it over, and reset the time. He matched the hole on the back of it to the nail coming out of the wall and straightened it. "There you go."

It had made Holiday sad to look at the clock as it was. He had reset it for himself, not the old man.

"Makes no difference to me," said Cook. "But thanks."

"So your El Salvador lady knows the correct time."

"All right, friend."

"T.C. . . ."

"What?"

"I talked to Ramone."

"You told me. He wouldn't make the call and find the identity of the patrol car's driver. I wouldn't have done it for you, either, you want the truth."

"It's not that. It's just, I sensed from his voice, the urgency in it, I mean, that he was getting close on the Asa Johnson murder."

"You don't think Asa Johnson's connected to the Palindrome killings, do you?"

"I just don't want you to be disappointed."

"I won't be," said Cook. "It's going to sound callous, I know, but I've had fun these past few days. No, *fun*'s not the right word. I've had purpose. When I've woken up these last couple of mornings, my eyes came wide open; do you know what I mean?"

"Yes."

"So let's just see where this leads us. Okay?"

"Yes, sir."

"And knock off that 'sir' bullshit, too. I never made it past sergeant, young man."

"Right." Holiday took a long swig of his coffee and placed the mug back on the table. "I've got to take off."

"See you at four," said Cook.

He stayed in the kitchen and listened as Holiday closed the front door behind him. Cook could hear the thin voices of the police Internet site, dispatcher to patrolman, coming from his computer. And something else: the faint sound of children laughing. Knowing that it was not possible, knowing, too, that he was not alone.

CONRAD GASKINS SAT ON the edge of his bed, rubbing one finger in small circles on the scar that ran down his cheek. Behind him, atop the sheets, was a duffel bag filled with damn near everything he owned. It was clothes, mostly, the majority being underwear, khakis, and T-shirts he wore to work. He had a couple of button-down shirts and a pair of slacks, but as far as nice shit went, that was it. Clothing, his shaving kit, one pair of sneakers, and the Glock Romeo had given him. He'd get rid of it later, but he wasn't gonna leave that behind. Another weapon was not something his cousin needed.

Too many beers the night before had caused him to sleep through his alarm clock. He had missed the pickup at the shape-up spot for the first time since he'd been lucky enough to find work.

Gaskins had phoned the foreman, the ex-con Christian who had seen fit to give him a chance, on the job site. And after he apologized and pleaded for the man to forgive him, he felt a rush of emotion come to him, and the words poured free.

"I am in a real bad situation here," said Gaskins. "If I don't get free of it I am going to die or get myself sent back to the joint. I don't want to die, and I don't want to kill no one. All's I want is to work an honest day and be paid honest in return."

Gaskins told the foreman, whose name was Paul, a little bit more of his situation but nothing too specific. He told Paul about his aunt Mina, Romeo's mother, and the promise he had made to her to look after her son.

"You've done everything for him that you can do," said Paul. "Grab your gear, walk out that house, and call me when you're ready. I'll meet you down at the end of your road."

"But where I'm gonna stay at?"

"I got a couch. Until you find something, you'll stay with me."

"You can take some money out my pay."

"Forget about that, Conrad. Just call me, hear?"

Gaskins had thought hard on it most of the day. He had made the call and now he was packed and ready to go. He'd considered Mina Brock and what he'd promised. Romeo hadn't even visited her for some time. He, Conrad Gaskins, would be her son now. She'd understand, even if she couldn't say it in words. He knew this, and still he felt guilt.

Gaskins Velcroed the straps of his duffel bag together, picked it up, and walked from the room.

Romeo Brock, not long awake from a nap, heard his cousin's footsteps. He rolled off his mattress and touched his feet to the floor. He stretched and looked at the two Gucci suitcases set beside his dresser. Then he went to the dresser, where he kept his wallet, keys, and cigarettes. He automatically checked that they were there every time he got out of bed.

Also on the dresser were his Gold Cup .45 and his ice pick. The tip of the pick was corked. Romeo liked to tape it to his calf. When he grabbed the handle and pulled it free, the tape naturally knocked off the tip. He might have seen this in a movie, but over time he had convinced himself that he'd thought of it himself. A man wasn't stupid who could invent a system like that.

Brock, shirtless, lit a Kool and tossed the dead match into the tire-shaped ashtray. He slid his wallet into the back pocket of his jeans and walked barefoot from his bedroom. He went down the hall, past his cousin's room, and out into the open living room. Conrad was seated on the couch, his duffel bag at his feet.

Brock took a drag off his cigarette, double-dragged, and let out a long stream of smoke.

"You dippin out?" said Brock.

"I'm done, Romeo."

"You ain't got the heart for it no more."

"Killin and robbing is easy. It's the consequences. . . . I don't want no part of it, man."

"We almost there," said Brock. "Least you can do is stay till we cut it up. Take your share and then, if you want to, go."

"That's blood money. I don't want it. And I don't want to be here to watch you go down."

"*Shit.* Me?"

"You don't think it's gonna happen? Even your boy Red Fury exceeded his grasp. When he was getting stabbed to death in that prison yard, do you think he was boastin? Was he prideful of his rep? Nah, cuz. He was cryin for his mama, most likely. The way all men do in the end."

"But I'm just getting started."

"You already done," said Gaskins. "A guy like you has success against chumps and kids, but there's a ceiling. You make a score like you did the other day, you start spending, and then you got a standard of living to maintain. So you gonna steal bigger and bigger until you step on someone's toes you shouldn't have. That someone then puts a contract out on you and, bam, it's over. Hell, boy, you might already have sealed your fate. You took that girl with you, you made a big mistake. That Broad-ass fella got to know where she works at. Maybe not today or tomorrow, but someday some killer's gonna follow her out to this house. Whoever's fifty grand was you stole, most likely. So, yeah, cousin. You done."

"Good thing I love you, man. I wouldn't let no one else talk to me that way."

"I love you, too. But I can't stay."

Gaskins got up off the couch and hugged Romeo Brock. He broke free and picked up his duffel bag.

"Take care of my mother," said Brock.

"You know I will," said Gaskins. "That's my heart."

Brock watched through the front window as Gaskins passed under the tulip poplar and walked on the gravel road toward Hill.

Brock could still catch up to Conrad if he ran to him now. Talk some sense into him, stop him from leaving. But he stood there instead, smoking his cigarette and tapping its ash to the hardwood floor.

THIRTY-TWO

RAMONE ENTERED THE video monitor room at VCB with a fried-chicken sandwich and can of soda in hand. It was late in the afternoon, and he had not eaten lunch. Rhonda had processed Aldan Tinsley while Ramone made the carry-out run.

Antonelli sat in a chair, his feet up on a table, his ankle holster and Glock fully visible. On screen 1, Bo Green was going at Dominique Lyons, who apparently had been informed of Darcia Johnson's on-camera testimony and cooperation. His face was contorted in anger, and he had been leg-ironed to the stool. Bo Green sat back, his hands folded on his belly, his expression neutral, his voice calm and soft.

"Bo just told Dominique that we've got the man who sold him the gun," said Antonelli. "And that that same gun was the weapon used in a homicide the night before. Check him out. Our boy don't look so pimpin now."

Onscreen, Dominique leaned forward and punched his fist on the table.

"Bullshit," said Dominique. "Y'all can't charge me on no other murder. I ain't stupid enough to buy a gun got a body attached to it."

"Beano told you it was clean?" said Bo Green.

"Damn right that motherfucker did."

"Where'd he get the gun, then?"

"I don't know. Ask *his* punk ass where he got it."

"We plan to," said Green.

Antonelli dropped his feet to the floor and nodded his chin at screen 2, where Rhonda sat with Aldan Tinsley. "Your booster's not saying much."

"He will," said Ramone.

"Rhonda hurt?"

"That door barely touched her. She went back like she'd been hit by a Mack truck."

"Woman's got acting skills."

"Along with everything else."

They watched Rhonda go back and forth with Aldan Tinsley and make no progress. Ramone ate his chicken sandwich with the ferocity of an animal, killed his soda, and tossed the can in the trash.

"Think I'll go in," said Ramone.

Antonelli watched the screen, saw Rhonda turn her head at a knock on the door. Then Ramone entered the box. He had a seat next to his partner and placed his hands on the table.

For the third time that day, Ramone loosened his tie. It was warm in the box, and he could smell his own body odor in the room. He had played basketball in these clothes a few hours earlier. He had wrestled with Tinsley. He felt as if he had been wearing this suit and dress shirt for a week.

"Hello, Aldan," said Ramone.

Aldan Tinsley nodded. His lips were swollen from where he'd hit the floor. He looked like a duck.

"You comfortable?"

"My mouth hurts," said Tinsley. "I think you loosed up one of my teeth."

"Assault on a police officer is a very serious charge."

"I apologized to the detective here. *Did*n't I?"

"You did," said Rhonda.

"I ain't mean to hit her with that door. It's just, I was upset. Y'all ain't say why you were there to see me, and I been having too many run-ins with the law lately. I'm just tired of it. Tired of being harassed, too. But listen, I wasn't lookin to hurt no one."

"Serious as it is," said Ramone, "the assault charge is the least of your worries right now."

"I want a lawyer."

"Dominique Lyons. You know the name?"

"I don't recall it."

"Five minutes ago Dominique Lyons told us that he purchased a gun from you on Wednesday night. A thirty-eight Special. The girl who was with him when he purchased the revolver has confirmed that it was you who made the sale."

Tinsley's lip trembled.

"The gun was used by Lyons in the commission of a homicide later that night."

"You ain't hear me? I *want* . . . a *fuck*ing lawyer."

"I don't blame you," said Ramone. "I'd get a whole team of lawyers, I was you. Felony gun charges, accessory to homicides . . ."

"Man, I ain't did no motherfuckin homicide. I buy things and I sell things. I ain't no killer."

Ramone grinned. "I said *homicides,* Beano."

"Nah. Uh-uh."

"I wonder if you can tell us your whereabouts this past Tuesday night."

"Tuesday night?"

"Tuesday," said Rhonda.

"I visited this girl on Tuesday night," said Tinsley, relief at the change of direction plain on his face.

"What's her name?"

"Flora Tolson. I been knowin her awhile. She can, like, verify that I was there."

"Where?" said Ramone.

"She stay up off Kansas Avenue."

"Where off Kansas?" said Rhonda.

"I don't know exactly. Above Blair Road."

Ramone and Rhonda exchanged a glance.

"What were you doing there?" said Rhonda.

"I was gyratin. What you think?"

"And you left her house what time?"

"It was late. We had a long visit. After midnight, I expect."

"And what, you drove straight home?"

"No, I . . ." Tinsley stopped talking.

"You walked," said Ramone.

"On account of that DWI you're carryin on your sheet," said Rhonda.

"You got no driver's license," said Ramone.

"Gyratin player like you, walkin to your dates," said Rhonda.

"I want a lawyer," said Tinsley.

"And the way you would walk to your home on Milmarson," said Ramone, "is through that community garden they got on Oglethorpe Street."

"Fuck y'all," said Tinsley. "I ain't kill that kid."

"What kid?" said Ramone.

"I'll take a gun charge," said Tinsley. "But not a murder."

Ramone leaned forward. *"What kid?"*

Tinsley's shoulders relaxed. "I *found* that gun."

"Found it where?"

"In that community garden they got on Oglethorpe. I always cut through it when I come back from Flora's. It's the shortest way to my mother's house."

"Tell us what happened."

"I was just walkin through. I came up on this thing, like, lyin in the path. I thought it was a man sleeping, at first. But when I looked down and let my eyes adjust, I saw that it was a boy. His eyes were open and there was blood around his head. It was obvious that he was dead."

"What was he wearing?" said Ramone, hearing the catch in his voice.

"He had on a North Face coat," said Tinsley. "I could make out the symbol they got in the moonlight. That's all I can recall."

"Anything else you remember about him?"

"Well, there was the gun."

"What gun?" said Ramone.

"The thirty-eight revolver that was in the boy's hand."

Ramone made a sound. It was a short, low thing that was close to a moan. Rhonda said nothing. They all listened to the air coming from an overhead vent into the room.

"Did you touch it?" said Ramone.

"I took it," said Tinsley.

"Why?"

"I saw money lyin there," said Tinsley.

"Didn't you realize that you would be destroying evidence at a crime scene?"

"Three hundred dollars was all I could see."

"So you stole it."

"Wasn't like that little nigga was gonna use it again."

Ramone stood out of his chair, his right fist balled.

"Gus," said Rhonda.

Ramone quickly exited the box. Rhonda got up and glanced at her watch.

"Can I get a soda, somethin?" said Tinsley.

Rhonda did not answer. Instead she looked into the camera. "Two forty-three p.m."

She left Tinsley there with his dread and walked into the offices. She found Ramone sitting and talking quietly with Bill

Wilkins by Wilkins's desk. Rhonda put a hand on Ramone's shoulder.

"I'm sorry," she said.

"Why didn't I see it?" said Ramone.

"None of us did," said Rhonda. "No gun on the scene. Any of y'all ever work a gunshot suicide where no weapon was found?"

"Left-handed mitt," said Ramone. "Left-handed, shot in the left temple . . . powder on the fingers of his left hand. He wasn't wearing that North Face because he was showing it off. He was carrying a gun in its pocket. My son saw him and said he was sweating. But he was crying. I shoulda fuckin seen it."

"You gotta admit," said Wilkins, "it's unusual, him killin himself."

"That's not true, Bill," said Rhonda.

"I'm sayin, black kids don't do themselves, generally."

"See, that's wrong," said Rhonda. "Black teenagers do commit suicide. Matter of fact, the suicide rate of black teenagers is on the upswing. One of the benefits of being admitted to the middle and upper class. You know, the cost of money. Not to mention easy access to guns. And a lot of black gay kids just know they're never gonna be accepted. Part of it's that unspoken thing in our culture. Some of my people gonna forgive you for just about anything, except that one thing, you know what I'm saying?"

"Think of how it was for Asa," said Ramone, "living with guilt in that kind of hyper-macho environment."

"He *couldn't* live with it," said Rhonda.

"Anyway," said Ramone, standing.

"Where you goin?" said Rhonda.

"Still a couple of things I need to sort out. Bill, I'll call you with an update later on."

"What about all the processing and paperwork?"

"Your case. Sorry, big guy. I'll talk to the father, if it's any consolation."

"Charges on Tinsley?" said Rhonda.

"Charge that motherfucker with everything," said Ramone. "I'll find a way to make it stick."

"We did some good work here today," said Rhonda.

"We did," said Ramone, looking at her with admiration. "I'll talk to you all later, hear?"

Out in the parking lot, Ramone phoned Holiday's cell. Holiday answered and said that he was out by National Airport, dropping off a client.

"Can you meet me?" said Ramone. "I gotta talk to you in private."

"There's someplace I need to be," said Holiday.

"I'll come to you right now. Gravelly Point, by the airport. The small lot on the southbound lane."

"Hurry up," said Holiday. "I don't have all fuckin day."

THIRTY-THREE

THE MAIN AREA of Gravelly Point, on the Potomac River and accessible from the northbound lanes of the GW Parkway, was a popular spot for joggers, boat launchers, rugby players, bicyclists, and plane watchers, as the runway of Reagan National was only a few hundred yards away. On the opposite, less picturesque side of the parkway was a small parking lot, used mainly by limo and car service drivers waiting for airport clients.

Dan Holiday leaned against his Town Car in the smaller lot. He watched as Gus Ramone's Tahoe pulled alongside his Lincoln. Ramone got out of his SUV and came to where Holiday stood. Holiday took mental note of Ramone's disheveled appearance.

"Thanks for seeing me," said Ramone.

"What'd you do, sleep in that suit?"

"I earned my money today."

Holiday removed a deck of Marlboros from his jacket. He shook a cigarette free and offered it to Ramone.

"No thanks. I quit it."

Holiday lit one for himself and blew a little smoke in the direction of Ramone. "Still smells good, though, doesn't it?"

"I need a favor, Doc."

"Seems to me I called you earlier today and asked for a favor. But you wouldn't help me out."

"You know I couldn't give you the name of that officer."

"I said *wouldn't*."

"No difference, to me."

"The straight man," said Holiday.

"It's moot now, anyway," said Ramone. "Asa Johnson was a suicide. His death had no connection to the Palindrome Murders."

Holiday dragged on his cigarette. "I'm disappointed. But I can't say that I'm surprised."

"Cook's gonna take it hard. I know he thought that this would reopen the case. That this murder would somehow solve the others."

"It's gonna crush him."

"I'll tell him," said Ramone.

"*I* will," said Holiday.

"Doc?"

"What?"

"That officer's name is Grady Dunne."

"You're too late. We got it already."

"Look, I'll find out why he was down there that night. Maybe it will help with the prosecution."

"Don't forget the perp in the backseat," said Holiday.

"Could have been a teenage suspect," said Ramone. "Or maybe it was just a lady friend."

"You think?"

"You tell me."

"Because I got a history of that," said Holiday. "That's what you're sayin?"

Ramone didn't answer.

"You never did ask me about Lacy," said Holiday.

"I would have. You turned in your badge instead."

"It was your screwup," said Holiday. "You should have grand juried her instead of giving her time to skip."

"I know it."

"The day your informant saw me talking to her, before she disappeared? The conversation wasn't about your dirty vice cops or anything else to do with your IAD case."

"What was it about?"

"Fuck you, Gus."

"I'm interested. You been wanting to tell me. So why don't you go ahead and get rid of it?"

"I gave her some money," said Holiday. "Five hundred dollars. Bus fare back to whatever Bumfuck, Pennsylvania, address she came from and some extra to get started. I was trying to save her life. 'Cause her pimp, Mister Morgan, would have found a way to cut her to shreds whether he was tied up with the law or not. He was that kind of asshole. But you wouldn't have known that, working behind your desk. If you had talked to me, man-to-man, you might have understood."

"You tanked my case. We never did get to prosecute those vice cops. And Morgan killed a dude six months later. All you did was fuck things up."

"I was helping that girl."

"That's not all you were doing with her. She told me all about it in one of our interviews. So don't get all high and mighty on me, all right?"

"I helped her," said Holiday. But he said it weakly and he couldn't look Ramone in the eye.

"I'm sorry, Doc," said Ramone. "I took no pleasure in what happened to you."

Ramone watched the sunlight shimmer off the water to the right of the lot, the river runoff that formed a pond. Holiday took a last hit of his cigarette and crushed it under his shoe.

"So what's the favor?" said Holiday.

"It's complicated. Asa Johnson's gun was stolen by a guy named Aldan Tinsley after Asa committed suicide. Aldan sold the gun to a Dominique Lyons, who used it in a homicide the following night. I got a confession out of Tinsley, but I shit the bed in the process. I roughed up Tinsley pretty bad, and I ignored his request for a lawyer three times. When the defense attorneys get ahold of this, and the testimonies mutate, I could have a problem. These are bad guys, and I'd like to see them go away."

"You need what?"

"I need you to positively identify Aldan Tinsley as the man you saw walking across the garden that night."

"I told you, all I saw was a Number One Male. I can't remember anything about him except that he was black."

"I don't care what you saw, Doc. I'm telling you, that's what I need."

Holiday grinned. "You ain't so straight."

"Will you do it?"

"Yeah."

"Thanks. I'll bring you in for the ID."

Ramone pivoted, heading for his car.

"Gus?"

"What?"

"I apologize for what I said about your wife. I hear she's good people. That was the alcohol talking."

"Don't worry about it."

"I'm envious, I guess."

"Okay . . ."

"A family just isn't in the cards for me." Holiday squinted against the sun. "You know, back when I was in uniform I was ordered to go see the department shrink. My lieutenant recommended it because of my drinking and what he called my excessive womanizing. He said my lifestyle was interfering with my job performance."

"Imagine that."

"So I'm there at the voodoo office, and I'm talking about my personal history. The shrink says, 'It occurs to me that you have a fear of separation,' or some bullshit like that, on account of I was fucked up for so long after my little sister passed. He's telling me that I tend to run away from lasting relationships because I'm afraid that I might, how did he put it, *lose my partner to circumstances beyond my control.* And I say to the shrink, 'That might be true. Or it might just be that I like strange pussy.' Do you think that's what it is, Gus?"

"And here I was," said Ramone, "thinking you were going to tell me a nice story, with one of those, you know, morals at the end of it."

"Some other time." Holiday glanced at his watch. "I gotta get out of here."

Ramone put out his hand and Holiday took it.

"You were good police, Doc. No bullshit."

"I know it, Giuseppe. Way better than you."

Ramone watched as Holiday opened the door to his Lincoln, reached in and got his chauffeur's hat, and placed it on his head.

"Asshole," said Ramone under his breath.

But he was smiling.

MICHAEL TATE AND ERNEST Henderson, well fed, waited in the lot of the Hair Raisers on Riggs Road until Chantel Richards emerged from the shop and got into a red Toyota Solara.

"Nice car," said Tate.

"For a girl," said Henderson. "What, you want one now?"

"I'm sayin, it's got style. Figures that she would be rockin it."

Chantel drove it across the lot and out the exit lane.

"Be real hard for her to lose us," said Tate. "Seein as how red it is."

" 'Less you let her."

"Huh?"

"What you waitin on?"

"I'm about to go."

"You ain't gone yet?"

They followed her into Maryland, through Langley Park and up New Hampshire Avenue. She got onto the Beltway and took it deep through Prince George's County. Nesto Henderson had been right. The color of the Solara made it an easy tail.

Chantel got off at the westbound ramp of Central Avenue and after a mile or so made a right onto Hill Road. Tate, behind the wheel, hung back, as the traffic had thinned. When Chantel parked behind another vehicle, on the berm at the crest of a rise, past a residential cluster that stopped at a large stand of trees, Tate slowed and put the Maxima to the shoulder a hundred yards back.

"What she doin," said Henderson, "walkin into the woods?"

"Nah, that's gravel. Can't you see it? Some kind of road."

"There's a car parked in front of her."

"Impala SS."

"Could be that it's our man's car. Could be he stayin in a house back in there."

"Okay, then," said Tate. "We did our thing. We followed her and we know where she at. Let's go back and tell Raymond."

"We ain't done." Henderson pulled his cell and began to dial in a number. "Ray's gonna want to come out."

"For what?"

"Get his money. That boy Romeo took him off for fifty." Henderson waited for the ring tone. "Ray Benjamin's quiet till you scheme him. He gonna get serious behind this."

Michael Tate's mouth went dry. He was thirsty, and he

wanted to run away. At the very least, he needed to be out of this car.

"While you talk to Ray," said Tate, "I'll go up in those woods, see what I can see."

"Right," said Henderson, just as Benjamin came on the line.

RAMONE PARKED HIS TAHOE on the 6000 block of Georgia Avenue, north of Piney Branch Road. He walked down the sidewalk, then turned right and took a few steps up to the iron gate that fronted the Battleground National Cemetery. Ramone lifted the latch on the gate, pushed it open, and stepped between two six-pound smoothbore guns and onto the grounds.

He went down a concrete walkway, past an old stone house that was a residence, and several large headstones, and continuing on to the centerpiece of the cemetery, an American flag flying from atop a pole surrounded by forty-one grave markers. There lay the Union soldiers who had died at the battle of Fort Stevens. Outside points of the circle were four poems mounted on brass plates, set up on stands. Ramone went to one of the plates and read its inscription:

THE MUFFLED DRUM'S SAD ROLL HAS BEAT
THE SOLDIER'S LAST TATTOO;
NO MORE ON LIFE'S PARADE SHALL MEET
THAT BRAVE AND FALLEN FEW.

Ramone looked around. It was quiet here, an acre of grass, trees, and spare commemoration in an urban environment. Despite the country atmosphere, the cemetery was visible from a highly traveled thoroughfare to the west and, on the eastward side, the residential block of Venable Place. There were less risky locations to meet partners. Ramone didn't think Asa would have come here for sex. It was probably the closest spot to his house where he could escape his home life and neighborhood and find a little peace.

Asa had told the Spriggs twins that he was headed for the Lincoln-Kennedy Monument. He had wanted them to remember it. He had wanted someone to find something he had left behind, and it had to be here.

Ramone went back to the entrance to the cemetery, where the large headstones sat, four in a row. And there he saw that they were not traditional headstones but monuments to Army Corps, Volunteer Cavalry, and National Guard Units from Ohio, New York, and Pennsylvania.

One monument that was topped with a peaked cap stood taller than the rest. Ramone stood before it and read its face: "To the Gallant Sons of Onondaga County, N.Y., who fought on this field July 12, 1864, in Defence of Washington and in the presence of Abraham Lincoln."

Ramone stepped around the monument's side. On it were listed the names of the killed and wounded. Among those listed was the name John Kennedy.

He looked at the ground surrounding the monument. He kicked at it. He went behind the monument and studied the turf and saw that a square of it had been placed or replaced there. He got down on one knee and lifted the square of turf. In the dirt beneath it lay a large plastic ziplock bag, the size used for marinating a piece of meat. A book with no letters on its cover or spine was in the bag.

Ramone took Asa's journal out of the bag. He went to a maple tree in the corner of the grounds, sat down in its shade, leaned his back against the maple's trunk, and opened the journal.

He began to read. Time passed, and the shadows in the cemetery lengthened and crawled toward his feet.

THIRTY-FOUR

DAN HOLIDAY SAT behind the wheel of his Town Car, parked on Peabody, watching the entry and exit space of the lot behind the 4th District station. T. C. Cook was up on Georgia, his Marquis along the curb and pointed north. He wore his faded brown Stetson with the multicolored feather in the chocolate band. He had put on a houndstooth sport jacket and a tie.

They had set the frequencies of their voice-activated Motorolas, and the radios were live. They had been there for the better part of an hour.

"Anything?" said Cook.

"He's gotta come outta there soon."

Using Cook's binoculars, Holiday had scoped Officer Grady Dunne pulling into the lot in car number 461 and watched him, in full uniform, walk into the station's back entrance. He was a six footer, lean and pale, blond and sharp featured. There was a practiced, military-issue confidence in his straight posture and step. He had not stopped to talk to his fellow officers who were hanging around at the shift change, shooting the shit and haggling over the most coveted cruisers.

"You see Detective Ramone?" said Cook.

"Yeah, I saw him."

"He update you on the Johnson case?"

"We talked about it." Holiday hesitated for a moment. "Nothing concrete yet."

The silence from the radio told Holiday that Cook knew this was a lie.

Two young men walked by Holiday's car. They wore shorts reaching to their calves, the edges deliberately frayed. The sleeves on one of the boys' T-shirts had been cut into strips and braided, the braids ending in tiny balls. There was a character drawn in glitter on the front of the shirt. The faces of the young men were identical. One of them smiled at Holiday as they passed. Holiday believed that despite his black suit and car, they had tagged him as some kind of police. That pleased him.

In the Marquis, T. C. Cook wiped sweat off his forehead. He had been feeling a little dizzy. He wasn't used to working, is all it was. The anticipation of the chase had ticked up his blood.

"Doc?"

"Yes."

"It's hot in this damn car. I'm sweatin, man."

"Drink some water," said Holiday.

He looked through the binoculars as the blond man came out of the station's rear door and walked toward a late-model deep green Ford Explorer. Dunne wore an oversize polo shirt out over jeans and wheat-colored work boots. Department regulations required officers to wear their gun at all times, even off duty. From the size of the shirt, Holiday assumed that Dunne's Glock was holstered at the small of his back.

"Get ready, Sarge. He's in his car and he's about to pull out."

"Right."

"If he goes north, I'll let you take point. Keep your cell on, in case these radios fail."

"Got it, young man."

"He's on Peabody," said Holiday. "He's coming up to Georgia."

"Copy."

As the Explorer turned right and headed up Georgia Avenue, Holiday said, "You."

They followed Dunne up the avenue. Cook kept himself back behind several cars but stayed on the Explorer, blowing yellows and one red light to do so. Holiday's mission was to keep Cook's Marquis in sight and in that way trust that Dunne was not far ahead. By radio, Holiday learned that Cook was on it.

Dunne crossed over the District line into downtown Silver Spring, a virtual canyon of growing congestion consisting of tall buildings, chain restaurants, new lampposts fashioned to appear antique, a brick street, and other town-center affectations. Dunne turned right on Elsworth and then hung a left into a parking garage.

"What should I do?" said Cook, holding the two-way in front of his mouth.

"Park on the street and relax," said Holiday. "I'll take it now and get back to you."

Holiday passed Cook, pulling into a space on Elsworth, and drove into the garage. He took a ticket at the gate and went up a ramp, going level to level until he saw the Explorer pulling into a space high in the structure. Holiday parked and watched Dunne as he got out of the Ford and went to a concrete bridge that ran between the garage and a newly constructed hotel.

To Holiday, hotels were for women and alcohol. He waited for ten minutes and then put on his chauffeur's cap and walked the footbridge, taking the same path as Dunne.

Holiday entered the hotel. The garage entrance led to a hall and a business office and then gave to an open area with a reception desk, sitting area, and bar. Dunne was at the bar, a glass of something clear before him. He was obviously alone, though there were others seated at the stick. Dunne's back was to Holiday, and so he moved with confidence to the sitting area nearby and took a cushioned chair near a small table holding magazines. It would not be unusual for a driver to be here, waiting on a client to come down from his or her room. Holiday opened a magazine and kept an eye on Dunne.

He's drinking vodka, thought Holiday.

It's got no smell. But it does. And it shows on you, too. You're sitting in a bland hotel bar because you're that kind of police. You've got no friends, other than your fellow cops, and you're not too sure about them. No family and no home to speak of. An apartment, but that doesn't count. You're alone when you're not riding your district. You've got nowhere to go. You're lost.

"Is everything all right, sir?" said a young man with a hotel name tag pinned to his chest. He had come up on Holiday and was standing before him with his fingers laced together.

"I'm waiting on a client," said Holiday.

"Would you like to use our desk phone to call him?"

"He'll be along."

Dunne finished his drink quickly, ordered another, and started in on it with intent. He had not turned around. With the exception of the bartender, he had not tried to make conversation with any of the people around him.

From across the room, Holiday waited and watched.

"WHERE YOUR COUSIN AT?" said Chantel Richards.

"Conrad's gone," said Romeo Brock. "He ain't comin back."

"Why?"

Brock tucked in the tails of his shirt.

Chantel had come from work and found Brock in the bedroom at the back of the house. He was buttoning his red rayon shirt, standing by the dresser as she walked inside. His gun was atop the dresser, along with a box of bullets, a pack of Kools, matches, a cell. Beside the dresser were the two Gucci suitcases. The one on the right held fifty thousand dollars. The one on the left held Chantel's clothes.

"Why he leave, Romeo?"

"He thinks we gonna have some trouble," said Brock. "He might be right."

"What kind of trouble?"

"The kind involves men and guns. But look, we gonna be fine."

"I didn't sign up for this," said Chantel.

"Sure you did," said Brock. "When you walked out of Fat Tommy's with me you bought a ticket for the full ride. But it's gonna be a good one, and we ain't even started yet. You know who Red and Coco was, don't you?"

"No."

"Well, that story's too long to tell. But I know you heard of Bonnie and Clyde."

"Uh-huh."

"Woman stood by her man, didn't she? They lived right and took no one's shit."

"But they died in the end, Romeo."

"It's how they rode on the way there." Romeo walked over to Chantel and kissed her soft lips. "Can't no one kill me, girl. Not till I made my rep. My name's gonna ring out strong before anything happens to me."

"I'm scared."

"Don't be." Brock stepped back. "I'm gonna go make a call, and then I'm gonna sit out there in the living room. You lock the door behind me and don't worry about a thing. We straight?"

"Yes, Romeo."

"That's my girl. My very own Coco."

He took his cigarettes, matches, and cell off the dresser and stashed them in various pockets. He picked up the Colt and the brick of ammunition and walked from the room.

Chantel thumbed in the push-lock on the doorknob and turned on the bedside clock radio, set on KYS. If she was going to cry, she didn't want Romeo to hear it. She had a seat on the edge of the bed. She laced her fingers together and rubbed one thumb over the other, and looked out the window to the small backyard bordered by a forest of maple, oak, and pine. If she could find the backbone, she'd run into those woods. But her courage didn't come, and she stayed in place, rubbing at her hands.

GUS RAMONE SAT IN Leo's, drinking a Beck's, his notebook on the bar. It was unusual for him to go anywhere but back to his family after work. He liked this place and the off-beat neighborhood crowd. That was part of why he'd come. The other part was, he just didn't feel like going home. He knew he'd have to talk to Diego. But he wasn't ready to tell him about Asa just yet.

Two men were beside him, talking about the song that was coming from the juke. They stopped to sing the chorus, and when the verse came they resumed their discussion.

"'Closed for the Season,'" said the first man. "Brenda Holloway."

"That's Bettye Swann," said the second. "Brenda Holloway did that song that Blood, Sweat and Tears made famous."

"I don't care if she did one for Pacific Gas and Electric. This is Brenda singin right here."

"Bettye Swann. And if I'm wrong, I'll kiss the star on your dog's ass."

"How 'bout you kiss mines?"

Ramone drank from the bottle and swallowed cold beer. Asa's journal occupied his thoughts.

There was no question now concerning the cause of death. Asa's last entry in the journal had been made on the day of his passing and was a veritable suicide note. He couldn't live up to his father's expectations. He hated his father and loved him. He was certain that he had been born gay and equally certain that his desires would never change. He couldn't bear the thought of his father's reaction if he were to find out. He didn't want to think about facing his friends. Asa could no longer live with who he was. He prayed that God would give him the courage to pull the trigger when the time came. He knew a quiet place were he could do it. He knew where he could get a gun. Death would be a relief.

The passages in the journal detailing Asa's homosexual experiences had unsettled Ramone. Asa had experimented first with phone sex and then, through the Internet and ads placed in local alternative papers, he had met men at predetermined locations near his home. At the end, he was seeing a partner, considerably older than he, whom he identified only as RoboMan. Asa wrote that this man was infatuated with him. For his part, Asa did not speak of his emotional feelings but rather the physical aspect of their relationship. They had engaged in oral and anal sex. There was no indication of rape or coercion. Ramone had to assume that the sex had been consensual. Consensual, perhaps. But not legal, given Asa's age.

Ramone opened his notebook on the bar. He began to read through the pertinent remarks he had recorded during his interviews.

RoboMan.

RoboCop. That was the first thought that came to Ramone. Could Asa's lover have been Dunne, the police officer he'd met at the crime scene? The same officer Holiday had seen driving by the garden the night he'd discovered Asa's body?

Then Ramone read something that he'd written just yesterday.

"Defensive," said Ramone, his voice unheard under the Bettye Swann vocal and sweet horns filling the room.

He raised one finger, caught the attention of the bartender, and ordered another beer.

He'd sit here at Leo's and drink this one slow. The next order of business was the gun.

THIRTY-FIVE

RAYMOND BENJAMIN PULLED over behind the Maxima on Hill Road and waited for Michael Tate and Ernest Henderson to come to him. He had phoned Henderson, told him he was nearby, and told him and Tate to bring their guns and get in his car when he arrived. He watched as they approached, Henderson with confidence in his step, ready to put work in. Tate looking more like a young man about to go clubbing or attend a fashion show than an enforcer.

Benjamin had been tight with Tate's older brother, a man named William who went by Dink, when both of them were full in the game. Dink had stood tall at Benjamin's trial, and because of that Benjamin had drawn a light sentence. Someone had rolled on Dink, so he took the full federal jolt, his lack of cooperation on the stand an added negative factor at his sentencing. Benjamin would never forget what Dink had done for him. He sent a little money to Dink's mother regularly and had put his younger brother Mikey on, even though he was unsuited for this type of work. He used Tate mainly in the car business. He took Tate with him to auction up in Jersey and allowed him to detail the vehicles before delivery. He had never used him for anything like this.

Tate and Henderson got into the backseat of Benjamin's S500. It was an immaculate, roomy, black-over-tan Mercedes with two DVD screens, well appointed with real wood and fine leather. Benjamin needed the space, as he was a very tall, broad-shouldered man.

"Talk about it," said Benjamin.

"Girl took that gravel road on foot," said Henderson. "Mikey went up there through the woods. He can tell you what he saw."

"Two houses," said Tate. "One at the head of the road, one far back. She went into the house at the back."

"Anyone in that first house?"

"Not that I could see. Wasn't no cars there."

"Looks like they all park out here, anyway," said Benjamin.

" 'Cause there ain't no way out back there," said Tate. "It dead-ends."

"Man's bein careful," said Benjamin, his eyes in the rearview on Tate. "Can you get there through the woods?"

"Either side is trees, all the way to the second house. Behind it, too."

"I'm not about steppin through those woods in the evening," said Benjamin. He feared no man but was frightened of snakes.

"We can wait," said Henderson. "Another hour it'll be full dark; we can walk right up the road."

"We need to do this now," said Benjamin. "I don't want to be sittin out here with guns in the car. Y'all are tooled up, right?"

"We're ready," said Henderson, lifting up his blue shirt and showing the checkered grip of a nine-millimeter Beretta holstered under his jeans. Tate nodded but did not feel the need to show Benjamin his gun.

"Okay, then," said Benjamin, still looking at Tate. "Mikey, you go on in. I'm gonna have you cover the back of the house."

"I can do that."

"That girl or anyone else comes out back, you know what needs to be done."

"You don't have to worry about me, Ray."

"Go on, then. When it's over, buck and run. We'll meet back here at the cars."

Benjamin and Henderson watched as Tate jogged down Hill Road and then cut right into the woods.

"He don't have it," said Henderson.

"But you do," said Benjamin.

Henderson burned with pride. "I'm hyped, Ray. For real."

"These motherfuckers took me off and shot my nephew."

"Said I was ready."

"Hold that attitude for ten minutes," said Benjamin. "Let youngun get to his position. Then we'll go in."

HOLIDAY AND COOK TAILED Grady Dunne back down into the District after he left the hotel bar. This time Holiday was on point. They speculated via radio as to Dunne's destination. He was taking his time moving through the city. He had made his way to Kenilworth Avenue, and then Minnesota, into Southeast.

"He's headed out of town," said Holiday, as Dunne got off Minnesota Avenue and hit East Capitol toward the Maryland line.

East Capitol became Central Avenue far inside the Beltway in Prince George's County. They were on the border of Seat Pleasant and Capitol Heights. They passed new developments, older homes, strip malls, young men walking down the road. It was less a suburb than an extension of Southeast, D.C.

Holiday eased the gas and faded back. Then he saw Dunne's turn signal and watched as he made a left into a gas-and-convenience mart up ahead.

"Holy shit," said Holiday into the radio.

"What's going on?"

"Get in your right lane and follow me into the lot of that strip mall."

As Cook got closer, he saw the convenience market, and Dunne's Explorer stopping at a pump.

"Goddamn right," said Cook. "That's where Reginald Wilson works."

"Hurry up and pull over."

Cook drove into the lot of the run-down strip mall. He pulled into a space alongside Holiday, facing Central Avenue. Holiday got out of the Town Car with binoculars in hand and slid into the Marquis beside Cook. Cook was sweating and his eyes were bright.

"I knew it," said Cook.

"We don't know anything yet," said Holiday, looking through the glasses as Dunne pumped gas into the Ford.

"Wilson's in there," said Cook. "There's his Buick, parked beside the market."

"Okay, he's in there. That doesn't mean the two of them are connected. For all we know, Dunne just stopped to get some gas."

"So, what, we're gonna do nothing?"

"No." Holiday lowered the binoculars and put them on the seat next to Cook. "Take these. Keep your eyes on the market."

"Where you going?"

"I'm gonna stay on Dunne. Figure out a way to talk to him. He'll be off guard. . . . It's the best time."

"And I'm supposed to, what, sit here on my behind?"

"Make sure Wilson doesn't go anywhere," said Holiday, who didn't want Cook slowing him down. "If he does, tail him."

"Stay in radio contact?"

"If I brace Dunne, I'm turning my walkie off. I don't want him to know I'm working with anyone. I'll report back to you when I'm done."

"All right."

Holiday looked at Cook, his shirt damp with sweat. "Why don't you take that jacket off, Sarge?"

"I'm working, young man."

"Suit yourself."

"Doc?" Cook extended his hand, and Holiday gripped it. "Thank you."

"Forget it," said Holiday. He left the Marquis and got into his Lincoln. He drove to the strip mall's exit and let the Town Car idle.

Dunne had entered the market. A few minutes later, he emerged from its front door, talking on his cell as he headed for his Ford. Cook watched him pull out of the lot, and he watched as Holiday waited patiently and fell in behind him on Central Avenue. Then both of them were gone.

Cook leaned his arm on the lip of the driver's-side window and put the binoculars to his eyes. He lowered them and stared at the Buick in the lot. He knew that Holiday had not told the truth about Ramone's progress. Ramone had broken through on the Johnson case, most likely. Now Holiday was pursuing Grady Dunne alone because he felt that he, Cook, was an old man. Too old to police. Baggage on a tail. Cook wasn't going to sit here and watch a parked car. Reginald Wilson wasn't going anywhere. He sure wasn't going home anytime soon. That's why Cook needed to get hisself over to Wilson's house. Make something happen now, show these younger men that he still had game.

Cook turned off his walkie and cell. He didn't want to talk to Holiday or anyone else. He'd had his fill of technology for one day. He ignitioned the Marquis and drove out of the lot.

Out on Central Avenue, Holiday kept four cars back from Dunne. Dunne stayed in his right lane and kept the SUV to ten miles over the speed limit. Holiday could see that he was still on the phone. He was preoccupied with the cell, an easy tail, and Holiday was confident that he would remain undetected until Dunne reached his destination. But Holiday had already decided that he would not let Dunne get that far.

He accelerated, even as Dunne slowed to observe a red light ahead. Holiday pulled up beside him in the left lane, stopped, and rolled down his passenger window. He gave his horn a short punch.

Dunne, his window open, looked over with expressionless eyes. "What?"

"Your right rear tire's about to go flat," said Holiday. "Just lettin you know."

Dunne did not thank him for the information. He said something into the mic of his cell phone, ended the call, and dropped the unit on the bucket to his right.

At the green, Dunne took off and soon pulled over to the side of the road, where a crab shack had been set up near a widened shoulder. Holiday followed and parked his Town Car behind Dunne's SUV. He turned off his radio and cell. Dunne was already out of his vehicle, checking his tire. Holiday exited the Lincoln and walked toward him. He reached for his wallet, and when Dunne glanced over and saw this, he instinctively touched the gun holstered at the small of his back.

He did not pull it. Instead, he stood and spread his feet. He was thin and taller than Holiday by a couple of inches. His blond hair was cropped short, and his eyes were a very light blue.

"Hey," said Holiday, his open wallet in hand. "No worries. I just want to show you my ID."

"Why?"

"Let me explain—"

"This tire's fine," said Dunne. "Why'd you tell me it was flat?"

"Name's Dan Holiday." He flashed Dunne his driver's license and made sure he saw the old FOP card fitted beside it. "MPD, retired. You're police, too, right?"

Dunne looked over at the Hispanic man working the crab shack, taking an order from a man through a drop-window set in a trailer. He returned his attention to Holiday.

"What do you want?"

"Oglethorpe Street, Northeast. The community garden. I was there after midnight, the early hours of Wednesday. I saw you with someone in the back of your patrol car."

Dunne's eyes registered recognition. "And?"

"You must know that a boy's body was found in that garden later that morning."

"What'd you do, follow me here?"

"That's right. I followed you."

Dunne's lip curled up into something like a smile. "The drunken chauffeur, sleeping one off. I remember you."

"And I you."

"What is this, a shakedown? Because I'll go to my superiors and tell them I was there before I give you a fuckin cent. I've got nothing to hide."

"I don't want money."

"Then what's your malfunction?"

"A kid was killed. I'm looking for answers."

"What are you, one of those jagoffs, listens to the scanner all day?"

"Did you know about the boy when you were there that night?"

Dunne shook his head slowly. "No. I found out the next day."

"Why didn't you come forward when he was found?"

"What for?"

" 'Cause you're police."

"I just told you; I wasn't aware of it at the time. So I had no information to contribute to the case."

"If you saw me parked there," said Holiday, "and you read me as drunk, why didn't you stop and roust me?"

"I was busy."

"What were you doing on a dead-end street with a passenger in your vehicle?"

"Who *are* you?"

"A concerned citizen."

"Go fuck yourself."

"What were you doing on that street?"

"Bustin my load into some whore's mouth. You happy?"

"You're no cop," said Holiday with naked disgust.

Dunne laughed and stepped close to Holiday. Holiday detected the sad and familiar smell of breath mint over vodka coming off of Dunne.

"Anything else?" said Dunne.

"Do you know a Reginald Wilson?"

Holiday looked into Dunne's eyes. There was nothing there, no recognition at all.

"Who?"

"The gas-and-go you just came from. Do you know the man working behind the counter?"

"Listen, asshole. I have no idea what you're talking about. I pulled into a station at random and bought some gas."

"What did the clerk look like?"

"Some kind of sand nigger, I guess. Who else works in those places? I didn't even notice him."

Holiday believed him. He felt his energy drain out.

"You're gonna be called in and questioned for Oglethorpe Street," said Holiday.

"So?"

"I'll see you around."

Dunne jabbed a finger into Holiday's chest. "You're seein me now."

Holiday didn't respond.

Dunne smiled through clenched teeth. "You wanna try me?"

Holiday kept his hands at his side.

"I didn't think so," said Dunne.

Dunne walked back to his Ford, got under the wheel, and drove away. Holiday stared at the Explorer's taillights until they faded from view. Then he went to his Town Car and drove back toward the gas station.

Dunne was a rotten apple. But he hadn't been involved with Asa Johnson and he didn't know Reginald Wilson.

It was over. He needed to tell the old man.

THIRTY-SIX

MICHAEL TATE MADE his way through the woods. Dusk was settling, and the trees and branches had lost their color and now were slate outlines against a gray sky. The forest was not dense, and he could see the house from his path. He walked with care and patience and made little sound.

He had a gun, a cheap Taurus nine that Nesto had sold him, holstered at his back. He didn't know what he was going to do when he got behind the house. But he did know that he wasn't going to shoot a girl.

In Raymond Benjamin's mind, Michael Tate was in his debt. Benjamin sent Tate's mother money every month. He had given Tate a job, even though Tate was not needed and did little more than apply tire shine and wheel cleaner to newly purchased cars. Benjamin believed that Tate owed him and that now it was time for Tate to go all in and commit the ultimate rite of passage, the taking of a life via a gun.

But in Tate's mind, he owed Benjamin nothing. Because Tate's older brother, Dink, had refused to testify at Benjamin's trial, Dink would be incarcerated for the next twenty years and come out a middle-aged man with zero prospects. The money sent monthly to their mother, a couple hundred dollars, didn't pay her grocery bills. No matter the amount, it could never compensate her for the loss of her son. Now Benjamin was about to bring Michael full into the life, as he had done with Dink long ago.

Michael had seen the results of such a move, in his family and in so many others where he'd come up. He wasn't about to step off that ledge. Besides, he didn't believe that killing turned a boy into a man. That was street wisdom, which most times equaled bullshit. The violent game had broken his mother's heart and stolen his brother's youth. That was all he needed to know. It wasn't gonna happen to him.

Tate found himself at the tree line behind the house. A light was on in one of the rear windows. He could see the top half of the woman. Some of her curly hair had come down about her shoulders. She was sitting, rubbing one hand against the other. She was a dark outline of a woman in a room, framed by the window, trapped inside that square. What was that word Tate was looking for . . . a *silhouette.* A silhouette of a woman, stressed and beautiful. Like a stressed and beautiful thing caged in a room.

Tate walked slowly out of the woods, toward the back of the house.

Chantel Richards felt a presence and looked up to a see a shadowy figure moving toward the window. She glanced at the locked bedroom door. She knew that she should open it and shout out to Romeo. Because surely this was one of those who had come to cause Romeo a world of hurt. But she didn't do this. Instead she watched as the young man's face came into view, and then studied it as he put it very close to the glass. She saw in his brown eyes that he was not there to hurt her, and she went to the sash window and pushed up on it so the two of them could talk.

"Chantel?"

"Keep your voice down."

"You *are* Chantel," said Tate, now speaking just above a whisper.

"That's right."

"My name's Michael."

"You come to kill us?"

"If you stay here, it's gonna happen."

"Then why ain't you shootin yet?"

"I'm giving you a chance to get out before it gets hot."

Chantel looked back into the room. Tate saw that her hand was shaking and he reached into the open window and held it.

"Come on, girl," said Tate. "What's gonna happen is gonna happen whether you stay or not. If you do stay, you *will* die."

"I need to get my suitcase," said Chantel.

"And the key to your whip," said Tate.

Tate watched her go to a dresser up against the far wall of the bedroom, where she looked down at something on the floor. She hesitated, then bent forward and came up with a suitcase in her hand. She returned to the window, and he took the suitcase from her and helped her out, taking her in his arms and easing her down until her feet softly hit the ground.

He looked at her feet. She was wearing a pair of single-band, leopard-print slides with three-inch heels. He had seen a photograph of this exact shoe in a magazine.

"We headin for the woods," said Tate. "Ain't you got nothing else in that suitcase you can put on your feet? Those Donald Pliners must go for two and a half."

"I didn't pack any other shoes," said Chantel, now looking at him with interest. "How you know these were Pliners?"

"I'm what you call fashion forward," said Tate. "Don't worry, I'm not funny or nothin like that."

"I didn't get that vibe."

"Let's go," said Tate, pulling on her elbow, guiding her toward the tree line.

"You better have a plan," said Chantel.

Michael Tate's plan was to sit far back in the woods and wait till the mayhem began. Then he and Chantel would get themselves down to Hill Road and take off in Chantel's Solara. To where, he didn't know.

"Trust me, girl," said Tate.

Her hand squeezed his as they entered the woods.

OFFICER GRADY DUNNE DROVE slowly up Hill Road. As he neared the turn to Romeo Brock's place, he noticed the numerous cars. There was Brock's SS, and the red Toyota that Brock had said was owned by the girl. And, much farther back, an S-series Mercedes and a new-style Maxima. Dunne pulled over and killed the engine. He thought of phoning Brock on his cell but decided against it. If the owners of the cars were the men who had come to reclaim their money, as Brock had predicted, they might already be in the house. Dunne would go with surprise.

He reached behind him, unholstered his MPD-issue Glock 17, and slipped it under the Explorer's seat. There he found his latest throw-down weapon, a ten-shot Heckler & Koch .45 with shaved numbers that he had taken off a suspect in Park View. He holstered it where his departmental Glock had been and got out of the SUV.

Dunne walked down to the gravel road, angered and adrenalized. That guy who claimed he was ex-cop, the extortionist chauffeur, had gotten his blood up. Not that Dunne had a thing to worry about. It had been exactly as he'd said it was that night on Oglethorpe. He had taken an informant, a whore dancer he knew, for a ride, and she had blown him down by the Metro tracks. IAD could jack him up for it if they had the ambition, but the girl would never testify. He hadn't known there was a body in the garden that night. When he found out about it, he'd gone to the crime scene, spoken to the homicide police, and was satisfied that no one knew of his presence the previous night. As for the man in the gas station that the chauffeur had asked about, Dunne had no clue.

Anger was good. It would keep him on point for the task at hand.

Romeo Brock had become a problem, though it was no fault of Dunne's. He had been careful about his dealings with Brock and his cousin Gaskins. Dunne's CI, guy name of Fishhead Lewis, had told Dunne about a young man, Romeo Brock, who had ambition and talked about it loudly in Hannibal's, a bar on Florida Avenue. Through Fishhead, Dunne would pass on information to Brock concerning independent, unprotected drug dealers or distributors who could be taken off with minimal fear of retribution. Dunne would not shake down these dealers directly or be seen with Brock or Gaskins. He'd learned from those two police officers in Baltimore, the ones who'd been busted earlier that year for making that mistake. They should have known that someone would flip on them eventually and end their party. Dunne was smarter than that. After the robberies, Dunne would drive by the area and make sure that all was calm. But he never participated in the crimes. Only in the profit.

Now Brock, eager to make a rep, had gone and shot a man for no reason and taken another man's woman. Dunne had intended to visit Brock and Gaskins this evening to get his share of the fifty. It was rare for him to meet them face-to-face, but Dunne didn't trust Fishhead with that amount of money. Then Brock had phoned him and said that Gaskins had skipped and there might be trouble. So Dunne found himself here, where he didn't want to be, pushed to potential violence and directly involved. He'd solve this thing, hopefully by intimidation rather than force, and get out of the arrangement.

Partnering with Brock had been a mistake, but it wasn't one that couldn't be fixed.

Dunne had found that he could do anything behind the badge and the gun. It was why he'd become a cop.

He turned and walked up the gravel road. He pulled the .45 and eased a round into its chamber. He was going straight in. He wasn't a criminal. He was police.

ROMEO BROCK STOOD on the front porch of his house, smoking a cigarette. His stomach was tight, and his palms carried sweat. He was aware of his fear and he hated it. A man like him, the kind of man he imagined himself to be, was not supposed to feel this way. Still, his hands were wet.

He looked out into the darkness. Night had come just about full. He was hoping to see Conrad walking back toward the house up the gravel road. Conrad, who was strong of body and will, would know what to do. But Conrad did not appear.

Brock had phoned Dunne again after speaking to him earlier, but this time his call went to message.

He thought he heard something from back in the house. It was his nerves talking to him, most likely. Could have been the radio Chantel had turned up loud. He supposed he should go there and check it out.

He stubbed out the Kool he had been smoking on the rail of the porch. He entered the house and did not close the door behind him. He heard his stomach talking to him as he went along. He walked down the hall to his bedroom door. He tried the knob, and it did not turn. He knocked on the door. There was no response, and he made a fist and pounded on the wood.

"Chantel! Open the door, girl."

Brock put his ear to the door. He couldn't hear Chantel's footsteps or anything else except for the radio. The song playing was one he'd heard many times. It was that "Been Around the World" thing. He liked that song, most times. But now it seemed to be laughing at him. Telling him about the places he would never see.

"Chantel," said Brock weakly. He rested his forehead on the door.

He felt the barrel of a gun pressed to the back of his head.

"Don't move. 'Less you want me to spill your brains."

He didn't move. He felt the man behind the voice take his Colt from where he'd put it, under the belt line of his slacks.

"Turn slow."

Brock did it. A young man with a blue Nationals cap tilted slightly on his head was holding an automatic on him with one hand and had Brock's Gold Cup in the other. Brock could see excitement in his eyes. He had no doubt that this boy wouldn't hesitate to kill.

"This way," said Ernest Henderson, holstering the Gold Cup in his jeans. He back-stepped down the hall, keeping his Beretta pointed at Brock's middle, and Brock followed. They came out into the living room, and Henderson motioned for Brock to sit in the chair that faced the open door.

Brock took a seat.

"Put your hands on the arms of that chair," said Henderson.

As Brock gripped the armchair, Henderson flipped the switch of a lamp several times. Soon a tall, handsome man entered the house. He held a Desert Eagle .44 Magnum at his side. He frowned at Brock.

"You Romeo?"

Brock nodded.

"Where my money at?"

"It's here," said Brock.

"I said *where?*"

"In the bedroom at the back. There's two suitcases—"

"Anyone else in this house?"

"The fat man's woman is in the bedroom."

"What about your partner?"

"He's gone."

"Go on, Nesto," said Benjamin, raising his gun casually and pointing it at Brock. "Check all the rooms while you're back there. Make sure this fake motherfucker ain't scheming."

Henderson went down the hall. Benjamin stared at Brock. Brock cut his eyes away. Both of them listened as Henderson checked the kitchen and the room where Conrad Gaskins had slept.

"Bedroom door's locked," said Henderson, his voice raised.

"Kick it in," said Benjamin.

Brock heard the young man try it several times, grunting with each effort. Then he heard the door crack open at the jamb. The young man returned with a Gucci suitcase in hand.

"Ain't but one," said Henderson. "Wasn't no girl back there, either. The window was up. If she *was* there, she gone now."

"Open that case," said Benjamin, speaking to Brock. "Turn it so we can see, and open it up."

Henderson placed the suitcase at Brock's feet and stepped back. Brock leaned forward and unzipped the lid. He opened the suitcase, and all of them looked at the women's clothing that had been packed inside it. For a moment, no one said a thing.

Mikey got the money, thought Benjamin. He got it and the girl and he's waiting down by the cars. He wouldn't think of robbing me. Not after what I did for Dink and their moms.

"Chantel," said Brock. He wasn't saying her name in anger. He was proud of her for what she'd done. She had fire. And here he was acting the punk. He looked up at Benjamin, a hint of defiance in his eyes.

"Yeah, Chantel," said Benjamin. To Henderson he said, "Cover his dumb ass."

Benjamin pulled his cell from his pocket and hit and held

the number three, which was the speed dial code for Michael Tate.

He heard footsteps, thinking, Here comes Mikey now. But when he turned, there was a white man coming from the darkness of the porch and walking quickly through the front door. A gun was in his hand, and his gun arm was straight.

"Police!" said Grady Dunne. He shouted the word again. His face was fierce and pink, and he moved the gun back and forth from Benjamin to Henderson. "I'm MPD! Drop your weapons to the deck, now!"

Benjamin didn't move. He didn't drop his gun. He held it at his side and looked at the H&K in Dunne's hand. It wasn't a police gun.

"I said drop those fuckin guns, *now!*"

Ernest Henderson kept his Beretta on Brock. He turned his head to look at the man who said he was police. He was blond, and a vein was standing out on his neck. Henderson waited to hear something, anything, from Benjamin. But Ray Benjamin did not tell him what to do.

"Drop your guns!"

Brock looked at the back of Henderson's neck. He studied the point where his neck met his shoulders. And he thought, That is where I will bury my pick. Directly into that boy's spine. They'll talk about me forever and say my name and what I did. How I went up against two guns with a tool made to cut ice. Me, Romeo Brock.

Brock pulled the ice pick where it was taped at his calf. As he expected, the action pulled the cork off the tip as it came free. He stood with the ice pick in hand, raised it, and stepped toward Henderson.

"Behind you, Nesto," said Benjamin in an even way.

Henderson turned and shot Romeo Brock in the center of his chest. The gun jumped in Henderson's hand as he shot him again. Brock went back over the chair. His arms pinwheeled through crimson mist as he fell.

Dunne squeezed off two rounds in the direction of Benjamin. The first slug went through Benjamin's shoulder and blew a fist-sized hole out of his back. The second, high from the recoil, nicked his carotid artery as it tunneled through his neck.

Benjamin fired his .44 through a cloud of smoke and arterial spray at the outline of the man who'd claimed he was police. He dropped, shooting again as he fell and hit the floor. He saw the man stumble against the wall as if thrown. Benjamin closed his eyes.

Grady Dunne staggered toward the door. He looked back at the Number One Male with the baseball cap, standing in the center of the room, still armed. The young man was shaking his head as if he could shake away what had happened.

Dunne tried to raise his weapon. His hand cramped open, and he dropped the .45. He said "God" and held his hand to his stomach, which was wet with blood now pulsing through his fingers. The pain was extreme, and he went through the door and tripped off the porch. There was air beneath him. He touched ground and spun as if he were dancing or drunk and lost his feet and landed on his back in the gravel road.

He looked up at the branches of a tulip poplar and beyond them the stars. He said, "Officer down." It was a whisper so faint that he could not hear the words himself. He tasted blood in his mouth. He swallowed the blood and breathed rapidly, and his eyes widened in fright. Into his field of vision came the Number One Male. He stood over Dunne and pointed his gun at his chest. There were tears streaming down the young man's face.

"Nine-one-one," said Dunne. He felt hot blood spill out of his mouth and pour down his chin.

The young man lowered his gun. He slipped it barrel-down behind the belt line of his jeans and pulled his shirt over the butt.

Dunne heard the boy's footsteps on the gravel. And then the sound of him running down the road.

Dunne listened to the crickets and stared up at the branches and the stars. I cannot die, he thought. But soon the sensations of sound and sight faded to nothing, and Grady Dunne joined Raymond Benjamin and Romeo Brock in death.

THIRTY-SEVEN

DAN HOLIDAY DROVE back to the lot across from the gas market on Central Avenue, only to find that T. C. Cook had disappeared. He tried to reach Cook on the Motorola and then on his cell but could not get him either way. He noted that Reginald Wilson's Buick was still parked beside the market. Holiday assumed that Cook had tired of the surveillance or was simply fatigued by the workday and had headed home. He thought he'd go to his house and check up on him, just to be safe.

Cook's Marquis was not in the driveway when Holiday arrived at his yellow-sided house on Dolphin Road. Holiday sat in his Town Car and dialed the home number for Cook but got the answering machine. A porch light was on, but Holiday guessed it had been activated by a timer or darkness. There were no lights on in the house.

He dialed the number to Ramone's cell.

"Yeah."

"It's Holiday."

"Hello, Doc."

"Where you at? It sounds like a party."

"Leo's, having a beer. What do you want?"

"Me and Sergeant Cook caught up with our police officer friend. Car four sixty-one? It turned out to be nothing."

"Big surprise."

"But I lost Cook somewhere. I had to leave him for a bit, and when I came back, he was gone. I tried his house, and he's not there, either. I'm thinking he got confused or something. I don't even know if he can read street signs."

"He had a stroke, not Alzheimer's. He'll turn up."

"I'm worried about him," said Holiday. He waited for a response but heard only bar sounds on the other end of the line. "Gus?"

"Keep me posted. I'll be here for a while."

Holiday hit "end." He sat in the Lincoln and thought about the old man and where he could have gone. There was only one place that came to mind.

T. C. COOK SAT BEHIND the wheel of his Marquis, parked on a side street in Good Luck Estates, a community off Good Luck Road in New Carrollton. He was looking at the ranch-style home of Reginald Wilson. There were no lights on in the house and few lights in the neighboring homes. The street was quiet and dimly lit.

Cook had been here for some time, thinking.

When Reginald Wilson came out of prison, he had moved into this house, which had been the home of his parents, both deceased. He had to have had his pre-term possessions in storage, or his parents had simply stored them here in this house. Cook knew that Wilson would never have abandoned his beloved collection of electric jazz albums. Maybe there was a clue to be found in all that vinyl. In any case, Cook surmised that Wilson would have kept the hair samples, his trophies from the Palindrome Murders, consistent with the behavior of this type of killer. Cook had to believe that those bits of hair, cut from the heads of Otto Williams, Ava Simmons, and Eve Drake twenty years earlier, were somewhere in the house that he was looking at now. Cook had convinced himself that this was a good time to see if he was right.

He knew that what he was about to do was a crime. But he felt that time was growing short. There was a good chance the hair samples were not in the house. But perhaps something was. Something that could link Reginald Wilson to the deaths of those kids. Enough of a something to warrant the reopening of the case. He was looking for an undeniable piece of evidence that would influence Detective Ramone to go to a judge and initiate DNA testing on Wilson. Cook was certain, as certain as he had been in '85, that Wilson was the one.

He retrieved his mini-cassette recorder from out of the glove box. He pushed the red "record" button and spoke into the microphone.

"This is Sergeant T. C. Cook. I am about to enter the home of Reginald Wilson in Good Luck Estates. I have reason to believe that there is evidence inside the house that will connect Mr. Wilson to the so-called Palindrome Murders, which occurred in Washington, D.C., in 1985. I'm looking for hair samples, specifically, that m-might have been taken off the decedents. I have no warrant. I am no longer an active-duty police officer. I've been working with a young man named Dan Holiday who is good police. But I want to state that he had nothing to do with this action I'm about to take. I am doing this of my own accord, hoping to bring some peace to the families. Also, to those beautiful children who were killed."

Cook recorded the time and date, and shut off the machine. He wanted all of this on record, in case he was mistaken for a burglar and shot while he was trying to enter the house. He didn't want his legacy to be that of a crazy old man, burglarizing homes, like some fool who'd wandered off the streets in his bathrobe. He wanted people to know his intent.

The night was cool, but Cook was sweating right through his jacket. He took it off, folded it, and laid it on the passenger floor. He removed his Stetson as well and looked at the perspiration marks on the inner band. He placed the faded hat on the seat beside him, next to the recorder. He flexed and unflexed his left hand and stared at it because it felt stiff and odd.

Cook opened the trunk, using a switch mounted low on the dash, and got out of the car. He stumbled a little, walking to the back of the Marquis. Once there, he unscrewed the lightbulb under the trunk's lid. He didn't want to attract attention and he didn't need the illumination. He knew where everything was.

Cook put on a pair of latex gloves. He found his Stinger flashlight and his jimmy bar and put one in each hand. He found it difficult to hold the flashlight because that arm was numb. He heard his own heavy breathing and waited for his heart to slow down. He felt sweat trickle down his back. He closed the lid of the trunk and walked toward the house.

Cook began to go around the side of the house. His plan was to use the jimmy bar on a rear door and, once inside, negotiate his way using the flashlight. But he was feeling poorly and he stopped walking.

He had become very dizzy and he felt the need to lie down. He went back to the car.

The backseat was inviting. He slid into it, dropped the jimmy bar and the flashlight on the floor, and closed the door behind him. He lay on his side, with his right cheek on the cool vinyl covering. His left arm ached terribly, and now the ache had traveled up into his neck and caused an awful pressure in his head.

This will pass, thought Cook.

He closed his eyes. Drool dripped from his open mouth onto the vinyl seat.

When T. C. Cook opened his eyes, it was daylight. He had slept the night away in the car. He felt better than he had before.

Cook sat up. He was back on Dolphin Road, parked in front of his house. The yellow siding was as clean as the day he had installed it many years ago. In the bay window that fronted the house he could see a woman looking through parted curtains. She looked like his wife. A boy and a girl were on the sidewalk, swinging ropes for double Dutch, and another girl was between them, jumping.

Cook picked up his Stetson, which looked brand-new. He fitted it on his head and got out of the car.

The sunlight was pleasant on his face, and he could smell lilacs in the air. His wife tended carefully to the tree that blossomed in the front yard. It must be April, thought Cook, as he walked toward the house. 'Cause that's when those lilacs bloom.

He approached the kids playing on the sidewalk. The boy holding the ropes on one side was fresh in his teens, with thick eyeglasses and a gangly build. The girl holding the other side was also young but had the lush curves of a woman. She had a hint of mischief in her eyes.

The girl in the middle, who was double-Dutching with ease, had beautiful dark brown skin and eyes. The sunlight winked off the colored beads in her braided hair. She jumped out of the ropes fluidly and stopped to stare at Cook, standing by the curb. She smiled at him, and he returned her smile.

"Hello, young lady," said Cook.

"Sergeant Cook?"

"It's me."

"We thought you forgot us."

"No, darling," said Cook. "I never did."

"You wanna play with us?"

"I'm too old. You don't mind, I'll just watch."

Eve Drake made a come-on gesture with her hand, and the kids resumed their game. T. C. Cook stepped toward them in the bright and warming light.

THIRTY-EIGHT

HOLIDAY PUT HIS fingers to the neck of T. C. Cook and found no pulse. The man's face was waxy under the Mercury's dome light. He had seen enough corpses to know that Cook was dead.

Holiday closed the door and went back to his Lincoln. He phoned Gus Ramone and told him what had happened and where he was. Ramone said he'd be there shortly.

Holiday returned to the Marquis, opened the back door, and stared at Cook.

I killed him, thought Holiday. He wasn't strong enough to work.

The latex gloves on Cook's hands and the jimmy bar and flashlight on the floor told Holiday that Cook had been planning a break-in at the home of Reginald Wilson.

In the front seat he found the mini-cassette tape recorder beside Cook's Stetson. He rewound the tape, pushed the "play" button, and listened to the recording. His emotions welled up as he heard the old cop speak his name and praise him. He pulled the tape from the recorder and slipped it into his jacket pocket. He took the gloves off Cook's hands and stuffed them in the same pocket. Then he took the recorder, the jimmy bar, and the flashlight and placed them in the trunk of his Town Car. While the lid was open, he transferred some items from Cook's trunk into his own, including some cop tools and a shop rag. He would use that later to wipe his prints from Cook's car.

He had been very quiet. No one had come out of a house and no one had driven down the street. Holiday sat down on the curb and smoked a Marlboro. He was working on another one when Ramone's Tahoe turned the corner and pulled up behind the Town Car.

Ramone sat behind the wheel, finishing his call to Regina. He had been speaking to her on his cell as he drove into P.G. County. When he was done telling her about Asa Johnson and the events of his day, including the death of Cook, he assured her that he would not be home too late. He asked her to keep Diego up if she could. He wanted to speak to him before he went to sleep.

Ramone killed the engine and got out of the SUV. Holiday stood to meet him. They nodded at each other but did not speak. Then Ramone went to the Marquis and examined Cook. Ramone returned to where Holiday stood leaning against the Lincoln.

"Why was he here?" said Ramone.

"That's Reginald Wilson's house over there."

"The security guard."

"Right," said Holiday.

"He was, what, surveilling him?"

"He was doing what he'd been doing for the last twenty years. He was looking for a break in the case."

"That's a long time to play a hunch."

"Cook wasn't wrong too often when he was homicide police. If you could DNA Wilson—"

"No PC."

"Fuck probable cause."

"It would be nice if it worked that way."

Holiday lit another smoke. His hand shook as he held the match.

"You call this in?" said Ramone.

"Not yet."

"When were you planning to do that?"

"After I move him off this street. I'm gonna take him up to Good Luck Road and park his car in a strip mall. I'll wipe my prints off and call in an anonymous."

"That's gettin' to be a habit with you."

"I don't want him found here."

"Why not?"

"Long while back, the *Post* did a feature on Cook," said Holiday. "The headline read, 'Years Later, Palindrome Murders Still Haunt Retired Detective,' something like that. The article quoted Cook as saying he strongly suspected a man named Reginald Wilson who by then had been incarcerated on other charges. It made Cook out to be half nuts. It's possible that some reporter's gonna go through the morgue material and connect Cook to Wilson and this street. The old man shouldn't go out like that. He doesn't deserve it."

"Maybe not," said Ramone. "But you're committing a crime."

"I shouldn't have taken him out with me. I owe him some dignity in death."

"He was a sick man, Danny. It was his time. It doesn't look like he went out with much pain."

"He went out not knowing."

"We might never know," said Ramone. "Chances are, the Palindrome case won't ever be closed. You *know* this. We don't always get to win in the end. It's not about slaps on the back and confetti."

"He wasn't looking for glory. He wanted to solve this for those kids."

"How do you solve a murder? Tell me. 'Cause I'd really like to know."

"What are you talkin about?"

"Would finding that killer raise those kids back from the dead? Would it bring closure to the families? What would it *solve,* exactly?" Ramone shook his head bitterly. "I lost the idea a long time ago that I was accomplishing anything. Occasionally I put assholes away for life, knowing they can't kill again. That's how I speak for the fallen few. But as far as solving goes? I don't solve shit. I go to work every day and I try to protect my wife and kids from the bad things that are out there. That's my mission. That's all I can do."

"I don't believe that."

"Well, you always were a better cop than me."

"No, I wasn't," said Holiday. "You say I was good, and so did the old man. But I wasn't."

"That's history."

"No. Earlier tonight I came up on the uniform I was tailing, and we had a little talk. Officer Grady Dunne. He didn't have anything to do with Asa Johnson or Reginald Wilson. But he was polluted. I'm sayin the guy had maggots crawling around inside him." Holiday hit his cigarette and blew smoke at his feet. "That was me before I got tossed. Shit, that motherfucker even looked like me."

"The poor bastard."

"I'm serious, man. I was looking at him and I was seeing myself if I'd stayed on the force. What I would have become. No question, I was headed for a bad end. You were right to go after me. I was lucky to walk away."

"Guys like him weed themselves out."

"Sometimes," said Holiday. "And sometimes they need a little push."

Holiday pitched his cigarette out into the street.

"You still thinking of moving the old man?" said Ramone.

"I'm doing it," said Holiday.

"Call me when you're done. I'll pick you up."

Holiday completed his task. Ramone retrieved him and dropped him back at his Lincoln. They heard the faint sirens of the squad cars arriving before the ambulance, and they shook hands.

"So long, Doc. I need to get home."

As Holiday walked to his Lincoln, Ramone drove off the street. He speed-dialed Regina at their house.

"Gus?"

"It is your man," said Ramone. "Everything all right?"

"Diego's still up," said Regina. "Alana's in her bedroom, talking to her dolls. We're all just waitin on you."

"I'm headed back to the mother ship," said Ramone. He told her he loved her and ended the call.

RAMONE ENTERED HIS HOME on Rittenhouse and locked his gun and shield in the usual drawer. The first floor was still. He went to a small table in the dining room holding bottles of liquor and poured himself a shot of Jameson. It went down right. He could have killed the whole bottle. If not for his family, it would have been easy to become that kind of man.

Ramone checked the locks on the front and back doors and went up the stairs.

In the hallway, he noticed the bar of light under his bedroom door. He walked into Alana's room and found her asleep in her bed, her Barbies, Kens, and Groovy Girls lined up on the blanket, their backs against the wall, all neatly spaced in a row. He bent forward and kissed Alana's cheek. He brushed a strand of damp, curly hair off her forehead and stood looking at her for a moment before he turned off her bedside light.

Ramone went to Diego's room, knocked on the door, and pushed it open. Diego was atop the sheets, listening to a Backyard CD on his portable system, keeping the volume low. He was looking through a *Don Diva* magazine but did not seem to be engaged in it. His eyes were hollow, and it appeared he had been crying. His world had been tilted. It would right itself, but never to the degree of comfort where it had been.

"You okay?"

"I'm blown, Dad."

"Let's talk some," said Ramone, pulling a chair over to his son's bed. "Then you should get to sleep."

A little while later, Ramone closed Diego's door behind him and walked down the hall to his own bedroom. Regina was in their king, reading a book under the light of a lamp, her head on a doubled pillow. They exchanged a long look, and then Ramone undressed and went to the bathroom, where he washed thoroughly and tried to get the smell of beer and liquor off his breath. He came back to the bed in his boxers and got under the sheets. Regina turned into him and they embraced. He kissed her soft lips once and again, and found himself hard and kissed her with his open mouth. She pushed him gently away.

"What do you think you're doing?" said Regina. "You getting greedy, going for two in a row."

"A guy can dream, can't he?"

"You better sleep before you have that dream. Comin in here back-to-back nights with liquor on your breath."

"That's the mouthwash. It's got alcohol in it."

"You talking about that mouthwash comes from Dublin?"

"Go ahead, Regina."

"You and your new drinking buddy, Doc Holiday."

"He's all right."

"What's he looking like these days?"

"He's got a little belly on him. They call it the Holiday Hump."

They embraced again. She fit into him exactly. It was as though they were one person, separated each day, brought back together at night. He couldn't imagine being apart from her, not even in death.

"You smell like booze and cigarettes, like you did when we first started dating," said Regina. "When you'd show up at my apartment after last call. What was that place you liked, where all those new wave white girls used to hang out? Constipation?"

"The Constable. That wasn't me. Least it doesn't seem like it today."

"Now we've got this. And all the challenges that go with it."

"And the good things, too."

She had turned off her lamp, and they were in darkness, their eyes slowly adjusting to the absence of light. Ramone brushed his fingers down Regina's arm.

"What are we going to do about Diego?" said Regina.

"I talked to him," said Ramone. "He can finish out the year in his old school. It feels right. Next year we can put him in one of the blue-collar Catholic high schools. Carroll, DeMatha . . . either one of those would be a good place for him."

"How're we gonna afford that?"

"It's not like it's a fortune. I'll sell the house in Silver Spring, I have to. Hell, the dirt alone's worth a bundle. We'll be fine."

"Did you talk about Asa?"

"Yes."

"How was Diego with it?"

"His world got rocked. He's probably stressing about all the times he called his friend soft or gay. Not knowing what that kid was going through inside."

"Can you imagine what it's like to be that way in this climate? Being told all the time that you're not wanted, that there's no place for you in this new compassionate world. All the hate we got out here, and the politicians throwing gasoline on the fire. I don't know what Bible those haters are reading, but it's not the one I was raised on."

"Forget about those fuckin idiots. What about everyday people who aren't about hate but still spread it? Diego didn't mean anything by those words, but now it's got him thinking hard on what comes out of his mouth. I been thinking on it myself."

"You and all your friends."

"You're right. Down at the office we go back and forth with that kinda shit all day. You'd look good in a dress, you've got gaydar . . . all that."

"So you gonna change your ways now, huh?"

"Probably not," said Ramone. "I'm just a man, no more enlightened than any other. But I am gonna think twice before I talk that kind of trash. I hope Diego does, too."

"What else you and your son talk about?" said Regina. "You were in his room a while."

"I was putting the last piece of the puzzle together on Asa's death. I was pretty sure I knew, but Diego confirmed it."

"And?"

"You know how I always told him to be aware of any firearms in the homes of his friends?"

"I know. That's your biggest fear."

"I've seen way too many accidents, Regina. Kids finding their fathers' guns and testing them out."

"Okay."

"Diego and his friends just have that knowledge. They read the gun magazines because they're boys and they're interested. The Spriggs twins know I have a Glock and that I keep it locked up. They *all know* these things."

"Oh, Gus . . ."

"Diego says that Asa's father kept a revolver in their home. He didn't know if it was a thirty-eight. But I'm betting that it was."

"Lord."

"The ultimate fuck-you to his old man," said Ramone. "Asa killed himself with his father's gun."

She hugged him tightly. They lay in the dark and neither of them could find sleep.

"Will you go to church with us on Sunday?" said Regina.

Ramone said that he would.

THIRTY-NINE

AFTER CHURCH, RAMONE took the family to a restaurant over the District line for lunch. It was family owned and had survived despite the encroachment of the chains into downtown Silver Spring. Diego ordered the Vietnamese steak, his favorite dish, and Alana drank fresh lemonade and walked back and forth through the beaded curtains that led to the restrooms. Church had been much needed, and this was a nice way to continue the afternoon. Also, Ramone was putting off what he knew had to be done.

Back at the house, Ramone stayed in his suit and told Regina he'd be back soon. He dropped Diego, who had changed into shorts, Nikes, and a Ronald Spriggs–designed T, down at the basketball courts on Third, where Shaka was waiting. He instructed Diego to keep his cell on and to call either him or Regina if he went anywhere else.

Ramone drove slowly over to the Johnson house. He

parked but did not immediately get out of the car. He had told Bill Wilkins that he would update Terrance Johnson on the findings of the case. Now he almost wished he had let Garloo take the lead. He was about to tell Johnson that his son had committed suicide and that he had done so with Terrance's gun. In addition, he had to tell Terrance that Asa was gay. There was no predicting Terrance's reaction. But this needed to be done.

Terrance must have known that his gun was missing, and he had to have suspected that Asa took it. His fear would have been that Asa had been robbed of the gun and shot with it. The death of his son, coupled with extreme feelings of guilt, had shattered him. But even with that, he could not have imagined that Asa had used the gun on himself.

Ramone had not told Wilkins or any of his other coworkers about the gun. If Wilkins were to enter it into his paperwork, Terrance Johnson could be charged with possession of an illegal firearm. Only police officers, federal agents, and special security types were permitted to own handguns in D.C. Johnson had bought the thirty-eight hot or he had been a down-the-chain recipient of a straw purchase originated in Virginia or Maryland. Legally, he was wrong. But Ramone wasn't going to report it. Johnson had enough to live with. There wasn't a point in piling any more misery on him, his wife, and their last living child.

He wasn't going to be entirely forthcoming with Terrance Johnson, either. Ramone had deduced the identity of Asa's older boyfriend, called RoboMan in the journal. Asa's math teacher had said that Asa had come to him for extra-credit work after school the day of his death. But there were no such papers in Asa's locker, book bag, or bedroom. RoboMan had to be a thinly veiled moniker for Robert Bolton. Ramone had found Bolton extremely defensive on the subject of stereotyping young black men when they had their conversation. But he had been defending Asa. Bolton was in love with him.

Ramone would mention his suspicions to the people who worked in Morals. This kind of thing was out of his bailiwick.

He simply didn't know what to do with what he'd found. He wanted to get rid of it.

He intended to keep information from his fellow officers in the MPD. He would keep information from the boy's father. It was like Holiday said: He wasn't so straight.

He got out of the Tahoe, walked up to the Johnson residence, and knocked on the front door. He heard Terrance Johnson's footsteps approaching. Ramone's impulse was to go back to his SUV. But the door opened, and he shook Johnson's hand and stepped into the house.

DAN HOLIDAY LIT A cigarette and tossed the match into the ashtray before him. It sat next to a vodka tonic on the bar. He stood in the middle of a group including Jerry Fink, Bob Bonano, and Bradley West. They were kidding themselves with Bloody Marys. Holiday had no such self-delusions. He needed a real drink.

Leo's was empty except for Leo Vazoulis and the four of them. Fink had just returned from the juke. A strong horn-and-backup-girl intro, and then a husky male vocal came into the room.

"'It isn't what you got, it's what you give,'" sang Fink, doing the girl part.

"The Jimmy Castor Bunch," said Bradley West, the writer.

"Nah, this was before the Bunch," said Fink, "and all that Troglodyte shit. Jimmy Castor was a soul singer before he was a novelty act."

"Okay," said West, "I got the Bunch thing wrong. But here's the five-dollar question. What singer did Jimmy Castor replace in a famous group, way back in his career?"

"Clyde McPhatter," said Fink. "From the Drifters."

"Wrong."

Fink grinned stupidly. "Bo Donaldson, from the Heywoods?"

"He replaced Frankie Lymon," said West. "As in, and the Teenagers."

"The little junkie," said Bonano. His cell phone, sitting on the bar, was playing Ennio Morricone's most famous theme, but Bonano was ignoring it.

"You owe me five," said West.

"You take credit cards, right?" said Fink.

"Leo does," said Bradley. "Just buy the next round."

"Ain't you gonna answer your phone, Bobby?" said Fink.

"Nah, it's just a customer."

"Another satisfied client of Home Butchers," said Fink.

"It's this bitch from Potomac," said Bonano. "She doesn't like the way I hung her cabinets. I'll show her something that's hung right."

"On account of you're Italian," said West.

"There used to be a natural bridge from the boot to Africa," said Bonano. "I ever tell you guys that?"

"Guy's got a vowel on the end of his name," said Fink, "he thinks he's Milton Berle."

"Berle was a Jew," said Bonano. "Like you, Jerry."

"His name ends with a vowel." Fink wiped vodka and tomato juice off his chin. "Uncle Milty was hung like a donkey, that's all I was sayin."

They paused to sing along with the Jimmy Castor tune, light smokes, and sip their drinks.

Fink looked over at Holiday. "Why so quiet, Doc?"

"No reason," said Holiday. "I'm a little self-conscious, is all it is. Listening to you Einsteins, I feel kinda inferior."

"Tell us a bedtime story," said West.

"I don't have one."

"He's just solemn," said Fink, " 'cause of all the violent crime we had in the area this weekend."

"Yeah, that off-duty police that bought it out in P.G. County," said Bonano. "You guys read about it?"

"It was in the *Post*," said Fink. "You saw it, didn't you Doc?"

Holiday nodded. He had read about Grady Dunne yesterday. The story said that an off-duty MPD cop had been shot to death in P.G. County, along with two other men. One of them was a fairly well-known ex-offender with drug distribution priors. The other man was only identified as a black male. Romero, something like that. Holiday could not remember his name.

Police were looking for a third suspect who was believed to be the shooter of the police officer. Tellingly, a spokesman gave no explanation for Officer Dunne's presence at the scene.

"Either he was undercover or sumshit like that," said Fink, "or he was involved with those guys, as in, he was as dirty as the doo-doo stains on my drawers. What do you think, Doctor?"

"I don't know," said Holiday.

"Ward Nine," said Bonano. "It's like Tombstone out in that motherfucker."

Holiday had also searched for news in the *Post* about Cook, and had found it in a single paragraph in Metro's "In Brief." He was only identified by his name, a man who had been found in a car in New Carrollton and appeared to have died of natural causes. The longer story would come later, when someone in the newsroom figured out who he was: that old detective haunted by the unsolved Palindrome Murders.

West signaled Leo for a fresh round.

"You in, Doc?" said Bonano.

"No," said Holiday, swallowing the last of his vodka tonic. He dropped a ten on the bar. "I gotta get to work."

"On a Sunday?" said Fink.

"People need rides on Sundays, too," said Holiday. He gathered his cigarettes and matches and slipped them into his black suit jacket. "Gents."

Fink, Bonano, and West watched Holiday walk from Leo's. They listened to the introduction to "Just a Little Overcome" by the Nightingales and bowed their heads in reverence to the beauty of the song as they waited for Leo to prepare and serve them their drinks.

A half hour later, Holiday sat behind the wheel of his Town Car on a side street of Good Luck Estates. Beside him were T. C. Cook's binoculars, a couple of granola bars, and a bottle of water. On the floor was a large empty cup into which he could urinate if needed. In the trunk of the Lincoln were a jimmy bar, a Streamlight Stinger rechargeable steel-cased flashlight, which could double as a weapon, a friction-lock expandable baton, a set of blued handcuffs, duct tape, a hundred-foot retractable tape measure, a digital camera, which he did not know how to use, and other tools and cop tools.

Several houses away sat the ranch-style, white-sided home of Reginald Wilson. Wilson's Buick was parked in the driveway.

Holiday had no particular plan. Wait for Wilson to slip up in some way. Or break into Wilson's home when he was at work and look for evidence. Toss the shit out of the place until he turned something up. Or plant evidence, if need be. Anything that would open the door to DNA tests that would link Wilson to the murders. Cook had been certain about his guilt, and that was good enough for Holiday.

He was prepared to sit here all day and, if necessary, the next day. Holiday had phoned Jerome Belton, his sole employee, and told him that he would be taking some time off. Now he had no immediate commitments. No family, no friends to speak of, no woman waiting for him at home. He had this. He'd fucked up damn near everything in his life, but maybe he could get this one thing right. He still had time.

DIEGO RAMONE AND SHAKA Brown walked south on Third Street. They had finished playing ball. Neither of them had been into it and they had only gone hard for one game. Afterward they had sat on the court with their backs against the chain-link fence and talked and reminisced about their friend, the secret he had lived with, and the way he had chosen to go out. Diego had promised his father that he would never talk about the gun, and he had honored his pledge by not speaking of it with Shaka. Mostly the two of them had stared out into the daylight or at the Spanish playing on the soccer field or the occasional neighborhood resident they recognized, using the park or walking by, because they could think of little to say.

"I better get home," said Diego.

"Why? You ain't got no homework."

"I'm startin back at my old school next week."

"That's next week," said Shaka. "It's not like you're in the middle of something."

"I been reading a book, believe it or not," said Diego. "It's called *True Grit*. My father gave it to me. It's pretty good."

"Go ahead, Dago. You know, soon as you go home you're gonna fall on the sofa and watch the Redskins. It's Dallas day, boy."

"True."

They walked along the commercial strip. Down by the barbershop, they gave each other a pound.

"Later, dawg," said Shaka.

"Later."

Shaka went west, in the direction of his mother's place, dribbling his basketball with his left hand, his right hand behind his back, as his coach had told him to do. Diego walked up the rise of Rittenhouse, toward the pale yellow colonial that had always been his home.

His mother would be in the kitchen, planning dinner or having a nap, what she called resting her eyes, on the couch in the living room. Alana would be reading her picture book about rabbits or doing the voices to all her dolls up in her room. And, hopefully, his father had come back home. He'd be in his chair right now, watching the Skins-Cowboys game, pounding his fist on the padded arm of the chair, yelling stuff at the players on the screen. Pushing his hair off his forehead and stroking his black mustache.

Diego stopped halfway up the rise. His father's Tahoe was parked out on the street, and his mother's Volvo was in the driveway. Alana's purple bicycle, with the streamers coming out the handles, sat up on the porch.

Everything was as it should have been. Diego walked to his house and touched the knob of his front door, warm in the afternoon sun.

1985

FORTY

DETECTIVE SERGEANT T. C. Cook took another look at the dead girl lying in the grass of a community garden near E Street, on the edge of Fort Dupont Park. Her eyes were fixed and reflected the strobing blues and reds coming from the light bars of the cruisers still on the scene. Cook closely examined the girl's braids, decorated with colorful beads, and saw that one was shorter than the others. There was no doubt now in Cook's mind. Truly, the decedent was one of them.

"I will find him, darling," said Cook, very softly so that no one could hear.

Cook labored to his feet. More often than not, it was an effort to do so. Well into his middle age, and after years of crouching down over victims, his knees were beginning to betray him. He shook a Viceroy out of his deck and lit it. He felt the satisfaction of his addiction as the nicotine hit his lungs. Cook nodded to the ME and stepped out of the immediate vicinity so as not to foul the scene with his ashes.

Walking away, he noticed that the superintendent of detectives and Captain Bellows had gone back to their offices. Knowing he would not have to deal with the white shirts relaxed him. He called them the Spaghetti Lids because of those silly strands of nautical rope decorating the brims of their hats. He had no time for their kind.

Cook walked to the crime scene tape, where two white uniformed officers stood, keeping back the spectators, reporters, and cameras. One was tall, blond, and skinny and the other was of medium height and build and had a darker complexion and hair. Cook had been rough on them earlier, but there was no reason to apologize. He had dressed them down for a reason, and now they were doing fine.

"Keep these people back," said Cook to the blond officer. "Especially the media, you hear?"

"Yes, sir," said Dan Holiday.

"Don't 'sir' me, son. I'm a sergeant."

"We'll do it, Sergeant Cook."

"I'm not playin. You let that girl through earlier, and she up and puked not ten feet from the decedent."

"It won't happen again," said Gus Ramone.

"You do your jobs right," said Cook, "someday you two are gonna be the police officers that you *think* you are today."

"Right," said Holiday.

Cook turned and studied the spectators on the other side of the yellow tape. There were several neighborhood kids, a couple of them on bicycles, and adults whose homes backed up to the community garden. An old lady in a housedress and an unbuttoned coat, her breasts sagging down to her belly. And a man in his twenties, dressed in a security guard's uniform, a Sam Browne belt around his waist and a red company patch on his sleeve, one hand in the pocket of his blue trousers. Cook looked them all over as he dragged deeply on his Viceroy, then dropped the cigarette to the damp ground and crushed it under his shoe.

"Carry on," said Cook. He walked back to thc corpse of Eve Drake, his fresh Stetson cocked just so on his bald head.

A young neighborhood lady with a high ass moving inside acid-washed jeans walked in front of Holiday, glancing at him playfully as she passed. He stood straight, and the corners of his ice blue eyes crinkled as he smiled.

"I'd murder that," said Holiday.

"She's a little young, Doc."

"You know what they say: 'Old enough to sit at the table, old enough to eat.' "

Ramone made no further comment. He had heard all of Holiday's nuggets of wisdom before.

Holiday began to imagine the young lady naked on his sheets. And then his mind drifted, as it tended to do, toward his aspirations. He wanted more than anything to earn the respect of a man like T. C. Cook. He wanted to be good police. And so he projected and fantasized about how his career would go. He saw commendations, medals, promotions. And to the victor, the spoils of war.

Ramone had no such ambitions. He was simply doing his job, keeping the civilians back from the tape. He stood there, his feet spread wide, and thought of a woman he'd seen standing on the edge of the academy pool in a blue bathing suit. Her figure and her warm smile had haunted him since he'd touched her hand. He planned to call her very soon.

AS HOLIDAY AND RAMONE worked and dreamed in Ward 6, Washingtonians and suburbanites on the other side of town spent their disposable income in restaurants and bars, eating prime-cut steaks and drinking single-malt scotch, the men in charcoal suits and red power ties, the women in padded-shoulder dresses, high-heeled pumps, and teased hairdos they had seen on Krystle Carrington. In the bathrooms of these restaurants and bars, Republicans and Democrats put aside their differences and came together to do many blasts of cocaine. "Money for Nothing" played from every radio, and Simple Minds were scheduled to perform in town. It was rumored that Prince would be shopping in Georgetown that weekend, and the wealthy "punk" kids at Commander Salamander were anticipating his arrival. Artistic types caught a double feature of *A Passage to India* and *Heat and Dust* at the Circle Theatre. At the Capital Centre, basketball fans watched Jeff Ruland, Jeff Malone, and Manute Bol take it to the Detroit Pistons. The applause in the auditorium and the laughter in the bars were raucous and deafening, and blinding, too. AIDS jokes were told at parties, and there was talk of a new drug that was coming to town, like cocaine, except that it got smoked and was meant for blacks. Outside of newsrooms and among local law enforcement professionals, the violent deaths of three black teenagers in Southeast were hardly discussed.

As these movers of the Reagan generation enjoyed themselves, murder cops and techs worked at a crime scene at 33rd and E, in the neighborhood of Greenway, in Southeast, D.C. On this cool, wet evening in December 1985, two young uniformed police officers and a middle-aged homicide detective were on the scene.

Near the crime tape, a security guard stood alone, fingering a braid of hair decorated with colorful beads that he carried in his pocket like a charm. Later he would return to his place, slip the braid inside a plastic bag and place it in one of the album sleeves of his extensive electric jazz collection, alongside the hair he had taken from Otto Williams and Ava Simmons. The album's title, *Live Evil,* was spelled the same way forward and back. It was the Miles Davis record that had been playing in the living room of his uncle's apartment, the very first time he'd been sexually abused as a child.

Soon it began to drizzle for the second time that night. The drops grew heavier and became visible in the headlights of the cars. It was said by some of the police on the scene that God was crying for the girl in the garden. To others, it was only rain.

IN MEMORIAM

Carole Denise Spinks, 13
Darlenia Denise Johnson, 16
Angela Denise Barnes, 14
Brenda Fay Crockett, 10
Nenomoshia Yates, 12
Brenda Denise Woodward, 18
Diane Williams, 17

ACKNOWLEDGMENTS

I would like to thank the officers from the Violent Crime Branch of the Metropolitan Police Department of Washington, D.C., who allowed me access to their world and helped make this book possible. Their kindness, generosity, and good work are much appreciated.